ECHO HOUSE

Books by Ward Just

ECHO HOUSE

WARD JUST

A Peter Davison Book

A MARINER BOOK

HOUGHTON MIFFLIN COMPANY

Boston · New York

For information about permission to reproduce selections
from this book, write to Permissions, Houghton Mifflin
Company, 215 Park Avenue South, New York,
New York 10003.

Library of Congress Cataloging-in-Publication Data

Just, Ward S.
Echo House / Ward Just
p.   cm.
"A Peter Davison Book."
ISBN 0-395-85697-3
ISBN 0-395-90138-3 (pbk.)
1. United States — Politics and government — 20th
century — Fiction. 2. Democratic Party (U.S.) —
History — Fiction I. Title.
PS3560.U75E24   1997   96-45283
813'.54 — dc21   CIP

Printed in the United States of America

Book design by Robert Overholtzer

QUM 10 9 8 7 6 5 4 3 2 1

To Sarah
and to Jennifer, Julie, and Ian

Contents

Prologue: Echo House

〜〉

THE STONE MANSION called Echo House had been owned
by the Behl family since 1916, the last year of the first Wilson
administration, a purchase made at the insistence of Constance
Behl, who saw for herself a brilliant future in the nation's capital.
She saw beyond the dull Southern village that it was to the
thrilling metropolis that it would become. With the triumphant
entry of the United States into the European war, the wider
world was gloriously at hand and her husband poised to embrace
it. Owing to the death of one member and the defeat of another,
Senator Adolph Behl was suddenly ranking member of his committee and already mentioned here and there as a likely candidate for the national ticket, some day, some way, if the cards
fell fairly. Constance craved a particular mansion on Lafayette
Square, but that was unavailable, so she settled for Echo House.

Towering high on the slope overlooking Rock Creek Park to
the north and the federal triangle to the southeast, Echo House
was the oldest of the great houses in that part of Washington.
Everyone agreed that it was ideal for the up-and-coming Behls
and something of a conversation piece due to its ingenious interior design. The architect was a follower of Benjamin Latrobe
and the landscapist an associate of the incomparable Olmsted.
The house was situated on a full two acres of land, well away
from the vulgar hustle of the downtown hotels and about as far

from Capitol Hill as geography allowed. Constance liked to say that politicians were like cats: they preferred to do their business in one place and sleep in another. Echo House was grand without being ostentatious, the sort of spacious, serious mansion that could accommodate a formal ball, an afternoon tea, or a masculine evening of cards, whiskey, and political conversation. In due course it would serve very well as a place where her son, Axel, could gather with his friends.

Moreover, the house had a history. One of the many inconclusive meetings between President Lincoln and General McClellan had been held in the library (the armchair in which the Great Emancipator was believed to have sat was roped off, a tiny card announcing its significance), and later the billiards room became a clandestine after-hours haunt of President Cleveland, on those evenings when he was weary of statecraft. At that time the house was owned by an attractive widow, famous for her peach sorbet and lively conversation. Senator Behl bought the house from the widow's dissolute grandson, on the eve of the young man's departure for the battlefields of France, paying full price despite its wretched condition. For the senator this was a matter of honor, and his wife was indifferent to price. In a stroke Constance had reached base camp of the summit of her ambition, which was to assemble Washington's greatest salon, the rooms where the capital's mightiest figures would meet and the place where careers would be made and unmade; and from which her husband would make his final ascent and her son prepare his own. Echo House reminded Constance of the country houses maintained by the Anglo-Irish gentry in her native Galway, except that it was much bigger.

The name derived from the repetition of rooms on the first floor, each room perfectly square but diminishing in size so that the effect was of a set of Chinese boxes clustered like the squares of a chessboard. The arrangement was imaginative but impractical, function following form almost to the vanishing point — living room, foyer, dining room, garden room, morning room, library, study, powder room. Constance had directed that each room be furnished in a different period, but in the event France of the megalomaniacal Second Empire seemed to predominate, its ambitions as lofty as Napoleon III. Many of these rooms remained unchanged into the nineteen-nineties, giving Echo House the atmosphere of a museum (by that time Lincoln's chair had gone to the Smithsonian Institution, where it had a corner of its own and a plaque describing its provenance, along with the usual congratulations: *A donation of Mr. Axel Behl in memory of Constance Barkin Behl and Senator Adolph Behl.*

Of course the kitchen was located in the basement; dumb-waiters linked it to the dining room. There were bedroom suites and another library on the second floor, more bedrooms and a gallery on the third floor, and the billiards room and Observatory on the fourth. The oval Observatory with its vast domed ceiling was one of the most remarked-upon rooms in the District of Columbia, its circumference identical with the President's office in the White House. There was a powerful telescope in the Observatory, but it was seldom used. Its precision seemed to diminish the subject. The view with the naked eye was breath-taking, and as charming and suggestive as any of Monet's or Pissarro's cityscapes. At dusk Washington seemed to float above the earth, mauve in the blurred and fleeting light, image chasing image as in an infinity of mirrors, and finally returned to the spectator himself, flattered at the sight of such seductive grandeur. This was Constance's view of things, sitting in the Observatory with her afternoon tea, corrected in the usual way. At night the sight was merely spectacular, inspiring in the manner of an imperial capital going about its imperial business, superbly confident, willful, giddy in its enthusiasm. L'Enfant's broad avenues connected to a dozen circles containing reminders of the tempestuous past — slender generals on horseback, admirals caressing spyglasses, heavy iron cannon left and right, parks deftly placed, symmetry triumphant. And indeed the White House and the Capitol were located according to the arrangement of the Grand Trianon and the palace at Versailles, the Capitol dome the highest point on the horizon, the symbol of the primacy of the people. That was the bountiful place where the big cats prowled and pawed and did their business and then came home, exhausted but content. Ireland was so dark and silent and earth-bound, and here the land was liquid and afire, the great floating monuments brilliantly lit and wrapped by the sparkling ribbon of the Potomac. And beyond the river, invisible but audible, the beat of the nation itself, the rumble of a mighty army, turbines, combines, printing presses, roads and rails stretching to the outermost edges of the realm. And — how provident that the spoils always returned to the capital city, protector and defender of the nation's birthright, repository of the U.S. Constitution itself.

From her armchair in the Observatory it seemed to Constance that the whole sumptuous metropolis was arrayed on a platter, its delicacies there for the taking; and the big cats would bring them to you, too, if you asked them nicely, flattered them, and fed them a treat. At twilight the city's ambiance was grave, its mood somber, as the workaday world wound down and ended with the bang of a gavel. And by night it came magnificently alive, as majestic as a cathedral and as vivacious as an operetta, with ominous aspects of the jungle as well. From the Observatory at Echo House it was easy to forget that Washington was just another glum city of government, like Albany or Sacramento, legislators and lobbyists and bureaucrats and their clerks working and reworking the sodden language of government in order to distribute the spoils. Instead, it was fabulous — and more fabulous in its reach and aspiration and promise and desire than any of the great capitals of Europe.

Naturally in so febrile an environment there were disappointments, schemes delayed or denied, the odds stacked against, ambitions unrealized. The capital's numerous checks and balances were formidable, and no less formidable for their subtlety; often a certain languid modesty won the day. All the same, Constance Behl thought Echo House auspicious. History had been made there; history would continue to be made. Peach sorbet would yield to oysters and Champagne as Washington continued to grow and prosper, extending its reach beyond the known world. Constance thought of her capital as a city-state like Venice or Genoa, the genius of its diplomacy and the weight of its treasury guaranteeing something like a golden age. She saw the great boulevards as canals and the White House as a palace, in due course her husband in the Oval Office, her son waiting his turn. It may not happen in her lifetime. But it would happen.

You nudged fate; you put yourself in the hunt. So Constance insisted on setting her table personally, the flatware, the crystal, the china, the candelabra, the flowers, all situated just so on creamy Irish linen. She attended to this chore with the energy and enthusiasm of a general preparing the battlefield, and indeed that was how she saw herself and saw the after-hours life of the capital. She believed that tables were the terrain of the common struggle. Life flourished on flat surfaces, desks, conference tables, lecterns, dinner tables, an indoor world; and as the general paid particular attention to his forward battalions, his artillery support and reserves and logistics, so Constance was concerned with the precedence of chairmen, which senator was across the table from which lobbyist, who was at her own elbows and who at Adolph's, the latter a delicate matter because he was not a lively partner, altogether too ponderous and self-absorbed, rarely contributing when she signaled general conversation. He did not roar as a lion should; not that anyone noticed in the prevailing din, and that upset Constance most of all. Of course the table glittered, but it had a businesslike quality as well, a commercial environment where practical conversation could flourish. She took special care with the placement of the candelabra, in that way encouraging cross-table discussion. Enfilade, the general would have called it. Constance thought the number twelve was just about right. That was the largest number that could be conveniently assembled within the range of one man's voice.

She believed it was cowardly to live in the capital city without participating in its intrigue, to be conspicuous at the table for the shuffle and the deal, to pay the ante whatever its sum, and to continue as long as there was a bet to be called or raised. A man was dealt a hand, and how he played it was a test of character; and so much depended on luck and the nerve to conceal an ace up your sleeve. You won or you lost but you stayed at the table, because the fabulous intrigue was there, and the intrigue would determine your own place in the volatile scheme of things. You lived in this manner for years, until one momentous night when all the chips were on the table, wagered on the turn of a single card — a vote in the Senate, a vote in the jury box, a vote at a national convention, a telephone call announcing that the White House was on the line. For a moment your world held its breath, your future poised on the cusp of the next rotation, and you were rewarded or punished. Yet this too had to be admitted, though Constance never did — such was the fundamental instability of Washington, and such was its fluidity, that there was always the suspicion of a more important game being played elsewhere, and the outcome of that game would have a mighty influence on your own. *Were you at the wrong table?*

Constance saw a passionate ballet of force and counterforce, a dance to music of opposing styles and tempi while the world watched and made its judgment. The world governed, and the world's judgment was decisive. In every family there's a moment seen as a turning point, the dancer dipping and weaving, moving center stage or into the wings, the music quickening or dying, the audience on its feet or on its hands, giving approval or withholding it. When things did not go well the reasons why were all too familiar; bad luck, bad timing, bad cards, bad judgment, false friendship, betrayal. No encore.

The unhappy event enters the world's memory and the family's as well, the facts becoming gray with age, misshapen as the legacy is passed from one generation to the next, described often in the language of the failed romance. If only you had loved me as I loved you, if only you had courage, faith, fidelity, trust — well, then, the world would be a different world. The family would have been a different family — more prominent, more respected, richer, healthier, happier, wiser. The failed romance, the unfortunate investment, the neglected medical appointment — or Adolph Behl's obsessive pursuit of the nomination for vice president of the United States. He confided to Constance that he was not in the first cut but he was the tallest tree in the second cut; and the vice presidency was the honor he wanted and would have. When she sneered that politics had nothing in common with the timber industry, he interrupted. More than you think, he said.

You've settled for second best, she replied.

You've ruined my life, darling.

The night Senator Behl's name would be put in nomination, Constance arranged a party in the Observatory. There was a terrible storm that night, rain falling in sheets, battering the windows. Someone said that the Observatory seemed like the drenched fo'c'sle of a ship, shuddering with each gust of wind. They were listening to the convention on the radio, the signal erratic even with the special antenna the Navy provided. Many good friends from Washington and elsewhere in the East were present; and Sir Charles Rath had sailed over from England. Constance presided; and there were seven other women, wives, enough for two lively tables of bridge in the billiards room. Everyone was in high good humor, because they all knew how long their old friend had sought his prize; they were happy for him and for themselves, too. The rising tide raised all the yachts. A private railway car was waiting on a siding at Union Station to take them north as soon as definite word was received, though that was only a formality, because Senator Behl had the support of the nominee, that support to be announced before the balloting. Everything was arranged and all that remained was the telephone call from the Man himself. Champagne was cooling in silver buckets in the billiards room, where the women were playing cards. The butler, old John, had stationed himself next to the telephone. In the deep shadows near the mariner's telescope, so inconspicuous as to be barely visible, stood young Axel Behl, summoned from school for the occasion. Constance insisted upon it, reminding her husband that it was the boy's birthday.

The room was loud with conversation, the men making plans for the coming campaign and the fine administration to follow. David Longfellow and Chairman Tyner of the House Banking Committee debated the economy. Senator Bilbauer and Judge Justin Aswell of the Appeals Court did not like the shape of things in the farm belt. Former Secretary George Steppe and Congressman Curly Peralta were filling jobs, a seat on the Interstate Commerce Commission or the chairmanship of the American Battle Monuments Commission, general counsel of this board or that agency, ambassadorships, the judiciary. George and Curly agreed that this President-to-be held his cards close to his vest, and that was a problem, because George Steppe wanted his son Georgie to be the U.S. Attorney in Boston, a post that vice president-to-be Adolph Behl could help secure — if he performed superbly in the campaign, and campaigning was not the senator's long suit. His own seat was so safe that he had never had to fight for it, and he was temperamentally unsuited to trench warfare in any case. Adolph Behl raised money and worked behind the scenes in the Senate and was at least as effective at one as at the other.

Slowly the rain began to end. Young Axel could see the misty lights of Washington far below. He put his eye to the telescope and listened to the exchange between the former secretary and the congressman, understanding little except that Mr. Steppe wanted something for Georgie and his father was supposed to help him get it when he was vice president. Axel turned to see his father deep in conversation with Chairman Tyner, the chairman talking and his father listening and nodding, every now and then glancing at the telephone. The radio was turned low, inaudible except for the scratch of static. From the billiards room Axel heard the women bidding, one club, one heart, one no trump, five spades, double, and then his mother's voice, Irish around the edges.

"Why don't they call, darling?"

His father grunted and did not reply.

"It's getting late. Don't you think it's late?"

"He'll call when it's time."

"I think it's late," Constance said, tapping her cards sharply on the table.

Constance resumed her monologue, a story her friends had heard many times, how as a little girl she had watched her father march off to war, Captain Barkin so handsome in his military kit, every daughter's dream. Jack Barkin was a man to be reckoned with. Of course the family name had been Anglicized to Barkin from de Barquin, Constance's grandfather having fled the Paris Commune in 1871, when aristocrats were shot on sight, arriving in Cork with the clothes on his back and little else except his good looks and his esprit de corps. God, he was a handsome man; all the de Barquins were tall and slender, *comme il faut*, irresistible to women, romantics by temperament. Her gallant father was off to the Transvaal to fight the Kaffirs. His charming letters home described each dangerous engagement, the troops massed on horseback — ah, he was a fine horseman — charging again and again, gloriously heedless of risk. Captain Barkin — Bar-canh, as Constance pronounced it — was put in for the Military Cross, but there was a tragic mix-up and before the mix-up was solved he was dead, killed by a lancer at Magersfontein, December 10, 1899. The family wept for days. The Queen herself sent condolences. Axel had the looks of the de Barquins, Constance concluded, most particularly the protruding upper lip, the de Barquin lip.

Chairman Tyner looked questioningly at Adolph, and Adolph said, "They weren't Kaffirs; they were Boers. He wasn't a captain; he was a conscript. And there was no mix-up, either, because there was no Military Cross. The rest of it, I'm not in a position to say."

"Aren't women extraordinary," the chairman said.

"Women live in a dream world," the senator replied bitterly.

When the call came at last everyone turned toward Adolph Behl. Curly Peralta began to clap and then all the men applauded, stopping abruptly when old John picked up the receiver and handed it to the senator. Adolph took it and stood at attention, listening, but it was evident at once that something was wrong, because after a few moments he began to cough uncontrollably and dropped the receiver. From the billiards room Constance asked what was wrong, darling. Someone stepped to the sideboard and poured Adolph a large whiskey, handing it to him carefully as if it were medicine. Old John retrieved the receiver and replaced it in its cradle.

Adolph stood motionless, the whiskey glass in his hand, the expression on his face unreadable. He looked like a classroom lecturer who had unaccountably lost his place and had forgotten what came next. He shifted the whiskey glass from his left hand to his right and in a sudden violent motion hurled it at the wall. Bits of crystal flew everywhere, but still he did not move. When his wife approached him he roughly pushed her away as if she were a tactless servant. *You bastard,* Constance snarled, loud enough for everyone to hear. Adolph's attention went quickly elsewhere, to his friends who were dumb with shock and dismay, except for Sir Charles Rath, who was too worldly to be shocked by anything and was rarely dismayed.

Humiliation gave way to rage, fury seeking to conceal insult as, many years later, the scar on the wall was concealed by a little Picasso sketch, a merry satyr in a loincloth scratching his cloven hoof. The senator was trembling, talking loudly to no one in particular, vowing revenge. His friends joined in because they too had been insulted. They all thought they were climbing to the top of the tree together, and when they discovered they weren't, they were furious. Adolph was still a United States senator and that counted for something, but his ambition was to be vice president. The nomination had been promised to him, and now the promise had been rudely withdrawn.

Curly Peralta managed, "What did he say exactly?"

Adolph mentioned a name, the young Midwestern governor, so well-liked in his own state and neighboring states, including Adolph's own state. He was the Man's choice, selected no doubt for his amiability and ignorance of national affairs; he would be a lap dog. Then Adolph murmured, "Alabama."

He meant that the Alabama delegation might revolt. He had good, close friends in that delegation, men he had known for years. He had attended their weddings, had stood godfather to their children, had hunted on their plantations as they had come to Echo House for billiards and conversation. Because it stood first on the roll of states, any Alabama revolt could turn the convention. The radio static had cleared, and George Steppe turned up the volume so that they could all listen to the balloting.

Adolph stared at the radio as if it were human and capable of any surprise. But Alabama was solid; no one broke ranks, not a single delegate. The head of the delegation bawled the unanimous vote to cheers in the great hall. Adolph had been an usher at his wedding and had managed a private bill through the Senate on his behalf; and now Adolph thought he heard laughter in the chairman's voice. And so it continued through the alphabet until the applause began to build — and then George brusquely switched off the radio.

For a moment no one knew what to do or say. They looked to Adolph for a lead, but he gave none. There was general movement in the direction of the sideboard; everyone beginning to talk at once while they prepared their drinks, agreeing that betrayal could not go unpunished. Curly Peralta decided that the nominee had sent a dreadful signal: his word could not be trusted, and in national politics a man's word was his destiny. A bad beginning, Curly said, and the nominee — the Man — must needs be taught a lesson. The means were near to hand, allies to be enlisted without delay, friendly newspapermen, finance people, Senate colleagues — for was this not an affront to the dignity of the Senate? — state chairmen, religious leaders, members of the bar. Each man had his own list of markers to be called when the time came. God, what a mess.

The women listened from the billiards room, where they had resumed their card game. Young Axel remained in the shadows, hearing the gathering of the tricks and the shuffle, the falling of the cards and the thick silence before the bidding, the scratch of a match when one of the women lit a cigarette. In the Observatory the talk trailed away, growing softer — and then someone laughed and the others joined in. The women looked at each other and continued their aggressive play, their conversation barely a murmur. Axel wondered if this was what his father meant by the dream world of women. Unsuited by temperament to the hard realities of government and politics, they lived in a half-light of illusion; they turned the facts to mean what they wanted them to mean, and perhaps in that way achieved their heart's desire. It would be a kind of freedom, amending or ignor-

ing the rules the men made, playing cards while the world came
to an end.

One no trump, Constance said, her voice soft as a feather.

Doubled, Ione Peralta replied.

Meanwhile in the Observatory the weather was changing.
Winter gave rise to spring, the hard ground suddenly loose and
receptive. The men commenced to talk about the ticket, its
strengths and liabilities, who would be with them and who
against them and how strongly. They were breaking the nation
down by region and class. They were dismantling it the way a
mechanic dismantles an engine, appraising each part by itself
and then as a function of the other parts. The ticket had appeal
to the middle of the nation and to farmers generally and white-
collar voters. The Northeast was a problem. New York was a
special problem, and the baby-faced Midwestern governor would
be no help there. No help in the parishes and synagogues and no
help in the union halls. They'd best hide the lap dog in the alfalfa.
The election would be a mighty struggle to be sure, and how
much better if the nominee had kept his word and chosen our
good friend as his running mate. But we can't walk back the cat.
What's done's done. If they were clever about it and campaigned
with energy. If they put their money into the right pockets in the
critical cities. If they stuck to the traditional principles of the
party — well, then, we're winners.

Axel looked at George Steppe. The young man had not failed
to notice that "they" had abruptly become "we."

"He doesn't know anything about Washington," Adolph said.
"He's never lived here. He doesn't know the way we do things.
He won't know who counts. He won't know how to preside over
the Senate. He's too green. These outsiders always muck things
up."

"He's not a quality man," George said. "But it's a strong
ticket."

From the billiards room came a tinkle of laughter, Constance's successful finesse.

"Bad show," Sir Charles put in.

"This wouldn't happen in Britain," David Longfellow said.

"Certainly not by telephone," Sir Charles said, and that drew a smile from Adolph.

And then, boats catching the freshening breeze, they were off again, plotting the course of the campaign, identifying natural hazards, predicting strategy and tactics, and, conspicuously, who would be involved and who wouldn't be involved. One of them called it the great American holy war, and you volunteered cheerfully, rallying to the din of the megaphone. Neutrality was a sin, and how much better to direct things from headquarters rather than in the stink and blood of the trenches. Any candidate would covet their experience and practical knowledge. They were veterans all, with campaign ribbons to prove it — including, as of tonight, a Purple Heart, ha-ha. The Man will need all the help he can get, Senator Bilbauer said. He needs us. He'll come begging. The phone will ring any time now.

Listening to them, it was obvious even to young Axel that there would be no revenge, not that night or any night. And from the look on his face, Adolph Behl knew it, too. So he gave them his full attention as they gathered around the sideboard with their drinks, helping themselves to shrimp and crabcakes, all the while talking themselves back from the precipice. The compass began its swing: high emotion had given way to chaos, and chaos back to judgment. These were practical men. Tomorrow held more promise than yesterday, and government was forever. There was more than one route to the top of the tree, and no one wanted to be left behind.

David Longfellow did not sense that the wind had shifted.

"God damn him," David said. "We're going to twist him the way he's twisted us, pardon my French. He's not clean. I happen to know about the woman he sees in New York and where he sees her. I know her name and where she lives and he knows I know. The Man's a whoremaster —"

"David," Judge Aswell said quietly. "Shut up."

"It's ammunition," the banker said lamely.

"Let's caucus," Curly said, rubbing his hands together.

"There's unfinished business here," George Steppe said, gesturing at the telephone.

"Yes," Curly said, looking at Adolph. But the senator did not turn from the window. Watching his father from the shadows, Axel could not erase the sight of his mother holding her arm and hissing, all burdened Galway in her distress, *You baaaassstard.* Now she was calmly dealing cards, telling another story as she stared coldly at her husband. He was standing alone at the rain-streaked window that gave out onto the rooftops and monuments of the capital. Low scud had moved in, and the darkness was as dull and restless as the surface of an ocean. He seemed lost in the humiliation of the telephone call. None of the others felt it as he did. They were his friends but like good horsemen they mounted again when they were thrown — or, to be exact about it, when a fellow rider was thrown. The race was not forfeit because a man fell off his horse, even if the circumstances were unfortunate or suspicious; the contest continued over the many, many furlongs remaining. This seemed to be the point that Curly Peralta was making, his high-pitched voice causing even the women to smile as they threw down their trumps. Everyone knew that revenge was a dish best eaten cold, but Curly was insisting that on this occasion it was a dish best refused.

"Don't you agree, Charles?"

They all turned to the portly Englishman examining the books in the low bookcases; they were books on the architecture of Washington, D.C. Sir Charles Rath looked up and muttered something noncommittal.

"Come on, Charles!" George Steppe's voice was loud. "Tell us your view of revenge. Do you take it or leave it?"

"Yes, Charles. Give us the benefit of your advice." This was Constance, her voice drifting in from the billiards room.

Sir Charles looked unsuccessfully at his friend for a signal. When Adolph gave none, he decided that tact was a virtue. "My friend will do as he thinks best," the Englishman said mildly.

"So loyal, Charles," Constance said. "You're so loyal. It's such a lovely quality in men. It becomes you."

"The unfinished business," George said softly to Curly.

"It's positively inspiring," Constance said, her voice ragged around the edges.

Adolph wasn't listening. He lifted his shoulders and let them fall. "Revenge," he said, looking across the room at Sir Charles. "I'll have it the way that our mentor said to have it, 'Without haste, but without rest.'"

Sir Charles smiled bleakly, recognizing Goethe's thought.

"That's not your business," Stanley Greene said loudly. He had been listening attentively these many minutes, his smile growing as the compass swung. His view of human nature was as wide as a column of type. The old cynic was rarely disappointed, and now he cackled maliciously. "Revenge is my specialty," he said. "Leave the revenge to me and watch Sunday's paper." The editor drew on his cigar and blew a huge smoke ring that floated across the oval room until it touched an upright rose in a fluted vase and collapsed. He looked inquiringly at David Longfellow.

"Leave it alone," Judge Aswell said.

"You wouldn't be wanting to interfere with an editor's prerogative? You of all people, Justin. You who've been so forthright in support of freedom of expression. David has the scoop!" The editor smiled broadly, the smile fading when he saw David Longfellow shake his head; and with that, the whoremaster disappeared for good.

Old John had glided to Senator Behl's side, a whiskey on his silver tray. The senator shook his head and they stood looking out the window at the scud, breaking here and there to reveal the Capitol building and the Washington Monument, conspicuous in pink. John had been with him for many years. They were about the same height and age and might have been brothers, so closely did they resemble each other. They shared a bookish temperament and a love of horticulture. They were united in their dislike of the swampy weather in Washington, a climate so thick and swollen that anything grew. Constance's English garden was an incoherent brawl that threatened everyone's peace of mind. Any blockhead could make a garden in Washington.

They preferred the disciplined and windswept prairie back in the Midwest, "the State," as Adolph always called it, his constituency. He and John gardened together in the spring, cultivating perfectly aligned rows of white and yellow roses, row upon row. They experimented with hybrid roses, one particularly successful, and they called that the Behlbaver rose. John's surname was Baver. Constance maintained that the rose was remembered by more Americans than any legislation her husband sponsored. Who cared about interstate commerce, the Behl Act? Only the railroads cared about it, and they didn't like it; Midwestern farmers liked it and forgot it. So they worked on their roses, loving the black soil and the harsh climate, a hard wind always blowing from the west ruffling the prairie grass. The senator thought the grass resembled the surface of the ocean, and the arrowheads he and John found no different from the bones of great fishes washed up on Atlantic beaches. Of course Constance hated it, so she always stayed behind at Echo House, or traveled with friends to the spa at the Greenbriar. The senator and John Baver always came back to Washington with stories of the swarms of butterflies that arrived in the spring.

They stood companionably at the window flanked left and right by the senator's favorite pictures, Childe Hassam's drypoint sketch of a middle-aged Henry Adams and a dense Edward Hopper etching of a farmer's field at dusk. The mariner's telescope was between them, its polished brass and antique fittings giving the scene a preindustrial look. Suddenly they turned their heads, leaning forward like commuters awaiting a bus. They sighed in unison and the senator slumped as if his bones had gone soft. In the distance were bright starbursts, flashes of red, white, and blue glittering above the clouds, disappearing into them when spent. They were fireworks along the Potomac, party loyalists celebrating the triumphant convention and its heroic nominees.

John continued to hold the silver tray with its glass of whiskey, and when at last the senator took it, John glanced at Henry Adams as if he expected that Adams, too, wished to be served.

Adolph said, "Thank you, Johnny." He turned now and looked across the room at the wall and the ugly scar his glass had made. He tapped his chest and slowly reached into his inside jacket pocket and withdrew a sheaf of papers folded lengthwise, his acceptance speech. He wordlessly handed it to John Baver.

"I'm so very sorry," John said. He slipped the speech under the tray, holding it with his fingers, and glided away to the pantry, pretending not to see Constance raise her empty glass, demanding a refill.

The party had been watching them at the window, waiting for John to leave so that the business at hand could be completed. Curly cleared his throat. "Senator," he said. "Listen to me a minute."

But Adolph did not turn from the window, where starbursts were still visible among the clouds.

"Listen to Curly," George said. "There's something we have to do here. It has to be done and you have to do it."

Curly said, "Make the phone call, Adolph. Make it while it still counts for something. Congratulate the son of a bitch, wish him luck, promise your support, make a joke, give him the usual mumbo-jumbo. Tell him you wish things had turned out differently and you look forward to meeting with him at the earliest opportunity, discuss matters of mutual interest and so forth and so on. You know the drill."

Judge Aswell nodded gravely. "Do it, Adolph."

"One club," Constance said, tapping her cards on the table.

Curly placed the call himself. He waited, then spoke a few words and extended the earpiece to Adolph. And in that gesture and the worldly smile that went with it was the essence of their politics: compromise and magnanimity. Magnanimity in defeat, magnanimity in victory, each requiring largeness of spirit and practical knowledge of the way the world worked. As Curly had said, the usual mumbo-jumbo. The gesture announced: We are not bitter-enders. We do not whine or bang the spoon against the porridge bowl. We do not take revenge in the heat of battle or its aftermath. We struggle, and if we lose, we give way. We congratulate the winner and we pledge our loyalty because there will be other struggles on other days and our opponent today may be our ally tomorrow. Above all, we do not burn bridges. This is the government, after all. Party loyalty counts for something and we stand with our brothers, always. It's bred in the bone.

Curly smiled broadly as he extended the earpiece to the senator, who was still looking out the window at the fireworks, fading now. There was some small noise from the telephone, a sound like the crackling of fire. The women paused in their bridge game, listening hard. Constance's fingers were suspended above the table like a seer's, her trump ready to fall, her expression unruly. Stanley Greene leaned carelessly against the mantel, his dark eyes hooded, watching Adolph Behl with the most open prurience; he seemed to be committing everything to memory. Curly extended his arm, exasperated, shaking the earpiece.

George said, "Come on, Senator. Get it over with."

No one was watching more closely or listening more acutely than young Axel Behl, still inconspicuous in the shadows. His father was almost close enough to touch, and then he turned from the window with an expression as confused as his son had ever seen; and he never saw it again. The senator looked around, blinking; the light caught his hair and turned it white. His hair seemed to rise in coils. He made as if to say something, and when no words came, he shook his head and strode from the room with no backward glances except to look with loathing at the crescent-shaped scar on the wall. Curly was left with the earpiece hanging in dead air.

Constance slapped her card on the table and called loudly for old John, but everyone was listening to Curly's soothing voice, My goodness, Adolph was here just a moment ago, he must have stepped out, but don't you worry, he's on board one hundred percent as we all are, though naturally he wishes things had been handled differently. You know how these things are, when you expect one thing and get another, naturally there's irritation. But the hard feelings will pass . . .

Curly turned his back and spoke privately, and then his high-pitched laugh ended the conversation.

"Let's open the Champagne, John," Curly said.

"Yes," Constance said brightly. "Let's do."

When John arrived with a tray of glasses and three unopened

bottles of Champagne, the company was silent, each man pondering Adolph's refusal to put things right. Was it an act of conscience? Vainglory? Simple anger? Perhaps he did not trust himself to speak, seeing betrayal on all sides. Perhaps all of the above, and perhaps none. Perhaps it was his dislike of the swampy weather in Washington, where any blockhead could make a rose grow. But his behavior was as out of character for him as it would have been for his great hero, Henry Adams. Not to mention Wolfgang von Goethe, Germany's greatest soul. This was not the first time in his long life in politics that a man had broken his promise and gone back on his word, so great are the temptations of public office. In politics the rewards of victory are tremendous. Nothing must be allowed to stand in the way of victory, because in politics runners-up don't count. The journalist's "gallant effort" reads nicely, but no one in the business cares about it.

Judge Aswell sighed. "Well, that's it. Adolph has decided to burn his bridges and ours too while he's at it. Our nominee's a vindictive bastard, likes his loyalties undivided, likes to scorch the earth when they're not. I can't imagine what got into Adolph. Has he lost his mind?" The judge turned to Curly Peralta for confirmation, but Curly was giving none. He only shook his head sadly while watching old John wrestle with the Champagne's wire and foil. His loyalty was to his old friend, no matter how badly the friend had mishandled the brief. Of course that did not mean that you went to war. The enemy of your friend had many friends who were also your friends, and the stakes were not small.

"He let his emotions rule," George Steppe said coldly. "And now he has to live with the consequences. The problem's his to solve. Trouble is, we all have money in the pot. What did you say to the Man, Curly?"

"The usual," Curly said.

George nodded decisively. "That's the way we do business in this house," he said to a murmur of agreement. "When a decision's made by our leader, we unite behind him. We make the call of congratulations and we promise our support because tomorrow is more important than yesterday. If we don't like the decision, we can quit. We can join the other side. We can sulk. But don't expect to be forgiven."

George Steppe's ringmaster's moustache flared, and Axel knew that he was in the presence of an impresario; the show went on, no matter what. He knew also that for his father tomorrow was not more important than yesterday. Probably for him it was the reverse; the sum of all the yesterdays equals tomorrow unless you believed in miracles. He surely didn't expect to be forgiven. Axel understood then that his father could be humiliated and that the insult was not political; it was personal. They had rejected *him,* and so he would leave the field and return to his Behlbavers and his butterflies and his committee chairmanship in the Senate. Of course he would redeem his bleak promise of revenge "without haste but without rest." Axel knew also that his father had tried to cross the Rubicon, and it was the wrong Rubicon. In any case, he was alone in his distress.

Old John opened the Champagne at last, turning the corks with his fingers so that they made no sound. The bottles were sweating and fuming at the mouth, the aroma of Champagne mixed now with eau de Cologne and bath soap. The women had assembled silently in the doorway, their faces as impassive as any jury's. They glittered with ornaments — necklaces, earrings, silver combs in their hair. The men waited patiently until the women were served, old John delivering the glasses one by one, finally to Ione Peralta and Constance. Then they helped themselves, and still no one spoke.

Constance motioned for Axel to join her. She put her arm around his shoulders, the company startled at how much they resembled each other, black hair center-parted, eyes that seemed chiseled from the same black stone. Constance raised her glass and smiled grimly.

"A toast to my son, Axel. To Axel, next in line. To Axel on his birthday."

Everyone drank and sang one disorganized chorus of *Happy Birthday,* the men suddenly subdued.

Then Curly Peralta stepped forward. With a sharp look at

Constance, he said, "To the nominees of our party, the next President and Vice President of the United States."

The men drained their glasses. Curly threw his into the fireplace and took another from the tray on the sideboard. The others followed suit, except for Constance, who neither drank nor broke her glass, yet stood in such a way that no one doubted who presided at Echo House.

Many years later Axel Behl told the story to his son, Alec, then a teenager. Old enough to appreciate the stakes. Old enough to grasp the ironies, as Axel said. The moment was morbidly apt. They had walked across the street from Echo House to Soldiers Cemetery and were standing before the stele that announced BEHL, a rose sculpted above the name, and below it an inscription in German, Goethe's *Art is long, life short; judgment difficult, opportunity transient.* Constance's selection, it went without saying; she had outlived the senator by five years, dying alone in the Observatory on the eve of Hitler's march into Poland.

Axel leaned heavily on his cane as he spoke. Alec was looking at him strangely, and he guessed that his right eye was drooping, the long scar on his face livid. His voice had risen, too, and he was sweating. He reached to massage his ruined knee and continued softly, "She was fierce, fiercer than he was. When she died I was out of touch. I'd been sent to Lisbon on war business. Curly Peralta handled the arrangements, and I didn't learn the circumstances until much later."

"I hardly remember her," Alec said. What he did remember were unforgiving eyes and a sarcastic tongue. She seemed to believe that life had let her down badly. Sylvia, his mother, called her a connoisseur of misfortune.

Axel reached with his cane to dislodge a bit of lichen on the stele. "So there I was in the famous Observatory, a shadow witness to how grown men behaved at a private moment of betrayal. I was invisible except when my mother, God bless her, proposed her toast. The king was dead, long live the king. And this much was true for me: in some unconscious way I chose my career that night, not the precise function but the form of it, where I would place myself in the scramble to the top of the tree. Meaning the government, because that's our family's milieu. That's what we do. That's what he did, that's what I do, and you will, too, when the time comes. We don't know how to do anything else."

And it had made them all so happy, Alec thought but did not say.

"Why, you were born the night Frank Roosevelt was nominated. Your mother likes to tell the story that when I called from the convention floor and the nurse said you'd arrived, I didn't ask whether you were a boy or a girl. I had to tell your mother about the five ballots and how California caved and what a great day it was for the nation. You know the story, a family joke."

Axel paused, out of breath. He took a tiny vial from his coat pocket, tapped a pill into his palm, and swallowed it dry. He sighed and bit his lip. Someone had wandered within earshot. In a moment the intruder was gone, and Axel spoke again.

"You're in it for the long haul. You give your loyalty to the *state,* don't you see? Nothing else matters. You know what the Stalinists say. Let them starve! Let them starve! The last two left alive will be communists for life. That's it exactly."

Alec said, "Your face is awful pale. Are you all right? Can I get you a glass of water?"

"My father disappointed us all, quitting as he did. And it was his own fault entirely. So inside the Observatory at Echo House that night I knew that I never wanted to be dependent on a promise that could be withdrawn over a telephone line — sorry to put it like this, Axel old boy, but I've made other plans, no hard feelings I hope, and let's stay in touch. I never wanted to learn the mumbo-jumbo and say that everything was fine when it wasn't fine. I suppose in that way only I am my father's son. I intended to be in the tree with my own juju. And I guess that's how it worked out, good for them, good for me. You know the story about the expert mimic? The one with the repertoire of a hundred voices in a dozen languages and in due course he forgot his own voice. He forgot what he sounded like and couldn't remember even in his dreams at night."

Alec said, "Dad, your face —"

"You never knew this, so I'll tell you now. Constance was determined that I take my father's place in the Senate, and when the time came put forward my own candidacy for President of the United States. She bought a little farm in Maryland so that I'd have a State to run from. That was her great dream, the ambition that would cancel her husband's lust for second best, the disaster that brought such shame on Echo House. And until that night in the Observatory, her dream was my dream, too."

"Honestly, you don't look well."

"But I've sold the farm, so you don't have a State. You'll have to make your own plans."

Alec was silent.

"You know about the Rubicon, Alec. It's only a little stream, even when Caesar crossed it. Only a few yards wide and a few feet deep, so narrow in places you could jump across. The Rubicon makes the Potomac look like the Amazon." Then Axel threw back his head and laughed loudly, tapping the stele with his cane. "Do you know what she gave me that night for a birthday present?"

Alec shook his head. He had no idea. His father was sputtering with laughter, his face ghostly white except for the livid scar. He reached to touch the stele, tracing the engraved rose with his fingernail.

"A pretty little nineteenth-century print," Axel said. "Not rare. Not valuable. You've seen it many times. It's in the Observatory next to Sylvia's merry satyr. A pastel, Constance's dream come true: the doge's palace at Venice in the early morning sunshine." And then Axel's smile vanished and he added, "The next day my father gave me his most prized volume, a signed first edition of *Democracy*. Some day it'll be yours."

PART I

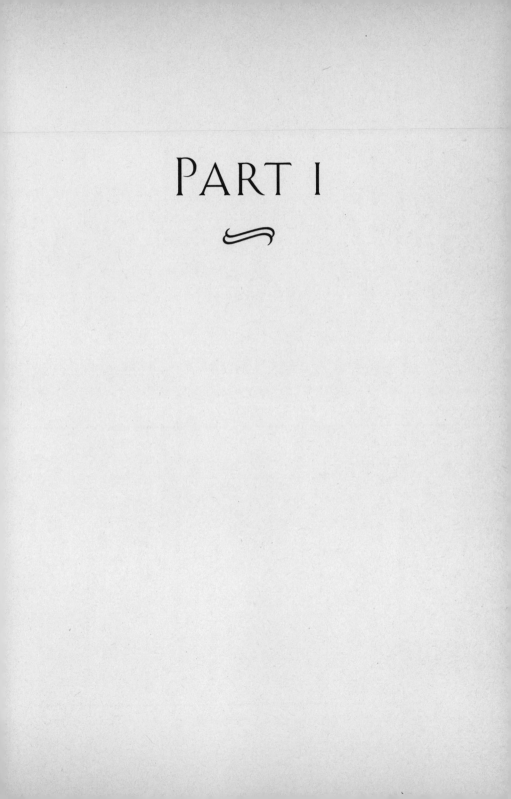

1

The Girl on the Bicycle

❦

AXEL BEHL and his son dined alone on Thanksgiving Day, 1947. Sylvia Behl had vacated in August, living in Europe, people suspected, though no one knew for sure except possibly Axel, and no one dared ask him. Sylvia was gone. Sylvia was a closed subject. She had written no one, not even young Alec; at least that was the rumor, and people who knew Sylvia believed it. She was a woman who burned her bridges.

The community understood. Sylvia was beautiful and high-spirited and, after 1944, Axel was neither. He admitted to Billie Peralta that his life might not be worth the effort it took to live it. However, the understanding did not include sympathy, for Sylvia was a handful, sharp-tongued, temperamental, opinion-ated, and slow to fit into the milieu. In fact, it was generally agreed that she had never really tried, an awkward situation all around, because everyone was so fond of her gallant husband. And the boy was a standout, the sort of well-mannered intelli-gent boy who was a pleasure to have to dinner. The community tended to take the long view and concluded that Sylvia's deser-tion was probably for the best. A Washington homily fit the situation: "That which must be done eventually is best done immediately."

So this was the first Thanksgiving without Sylvia, and a desul-tory affair it was, despite the best efforts of the kitchen staff; but since they were French the meal had a saucy quality that owed more to Périgord than to the federal city. After preparing dinner, the servants had been given the evening off, leaving only Axel and Alec at home, picking through the spicy dinde with its tangled collar of green beans and au gratin potatoes and puréed mushrooms and foie gras; but no stuffing or cranberry sauce or pumpkin pie or the creamed onions that were Sylvia's specialty. Father and son sat in silence, listening to the clock tick.

Axel had turned down half a dozen well-meant invitations from friends to come up to New York or down to Middleburg or The Plains. In early October he had had another operation on his back and was still in pain. That operation had not been a success any more than the others had been. The surgeons at Walter Reed remarked that he was very fortunate to have such a high tolerance for pain; he thought they would kill him in their heroic efforts to keep him alive. So this was the last operation, permitting him the dubious consolation that he would not have to be cut again; in that one sense the operation reminded him of his marriage. And the boy bravely insisted that he would rather be alone at Echo House with his father than with friends, whose kindly concern he found embarrassing, particularly since no one would mention his mother's name. He was not in the mood for another family's feastly hilarity with its specific rituals like charades or Monopoly. And the table conversation would be politics, everyone expected to contribute, whether they had anything to say or not; and God help you if you got a fact wrong, the number of congressional districts in Iowa or the identity of the governor of Kentucky or the number of Reds in the French National Assembly. So at six in the evening Alec found himself toying with his food, moving the potatoes around the beans and the mushrooms around the dinde, thinking about the long train ride back to school in Massachusetts two days hence. His father had offered to fly up to Boston so that they could have Thanksgiving at Locke-Ober with the Aswells, but the boy had said no thanks to that, too, not wanting to trouble his father. The last operation had left him looking haggard and frail, in no condition for a three-hour journey in an airplane. And it was bitter cold in Boston.

Candle wax was dripping on the tablecloth, and the boy moved to reposition the candles, which had begun to list. The dining room was warm and the silence oppressive. He thought he might slip out for a movie, since his father would surely retire early. There were war films playing on a double bill downtown, leathernecks assaulting a Pacific island. That would surely take care of the rest of the evening, leaving only Friday and Saturday before departure on the crowded midnight train to Boston. He glanced into the oval mirror over the sideboard and saw his father's face, gaunt in the flickering candlelight. His father looked colorless and insignificant in the vastness of the room. His head was thrown back and his eyes were closed, but he wasn't dozing, because his lips were moving and he was massaging his lower back. Framed in the mirror, Axel Behl's white face had the dour aspect of a seventeenth-century Dutch portrait; and the artist was no friend.

"Can I get you something?" the boy asked. "More turkey? Mushrooms?"

His father waited a moment before replying, in a dusty voice, "Pour me a glass of whiskey, please."

The boy went to the sideboard and poured whiskey from a decanter into a glass, looking again into the mirror, his own face up close and his father's in the background, flickering yellow light all around. He handed the whiskey to his father, who took a sip and set the glass carefully on the table.

"Pretty awful, isn't it?"

"It's not so bad," the boy said. "It's a French Thanksgiving."

"I asked Billie Peralta to tell them what to do and how to do it, but Billie doesn't speak French very well and Jacques wouldn't've listened anyhow. He only listened to your mother. Reluctantly." Axel sighed, leaning forward to massage his back. Little beads of sweat jumped to the surface of his forehead. "I suppose we should have taken Billie up on her offer, gone out to Middleburg for turkey. And charades after."

"'This is fine," the boy said.

"I hate charades," his father said.

"So do I."

"She would have been thrilled to have us, though. She likes to take people in. And she never liked Sylvia."

"I know," the boy said. He ate a mouthful of turkey.

"She said Sylvia's bite was worse than her bark."

Alec nodded, not knowing where his father was headed with this conversation but dreading it.

"Washington's hard," Axel said. "We all know each other so damned well and everyone has a past with everyone else. You either fit in right away or you don't, and if you don't you never will."

"She said she missed London," Alec said. "But I don't know what the great difference is. They both have a river and a legislature and the men wear hats."

"The difference is." Axel paused. "Heat."

"I like Washington," Alec said loyally.

"Maybe your taste in cities will change."

"Not mine."

"Well, you're young. You can keep your powder dry."

"She used to say that Washington was dry. She said it was a dry bath. What did she mean by that?"

"She thought that Washington was old. London was young. Sylvia always took a contrary view. She liked to turn things inside out. We Behls are attracted to women who turn things inside out. Trouble is, it's not a quality that wears well, long term. It's tiresome." Axel took another sip of whiskey, holding the glass to the candlelight and looking through it.

They were silent again. The boy was not certain what his father meant about turning things inside out. At that moment he was certain he would never live anywhere but Washington. He could not imagine living anywhere else, certainly not bombed-out London, with its frightening memories. Echo House was home for him, as it had been home for his grandfather and his father.

"Son." The boy looked up. His father was staring into the

middle distance, as if what he had to say could only be thrown into neutral territory. "I have a number for her, if you want to call. She's in London. At least she was in London last week."

"Did you speak to her?"

"No. But I have a number."

The boy was watching his father in the oval mirror, the older man in a soft tweed suit, blue shirt, and regimental tie. It was an old bespoke suit and it fit him badly, loose around the shoulders and waist; but of course it had been made for a larger man. It was the suit he always wore at Thanksgiving and Christmas. Now, as usual when he was speaking of personal matters, his hand moved to the deep scar that ran from his hairline to his jaw. He took another swallow of whiskey and the boy knew that the pain must be very bad, because his father seldom drank. He had not touched his wine.

"It might be a good idea if you called her."

"I'll think about it," the boy said.

His father reached into his pocket and put a file card on the table. The boy took it and put it away without reading it, though he noticed that there was an address along with a telephone number. He had assumed that his mother was in London, her favorite city in the world, where she had many friends and fine wartime memories and no family. "Five hours time difference," his father said.

"I remember," the boy said.

"Do you miss London?"

"I hated the school."

His father nodded; that was old ground.

"And then you went away."

Axel smiled wryly. "No question. That was a big mistake."

He had gone away and returned a casualty of war, so broken and torn up that he was unrecognizable. Their London house, which had been so full of life before the war, was suddenly silent and blue, his father upstairs in the wide hospital bed, his mother below. Nothing had seemed beyond Axel Behl's reach, a ticket to Wimbledon or a box of Belgian chocolates or an American convertible or an introduction to Glenn Miller; suddenly he was helpless, unable even to speak coherently, assisted by nurses every day and night. Alec said, "Where did you get the number?"

"Son," his father said. "Please. I have friends and they have friends. It wasn't very hard to do."

Then why did it take so long? "Okay," the boy said.

"Well." His father sighed heavily, smiling slowly. "What are your plans for the evening?"

"There's a double feature at the Circle."

"What's playing?"

The boy hesitated. "I forget."

Axel looked at him sharply. "The morning paper's in the library. You can check the listings."

"It's a John Wayne double feature."

"John Wayne goes to war?"

"I guess so."

"Germans or Japanese?"

"Japs, I think."

Axel Behl was silent a moment, leaning back, his hands flat on the table.

"It's only a movie," the boy said.

"I saw one once," he said. "The White House last summer. Mr. Truman invited us over. I made myself go and it wasn't easy. I swore I never would, but when you're invited to the White House, you go. Such tripe. One lie after another, and when you added up all the little lies you had a big lie the size of the Matterhorn. I left halfway through, pleading fatigue. Couldn't stand it. Hated every minute." He began to drum his fingers on the table, looking again into the middle distance.

"I know," the boy said. Talking to his father was like walking through a minefield: one false step and you were on your back, minus an arm or a leg.

"No, you don't."

"Then tell me," the boy said quickly, the words out before he could bring them back. His father had never spoken about the war and made it clear he didn't want to be asked about it. His war was so profoundly intimate that it could not be shared; at least he did not share it.

"Propaganda," he said suddenly.

"What's propaganda?" the boy asked.

"A rhapsody," Axel said. "A bully's love song."

"You walked out of a movie in the White House?" The boy wanted his father to keep talking, to tell him about the war even if it was his own false rhapsody. He had the right to tell any story he wanted, at whatever length or to whatever purpose. He could use the historical facts or invent his own; it wouldn't matter. But he did not have the right to remain silent, keep things to himself, withhold evidence. What had happened to Captain Axel Barkin Behl in the war was their common property. They both lived with the consequences and would go on living with them. This was the way the world worked, and this was their fate. His father was crippled and his mother was gone and there remained only the two of them to face the wide world. And the world was not indifferent.

"Do you remember which movie it was?"

But Axel was silent, his eyes half-lidded, his fingers again tracing the cicatrix that carved his face. He had been startlingly handsome as a young man before the war. Everyone said so and the family photographs proved it, Axel in black tie, Axel in tennis whites, not a hair out of place, the part in the center of his skull as straight as a sword's blade. But it was hard for Alec to recall the prewar years. What he remembered was a private hospital in Belgravia, its cream-colored façade suggesting a villa in the Levant, his father on the third floor bandaged head to foot, his eyes glazed and staring from a hole in the rough gauze. His mother's gloved hand pushed him forward to give Daddy a kiss. But she did not say where, so he kissed the bandaged cheek and watched his father wink. Later, when Axel was home with most of the bandages off, Alec did not want to remember him as he had been. That memory was indecent.

The silence lengthened. The boy looked into the candlelight and willed his father to speak. How difficult could it be to give voice to the events of your own life, to speak so that others could understand the shadow-line that divided youth from maturity? Did it involve betrayal? Was it simple stupidity or plain misfortune, obvious bad luck of the sort that everyone encountered every single day? He had gone away a healthy young man and returned a wretched old one, and this seemed to happen overnight. The circumstances were mysterious, and his silence only made them more so, and sinister besides.

Axel smiled. "They say that good judgment comes from experience. And experience comes from bad judgment."

Alec laughed even though he had heard the expression many times.

Axel said abruptly, "As you know, I went to France in early 'forty-two. Fred Greene and I were put ashore in Brittany. You might remember Fred, big redheaded fellow, hot-tempered. Wonderful pianist; he knew everything about popular music and classical music, too. After the war he intended to make his living playing in nightclubs. Fred was my closest friend; we'd known each other since we were schoolboys. His father was an editor and a great friend of the senator, wrote speeches for him. We had been in Spain together, not to fight but to study German aerial tactics, the bombardment of civilian targets mostly. Spain was a war of fire and maneuver, the tactics not much different from Lee's at Antietam, except that Lee was a genius and there were no military geniuses in Spain. The difference between Antietam and Teruel is disciplined butchery and undisciplined butchery, plus of course the airplanes. Spain was modern war and old-fashioned war at once, so we stayed on longer than we should have, learning what we could, and we learned quite a lot. Fred's wife was even less enthusiastic about this adventure than Sylvia, and in fact she left him because of it. Fred didn't understand her and neither did I, because our work in Spain was important. People were *dying,* Spain was bleeding to death." Axel paused, thinking about Spain in 1938; there was more to be said, but he didn't say it.

"Later on we went to work for Colonel Donovan and volunteered for France. That was when you were sent to Scotland to school. You were much too young for boarding school, but that couldn't be helped. Sylvia had a job in the war, too, and as you have cause to know, caring for small children was not her long suit. Baby-sitting was not in her repertoire. Nannies were impossible to find in London, and Sylvia dismissed the ones we did find, and the blitz was in progress and so forth and so on. It was very dangerous. So you went away to Scotland, Sylvia stayed in London, and I went to France with Fred Greene in a small boat."

Axel stopped talking, drumming his fingers on the table again, leaning back and looking at the ceiling and then at the three portraits on the far wall. His father and grandfather were there, along with Constance. The family resemblance was striking; all the men had high foreheads and heavy eyelids over liquid dark eyes and thin lips, and they were scowling. Young Alec was unmistakably of this tribe, except that he had his mother's fair hair and gray eyes, and his build was slender. He had a way of leaning forward on the balls of his feet when the conversation interested him, a trick of Sylvia's as well. There was much of Constance in Axel. His extraordinarily large hands could have belonged to a farmer or blacksmith. He had her stony black eyes, but they were set in his father's face; the de Barquin lip was conspicuous also.

When next Axel spoke it was in a voice as dry as an accountant's, and his manner and tone suggested that the words were costly. He did not give them up easily. Truthfully, he did not want to give them up at all. So his son had better listen carefully, because they would not be repeated.

How much there was to remember. This much was known for sure.

They formed up with Allied troops after D-Day and were ordered to report to Patton's command, assigned to his intelligence section. This was logical; they knew the countryside very well, having lived off it for the past two years. They knew where the Germans were and where they weren't and which French units were reliable and which were bandits. The politics of the Resistance were complicated, as complicated as the various lines of command in the Spanish war; so they tried to avoid politics, claiming indifference or ignorance, depending on the situation. Fred Greene was fluent in French, and Axel was fluent in German and passable in French. Patton was short of translators, and while he distrusted OSS characters generally, he had known and admired Adolph Behl and someone had told him that Fred was all right, so he asked for them by name. That was the way things were done. Someone knew someone and the word was passed down, your orders were cut, and you went off in a Jeep to join George Patton's intelligence section.

They began in Anjou, following Patton's line of march east, the road littered with empty jerry cans and C-ration cartons and the occasional disabled tank and rotting corpse. The region was thick with land mines and remnants of German units, because Patton had not bothered to stop and mop up, perform the usual housekeeping chores. Housekeeping (Axel's term) was not in the general's repertoire. From the look of things, he had destroyed everything in his path, so it made for a dispiriting ride. The litter and the stench.

Axel was driving very fast, and when he came to a crossroads he veered south, turning on impulse into a part of the country that had not been touched by blitzkrieg or invasion or Patton's stampede. Axel was disgusted by the corpse-smell and the helter-skelter of war's residue, and when he saw the turn he took it without thinking. When Fred looked at him in alarm, Axel said he was taking the scenic detour. He said they were owed one. Just once in the miserable year 1944 he intended to behave irresponsibly, and if Fred didn't like it he could get out. If they were lucky they would find a bottle and a wheel of cheese, have lunch and a snooze, and pretend they were in Rock Creek Park on a hot Sunday afternoon.

Fred shrugged and pulled his helmet over his eyes, a gesture that said, more plainly than words, Bad idea.

The unfamiliar road was winding and treacherous, but there was no sign of the Wehrmacht. They crossed one river and then another and entered ancient Aquitaine. Suddenly there were no more road signs. Axel drove more slowly now, elated to be motoring through the quiet countryside at midday. In that part of France the light is thick and milky, shadowless where it touches the earth. The atmosphere is heavy, almost dreamy; you can imagine a knight on horseback or a traveling carnival. The land was deserted and undisturbed, except for a few small farms and orchards. Many of the fields were overgrown and the farmhouses in disrepair. Axel wondered aloud if the inhabitants had fled, though there was no sign of military activity. Even the usual graffiti were missing. It was as if they had stumbled into a France of another century.

They drove south for many hours, the countryside growing wilder and less civilized and at the same time drowsier. Late in the afternoon they came over a rise and saw below them an exquisite medieval village crouched in the shadow of a narrow valley, a noble Romanesque church with its heavy walls and bell tower set in a square beside a meandering stream. Atop a low hill was a diminutive château with vineyards all around, motionless in the milky light. They stopped the Jeep and gaped, forgetting utterly about the war and their destination west of the Rhine; and they felt now that they were surrounded by the century before, having somehow stumbled into this undiscovered or forgotten valley, some place far removed from the industrialized and self-aware twentieth century. It's the simple truth that many strange and inexplicable things happen in wartime. Ask any soldier.

They motored down the road slowly, because they had no way of knowing the politics of the village, who occupied it, and whether they were friendly. They crossed a stone bridge spanning the slow-moving stream and stopped in front of the church. In the square a half a dozen old men were playing boules. The men looked up at the approach of the American Jeep but did not pause in their game. They moved ponderously, their arms swinging like pendulums, the heavy balls lofted and falling with a thud to the bare ground. From the terrace of the café across the square, a waiter was motioning. Axel and Fred left the Jeep where it was and walked to the café, carrying their carbines.

I am the *patron* of this café, the Frenchman said.

I am also the mayor of the village.

You are welcome here, but you will have no need for weapons.

The mayor offered bread and cheese and a carafe of the local wine, coarse as sandpaper. He remarked on the weather, warm even for August. The night would be warm as well. Wouldn't you prefer to wear something more comfortable? Then he offered the traditional blue trousers and smocks worn by working-men. The mayor seemed eager to avoid any reminders of the nearby armies. Anonymous in blue, rifles stowed in the Jeep, the Americans sat at a table on the terrace of the café and talked with the mayor, an obviously well-fed mayor. Yes, there had been Germans in the vicinity, but they had departed without warning early one morning the previous week. In any case there had been no trouble with them.

Enjoy yourselves, gentlemen, the mayor said and disappeared into the interior of his café. In the square behind them the old men continued to play boules.

Dusk came suddenly. It did not occur to Axel and Fred to get on with their own journey. General Patton had got almost to the Rhine without them; he could persevere a little longer. Perhaps, if left alone, Patton would be in Berlin by Halloween. They had been in France for so long, they had begun to think of it as home; its fate was theirs also, and they felt entitled to a few hours' leave.

Axel asked for another carafe and they wandered away to the stone bridge. Downstream they heard the murmur of women's voices and the splash of water. They stretched out on the grass below the bridge, growing drowsy as the sun failed. The wine had taken a toll, and this countryside was unimaginably peaceful. Axel lay back, dozing, lulled by the movement of the stream. He wondered if his sense of well-being was an ancestral memory, the de Barquin blood that his father insisted was an Irish fantasy. He thought about Echo House, feeling a tremendous nostalgia for it, its many nooks and crannies and dubious history. Then he thought about his own flat in London with his wife and son, Sunday mornings with the newspapers in Regent's Park and afternoons at the Victoria and Albert or in the country. He knew his son was safe and healthy in Scotland and that the blitz had all but ended. He had not heard directly from his wife in months, and they had not spoken in more than two years. Axel had no trouble remembering the look in her eyes or the way her hair fell or her voice, and their intimate life; but he had been gone a very long time, and people changed, even their voices. Only a few hundred miles and a channel separated them, with the war in between. Axel wondered what she did with her nights, where she went and who she went with and what she did when she got there. And, when she got home, if she still stayed up until dawn composing verses. Sylvia was a beautiful woman, always the life of every party. She would be much in demand, and under such circumstances it would be easy for her to neglect her writing. Naturally he wondered if she had been faithful to him and knew at once that she hadn't been. This was wartime. All the rules were being rewritten and some of them weren't strict to begin with; and they had never bothered much about rules.

Fred stirred and said he was going in search of a place to spend the night.

Good luck, Axel said.

The women dispersed and the countryside was quiet except for the swish-swish of the stream and the far-off call of black-birds wheeling high overhead. The ground was damp with a locker room's sweat-smell. Axel stretched out flat, the coarse French cloth rough against his skin, a welcome sensation. The birds described great arcs in the pale blue sky, climbing and falling, sliding on the wind currents. Suddenly the world seemed made of flesh and blood, a thick overheated physicalness, things in motion, a kind of silent deluge.

Fred returned with the red-faced mayor. It seemed he had a problem only the Americans could solve. They followed the mayor along the road by the stream until they came to a stone building with a wide wooden door. They could see lights inside. The mayor unlocked the padlock, and the door swung wide, revealing a German staff car. Lanterns hung from the ceiling and in the shadows were three men of the village, evidently the guardians of the car.

It won't run, the mayor said. We thought you could help us. Americans know everything about automobiles.

Where did you get it? Fred asked.

There have been Germans here, the mayor replied.

And where are they now?

They went away, the mayor said.

Where did they go? Axel asked.

East, the mayor said. They said they were going east.

Valhalla, Fred said, and one of the men laughed unpleasantly.

It took a minute to open the hood and another few minutes to arrange the lanterns so that they could see the engine. Fred asked for a wrench and began to hum to himself, testing wires and prodding the engine's parts. While he was working, Axel looked into the interior of the car, but there was nothing of interest. It was just an abandoned scout car, in near-pristine condition. There were no signs of battle on it. Fred was inspecting the carburetor under the light, turning it this way and that. He was humming *Blue Skies* and grinning while he tinkered. At last he nodded and tightened a screw and replaced the carburetor. The mayor and the men in the shadows were watching him intently, saying nothing. When Fred asked one of them to start the car, it fired up immediately with a pop-pop-pop, then settled into a low rumble. Fred stepped back and cleaned his hands on a piece of cloth, still humming Berlin.

We are indebted to you, the mayor said.

It's nothing, Fred said.

You were a mechanic in America?

No, Fred said. As you say, all Americans understand about automobiles. Introduce us to your friends.

What is your destination? one of them said.

East, Fred said. We too are headed east.

Where the Germans are, he said.

That's right, Axel said.

I suppose it's necessary, the mayor said. But it's a waste.

Why are you here? said a voice from the shadows.

There was an invasion, Axel said. In Normandy. There are thousands of Americans in France now and more on the way.

Why are you *here?* the voice repeated.

We took a detour, Fred said. What's your name?

Gaston, he said after a moment. Do you have a cigarette for us?

Fred shook cigarettes out of his pack and handed them around and lit them with a Zippo. He took one himself and handed the pack to Gaston.

We must go now, the mayor said nervously.

Where are we going? Axel said.

East, Gaston said. I thought you said you were going east.

The château, the mayor said quickly. The count insists that you spend the night with him in the château. You will be very comfortable there. Monsieur le Comte has prepared rooms and a fine supper and is pleased to welcome you, two Americans who have wandered into his domain. It's all arranged.

What do you think? Fred said in English.

Better there than here, Axel said.

It's a piece of luck, he said. A hot meal and a bed. Why not? Do you suppose there's a countess, too?

Probably, Axel said. What's a count without a countess?

Maybe there's a little contessa, too, Fred said.

Speak French! Gaston said loudly. This is France. We speak French here.

Axel said to the mayor, What's the matter with your friend?

He's all right, the mayor said. He can't understand what you say and it makes him suspicious. We can go now. It's best that we do.

Goodbyes were perfunctory. Outside, dusk still lingered. The mayor led them back up the road beside the river until they came to the church. When he turned to face them, his expression showed almost fatherly concern.

He said, You are welcome to remain here. It's safer than in the East.

General Patton wouldn't like it, Axel said.

In your blue trousers you look like one of us, the mayor said. And you speak very well, although your accents are not of this region. Alsace, perhaps, or the Jura. Have you ever worked in a vineyard?

Alas, Fred said. Patton shoots deserters.

You shouldn't smile, the mayor said. It's not funny.

Don't you want the Nazis out of France? Fred said.

The mayor looked at him blankly and shrugged. There are no Nazis here, he said. Do you see any Nazis?

We thank you, Axel said. But it's impossible.

The château, Fred began.

The young woman will show you the way, the mayor said.

And that was when they saw the girl on the bicycle, poised to pedal away up the hill. She was wearing a red beret and a summer dress that looked a size too small. She stared at them with an unfriendly expression that seemed to say, Keep your distance. It was evident she intended to keep hers. Axel wondered what she had heard about American soldiers. In the gathering darkness they could not see her clearly, except for the unfriendly expression. She motioned impatiently.

Before they got the Jeep in gear she was halfway up the hill, pedaling furiously in the direction of the château, gaunt against the night sky, dull lights within. When they pulled up behind her, she slowed down. The way was steep and the road rutted. Fred banged his hand against the wheel and said something obscene, then reached under the dash and extracted his little Leica camera, squeezing off two quick shots. He had only the headlights to work with, but any photograph was worth the chance. She was a sexy girl but unapproachable, lost in her own thoughts. Still, in a remote village in the middle of a war, her appearance seemed miraculous. She never looked back but stared straight ahead, standing up on her pedals, working hard climbing the last few hundred yards. In the yellow glare of the headlights her dress was transparent, and as she swayed from side to side it was evident that she was beautifully built and supple as an athlete. But she didn't look like a contessa. She didn't look like any of the hungry village girls the Americans had seen in the past two years, girls so lonely they took suicidal risks in pursuit of what they wanted; or so terrified and broken down they refused to take any risks at all.

This girl slowed down and then stopped, leaning forward on her bicycle and sliding off. The back of her dress was soaked with sweat, though she did not seem winded. She stood with her back to them, her head raised as if waiting for a summons; and then she ran her long fingers through her hair, looking into an invisible mirror. Fred turned off the engine and they waited in silence, the girl garish in the glare of the headlights. In the thick night air they could smell the perfume of the vineyards and something else besides, the French girl's ripe sweat.

She parked the bicycle at the base of a wide stone porch, pointed at the front door, and disappeared around the corner of the château.

'Bye, Fred said.

Don't forget to write.

French bitch.

They waited a moment in the silence and then alighted, carrying their weapons. A servant met them at the door and conducted them to adjoining rooms on the second floor. He said there was hot water if they wanted to bathe and clean clothes in the closets. All normal sizes, he said with a smile, calculating Fred's height. Take what you need, the servant said. Dinner will be informal. The count expects you downstairs in one hour.

While Fred drew a bath, Axel went to the window and looked over the village and the countryside far below, so peaceful in the moonlight, the terrain reminding him of the Blue Ridge near Middleburg. The hills rolled back in various shades of gray and dark blue, fading at the horizon. He listened for the far-off thunder of artillery but heard nothing except the movement of insects and the occasional call of a bird. The birds wheeled and pitched, watched by a hawk circling at great height. A nocturnal spider as big as a thumbnail sat on the edge of its web in the corner of the window casement; and when Axel moved the web it seemed to arch its back, poised for a reconnaissance. Fred said something from the bathroom, but Axel could not make out what it was and did not reply. He was watching the spider, moved now to a defensive position as he continued to tug at the web. All this time the birds rose and fell, pursued by the hawk.

Looking up, Axel saw the battlements of the château, a sickle moon sitting like a crown on one of the turrets. There were no lights anywhere below. He wondered how it would be to spend the war in this remote village, working the vineyards and otherwise leading a blameless rural life; and later to appear in Patton's tent with a harrowing tale of capture and torture by Nazi SS. No one would believe it, though. They would think it more OSS la-di-da, Behl and Greene finding themselves in a petit château in ancient Aquitaine, avoiding the war, shuttling between the bedroom and the wine cellar, overseen by comely countesses who were eager to share their bodies while the rest of the Third Army was face down in the mud. There were remote villages all over France that had avoided involvement in the war; they avoided it the way you did the eyes of a surly stranger in a dark alley.

No horseshit from this bastard, Fred said from the bathroom.

What do you mean?

How do we know who he is?

He's Monsieur le Comte.

He's probably a collaborator, Fred said. Living it up in his château while France burns. A profiteer selling his filthy wine to the German army at exorbitant prices.

Water hot enough for you, Fred?

Fuck you, Fred said.

Plan to give him a civics lesson, Fred? Tell him what's what back in the arsenal of democracy? Because if you do, please save it for after dinner. I think, from the smell of things, that he's serving roast lamb.

Axel went in to bathe, thinking about the girl on the bicycle, the look she had given him before beginning her trek to the château. She seemed to him to be the pulse of this lost, forgotten, unsupervised province in which so much seethed beneath the surface. Its obscurity gave rise to an excess of imagination, as if they were at the outermost edges of the known world. He and Fred were the law here. They stepped lightly but they took what they wanted. They were guests of the nation but also the advance party of the liberation. They did not take orders. No authority touched them except the alien German authority. The girl's hostile look infuriated and excited him. Surely this was not a random encounter but something fated; otherwise, why were they directed to this place? Axel dressed and returned to the open window. He watched the spider move forward from the margins of its web to the center, sure, swift strides and then a pause. The spider was moving forward like the point man of an infantry company. Axel tugged at the web, still thinking about the French girl and wondering when he would see her again.

It was then that he heard a familiar sound and looked out over the dark village. He watched the twin taillights of an automobile ascend the road from which they had come, hesitate at the top of the hill, then disappear. The night was so still that he could easily hear the rumble of the engine, and he knew at once that it was the German scout car. Greatly uneasy, he wondered where it was bound and why. The car's rumble vanished and he resumed his watch over the spider, now only inches from his thumb. He was remembering the way the girl moved and thinking about the scout car and deciding to say nothing to Fred about either one, when the insect lunged. The spider was quick but Axel was quicker and when next he looked at the web, the spider was gone. The sickle moon had slipped behind the château, the birds had disappeared, and it was too dark to see the hawk. He was suddenly fatigued. Then Fred was in the doorway, gesturing impatiently at the clothes closet. It was time for dinner.

Dressed in wool sweaters and English slacks, they arrived downstairs at the appointed time. The château was damp and chilly despite the fire roaring in the huge hearth. The count was standing before it, staring glumly into the flames. Axel and Fred exchanged glances. Whatever they expected — Louis XIV in a powdered wig, the Marquis de Sade in platinum underwear — it was not what they got. The Frenchman was young, younger even than they were, and half a head shorter. He looked like an American college boy from the Ivy League, handsomely turned out in a blazer and ascot and gray flannel trousers. His hair was short and curly and he was smoking a Gauloise. The war seemed to have done him no harm; he was as plumped and groomed as a pet partridge, and as high-strung. The count had a tremor that was not college-age.

They shook hands and Axel handed him a carton of Lucky Strikes, which he accepted with a nervous laugh. In Europe in 1944 a carton of Luckies could buy you about anything you wanted, even, or especially, the things that were out of reach for a young count with an old château. When he announced that he spoke English poorly and would prefer to converse in French, Axel and Fred agreed at once; the count visibly relaxed then. The servant arrived to ask about drinks, indicating the sideboard, with its thicket of bottles. There looked to be an international selection of spirits, including Kentucky bourbon. They took malt whiskey neat. The count drank schnapps.

You found your way, he said, smiling dryly to acknowledge the absurdity of the question. No one could miss the château.

We had a guide, Fred said.

An extraordinary girl, Axel added.

Yes, he said. She's very beautiful, isn't she? Her name is Nadège. Her father manages the vineyard, as his father did before him, and his grandfather. She helps out in the kitchen while her husband is away.

Where is her husband? Fred asked.

He's a soldier, the count said sadly. She calls him a patriot. He was commander of a Maquis unit, captured near Orléans in 1942 and sent to one of the German camps. He's there now, somewhere in the East. Probably Poland. Isn't that where their camps are? She gets word from him from time to time and she is able to pass messages. The conditions in the camp are dreadful, but he's alive, it seems. They're very close, Nadège and her husband. She's only waiting for his release and then they'll return to their farm.

It won't be long now, Fred said.

Are you certain?

Positive, Fred said.

Why are you positive?

Because Patton's almost at the Rhine. The Germans have had it. Morale is shot. The Russians are slaughtering them in the East. We'll be home for Christmas. So will Nadège's husband, if he's still alive.

Axel listened to this without comment. They knew nothing of the course of the war, and little enough about military operations. Their work in France involved identifying targets for sabotage and then organizing the sabotage. They arranged weapons shipments. The work was dangerous but it involved finesse as much as it involved anything. They had had close encounters but had never been wounded or even shot at. They worked with partisans who were killed, and some who were captured and tortured and their families tortured also. That was a bad bargain and required tremendous fortitude, along with indifference, and they never asked about it. They worked in the shadows, trying to gather intelligence and satisfy London. So Fred didn't know what he was talking about, but that didn't stop him.

He was looking around the room as he spoke, embellishing the strength of the Allied forces. The room was so large and ill-lit that the corners were in shadows. Tapestries concealed the stone walls, and long candles threw little darts of light. The chill was easing, though perhaps that was only the whiskey. They could smell the lamb cooking.

I hope you are right, the count said.

Have no doubt, Fred said.

I'll try, the count answered.

Fred said, Why weren't you occupied by the Nazis?

We are very far out of the way here, the count said. We don't have many visitors of any kind. There would be no reason to occupy this village. We're very poor. There's nothing for them here.

Your château, Axel began.

He shrugged, as if the château, too, was poor and therefore of little interest.

No Germans at all? Fred asked.

The count took a patient sip of his schnapps and looked into the fire. He said, Germans are everywhere in my country. We are a defeated nation, after all. We live day to day. As they say in your country, beggars can't be choosers. A squad of them came here last month, looked around, and went away. They did not bother me. I think they were on the run from General Patton and fetched up here by accident. I believe the people of the village frightened them, so they did not stay.

Came and went, did they? Fred said.

They were wise to leave quickly, because Nadège was planning to kill them all. She was organizing an — ambush. The count raised his eyebrows and laughed his dry laugh.

Would she have?

Oh, yes, the count said. Certainly. She knows all about military operations. She too is what she calls a patriot. For a while she trained with her husband.

Good at ambushes, is she? Fred said. His tone was belligerent, and the count did not reply. She was standoffish with us, Fred went on. Does she dislike Americans, too? Or only Germans?

The count was silent, turning now to the fire and stabbing at it unsuccessfully with a poker. Axel realized then that he was much older than he looked. His skin had an unhealthy pallor and his hands were not those of a young man. His blazer was threadbare and looked to be a size too large. His curly hair could have been dyed.

She knows no Americans, the count said.

Tell us about the Germans, Axel said.

The count paused for a moment's reflection. He said, One of them was injured and I dressed his wounds here. I have had some medical training. The wounds were not serious but they were very painful. Nadège wanted to kill him in his bed but I told her that if she did, the Germans would find out and then discover the identity of her husband and it would go badly for him in Poland. They were just boys in a strange country. Let them go in peace, I said. And she did.

You treated a German soldier?

Of course, he said.

Why did you do that?

He was injured. I was able to help him.

You repaired him, Fred said. Put him back together again.

I did what I could, the count said. It wasn't much. The operation was very painful for him and we had no proper anaesthesia, so we used this. The count held out the glass of schnapps, tilting it back and forth. His hand trembled slightly but it did not seem to be fear, because he was speaking normally, as any man would in his own house with guests.

It wasn't effective, he added. The schnapps.

Fred stepped to the sideboard and filled his glass with whiskey and then turned to face the count. He was flushed with anger and his voice was harsh. Boo-hoo, he said, my heart's bleeding. Thanks to you that bastard is probably back in the line at this minute. That Kraut bastard is shooting at Americans right now.

The count said to Axel, Please, help yourself to whiskey.

Axel said, Surely you must have known that.

He lifted his shoulders and let them fall. He lit another Gauloise.

Shooting at Americans, Fred said again. Probably shooting at French also. Thanks to you.

I doubt that, the count said mildly. I doubt that very much. I had to amputate his hand.

Fred turned away, not believing a word of it.

You said the wounds weren't serious, Axel said.

The count said softly, You would see things differently from the way I do. You would have another point of view altogether. The Germans arrive in my country every few generations. They arrived in 1871 and again in 1914 and 1940, and those are only the invasions within memory. We expect it; the Germans are part of our national life. They are as much a part of French culture as Joan of Arc. The sun makes its transit. The moon rises. The tide goes in and the tide goes out. And the Germans invade. Perhaps it's revenge for Bonaparte; perhaps it's their own disquiet that sends them over their borders again and again. They are a restless and romantic people. They are never satisfied and this is understandable. They are descendants of the horse people. It is in their nature to move violently from place to place. In another thirty or forty years they'll come again, regardless of whether your General Patton crosses the Rhine this month or next month or next year. Or never crosses it. We French think of the Germans as a natural phenomenon, like the mistral. So when they arrive my family does its best to accommodate them, since we know they will return; they always have before. I have had to make my own rules within our particular family tradition. We have properties in the north also. We have a petit château near Sedan that has been a German headquarters in three wars. It is a German headquarters now, unless your Patton has liberated it for his own headquarters. My maternal uncle, who occupies the Sedan château, is a droll fellow. He considered adding a German library to the one already there, cautionary tales like those of Musil and Joseph Roth. Now perhaps we can add an American library, Twain, James, and Melville. Perhaps you too will return in a generation. No doubt you will.

The count poured himself another schnapps and looked directly at Axel, his eyes alive with a bright worldly glint, eyes that found irony wherever they lit. He apparently had chosen Axel as the senior man. He said, We have had a great deal of experience with wounds, my friend. We have seen many hundreds of wounds in the 1871 war and the great 1914 war and this war also. And I am bound to tell you that losing an ordinary hand is not a serious wound, not serious at all, when you consider the many possibilities.

My family has occupied this château for five centuries, the count concluded almost as an afterthought, no doubt to give the Americans valuable perspective on the inventory of wounds, grave and trivial, from sticks and stones to maces and lances and arrows and boiling oil to bullets from machine guns and thousand-pound bombs from planes in the air, each with its specific signature.

Axel looked him up and down, so nonchalant in his soft country clothes, so elegantly threadbare. He thought he had been listening to a relic from the dim past, but now he wondered if the count wasn't the immediate future — worldly, unmoved, sardonic, unsurprised, aloof from the common experience, coolly neutral unless the knife was drawn across his own throat. Axel believed that his generation of Americans would have to be responsible for the Europeans, because the Europeans would not be responsible for themselves. The Europeans had too much to explain to their own children. Of course for the count explanations would be a luxury, superfluous; they had been superfluous for five centuries. He and Fred had had many earnest discussions concerning the moral rearmament of Europe, the better to stand against the Soviets; and had decided they would have more luck with America, for America had so much more to lose. He did not see just then how they could go about morally rearming this count.

Axel poured another whiskey, tipping the glass in salute.

It's good whiskey, he said.

A gift from before the war, the count said. We had English partners.

For your wine, he said.

Our wine was popular in England, he said.

I can imagine, Axel said.

It's ordinary wine, he said. Not too expensive.

Your family is with you here?

My father is with the government at Vichy, the count said. He is a legal administrator. He is what you call a collaborator but he believes in Pétain. He was with the old man at Verdun in the last war, so they are comrades. They share the burden of eight hundred thousand casualties in seven months. Soon we will have General de Gaulle, so I do not know what will happen to my father, but I expect it will be nothing good. I have a brother who is a *résistant*. He's somewhere in the countryside doing whatever *résistants* do, sabotage and assassination, espionage of one kind or another. He likes it. It suits him. He has his own group and excludes no one, not even communists. His wife is with him. And their children are in England. My older brother works in Zurich with the Americans. I have no idea what he does, but I assume that it's unwholesome. He has always wanted to emigrate to America, and now I suppose he will. He wants to marry an heiress and live in California. Do you know any heiresses? He's very attractive. He speaks excellent English.

That would be the way to do it, Axel said.

You've covered all the bases, Fred said in English. And then in French, You're a lucky man. You're drawing water from all the wells. No matter who wins, you're covered.

Certainly, the count said with a look of surprise. Of course.

Against all odds Axel found himself drawn to the Frenchman, his candor, his fragile dignity, his utter imperturbability. He believed his duty was to survive at all costs, and in this distant region he was landlord-by-right. And you, he said. Monsieur le Comte, what's your role in the family scheme of things?

I am here, as you can see. Someone has to occupy the château and supervise the vineyards. The village depends on this domain for its livelihood. So that is my responsibility while the others are away. We go on as before. We get on as we have always gotten on. It makes no difference to us who is in charge at Paris. It made no difference in 1789 and it makes no difference today. The tumbrils never got this far south. They never will. There is only one road into this village, and you go out the same way. They do not care that we are here and we do not care that they are there. It is our duty to get on as best we can, theirs too. Sometimes it is a struggle, as when the Germans come. But my duty is to preserve and protect what we have and I do in my way what my father and brothers do in their ways. Sooner or later they will return, except for Alain, who I expect will emigrate to America. He has always wanted to be an American. When you have lived on one piece of land for a very long time you become proprietary about it. There is no difference between it and you. So you become stubborn.

Sure of yourself, Axel said.

Cowardly, Fred said under his breath.

Shall we go in to dinner? the count suggested.

They did not talk about the war at dinner and obviously avoiding Nadège was difficult. She was as lovely up close as she had been at a distance. Her hostility and sexual heat filled the room; and she was aware of this. She served the plates, filled the glasses with wine, and withdrew, strolling as if she heard music somewhere and wanted to join the dance. She sang softly to herself, her music easily heard over the desultory conversation, something to do with a pest that was attacking the grapevines. The candles began to gutter and throw fantastic shadows. The count droned on as Axel lost himself in his troubled thoughts. When

Nadège removed the dinner plates, she seemed to glance fondly at the count, brushing his shoulder with the tips of her fingers; but he took no notice and did not look at her. Had they become lovers in the absence of her patriot, and was that the cause of her extraordinary aplomb? Absence usually created its own demands, especially when the rules were rewritten.

Axel watched her turn and look through the door. She stared at him with high disdain. He thought she had suddenly recognized him as the enemy of her future, not liberation at all but occupation. America's future would be her future as well, this valley a part of the American empire no less than the Blue Ridge near Middleburg. And then her eyes slid away and she returned to her kitchen chores. The count and Fred Greene were debating modern French and German music, Massenet and Mahler, and which was the more timely. Axel apathetically sipped his wine, filled with an exhaustion that was close to despair. What was he doing in this place while armies raced across famished Europe? In Russia and the Pacific the corpses were accumulating in a vast hecatomb. Civilians were exiled or imprisoned or slaughtered where they slept, whole cities torched and liquidated. Nothing again would be as he had known it. People and places and the emotions that connected them would disappear, except from the memory of those who could bear to remember. The West would set about reassembling its history. Fred was making some point about *The Song of the Earth*. Axel promised himself that if he survived he would make his life count for something, to bear witness to what had happened in the war. He realized he had never before thought about surviving.

He stared across the great dark dining room to the heavy door slightly ajar and saw Nadège at the kitchen counter slicing strawberries, her face lit by a bare overhead bulb. The crimson juice of the strawberries flowed over the cutting board as she stared at it, savagely slicing the fruit with a huge knife, the juice on her fingers and the cutting board. He could not fathom the look on her face, and then he thought he knew. She was waiting for one who would never come. She would wait forever, her lover always out of reach. Even when he returned he would be out of reach, because she would never be able to imagine his days in Poland. He would not be able to explain them and she would not be able to imagine them. And he would be unable to grasp how she had lived in their remote village. Axel knew that he, too, was out of reach, an American on foreign soil. Only the war was near to hand, and if the count was correct — and who would daresay he was wrong — it would not be the last. And Axel was not yet forty.

The table was silent now, the count and Fred having reached no agreement on Massenet or Mahler. Nadège delivered the strawberries and did not appear again. The kitchen was dark. At the count's invitation they returned to the fireplace for coffee and Cognac, but after only a few minutes he announced that he would have to retire. He was obliged to be up early on business and, alas, would be unable to see them off in the morning. He wanted them to know that they were welcome to stay on. They could stay with him in the château or in the village. There was much to be done in the fields, and anyone familiar with machines was a godsend. Of course they would be paid for their work. Even Americans needed a respite from combat, and there was no more secure location in all France. This was logical, but the choice was theirs.

Unfortunately, Axel said, they were expected at the war. Personal invitation of General Patton.

As you wish, the count said.

They shook hands and he walked off, pausing at the staircase to look at Fred. His expression was impish.

It is not cowardice, Monsieur Greene. You should be clear on that point. Cowardice is a simple thing, and we are not simple here. No, it is a more complicated thing altogether.

And then he was gone.

The Americans remained a few minutes longer, finishing their Cognac. Fred wanted to replay the evening. He was especially caustic about Jules Massenet, sentimental moron. He had less to do with the modern world than Renoir, that illustrator. The German genius for dissonance and excess in music accounts for their military brilliance, wouldn't you say? But Axel was distracted and answered him in monosyllables. They were very good at reading each other's moods, so Fred did not press except to say that his friend looked tired. Why are you weary, Axel? Are you tired of our horseshit life? Are you tired of thinking about Germans? Do you want to spend the rest of your life in this leet-le château with ripe Nadège? Working the fields like two characters in a Millet canvas? Maybe we'll find God as they do in Victor Hugo's novels. If we remain, Fred said, no doubt we'll learn the subtle qualities of endurance so prized by Monsieur le Comte. Count Coward.

It was midnight. They refilled their glasses and took them upstairs. Axel checked to see if the spider had returned to its web and was gratified to find that it had. A fly was struggling in the threads, and he removed it with a fingernail and watched it dart away. He lay down at once, but sleep did not come. He lay in the nervous interval between the quiet and the frantic, heavy with desire that he knew could not be satisfied. He swallowed the last of the Cognac and put the glass aside, wishing that he had another, because he was on the spike of the present moment, the future unknowable and the past out of reach. As the French say, he was *coincé,* cornered, in that small room high above the valley. Moonlight fell through the open window, the air redolent of the vineyards. He was wide awake with his eyes closed, wrapped in a cocoon of his own making. As he often did during those years in France, he sought to penetrate his eyelids to discover the world beyond the nervous interval. He counted the countries he had lived in or visited, working backward from the most recent. There were twenty-six altogether, and soon he found himself on his long honeymoon voyage to India, Ceylon, Burma, and Siam.

In India they had had letters of introduction. They were invited to visit the archives of the museum at Calcutta. The curator showed them statuary and temple rubbings, many of them pornographic. When Sylvia laughed loudly, the curator was offended; then he too began to smile. The naïveté of Americans amused him. They stayed at the museum all morning, then walked back to the hotel in the furnace of midday, Sylvia still convulsed. Axel thought she was behaving like a schoolgirl. She admitted later that she had been caught unawares, off guard, and asked him if he had ever seen such things before. Of course, he said. The British Museum, the Dahlem, even the Corcoran in Washington. Why didn't you tell me? she demanded. This became a great issue with her. You're so secretive, she said. You never tell me anything. I know nothing of your thoughts. She worried the matter all the way to Siam.

In that way the early morning advanced at its usual pace; and in due course Sylvia left and Nadège arrived, and still he could not see beyond the next tick of the clock. He thought that when sadness closed its fist around your heart, it would never relax until it had squeezed you dry.

They departed at dawn, driving into a gorgeous sunrise. There was no one about in the château or in the village. They went out the way they came in, but in no time were lost, driving along a country road no wider than the Jeep. After an hour Fred stopped and Axel climbed on the hood with field glasses to search for a landmark, anything that would point the way to a town. In the saddle of the next low valley was a church spire and a few crabbed buildings. A thin ribbon of smoke rose from one of the chimneys. Many birds were gathered round and about. Even at a mile or more away Axel could see them perched on the steeple and swarming nearby, tiny as insects. With the glasses he saw that the stained glass windows of the church were intact and the steeple unmarked. Townspeople were seated in the little graveyard beside the church. Fred put the car in gear and proceeded carefully. They had no idea what they would find or if they would be welcome.

The cries of the birds grew shrill as they approached, but there was no other sound, because this was a city of the dead. The people in the graveyard had been shot and left to die where they fell. The parish priest was impaled on a bayonet and abandoned on the church porch. There were other dead in the streets and on the front steps of houses and littered like garbage at the base of the World War One monument. Huge blackbirds had collected on the tables in front of the café, walking over the bodies of the dead. More people lay across chairs and under the tables, some shot and others hacked to death. There were women and children, some infants, and men young and old. A dog prowled among the corpses, and as the Americans watched, he too collapsed and died. There was no evidence of any weapons or any resistance. There looked to be forty or fifty dead; probably there were others in the houses.

What went on here? Fred said.

But Axel only shook his head. He said, Remember . . . but he had forgotten the name of the village in the Sologne that had been destroyed by the Germans after they learned it had sheltered a unit of the Maquis.

This is like that, Fred said.

This is worse, Axel said.

Fred reached into the back seat to fetch his carbine, checking to see that the clip was loaded and engaged, and the safety off. The birds continued to cry, stretching their wings as they pranced among the dead. White smoke spilled from the doorway of the café, the smoke sliding between the tables and chairs, obscuring the dead. Something was burning inside the café and it looked for a moment as if the bodies themselves were smoldering. Abruptly a demented cat shot from the doorway into the square, running in circles and screaming. Fred lowered his carbine.

We should do something about the priest, Fred said.

There's nothing to be done about the priest, Axel replied.

I don't know, Fred began.

Say a novena if you want, Axel said.

They drove slowly around the square and up the main street, where there were more dead in alleys. They did not know what to do; there were many too many to bury. The Germans had a word for an action of this kind, *Schrecklichkeit*, frightfulness. They continued driving very slowly through the village. The cries of the birds receded, and soon a kind of immaculate stillness ruled beyond the cough of the car's engine. The milky light of Aquitaine cast no shadows, and the heat rose in waves.

Ahead of them was the tiny mairie, with its tricolor hanging from a staff over the entrance, and under the tricolor was a squad of German soldiers, all down. They had been placed against the wall of the mairie and shot, their bodies torn to pieces by the fusillade. Many had been shot full in the face at close range. Their weapons lay scattered here and there. The German soldiers looked scarcely older than schoolboys, even the lieutenant in charge. Their haircuts and soft skin gave them away.

Fred braked and they sat looking at the mess. They could hear low moans, death rattles from the mortally wounded, and other human sounds they did not identify. Axel forced himself to look closely, and remembered then something that he had heard from one of his officers in Scotland. Such moments produce in the witness a kind of megalomania, because you are alive and everyone else is dead. A dangerous time, the officer added. A time to behave with modesty, and to believe only what is in front of your eyes. The officer was a fool, but Axel remembered what he said.

Then Axel heard Fred's noisy breathing as he opened the door and got out, leaning against the hood, bracing his elbows to focus the Leica. His hands were shaking so badly he could not get the camera properly to his eye. At last he squeezed the shutter with his arms held straight out and his face turned to one side, as if he were warding off an attacker. His eyes were closed. He took off his helmet and hurled it into the back and put the carbine on the seat and stood silently a moment, undone, disarmed, and unprotected, the useless Leica in his trembling hand.

Partisans, Fred said softly. Outstanding, just outstanding.

Didn't they do a fine job, he went on. The Germans massacred the villagers and the partisans massacred the Germans.

That's the logical sequence, he said.

There can't be any other explanation.

And it's impressive, he added. An outstanding job they did.

Shall we liberate a Schmeisser? he asked. His voice was high and trembling, almost like a child's. It's a fine weapon. It's better than anything we have. These carbines are toys.

But Axel did not want to liberate a Schmeisser or anything else. He wanted to get out of the city of the dead. The stench of it, rising each minute with the sun, was suffocating. And he did not believe Fred's sequence of events, at least not in the logical, matter-of-fact way he presented them. Something else had happened here, to sweep clean the village, to come through it with a scythe and kill everything that moved, even the animals. He touched the stock of the carbine, seeking reassurance.

Get moving, he said. Right now.

They were exposed, as exposed as the villagers or the Germans, and unless they escaped at once they would forfeit life, too. There was nothing more to be done in this place. But Fred remained standing in the road.

Do you mind driving? he said. I'm not myself.

Fred shuffled around the car to the passenger's side while Axel heaved himself behind the wheel. He placed the carbine across his lap. Fred was utterly withdrawn now, sitting quietly with his hands in his lap, humming some Broadway show tune. Axel put the Jeep in gear and moved off past the mairie, and it was then that he saw the German scout car parked at the side of the building. Three men lounged inside it, smoking cigarettes, Gaston and the two others they had met the night before when Fred fixed the carburetor. Nadège stood beside the scout car, her arms folded across her chest, watching. They had been there the entire time, just out of sight around the corner of the mairie. Nadège seemed to be in charge.

Hello again, Fred said. What do you suppose she wants? What is she doing here at this time?

Axel said, Be quiet.

Only twenty yards separated them, but Nadège and Axel stared at each other across a chasm. No question here who the intruders were, who belonged and who didn't belong, and who would be made to give way. The steady malevolence of her glare was unambiguous, and Axel knew without a doubt that she wished him dead and was entirely capable of seeing to it herself. He put his hand on Fred's arm, warning him to be still and to make no sudden movement. Gaston and the two others were nervous, and there were already so many dead.

Nadège seemed too young to be so fierce and self-possessed,

but of course for years she had managed on her own, guarding secrets, her own secrets and the secrets of her community, this distant valley in Aquitaine with its churches, vineyards, and villages. The war had transformed it utterly, but the war would not last forever and when the war ended life would resume as before, except that there would be many more secrets. Axel was suddenly at a loss — and beside him was Fred Greene, he who had always been so resourceful and steadfast, grinning and humming one of Cole Porter's society melodies.

The three men climbed from the car and stood beside Nadège, the four looking like statues in a village square, some muscular tableau by Rodin, implacable in defense of what was theirs — the results of the revenge they had wrought. This was private, having to do with them alone. Permissible under the rules they lived by, but private also. Surrounded by dead boys, it was obvious they believed themselves heroic. They were so few and their enemy so numerous. When one of the Germans cried out in a high trill of pain, Gaston looked at him, reached into the scout car, shouldered his rifle, and shot him where he lay. The trill ceased, and they were alone again in the appalling echo of the explosion. Fred put his hands over his eyes and bent his head.

Nadège had not moved. She remained standing, head forward, arms crossed on her chest. In her summer dress and red beret she seemed a stranger to this environment and opposed to it, the dead and dying soldiers in their heavy uniforms and ugly weapons. She occupied another space altogether, yet seemed entirely at ease and familiar. She had not looked at the German soldier before Gaston fired and did not look at him now. She seemed purely unafraid and relaxed in her own zone of profound indifference. The soldier had surely found his Valhalla, good luck to him. The Germans had no place here, so distant from their homeland. They were the invaders, and according to the rules of war deserved their fate no less than an arsonist caught in his own fire. In war, force rules. Yet — this, too, had to be said, although Axel did not say it — they looked so young, too young to have paid such a price. They were boys who had loved their country, had loved it in France no less than in Germany.

Nadège took a little hitch in her skirt and opened her mouth to speak. Axel waited for her words, Rodin's beautiful heroine finding voice at last, words to explain these dreadful events. He imagined what they were before he heard them. *Malevolent forces oppose us and these forces are more powerful than we are. They are unyielding. They are incoherent. But we understand them better than we understand ourselves. When we are put in the way of events we cannot fathom, among people whose souls are mysterious, then we must alter the events or eliminate the souls. We carelessly stray beyond our boundaries to a place where we do not know the rules. We are far from home and our duties are only abstract and half-remembered. But we cannot decide, just this once, to neglect them. Our own survival is at stake, meaning the future of the known world* . . . Nadège smiled. Gaston and his two comrades elevated their weapons, and then Axel heard the click-click of the Leica. Fred was taking their portraits, an act so startling that they ducked their heads and scrambled behind the scout car, all but Nadège, who remained patiently standing as if she were prepared to wait for a thousand years.

Axel's fingers closed around the stock of his carbine. His head swam in the heat, his vision blurred and fractured. The sun was directly overhead. He believed he would have to kill her, but he did not see how he could go about it. There were only seconds remaining and then he would have to decide. On the margins of his vision he saw general movement among the young Germans lying under the tricolor. First one and then another, the dead were rising before them, rising painfully but with purpose, rising on wrecked limbs, rising woodenly as if hauled by invisible wires. The lieutenant was looking directly at Nadège in her summer dress. He had a gaping wound in his neck and croaked when he spoke, trying now to rally his command, who were swaying like wraiths as they gained their feet. He held a Schmeisser in one hand, and the other was missing, the wrist sealed by a leather plug. He awkwardly raised his arms, pointing the heavy Schmeisser at Nadège. She did not see him. She appeared to see nothing at all as she stood motionless in the heat, German infantry coming to life around her.

Axel whispered a warning before the first shots were fired. In the pandemonium she dropped from sight. He knew in his heart she was hit. Her head jerked forward, the red beret filling and pluming, and then she was down. She was unarmed, without means to defend herself. Gaston and his comrades began to fire from positions behind the scout car. Three Germans were standing and they never retreated or sought cover or bothered to aim their weapons, moving the gray barrels from side to side as you would a common garden hose. Axel hesitated only a moment, then threw the Jeep into gear and raced away. There was more firing before they were around a bend in the road and out of sight. Beside him Fred Greene continued to snap pictures, humming loudly. Axel recognized a march from one of Gustav Mahler's symphonies.

They drove off into the milky noonday sun. Neither of them looked back or spoke. Axel was incapable of speech, his thoughts in memory's shadow, the shadows deepening. He was no longer certain of what he had seen and its meaning. He drove erratically, the Jeep spinning from side to side, catching ruts and hurtling off center. The wheel was hard to hold. Axel could not find accord; his body refused to synchronize as the shadows grew darker still. He wanted Fred to shut up but could not find voice. Two miles up the road Axel jerked the wheel, steering the Jeep onto the rough shoulder of the road, where it swung left and right, skidding, and then detonated the land mine.

The chassis was thrown high in the air and landed in the ditch upside down. Fred Greene's skull was crushed, but it took him a while to die. Axel was luckier. The windshield missed his chest by a foot, and he survived, terribly injured. Later, at the inevitable inquiry, the partisans claimed no knowledge of the accident. Americans were not in the vicinity. Among themselves, they called it justice, revenge of a kind. Gaston had placed the mine early that morning, and the Americans were merely unlucky.

"You asked me what happened. And the answer is: I don't know what happened. I don't know to this day. After we left the city of the dead, my mind's blank. They said it was a land mine, and maybe it was. They told me the Jeep was mangled and that there was barely enough of poor Fred to carry away. A friendly gendarme took me to the provincial hospital, where I remained for weeks, unconscious. Once they discovered my identity and determined that I was able to travel, they sent me to London for the very finest in medical attention, et cetera. Where there were surgeons familiar with wartime wounds. Where my devoted family would be nearby. And I remained unconscious until the moment I heard your mother's voice —"

He remembered the humidity and medicinal aroma and Sylvia looking at him with the quizzical expression she favored at moments of high emotion. Moments later the pain began. When she spoke — not to him but to someone else in the room, her voice as seductive as ever, speaking as she would to a very close friend — he suspected the worst. So he did not move. He did not let them know he was awake and listening hard, listening for subtext and nuance, for he believed they never told the truth in hospitals. It was necessary to lie quietly and eavesdrop and then crack the code, as in a clandestine operation.

They stood near an open window. There was a soft breeze, and Sylvia was smoking one of her English cigarettes. He held his breath, not moving, and then he heard her say that he had never been sick a day in his life, had never experienced the normal anxieties and reversals. He was a man who did whatever he damn pleased and was unaccustomed to restrictions. Then she laughed brightly, and the man she was with, evidently the doctor, asked the obvious question, to which she replied, No, Axel Behl was not a professional soldier. He was not a professional anything. He went places and advised people. He was very good at giving advice. He wanted to be a professional politician because politics was the family business, like a Southern plantation or a bank. Sylvia laughed again without mirth. She said, "He protested, denied it up and down, but I know he wanted to be President of the United States. Can you imagine? My husband never thought small; give him that. When Axel saw something he wanted, he saw no reason not to take it. Have you ever been to Washington, Doctor? It's the midlands with monuments. A dreadful small-minded provincial town where the President's a kind of doge presiding over a Council of Ten. Lives like one, too, in a white palace in front of a huge square, and Axel wanted that more than he wanted anything." He could not hear what the doctor said next, and perhaps he said nothing at all. But he remembered very clearly Sylvia's long equivocal sigh, a kind of yawn, the sound a cat makes when it awakes from deep sleep. "Thank God there's no chance of that now," she said.

Axel was silent again. His voice had grown so soft that his son had to strain to hear him. He picked up his glass of whiskey and set it down again, looking searchingly at Alec, then shaking his head, as if he had suddenly remembered something much more important.

He said, "As the count told us, human beings are fragile."

"The count," Alec began.

"Amnesia can be a blessing," Axel went on. "But you can't have it any time you want it, and when you get it, it's there to stay. It's the man who came to dinner and won't go home. He's there every hour of every day, blocking the view. He will not be moved."

Alec was back in the city of the dead, the birds picking through the bodies, the dog collapsing, the French girl and the one-handed lieutenant, events without a logical beginning or end. There seemed to be no rational cause for any of it, unless the cause was the war itself, in which strange things happened, as every soldier knows. His father seemed to have found something nearly supernatural in a city swept clean of life, implying that God had stumbled and crushed the city as thoughtlessly as you would an anthill. But God had nothing to do with it. Alec thought of the townspeople and the German soldiers, and then suddenly did not want to think of the city of the dead any longer. It was his father's story, and his father was welcome to it, especially Nadège. Alec regretted knowing the details and wished his father had kept them to himself. He wished that he had not asked his question.

"We were outgunned, you see," Axel said.

Alec nodded at this non sequitur.

"And Fred was so god damned useless."

"I'm sorry," Alec said, not knowing what else to say.

"It's all incredibly vivid," Axel went on. "The mayor, the count, the slaughter in the square and the Germans in the court-yard of the mairie. And Nadège, and Fred breaking down."

"Almost like a dream," the boy said.

"Not exactly a dream," his father said.

Alec heard the sarcasm and colored.

"I don't know what happened to her," Axel said. "She was there one minute and gone the next and there wasn't anything I could do about it. I'm sure she survived." He looked up and smiled, his fingers touching his chin. "It seems to me that she tipped her beret before she disappeared. That's what I'd like to believe. And I'm sure that's the way it was. God, she was a strong character. A beautiful young Frenchwoman trying to get through the war. Did I tell you that her husband was in one of the German concentration camps?"

"Wouldn't you like to know what happened to them?" Alec said hurriedly. "The count? Nadège and Nadège's husband?"

Axel shrugged.

"To know if they were ever reunited?"

"I'm sure they were," Axel said. "They'd been through so much, it would be unjust for it not to work out for them. I doubt I can find the village, though. We were to the back of beyond. We'd lost our way."

"You probably could," Alec said. "Sure you could."

"It's somewhere in Aquitaine," Axel said doubtfully. "That's all I remember. I do have Nadège's photograph; the only undam-aged object they found in the wreckage was Fred's Leica. Except at the end the film had run out and poor Fred was shooting with an empty camera." Axel went on to describe the Leica, beautiful thing, small enough to fit in your hand, made in Germany before the war.

The boy had pulled his chair up close to his father, the better to hear each word. It was easier now, listening to him talk after the fact. Before, it was as if he were still in France, describing an incident that had happened the day before. He knew there were gaps in the story, but that was inevitable, natural in the circumstances. War stories were volatile affairs, even in the movies. Still, Axel was more animated than he had been in months. He seemed to have forgotten the pain in his back and the other pains here and there. His scar was not so pronounced. Alec remembered his father in the English hospital, motionless in bed, unable to speak. The boy had no idea what had happened to him, except that he had been badly wounded and was lucky to be alive. The hospital was crowded with wounded, many of them sightless or without limbs. It was an atmosphere thick with violence and pain, and at times they seemed to be the same thing. It was all so mysterious. When he asked his mother for an explanation, she put him off; later, dear, when you're older. When he was home from school they talked in the early evenings, while she had a cocktail before going out to dinner. The room was thick with smoke from her English Ovals, and they listened to Eddy Duchin on the phonograph. This was their time together, and whenever he spoke of his father she either changed the subject or replied with an anecdote from before the war. He remembered her cocking her head, listening to Duchin, tapping her foot as if she were in a cabaret. Then the doorbell would ring twice and she would stub out her cigarette, kiss him goodbye, look into the mirror, and disappear into an automobile idling at the curb. She always looked lovely, blowing him a kiss from the doorway. And when she returned, sometimes early, sometimes very late, she would go at once to her room and write in her journal. She never rose before noon.

Remembering those days now, Alec was filled with remorse and confusion: his father near death, his mother so melancholy. He was unable to connect that time with this one and wondered if there was no connection. Did life pass in episodes, each episode complete in itself and without obvious direction? Did the events of a life drift like rafts on a featureless sea, pushed by random winds and pulled by a remorseless tide? His father and mother had floated far apart, but it appeared to him that he was nominated to keep them both in sight. It seemed to him that they had changed utterly and he had not changed at all. He was a little boy then and a young man now but had not changed inside, except that he was alert to winds and gales. He did not understand why his parents were at such odds; collapse had come so suddenly. Alec looked across the table to the portraits of Behl men on the wall above the ruins of the Thanksgiving turkey in its tray on the sideboard. His father had finished with the Leica and now was silent, staring at the ceiling. He was very far away, his finger moving to the beat of the clock's pendulum. Alec put his hand on his father's arm, conscious of the rough tweed and the soft muscle beneath.

"Why did she leave?"

"You have the number, Alec. You can ask her."

That was not the answer he had hoped for, but he was not discouraged. "I'd hoped that you might say."

"Poor Sylvia," his father said after a moment.

The boy started at this unexpected remark.

"Sylvia loves beauty, the perfect form, the more unfamiliar the better. But I'm not beautiful anymore. And I was always predictable."

"That's not true," the boy said.

Axel pushed his chair back, pausing, gaining time. The boy looked so much like his mother that it was almost indecent. It took your breath away. In candlelight he could have been her twin; and then he would narrow his eyes or make a gesture with his hands that was unmistakably Behl. Axel knew the boy had a good heart. He was not divided against himself as Sylvia was, and his ego was under control. The boy had good values, meaning a sense of community and a democratic spirit. He had never heard him utter a snobbish remark. But Alec was without direction or a sense of purpose or destination. He had no idea how dangerous the world was, and how disappointing in its rewards.

And it would become more dangerous still. You would need a suit of armor to maneuver in it, and the outcome would always be in doubt. Alec did not apply himself in school, yet he had an inquiring intelligence and a willingness to listen. Listening was not one of the things that Sylvia was good at. Axel sighed and began again.

"She had the life she wanted in London, a careless life, each day a solo flight. A solo adventure. At night she wrote her poetry, sitting in our bedroom window and looking into the garden. You remember it, Alec, the English garden, her creation, with a design that had meaning only for her. The first of many English gardens, I'm afraid. Strange thing is, Constance, your grandmother, was a connoisseur of English gardens. It must be a female, Anglophile thing, something in the genes. 'It goes with my temperament,' Sylvia said. I thought her garden looked like a technicolor pandemonium, and I'd had enough of that. I'd had enough of that to last a lifetime. Whether her poetry was any good I'm not in a position to say. She thought it was very good and she was the one who was writing it, so I suppose she ought to know. You have to take her word for it. She worked hard on her poetry during the night and on her English garden during the day. So I came back from France and didn't fit into this world she'd made and the people she'd made it with. And she didn't fit into mine, God knows." He looked at the boy, who was listening hard with his chin in his hand. "I should say *our* world, yours and mine, because we were a family after all. And it wasn't a question of not trying, on my part or on her part either. She tried, but she was working like a heretic striving mightily for faith. You have to talk yourself into it and believe that the search is worthwhile. This was an impossibility for her and for me, too. And she knew it and I knew it."

"Yes," the boy said doubtfully. "And she left then?"

But his father did not hear, or if he heard he gave no sign. He said, "And when the war ended we returned to Washington, back to Echo House, my work in the government. I had to give back, Alec. When you fight a war and win it, you own it. And it owns you. The price is never cheap and you have to protect the

victory, as you would any investment. The winning cost too
much blood, don't you see? You can't walk away from it and
simply allow people to bleed to death and create the very conditions you fought in the first place. And if you don't think
the government can break your heart, walk over to Mr. Lincoln's memorial sometime and look at his face." Axel opened his
mouth to say something more, then didn't. It was easy to explain
that government was noble work, the only work worth doing. If
you had a talent for it, you had to do it. If you could afford to do
it, you had a duty to try. But it was not so easy explaining the
way you went about it, the evasions and compromises. Sylvia
called it the civics lecture that concealed the raunchy joke. Axel
wanted to control things and people, and the government was
the officially approved way of going about it; making the world
safe for democracy meant making the world safe for him and
his ilk.

Axel, she'd said, you don't tell yourself the truth. You've gone
soft in the head; you won't examine your own life, the choices
you made and what you felt while you were making them. Mo-
tives, darling. Something other than "bad cards" or "mistakes
were made." Government's the opiate of the patrician masses,
don't you think? You've had too many séances in the Oval Office
with a movie; later, cookies and bourbon and classified talk. Too
many secrets, not enough mystery. There's no beauty in it, no
beauty at all. You've teamed up with the hollow men, and if
you're not careful, you'll become one yourself. But maybe that's
what you want for yourself. Maybe that's your beau ideal.

That was one of their last arguments, and a week later Sylvia
was on her way to London.

"Hard to explain about the government, Alec. It's a religion, I
suppose, and you either believe in it or you don't. The people
who don't believe in it think it's an opiate. Too bad for them."

The boy nodded as if he understood completely, but he didn't
understand at all. He didn't know what the government had to
do with his mother, who only wanted to write her poetry. She
was devoted to poetry the way his father was devoted to the
government, and he did not know why these two objectives

were so in opposition. They seemed to be fire and ice. He looked at his father and thought that their rafts were very far apart now, and his mother's was out of sight. What would she have said, had she been present? He knew he could mediate between them if only they would give him a chance. He knew also that his father was withholding something important and was not at all certain that he wanted to know what it was. Yet he leaned closer, waiting. His father had turned gray and was rubbing his back again, staring bleakly at the glass of whiskey.

"You'll hear stories," Axel said sharply.

"What kind of stories?"

"Stories!" he said loudly, speaking to the room. "About me, what the war did." Axel scratched his cheek and sighed. There were limits to how much you told a boy who was barely out of short pants, even a boy with an even temper and an inquiring intelligence and good values and the rest. He had already said too much at great length and Alec hadn't understood half of it, and he'd never know which half. When he was telling the story, he had forgotten where he was and whom he was talking to and why. God, Sylvia was a bitch.

Alec nodded, blinking.

"That I was so badly hurt that your mother and I were unable to have a normal life together," he said at last, looking sternly at his son, who turned away in embarrassment and confusion. "Don't believe the stories." And they were false, at least in the commonly retailed version that had him kin to Jake Barnes. It was only that his body had been so badly torn, long lumps of scar tissue, bits of iron under the skin, the flesh raw and discolored. He was frightful to look at, his body repulsive; and things were no better with the lights off.

"I haven't heard any stories," the boy said.

And perhaps that was the truth; they were a closed community and looked after one another. There were the normal rivalries and disagreements because there were only so many nests at the top of the tree. But they were a closed circle. When there was menace from the outside, they closed ranks in a phalanx of denials or evasions; and if someone had made a public error of

judgment, he was allowed a plea of nolo contendere, an acknowl-
edgment that whatever the mistake, the situation was in hand
and the error, if that was what it was, was inadvertent and would
not be repeated. If there was an event that related to work in
the war, that was off limits absolutely. *Omertà* about war-related
events, injuries or indiscretions; that was the rule, the only excep-
tion being cowardice.

Everyone had a loyalty to the work of the nation, and the
personal side of things was only that — personal and of no relevance or consequence unless it interfered with good judgment,
as it sometimes did. The pressure of public service was tremendous, and it took good, close friends to identify the tiny cracks
that became fissures that turned into great fault lines that could
be clearly seen by enemies who were waiting to exploit any
sign of weakness or disarray. You discussed the personal lives
of friends only with other friends and never, ever with outsiders, the better to further the work of the nation. It was essential that confidence be maintained, that steady hands be on the
wheel. Everyone needed elbow room, and too much scrutiny
was worse than none at all.

"She said you hit her," the boy said softly.

"Never," his father said quickly. "She said that? When did she
say that?"

The boy nodded miserably. "Before she left."

"What did she say exactly?"

The boy shrugged and turned away.

"She'll say anything," Axel said.

"That was what she *said*," the boy insisted.

"Did you believe her?"

"No, sir," the boy said.

"Did she say this to anyone else?"

"I guess it was just me," Alec said, his voice almost inaudible.
Then, "I'm sure she wouldn't have told."

Axel nodded. He believed that his wife meant to destroy him,
in her terms a kind of poetic justice, a strophe for Axel. But he
knew equally that she would not succeed. Sylvia was not a subtle
woman and would not know how to go about a campaign of

character assassination, a plot that required Florentine patience and skill. Not that she wouldn't try; if she had told Alec, she had told others, Billie Peralta certainly, probably the wretched and mischievous Mrs. Pfister as well. Sylvia understood the difference between public and private, what belonged to you and what belonged to the world, except that her definitions were elastic and she tended to reverse the two. But she wouldn't succeed; too bad for her. When you embarked on such a campaign you had to know how to go about it or you would fail as surely as if you had walked in front of an express train; and you would deserve what you got, because you had been careless. She had no allies, no one she could count on. She had no loyalties. Sylvia never saw beyond herself, and so she invented stories and retailed them to anyone who would listen, even her own son. In that way she was promiscuous. The truth was, Sylvia had never seen the hard way of life. She had not learned the hard lessons.

The room's heat had grown oppressive, and the boy's stomach was moving in circles. He wanted to open the window but dared not leave his seat lest he be misinterpreted. He set about pinching the candle wax, collecting it in little piles, leaving his thumb prints. He wished he was at the movies downtown, John Wayne and his company of leathernecks — and if it was a rhapsody, so much the better. There were things in the world that you had to see for yourself, and his father could not understand that; anyhow, he didn't. Whatever the film, it would be an improvement on the picture he had in his mind now, the garden room at Echo House late at night, his mother in tears, her words tumbling over themselves, incoherent through the tears, except her accusation, again and again: *He did this to me.* She was disheveled. Heavy makeup concealed the bruises above her eye and the scratches on her cheeks. She talked and he listened, horrified and scared. He had no idea what to say to her, and truthfully he had no wish to listen. She talked on and on, and when she finished, she apologized but said she had no one to confide in. The next day she was gone.

Alec sneaked a look at his father, who had been silent these many minutes. Axel was perspiring and his eyes were closed. His lips moved fractionally, as if he were telling a story to himself. He was gripping the table's edge, his hands gray and frail but beautifully manicured. To know another was impossible. It was hard enough knowing yourself. His father would forever be a mystery, the facts of his life in dispute, as much as any character from antiquity. His father's hand slipped, his head bobbing —

Axel felt his chair move and he looked up, blinking. Alec was rising, saying something in a kindly voice, standing behind him now, his hands on the slatted back of the chair. Axel had fallen asleep.

2

Mrs. Pfister

∽

THE COMMUNITY saw Sylvia as a creature of Axel. When they met, she was barely twenty years old, while Axel, though not much older, seemed already to have found a settled middle age. Billie Peralta was reminded of the perverse Escher design where a white dove evolves from a black sparrow, or the reverse, depending on beholder's eye. No telling which came first, according to Billie, who freely admitted her bias. She and Axel had walked out together the year before her marriage to Ed and she knew that his reputation was as carefully crafted as a press release, the sober reflection of his blameless daylight hours — the nondescript office at the State Department that seemed to be a kind of clubhouse for younger foreign service officers, the men-only lunches at the Grill Room, tennis on Saturday afternoons, services at the National Cathedral on Sunday mornings. Of course he had been coached by an expert, the ambitious Constance, who monitored his every move, with and without his knowledge.

Billie had met Axel at one of her parents' dinner parties, an agony of bland food and polite conversation, two ambassadors, an admiral, someone from the National Geographic Society, their mousy wives, and Axel Behl. Her parents always liked to have someone younger to liven the table. In fact the young man was expected to listen and contribute only when asked. The talk that evening was spirited, if you were interested in the midterm congressional elections. Axel spoke only once, to observe that the Republicans would retain control of the Congress but that the young New York governor would win the presidency in two years because the economy would fully collapse. If Frank Roosevelt won the nomination, he would win the election and take the Congress with him, and the twelve-year drought would end. The company listened to him respectfully, and then pounced.

No, no, it was much too early to tell.

Roosevelt was a cripple.

Hoover would see things through.

Her father told a story. The admiral told another story.

Axel listened politely; then when a lull came turned to Billie and asked her which character she liked best in *The Great Gatsby*.

She said Daisy, of course, because with all her faults she was the one who was truly alive. She was not "nice." She used people. But, really, all she wanted was some excitement and affection, someone to care for her.

But she married that oaf, Axel said.

Sometimes people do. Marry oafs.

She could have married Gatsby, Axel said.

Gatsby didn't want a wife, Billie said. He wanted a slave.

He wanted her on a pedestal, Axel said.

It's cold on a pedestal, Billie replied. And it's hard to keep your balance.

I thought all women wanted to be on a pedestal, Axel said.

That would depend on the woman, wouldn't it?

When he laughed, she saw that he was not the cold customer that she had assumed he was. His laugh came from deep in his throat and he was looking at her all the while through the deepest black eyes she had ever seen, or anyway noticed. She could smell his aftershave and the wine on his breath. His hands were huge and when he touched her wrist, she did not pull away but moved closer, intrigued. She was flattered that he had turned to her and asked about Gatsby, not wondering if she had read the novel but assuming that she had and would have opinions about the characters. Conversation rose around them but they occupied a private zone inhabited by Nick Carraway, Gatsby, Daisy, and Tom.

And you, she said at last. Who's your favorite? As if I didn't know.

Not Gatsby, he said.

Surely not Nick —

Nick's a bore, Axel said. Nick Carraway spends too much time wrestling with his conscience and losing. I prefer Jordan Baker.

Billie had to think a minute, trying to recollect Jordan Baker, Daisy's friend. You mean the golfer, she said.

The golfer who was caught cheating, Axel said.

"Some unpleasantness," Billie remembered.

She moved her ball, Axel said.

And what happened to her?

Nothing much. But she's the most unhappy person in that deeply unhappy book.

Because she cheated? Billie asked in surprise.

That, too, Axel said. Everyone has to look out for themselves, you see.

The party broke up at ten-thirty. When Axel asked if she would like to go to his club for a nightcap, she said yes indeed, she thought she would. She had noticed her mother looking at her strangely, and now she remembered the conversation in the living room before everyone arrived, how well-mannered and smart and attractive and potential young Mr. Behl was, and how much she would like him if only she would give him a chance. She had not paid attention, because she and her mother had different definitions of "smart" and "attractive" and what constituted potential and the value of good manners. Axel Behl seemed to be a man who had different speeds for different ages, and for men and women as well. Billie blushed when her mother nodded happily and said she'd leave the light on and not to worry about the hour and thank you ever so much for coming to dinner, Axel.

I'll bet you five dollars that Frank Roosevelt never wins another election, her father said with a huge guffaw, shaking hands with Axel and patting him on the back as if he were already a member of the family.

Remember us to your parents, her mother said.

Billie thought she had made a terrible mistake. But in the car Axel took her hands in his and allowed the silence to gather, looking at her with his black eyes and smiling thoughtfully. Then he gently pulled her toward him, letting her know that if she resisted he would stop at once, no harm done, except for the irretrievably lost moment, and how many were there in a life-time? She didn't feel like resisting, so they kissed and kissed again, his hands quietly on her back pressing her close until she could feel the beat of her own heart. This was so exotic and unexpected, necking on the street beneath flickering gaslamps within sight of her bedroom. The night was balmy. He took off his coat and unbuttoned her dress and suddenly she was bare-chested and he kissed her again.

She had never been undressed in an automobile, but she liked the sexy carelessness. This was something Daisy Buchanan would do, not with college boys or the oafish Tom but with Gatsby himself, her true and only love. College boys were all thumbs and urgency and you never felt secure with them. She liked the light of the streetlamps on her breasts while a few yards away the good people of Georgetown were preparing for nighty-night. When he put the car in gear he did not turn in the direction of his club but north to Rock Creek Park, driving very slowly through the deserted streets. In a moment they were swinging into the driveway of the famous Echo House. She was still bare-chested, leaning against him, feeling his soft shirt against her skin. She kissed his neck. Seconds later they were moving hand in hand through the front door and across marble floors into the kitchen and up the back stairs to his big bedroom, where they tumbled to the floor and began to undress each other slowly and then make love more slowly still, until the very end of it when they were flying.

Of course she was swept away. Who wouldn't be?

The affair burned for a summer, and then it didn't burn. Axel was working, Axel was in Cuba, Axel was on business in New York, Axel had an evening meeting, Axel had accepted an embassy dinner, Axel had promised an evening at home with Constance and the senator. Billie heard stories that he had been seen here and there, always with an attractive woman on his arm, older women, younger women, short, tall, blond, brunette women. And wasn't that Axel to a T, never serious about anyone, never faithful to anyone. Axel Behl was absorbed in his work, his whatever-it-was at the State Department, and women were an inconvenience. Axel had too many irons in too many fires. He was one of those organized men who didn't need women, Alice Grendall said.

Billie didn't think she was in love with him, and she couldn't imagine marriage to him. She was mightily attracted to him, the way he looked and moved, and his command of things. He sailed through life with the confidence and élan of a young prince. He had the mystery of one, too, as if Echo House were the capital of some vast and turbulent realm that required constant supervision. When he told her he would be away for a week, New York and then Chicago, she said that as it happened she was going to Chicago also, to see her aunt. He thought a moment and asked her to join him on the Twentieth-Century Limited. She could see her aunt, he could do his business, and they'd rendezvous and complete the round trip together. There's nothing like a fast train, he said.

She did not tell the story for many years, and she and Axel discussed it only once, to no satisfactory conclusion. Axel humiliated her in the most public way, the humiliation greater because he seemed to have no recognition of it and took no responsibility for it. When she reminded him, *You were a bastard to me, Axel, an absolute bastard,* he professed confusion and ignorance; and then he conceded yes, perhaps he had behaved badly but he had no choice, given the situation. From the flustered look on his face she was convinced he was apologizing only to have done with the conversation. If he apologized, he would not have to explain. And this was also true. If she had not known him so well, she would have said, at that moment, that he was frightened of her.

He said he would be late so it was better if they met in the bar car. When she arrived thirty minutes before departure, she was surprised to see his bags already in the compartment, his clothes neatly hung in the tiny closet, his razor and shaving bowl and aftershave and comb laid out on the basin. She tipped the porter and changed into her traveling ensemble, a clingy print dress and the gray cashmere sweater he had given her, no jewelry except for the plain gold bracelet. She lit a cigarette and stood for a moment looking out the window at the platform traffic, men in business suits and fedoras, women in furs, everyone hurrying though there was plenty of time. She was happy and excited, thinking of cocktails in the bar car and dinner later, and returning to the compartment, the bed turned down and welcoming. By then they would be in Ohio. She had bought him a little clock at Peacock's and placed it on the basin next to the aftershave.

When she opened the door to the bar car, she could not see him. There were two men reading newspapers but neither of them was Axel. Then she heard his voice at her elbow. He was out of sight at a table backed up to the barman's pantry. She could see his shoe and his black sock with the narrow ribbing.

You wouldn't like it, he was saying.

How do you know? The voice was a woman's, a low, teasing voice.

It's a haunted house, he said.

Ghosts? she said. Bats? The dead rising from their graves? What?

It sits high on a windswept hill. The wind howls at night. There's a cemetery across the street.

She said, Gosh.

I can't believe you've never been to Washington. Come to Washington; I'll show you the sights.

Tell me about the sights, she said.

Such sights. Washington is like Venice except that we have boulevards instead of canals. They are the widest boulevards in America. We have an obelisk. We have — bell towers. We have grand palaces. We have intrigue. Do you want to visit the White House?

I wouldn't mind, she said. Do I get to see the haunted house, too?

Permit me to give you the guided tour. It has eight rooms on the first floor. The rooms diminish in size until you get to the broom closet. It has an Observatory with a telescope. Like roses? My father cultivates roses. He has a rose named after him.

That's what he does?

When he isn't in the Senate, Axel said.

He's a senator?

That's what he does, Axel said.

Does that mean you'll be a senator, too?

No, it doesn't.

Good, she said.

You don't like senators?

The Senate would not become you, she said.

It's very formal, he agreed. It's tedious. But the vacations are long.

I suppose you work for the government?

I have an office there, yes.

In the White House, I suppose. So you'd be at the center of the intrigue.

The Department of State, he said.

What do you do at your Department of State?

Raise money for Franklin Roosevelt.

Doesn't he have money of his own?

He's running for President.

He is?

Yes, Axel said.

Will he win?

Do you think he should?

I have no idea. I like his wife.

Will you come to Washington then?

Yes, of course.

In the little silence that followed, Billie tried to collect herself. Their voices had lowered until she had to strain to hear. She stood as still as she was able to, listening to their inane conversation. The words bore no relation to their subjects. Axel and this woman were seducing each other, and he had told her things he had never told anyone. She did not know he was raising money for Franklin Roosevelt. She had never heard him compare Washington with Venice, a ludicrous idea. She wondered if he had come on board with this woman or had picked her up in the bar car. Probably he had met her somewhere in Chicago. She recognized his tone of voice because it was the same tone, breathless yet edgy, that he had seduced her with.

I don't know your name, he said.

Sylvia, she said.

Axel Behl, he said. I never met a Sylvia before. You're my first Sylvia.

Billie watched the barman approach.

Axel, Sylvia said, and gave a muffled laugh. What's your sign, Axel Behl?

My sign?

Of the zodiac, she said.

Lion, he said.

Ram, she said, laughing again.

The barman said to Billie, May I seat you, miss?

I belong here, Billie said, looking around the corner of the pantry to the table where the lovers were. The woman was very young, nineteen or twenty, an age that did not go with her voice. She was very pretty in an exotic way, not at all Axel's type. This Sylvia was a recognizable New York type, well-built, with short fair hair and too much jewelry, an aggressive manner. They did not look up when she appeared around the corner, the Lion and the Ram tête-à-tête across the narrow table. Their fingers were touching and they looked as if they had been there together for a century. Axel began to speak again, so softly that Billie could not hear what he was saying. He was talking into her eyes and as he spoke he moved his fingers slowly across her bright red nails. Her head was tilted slightly as she looked at him, her chin in her palm. The barman shifted awkwardly but still the two did not move, absorbed as they were in their own zone of enchantment.

Sylvia was the first to notice that they were no longer alone. She raised her eyes and looked first at the barman and then at Billie, her eyes narrowing when she saw Billie, whose hand rested now on Axel's shoulder. The barman asked if he could serve them a cocktail or a glass of Champagne or perhaps they would prefer to see the list of mixed drinks and he would return to take their orders when they had decided, certainly no hurry, take all the time you need —

But Axel was already rising to his feet, bending forward to take Sylvia's arm as if it were fragile as porcelain. She rose with him, and standing there in the aisle, they looked like two sleepwalkers.

Axel! Billie said loudly, mustering all the indignation that had been building inside her these many minutes.

But he did not seem to hear and when he turned to look at her fully he gave no sign of recognition and indeed looked questioningly at her hand, still resting on his shoulder. From the expression on his face, she might have been a block of wood.

You must excuse us, he said pleasantly.

Yes, Sylvia said.

There's been some mistake, Axel said.

Mistake? Billie said.

We're expected, you see.

What? Billie began.

Now they turned and moved up the aisle at a run, swaying a little because the train was under way. It gathered speed, rocking definitely now, and the last Billie saw of the Lion and the Ram was through the window of the rear door of the bar car, wrapped tightly, kissing ferociously. The girl was massaging Axel's head, standing on tiptoe to reach him, leaving Billie — as she admitted to an enthralled Alice Grendall many years later — as lonely and forlorn and chaste and discouraged as any sullen little virgin.

Bastard, she said. Who did he think he was? He looked through me as if I didn't exist.

What did you do? Alice said.

If you think I went back to my compartment and wept bitter tears, think again. I had heard about the *coup de foudre* but I'd never seen one. Now I had seen one and it was just about what I imagined. So I had a cocktail and then another cocktail and after the cocktails I had dinner and went to bed alone. Truth was

— and these many years later Billie was able to summon a strangled little laugh — I think I was envious. I still am.

The community watched the affair with fascination and delight, the strait-laced prince of Echo House and the ravishing princess of Gramercy Park, who at a certain angle bore such a startling resemblance to one of Modigliani's demimondaines, an oval face with eyes turned down at the corners, a lovely long neck that sprouted from sloping shoulders. She was trim and voluptuous at the same time. She was so very young and unselfconscious, her bright laughter an antidote to Axel's grueling solemnity. Harold Grendall believed they made a superb match, not the first time nor the last that he let his head rule his heart. Axel had always had just a little bit too much of everything and it was good for him — eat your spinach, Axel — to want something that couldn't be had at the snap of a finger or his signature on a check. If Sylvia was a little too cavalier about the capital — well, it had to be admitted that Washington took itself too seriously and often closed in on itself in unhealthy ways. It was essential that she learn about the government and how it functioned, and to that end someone suggested some courses at G.W., a suggestion laughingly declined; and that was a storm warning. Whatever would Sylvia *do?* Their circle was tight and when she vowed to let some air in, introduce New York's cosmopolitan spirit to the monotonous city of government, people objected. Washington liked its own spirit. It had something of the satisfied atmosphere of the undiscovered resort and didn't need blasé New Yorkers telling everyone how to behave.

They were the couple that other couples talked about, the word spread by the usual tom-toms, Harold and Alice and Ed and Billie tapping out the messages; there was nothing to be done about it. They all had connections, each to the others — as Judge Justin Aswell tactlessly pointed out at the rehearsal dinner. Justin had been given the chore of keynoter and took the occasion to instruct Sylvia and her family on exactly how connected everyone was. Ed Peralta's father, Curly, was Senator Adolph Behl's closest friend. Harold and Ed and Axel had been in school together. Billie and Alice grew up around the corner from each other. Justin's charts showed just how close they all were, related by blood or by marriage or by school or university, in-laws and stepchildren and stepparents and cousins, roommates, clubmates, teammates, friends from summers on Cape Cod or Long Island or Mackinac. Justin had connected Alice Grendall to Sylvia, via Sylvia's great-aunt and Alice's brother's first wife's grandmother. Axel and Lloyd Fisher were related in some fashion that Justin found difficult to explain, perhaps the bar sinister. By then he had taken on so much Champagne that his attention had begun to wander.

He ended by saying that in times of crisis these connections were an advantage, everyone pulling together believing that an attack against one was an attack against all. Moreover, the connections were not coincidence. They represented a kind of natural selection. Justin had an idea that there was a specific gene that predisposed a man to public service, a life inside the government, a gene not unlike the one that determined musical talent. Otherwise, why did so many men of the same woof and warp opt for the judiciary, the foreign service, or the military, badly paid posts that were under the scrutiny of a venal Congress and the wretched newspapers, and the answer was the gene and the determination to participate in the political life of the nation.

They finally pulled him down and Axel rose — out of turn, it had to be said — to deliver a graceful little essay describing the tremendous affection he had for his wife-to-be and her charming parents, who represented the best of old New York, and how many happy afternoons he had spent at their lovely apartment on Gramercy Park. Axel's words were an attempt to reassure Sylvia, but everyone there could see the stricken expression on her face, the look of someone who has heard a dismal weather report; she had thought that it would be she and Axel against the world and now believed it would be the world and Axel against her. She smiled a little at her father's brief and pointed response: Harry Walren hoped and believed that his daughter would be well protected in such a — he paused here, showing steel for the first and only time that evening — serious and important and strenuous environment, so charged with possibility, so vital to the American democracy. Axel and Constance applauded heartily, but old Senator Behl did not, knowing cosmopolitan sarcasm when he heard it.

After the honeymoon that took them halfway around the world they returned to Washington, where Axel worked on German affairs for the State Department when he was not raising money for Franklin Roosevelt's presidential campaign; young Alec was born the night Roosevelt was nominated. They were living then in a house near Dupont Circle, Axel walking to work each day and Sylvia remaining at home with the baby. She began to write seriously for the first time and in due course began to publish. She told no one, not even Axel. The poems were private; they were between her, her pen, the page, and her anonymous audience. Axel was often away, and despite the community's best efforts, Sylvia withdrew, traveling frequently to New York and leaving the baby in the care of a nanny, whose only instructions were to be present at all times when Grandmother Constance came to call.

I don't give that marriage six months, Alice Grendall said. Poor Axel.

Poor Sylvia, Billie Peralta said.

Things seemed to improve when Axel was posted to England, but almost immediately he left for Spain with Fred Greene, who was not a suitable companion for such a journey. Sylvia was disgusted by the Spanish adventure, though she conceded that the stakes were high and the Republicans worthy of support. When she asked Axel what happened to García Lorca, he replied that he did not know. Who's García Lorca? After he returned to England, things were very bad and only got worse when he was wounded in France.

Both Grendalls were in England during the war. Sylvia had pleaded with Harold to allow her to do something serious for OSS. She thought she had a natural talent for codes and ciphers; perhaps there was something in that line or in propaganda. She had done some writing — it was the first anyone had known of that — and wanted to contribute. Was it true that the British had faked the photograph of Hitler doing a jig outside the railway car at Compiègne? Anything sensitive was out of the question — Sylvia Behl, my God no, the woman's unreliable — so she was put to work as a file clerk. Rebuffed, she slipped into London's wartime demimonde, where everyone arrived without a past and left the same way. Harold and Alice saw less and less of her, and when someone finally noticed that she had not shown up in Files for a week, she was quietly let go.

Sylvia was unrecognizable as the girl who had walked into Axel's life fifteen years earlier, younger than springtime and oh so naïve. Suddenly she knew too much. Her high spirits had been replaced by weariness or fear or boredom or some combination of the three; no doubt she had realized that her marriage was a misalliance, the white dove evolving into the black sparrow and vice versa. Harold thought that she and Axel and the boy were like a ravaged nation in the aftermath of a war, disoriented and without leadership or hope for the future, or resources to begin the reconstruction.

After the war they returned to Echo House, Axel wasted, looking starved, ten years older than his age at least — degraded, Harold said. Axel was seen here and there between visits to Walter Reed, and in time did seem to improve. But Sylvia had virtually disappeared, "in seclusion," she said. Naturally the rumors multiplied and as usual Alice Grendall brought the news.

I saw her car the other day, Alice said to Billie Peralta. She's visiting someone in Falls Church.

Alice explained that she had had to drive her maid home and saw Sylvia's car, the dinky green MG with the right-hand drive, parked in front of a nasty little bungalow, shades drawn and a dog on a chain in the front yard. When Billie said she couldn't believe it, no one they knew lived in Falls Church, for heaven's sake, Alice replied that army sergeants lived in Falls Church. Her maid's husband was an army sergeant. So Mrs. Sylvia-more-mysterious-than-thou Behl had found herself an army sergeant.

Billie was silent. The story was implausible.

Of course you couldn't see in the house, Billie said.

So it could be anything, she added.

I suppose she thought no one would discover her in Falls Church.

Still, Billie said. A sergeant?

It was predictable, Alice said.

To which Billie replied with an obscure remark about lambs lying down with lions.

When Alice informed her husband that night at dinner, Harold Grendall sighed and muttered something complicated in German. He said, *Wir müssen wissen; wir werden wissen.* We must know, we will know. Their community was so tight and everyone knew each other so well. Curiosity was natural. And of course Sylvia had to drive a bottle-green MG with right-hand drive, a vehicle no less conspicuous than a fire engine, and had to park it on that specific street the day Alice drove by.

What did you say? Alice said.

Nothing. I'm thinking, Harold replied.

About her? Alice said.

Harold sighed again. The women had excellent instincts and a natural nose for scandal, not unsurprising, since most of them had volunteered for intelligence work during the war and were trained to be suspicious, working always on the sound assumption that nothing was as it seemed. They were quick to judge Sylvia because they sensed her otherness, her incongruity and appetite and independence, her refusal to play along. Poor, frustrated Sylvia; you would have expected her to pick the tosspot columnist who was always at Echo House for Sunday lunch or even the dissolute South American ambassador so deft with the tango.

Yet Harold doubted that an army sergeant figured in Sylvia's afternoon disappearances. Sylvia lived by her own strange standards, but he could not imagine her driving to Falls Church for a liaison in a bungalow. Of course you never knew for a dead certainty; people's private lives were always mysterious and there were skeletons in every closet, his own included. Bad luck all around.

I hope you keep quiet about it, Harold said. We don't need another scandal. There's very little of consequence that goes on in this city that Axel doesn't know about, so the odds are good that he knows about Sylvia and her sergeant, if that's who it is. Personally, I doubt it. I'd say it's another set of crockery altogether and that Axel has decided, for his own reasons, to do nothing about it. Say nothing and do nothing.

They've had a hard time lately, Harold said at last. But they've been together a long time and there's every possibility that they'll fix things up. Stories get out and the fact that they're out changes things. The people involved look at the problem differently when they know it's common coin. Same thing in government. When the secret's out it's a different secret because it's no longer confidential. Daylight gives it a different shape and significance and it's hard to see the thing as it was originally, as a secret. So keep quiet. Axel and Sylvia are quality people and have to be given a chance to work things out themselves, with no interference from friends.

Alice looked at him skeptically.

That's what we do in Washington, Harold said with sudden emotion. We fix things up. We compromise; that's the essence of our society. We give a little and get a little and out of the chaos comes an order that we can live with. It isn't perfect. But it's what we do.

As it happened, Axel knew everything; and Alice's lurid speculation was false, at least the part about the sergeant. On Thursday afternoons Sylvia drove across the river to Falls Church to see Mrs. Pfister, a clairvoyant whose uncanny observations were attracting an eclectic clientele. Sylvia first heard her name from Belle Aswell, who had heard it from her son-in-law. Belle did not approve of her son-in-law and cited the weird Mrs. Pfister as evidence of his unreliability. Axel had heard of her, too, the expression on his face bemused when he disclosed that she was in vogue with the wives of several Asian specialists at the State Department. The specialists sometimes went along to listen to the uncanny observations. She's odd, Axel said, indicating vaguely that she had come to the attention of intelligence officers.

The usual concerns, Axel explained.

I think I'll go see her, Sylvia said.

We haven't figured out how she does it, Axel said. She predicts things. She predicted the Republican Congress in 'forty-six. She predicted Jimmy Byrnes. And she goes backward, too. She re-played a conversation between de Gaulle and Anthony Eden back in 'forty-one that was correct in every detail, and I should know because I was in the room. Mostly people go to her for personal things, their love life or their health or finances. She casts their horoscopes or investigates the zodiac or deals the cards or whatever it is that summons the spirit world. Apparently she has different techniques for different clients. She's not dumb; that much we know.

Sylvia looked at him closely. We? She said, You seem to know quite a lot about her.

Word gets around, Axel said.

She nodded doubtfully, still looking at him.

A strange woman, Axel said. She showed up from nowhere a few years back, theoretically a refugee. She's built up quite a practice. And it's growing every day. If you see her, be careful what you say.

Isn't she discreet?

She's discreet, Axel said. All the same, be circumspect.

Sylvia smiled. It wouldn't make much sense to go to a clair-voyant and be circumspect; but Axel would not understand that.

She said, I'll let you know what I discover.

Do, Axel said thoughtfully. By all means, do.

Mrs. Pfister sometimes used the tarot, sometimes ordinary playing cards. Often she went into a trance and spoke rapidly in tongues or voices not her own. She was young; Sylvia guessed in the vicinity of thirty-five. Her blond hair was her own and she had extraordinary skin and shiny gray eyes. Her voice was soft and vibrant as a cat's purr, with an accent that seemed to be Slavic in origin. Mrs. Pfister's manner was formal and so imper-sonal that she did not immediately inspire confidence. She al-ways took her time, refusing to be hurried in any way.

They sat at a plain metal bridge table, Mrs. Pfister fussing with the cards, shuffling slowly and then turning one card after another, watching the cards as she spoke. This was Sylvia's third visit and she had an idea it would be her last; little of value had been disclosed. Tell me why you are here really, Mrs. Pfister said after Sylvia was seated. Speak to me sincerely. Do not be afraid. Sylvia said she wanted to uncover the past so that she could observe the future, read the tea leaves, she said, smiling at Mrs. Pfister. She knew there was coherence, a thoughtful plan as in a poem, one line leading to the next as one card led to another. Sylvia paused, overcome suddenly by emotion. She said, Perhaps this is too much to ask. All desires cannot be fulfilled. I don't know what it is that I want to know, but I want to know it very badly because my heart is breaking and I believe I am the cause. She told Mrs. Pfister that her marriage was collapsing. She and her husband were not intimate, in the usual sense or any sense. He seemed to have — some virulent field of force surrounding him that she could not breach.

Sylvia watched the woman across the table turn cards, searching her face for some sign. She did not know what to say next. She looked at her hands and said she felt boxed in by her wretched and inglorious life in Washington, yet that was not the cause of her great unhappiness. Probably it was a symptom. She believed that the terrible difficulty between her and her husband lay elsewhere, years back, when he was at war and she was living —

"In London," Mrs. Pfister said softly. "With your little boy. In a maisonette with a garden in the rear. Weren't roses climbing a trellis? An elderly couple lived on the top floor. Gardening, you wore a blue sweater that was out at the elbows. And your husband was away in France. He had an experience in France."

"He was wounded badly," Sylvia said. "He was with a friend."

"Not that," Mrs. Pfister said crisply. "This occurred before he was wounded. This happened before the accident."

Sylvia made a helpless gesture. Perhaps this was a mistake after all. Axel had never told her how he was hurt, insisting that he remembered nothing. She was aware that Mrs. Pfister was watching her, awaiting some reply.

"I don't know," she said.

"There were many casualties."

"No." Sylvia shook her head emphatically. There was no elderly couple on the top floor of the maisonette either. She said, "There was only Axel and his friend Fred Greene. Fred was killed."

"Many dead," Mrs. Pfister repeated, "and one of them was a young woman, a Frenchwoman your husband cared for."

Sylvia opened her mouth to say something, but no sound came. She was too astonished to speak. She watched Mrs. Pfister turn one card and then another, looking at them closely. They were anonymous cards, a six of clubs and a four of diamonds. And then a seven of clubs fell.

Mrs. Pfister stared at the card a moment and sighed. "I think this young woman is the field of force you spoke about, the current that surrounds your husband." She paused again, staring intently at the seven of clubs. "They were not lovers," Mrs. Pfister said at last.

"I don't believe that," Sylvia said.

"I am certain of it," Mrs. Pfister said.

"Does it matter whether they were or they weren't?"

"It always matters," Mrs. Pfister said. "In this case —"

"Not to me," Sylvia said. "Her 'current,' as you call it. Is what matters. They were lovers in every sense that matters, isn't that true?"

"Perhaps not in this case," Mrs. Pfister amended. "Perhaps not in the way you mean."

What way was that? Sylvia wondered to herself, watching Mrs. Pfister turn cards. She said, "Where did they meet?"

"In France," Mrs. Pfister said.

"Well, of course. But *where?* Under what circumstances?"

"I can't say," Mrs. Pfister said. "My vision is blocked. I see a heavy stone wall."

"Was she pretty?"

"I see her standing beside a stone wall, leaning her bicycle against it, looking over her shoulder. She has an unfriendly expression on her face. She does not approve of your husband's friend, who has offended her in some way. She is quick to take offense, and she is looking at him in order to avoid looking at your husband. Yes, I suppose that men would consider her pretty."

Sylvia said impatiently, "And how did this woman die? And does she have a name?"

Mrs. Pfister did not reply immediately. She gathered the cards and commenced to shuffle them slowly seven times, concentrating on her fingers. She said, "There was confusion, gunfire, a skirmish of some kind."

"A skirmish?"

"Something of that sort," Mrs. Pfister said vaguely.

"You don't see it clearly?"

"Not very clearly," Mrs. Pfister said.

Sylvia said, "Did Axel kill her?"

Mrs. Pfister looked up in surprise.

"Axel was present."

"It would seem so. He and his friend."

"He's capable of it," Sylvia said.

"I have no doubt," Mrs. Pfister said.

"He's capable of anything."

"Yes, of course."

"This is what the cards tell you?"

Mrs. Pfister moved her head, yes and no.

Sylvia was trying to get the events straight in her mind. She had never heard this story or anything like it. Axel never talked about the war, at least his part of it, and had always maintained that he had no memory of the day he was wounded. She had no idea how he and Fred had lived before August 1944, or whom they had lived with. They had worked under cover, after all. She assumed he had killed, and imagined that he had done it with the coldness and efficiency that he did everything else. Axel had been an invalid for so long and when he was himself again he avoided her questions, saying that those years were better left undisturbed; he knew nothing that he cared to tell. Not that she insisted; and he had not pressed her for details of wartime Britain except to ask if Alec had been frightened by the German bombs.

She would have told him about her life if he had asked, but he never did. After the war years they were so divided in their emotions that questions would have been difficult and answers clumsy. The answers would have been incomplete. They had lived under wartime discipline that seemed practical at the time, though later they would understand how abnormal it was, and how strenuous.

Sylvia said, "How strange it is to hear all this."

Mrs. Pfister continued to turn cards until she found one that spoke. "I believe this Frenchwoman was married. Her husband was not with her. They were not together."

But Sylvia was not interested in a husband, present or absent. "The skirmish," she began.

"They were witnesses to it," Mrs. Pfister said.

Sylvia waited.

"I can see her falling," Mrs. Pfister said.

"Where?" Sylvia said. "Where was this?"

But Mrs. Pfister shook her head. She did not have that information.

"It's all so unsettling," Sylvia said. "I feel you're describing an incident from my own past, a memory I had mislaid or caused to cease to exist, but that's been with me always, at my elbow without my knowing it. As you said, a current." She turned then to look at the pale stripes of light falling through the blinds. From far away she heard the high whine of a police siren. She had been sitting at the bridge table for an hour or more, asking questions and listening to the answers that came between long pauses, each answer more unnerving than the last. Yeats spoke of an existence between sleeping and waking, neither one nor the other but a shadow realm of high purpose and resolve. Yeats accepted the spirit world of the fairies, and accepted also the disciplines of astrology and magic. He believed that the borders of the mind were ever-shifting and that one mind could flow into another, and that memory worked in the same way. If Yeats were sitting at this bridge table with Madame Blavatsky —

Yet Sylvia also knew, without the slightest doubt, that Mrs. Pfister had hold of something vital.

She said, "There was no elderly couple on the top floor of the maisonette. A British army colonel and his mistress lived there."

Mrs. Pfister nodded.

"And my sweater was red, not blue."

Mrs. Pfister continued to turn cards, frowning now.

Sylvia said softly, "How did they meet? I mean where and under what circumstances. Under whose roof? Was she a *résistante* with a black beret and a bomb in her knickers? Did she work for him? Was she one of his people, who helped him derail troop trains and cause havoc in the countryside? Who was this Frenchwoman he cared for? *And what was her name?*"

"I am not able to say," Mrs. Pfister said. Sylvia thought she detected a slight smile, not unkind or sarcastic. It was as if she had suddenly welcomed a new thought. Again Mrs. Pfister began to turn cards, and that was the only sound in the room, the snap of pasteboard. She remembered that Yeats had no use for cards, preferring the signs of the zodiac.

Mrs. Pfister said, "It's possible she lived behind the stone wall where she parked her bicycle."

Sylvia said irritably, "That was her home? Behind a stone wall?"

Mrs. Pfister turned one card and another and a third, not looking up. Outside, a dog began to bark.

"Once Axel mentioned a château."

Mrs. Pfister nodded.

"Where he and Fred Greene stayed for a night late in the war. A château with a vineyard. He said something about a count. Perhaps this woman he cared for belonged to the count."

"Did he mention a town or a region?"

"No."

"Or what he was doing there?"

"War business," Sylvia said.

"Dirty business," Mrs. Pfister said.

"He was on his way to join General Patton."

"I would say this girl was a country girl," Mrs. Pfister said after a moment.

"Not a girl from a château," Sylvia said.

"It seems not."

"And my husband's infatuation —"

"Infatuation?"

"Yes, my husband's infatuation."

"That is not the word I would use, Mrs. Behl."

"What word would you use, Mrs. Pfister?"

"Not that word."

"Well, then. Obsession?"

Mrs. Pfister paused fractionally before she said, "Hope."

"What does that mean?"

"It means your unhappy husband found hope."

But Axel had never lacked hope. His American optimism was well known. He had hope enough for a dozen men, and if he found himself bereft, he would never go looking for a woman. Sylvia tried to imagine the country girl, her size and coloring, her hair and the way she carried herself and the timbre of her voice, a woman quick to take offense, parking her bicycle and looking over her shoulder at Fred Greene. Surely it had been Fred who had made a lewd remark. Fred could not look at a woman without wanting to sleep with her. But Sylvia, trying to stare into the shadow realm, could not summon an image. The woman was as amorphous as the word Mrs. Pfister had used to describe her. Sylvia bent her head to look at the cards, face up on the bridge table; but the light was poor and she could not make out the numbers.

"And then she was killed," Sylvia said.

"She died," Mrs. Pfister corrected.

"A death witnessed by my husband."

"I believe he was present, yes."

Sylvia leaned forward, formulating a question.

But Mrs. Pfister spoke instead. "What does he do, your husband? What is his work?"

"Government work," Sylvia said without thinking.

"Secret work," Mrs. Pfister said.

"I suppose it's secret. He doesn't talk about it. But he isn't forthcoming about anything, so it's not surprising." She hesitated and when next she spoke it was in a whisper. "And how did he react when the French girl died? He was there, wasn't he? What did he do when she died?"

Mrs. Pfister fanned the cards, concentrating hard. She closed her eyes and moved her head from side to side, stretching her muscles. She was silent a long moment, and then she sighed heavily. Her eyes popped open. She said, "Forgive me, I'm tired and the cards are tired. That will be all for today."

"Of course," Sylvia said. "I understand. This must take a tremendous effort. You can't know how much I appreciate it. But what did he do, after? Did he try to save her? Did he run away?"

"I cannot say," Mrs. Pfister said. She collected the cards and set them decisively to one side.

"Cannot or will not?"

"Whichever you prefer," Mrs. Pfister said mildly.

Sylvia tried to imagine the French girl and Axel together and found she could not. She was handling a few fragments of an object and trying to imagine the whole from the parts, while around her swirled ghosts from another place and time. The small room seemed to contain multitudes, the worried souls who visited to ask about their love life or their health or their finances. Be careful what you say, Axel had said. Suddenly Sylvia had the fantastic idea that Mrs. Pfister was taking Axel's side, that Axel was her real client and she was protecting him, refusing to complete the narrative that she had begun. She had left the story in midair, to Axel's advantage. Sylvia leaned forward to ask the question — Is the country girl in his thoughts now? But she knew the answer to that.

She said instead, "Why do you want to know about his government work?"

"Sometimes it helps me, knowing."

"He said I was to say nothing about it."

"He knows you're here, then?"

Sylvia looked at her with surprise. "Of course."

Mrs. Pfister had risen from the bridge table and was standing at the door, waiting.

"I don't know what he does, really."

Mrs. Pfister nodded.

"May I come back?" Sylvia said.

Mrs. Pfister said of course.

"It's important to me," Sylvia said.

Mrs. Pfister opened the door. It was dark outside.

"It's important that I know about my husband's war."

Mrs. Pfister waited.

"There's much that's unexplained."

"It's possible that your husband does not know that the Frenchwoman is dead," Mrs. Pfister said and closed the door.

That night Axel came home later than usual and after changing his shirt went directly to the garden room. He was surprised to find the ice bucket full and a tray of hors d'oeuvres on the sideboard, a fresh Stilton surrounded by English biscuits and pale pâté de foie gras with toast. Sylvia was puttering among the plants and seemed more cheerful than she had in months, though Axel did not make much of it; he had had an exhausting day moving paper from the White House to Capitol Hill and back, an ambassadorial appointment that was proving difficult enough that they had asked him in on an ad hoc basis to work the usual magic. When Sylvia asked him how his work day had been, he replied, A little of this and a little of that. He was worn out and his back hurt but he believed he had saved the nomination, no thanks to the nominee, who was pig-stubborn even by Wall Street standards. He was refusing to supply a biography to the Foreign Relations Committee on grounds of privacy, and if they didn't like it they could go shit in their shoes, pardon my French. He was the one making the financial sacrifice. They should be *begging* him. But Jimmy Longfellow was a very old family friend and it was important that he be installed in Lisbon as quickly as possible and with a minimum of fuss. Axel had offered his services, something he rarely did, and the White House was grateful. He made a drink for himself and one for Sylvia and turned on the phonograph, one of the Broadway albums she liked. He opened *Time* and saw a picture of the nominee with his new wife.

Before he had a chance to read the piece, Sylvia was demanding his attention, rising from her plants, fetching her drink and talking rapidly, describing her ride to Falls Church, describing Mrs. Pfister, describing the séance, and her own amazement at the accurate recall of details of their London life, the pretty maisonette in Regent's Park with the roses on the trellis and the apple tree and all the rest. The afternoon shade, the stone birdbath.

"Things no one else could have known," Sylvia said. "Of course there were mistakes, a blue sweater instead of the red. You remember my old red sweater, Axel? And she misidentified the brigadier and his mistress in the top-floor flat."

Axel looked up. "What brigadier? I never heard about a brigadier and a mistress."

"They moved in after you left for France. We played backgammon on Sunday afternoons at that club in Mayfair, what's-its-name. I usually won, too. Meta Fitzgibbon didn't know how to attack with the doubling cube, and Alfred was always drunk."

"Sounds charming," Axel said.

"It was uncanny, the things she knew. It gave me the creeps."

Axel fingered the pages of *Time* as he listened to her. Someone had told him they had inside information, and now, glancing at the photograph, he knew what it was. The new wife looked like a chorus girl, except that she was young enough to be called an ingénue. TYCOON & WIFE, the caption said. The smirk was in the ampersand.

"She knows you, too," Sylvia said.

"Who?" Axel said. "Who knows me?"

"Mrs. Pfister," Sylvia said.

He sipped his drink, alert now.

"She knows about your wartime life."

"What does she know about my wartime life?"

"That you were in France and that you were injured. And lots more besides." Then Sylvia described the country girl leaning her bicycle against the stone wall and glaring at Fred Greene, offended at something lewd Fred had said. It was a wall to a house and the girl lived in the house, apparently. "She was a lovely French girl. Didn't you tell me once that you and Fred put up for a night in a château? Did the girl come with the château?"

Axel looked at his wife without expression.

"Later, there was gunfire and a skirmish of some kind. General confusion. Her word, Axel. 'Skirmish.'"

Axel nodded slightly.

"You witnessed it," Sylvia said. "You were *there,* you and Fred. Mrs. Pfister didn't know what the skirmish was about or who was involved but she said she could see the French girl falling" — Sylvia was watching Axel carefully but his face betrayed nothing — "but would not say what happened next. At any event, she didn't say. Perhaps the cards refused to speak; she wasn't specific. At first I thought you were involved in some way; it was a war after all and you were behind the lines. Anything can happen. But you were only a witness, according to Mrs. Pfister. So you can tell me now what happened, how these events came about. And what they mean to you."

He was appalled at her enthusiasm, an almost childlike delight in ransacking his life and discovering the money in the mattress. He said, "Shut up."

But Sylvia, engrossed in her own narrative, assembling the fragments as best she could, did not hear him.

"For example, she had a husband. Did you know that?"

"I knew it," Axel said.

"And you never said anything to me."

"Why would I?" Axel said. He was staring coldly at her and did not notice the magazine fall to the floor.

"Not one word," she said.

"It wasn't your business," Axel said. "It still isn't."

"Not a word to me or to anyone, an affair so private you couldn't mention it. And it's been between us all these years and I never knew she was there, this French girl you fell for. To me she was one of those unk-unks you're always talking about, the unknown unknown that's discovered too late or not at all. I don't even know her name. And if it isn't my business, whose business is it? Thank God for Mrs. Pfister."

Axel moved his hand and whiskey spilled from his glass.

"Do you still think about her?"

"Go to hell," Axel said.

"Of course you would," Sylvia said. "Mrs. Pfister insisted that you and the unk-unk hadn't been lovers, but who could believe that?"

Axel remained silent. He wondered who had gotten to the psychic or whether she had made one connection and guessed at the rest. People talked too much, always had, always would, about matters they didn't understand; of course there were files, and conversation about the files, but none of her clients would have access to either one. Something malignant was at work, unless Mrs. Pfister was exactly what she claimed to be, and that was unacceptable.

"Mrs. Pfister said she surrounded you like a field of force, an electric current. Mrs. Pfister said your unk-unk represented hope, and I said that was unlikely, because you never lacked hope. My Axel has always been an American optimist, but now I'm not so sure and wonder if that was another deception. I've been thinking about that remark my father made, the one I disagreed with and fought him on. Axel Behl's an adventurer, he said. He's an adventurer just like me. But you weren't like him at all, and that's why I fell in love with you in the bar car of the Twentieth-Century Limited and stayed in England while you played soldier in France. And now I find you've had someone else all this time, while I was blaming myself for our troubles. We don't know each other at all and I'm afraid that's the way we'll always be, because that's the way you want it."

She paused, looking out the window into the darkness, aware of the amber glow of the city below the roof lines of the neighbors. She suddenly remembered a cocktail invitation she had accepted, friends of Axel's.

"There's one other thing," she said.

"I don't care what it is," Axel said.

"I think you'll care," Sylvia said. "At the very end when I was pleading for information because so much had gone unsaid, Mrs. Pfister volunteered that it was likely that your French girl was dead. And it was possible that you did not know that. Go ahead, you can shake your head yes or no if you don't care to speak, if speaking's too painful. Apparently she died after you left the skirmish. Or perhaps there was another skirmish; Mrs. Pfister wasn't clear on that point. She said her cards were tired. So much is mysterious and incomplete. I'm returning next week for the rest of the story, though why is it that I have the feeling that I have all I'm going to get? She left me on tiptoe, Axel."

Sylvia raised her heels and let them fall.

"But that's the way she is, I guess. At the end she was so tired, exhausted really, that she could not go on. But there's no doubt she admires you. The way everyone does, even my father. She was in no way critical or disparaging of your role in things. And you can bet I was discreet when she asked about your work, who you are exactly." Sylvia smiled to herself when she saw him frown, his jaw working. "For a while I thought she was taking your part as she described the events and her very clear picture of the girl falling. How do you suppose she got her gift? Who gave it to her? She seemed to imply that there was a coherence or pattern to the events and that they had worked out according to some plan, though whose plan it was she didn't say. God's plan, I suppose. Of course now that I've established the past I'm looking to the future. That's the main thing, isn't it, Axel? And the cards will speak to that point also, I assume."

He was no longer listening carefully, but his eyes never left his wife as she moved back and forth in front of the sideboard, her hands describing tight circles and her hips swinging seductively with each step; but that was her normal strut, high heels snapping sharply on the parquet. She had never looked more like one of Modigliani's demimondaines nor sounded more like her mother. He glanced at the copy of *Time* at his feet, TYCOON & WIFE. He remembered to take a sip of Scotch, then allowed his attention to wander.

"Why is it that you can never say what's in your heart? I have no idea what's there, this locked room you have —"

He was remembering Nadège, the set of her mouth, the way she wore her beret, her coloring, her stride, and the unquiet emotions buried beneath her skin. He saw her as a philosopher saw an idea, now clear, now vague, always within reach but never entirely grasped. Now somehow Nadège had been summoned to a bungalow in Falls Church and made to perform for strangers. Her sleep had been disturbed. He could do nothing for her; she was beyond his protection; and now more shadows crowded in upon him. He was unable to separate her from the city of the dead or the château or her bicycle. They had never addressed each other by name, had never touched, had never laughed together or quarreled. If she was dead, it was God's will. By rights he should be dead, too. He believed Nadège was present in his memory in order to remind him of the ghastly afternoon in the summer of 1944 when so many died under such appalling circumstances, except him. He lived. It was a simple fact that in wartime your imagination ran riot.

"But what I want to ask," Sylvia said. "Were you responsible?" She was quiet now, waiting for his answer.

"Was it something you did? Or didn't do?"

He looked beyond her now, to the croquet court in darkness, the soft glow of the capital on the horizon, the city Sylvia said had the heart of a hangman and the soul of an accountant. He wished Nadège had been left in peace with her patriot. She had no business in Falls Church. It was true that her name derived from the Russian Nadezhda, meaning *hope*. So the psychic was correct in that sense if not in any other. The name hadn't done Nadège any good, though. Everyone knew that in combat events worked according to their own logic, which was never foretold. Angels and demons hovered over every battlefield, directing events. It was not a matter of doing or not doing. Axel saw her very clearly now, bending over the cutting board. He was watching his wife, but Nadège was present, moving in Sylvia's shadow cast by the two bright lamps on the sideboard. The two were indistinguishable; and then she was gone, vanished utterly. Sylvia remained.

Her voice was low and she was speaking rapidly, something about Mrs. Pfister's Slavic accent and regal bearing. Sylvia was wearing a tight blue skirt and a white silk blouse and her mother's pearls. Gold bangles clicked when she moved her arms. He remembered buying them for her in Calcutta before the war, the day after they had been to the museum. She showed them off to everyone they met, extending her arm, pointing out the chasing on the gold. He glimpsed the narrow straps of her bra touching the silk and marveled again at her lithe youthfulness; she was supple as a whip and he was so clumsy. Sylvia seemed never to age and looked almost girlish now as she tossed her head and refilled her drink. She had no gray hair at all and scarcely a line in her face, even around her eyes when they narrowed, and when she spoke it was with an immature intensity, words italicized for emphasis.

She said, "You never react, do you, Axel?"

Her body had not matured and her emotions had not matured either. How could she know so little when she felt so much? Now she believed in magic, a seer with a deck of cards and an overheated intuition; and someone had talked out of turn, not much doubt about that. Bewitched, Sylvia thought she had deciphered the Rosetta Stone. She did not believe that a human being had a right to his own memory, the right to preserve and protect his own past.

She said, "If only you had some imagination, then we might find a way to talk to each other."

When he did not reply, she said, "You think everyone can read your mind, know your thoughts as intimately as you do. Axel, what happened to you over there? Something must have happened, or is it just this little French tart whose existence I didn't know about until a few hours ago, and now I find she's a guest in my house —"

Axel's hand was shaking when he brought his glass to his mouth, all the while watching her as she moved back and forth in front of the sideboard, her voice a bird's shriek. Blood rushed to his face. He put the glass aside and rose, faltering, groaning from the pain in his back —

Hit her? He could have killed her.

3

Equilibrium

∽

Echo House was empty now, Alec back at school and only old Mrs. Johnson there to clean and prepare dinner on those evenings when Axel dined in. After Thanksgiving he had dismissed the French staff, his hours too erratic to accommodate a temperamental chef who insisted that dinner be served at nine sharp, no exceptions. Axel enjoyed being alone at table, often reading as he ate, and alone later in his study listening to Django Reinhardt or Benny Goodman while he studied the government documents he had brought home in his briefcase. Axel had no formal title but operated quietly as a fixer without portfolio. He thought of himself as a mechanic. They had offered him space in the War Department building, but he preferred his own office near Farragut Square, because his own business so often intersected with government business.

Axel insisted that there was much to recommend the bachelor life, its stillness, leisure, and freedom — well, not freedom precisely; *liberty*. He lived happily among men, the musicians on his phonograph, the artists on his walls, the authors of his books, the officials whose observations he read each night in documents, his own comments written in a headmasterly hand, well done, incomplete, good idea, bad idea, see me. Often he would look up when the arm lifted from the last disc, Django's run echoing in the study, and hear the clock ticking in the dining room. His house was utterly still except for the clock's pendulum. If the moon was full, the yard was flooded with light, almost bright enough to read by. The light had a kind of murmur to it, as if the angels were gathering round. At such moments he was filled with well-being.

Once a month or so, round about midnight, Axel would limp to the garage, climb into his black Packard, and drive downtown to the Lincoln Memorial in order to contemplate the ruined face of the President. Axel looked at the great head and saw the barrel of a revolver touch the skull, Lincoln's eyebrows lifting in recognition, an immense sadness settling. Surely at that moment he saw the face of God. He had preserved the Union, but his knowledge of the terrible price cast an eternal shadow on his soul, an ocean of blood to secure an idea, a free, liberated, and undivided nation. Abraham Lincoln had known the cost to the last corpse, and still he persevered. The identical task awaited Lincoln's successors. The demands differed and the price varied with the demand, but it was always paid in blood. The task in the present decade was no less sublime and the cost would be as high. Lincoln's memorial belonged in Washington, a reminder every minute of every day that America's ordeal was to know itself. Thus consoled, Axel Behl put his car in gear and went home.

When the Senate was in late-night session he often drove to the Hill and slipped into the visitors' gallery. These sessions came at the end of the term, the rush to adjournment, legislation fed into the mill helter-skelter, everyone exhausted, the chamber filling with blue smoke from cigars and cigarettes. A man with a connoisseur's nose could detect the odor of whiskey as well. The Senate chamber had an antique feel to it, all carved hardwood and figured carpets, tiny mahogany desks, each with its own brass spittoon, pages in black knickers standing at attention near the rear doors like obedient sons, scribes in business suits taking shorthand on folio-sized sheets of creamy foolscap, earnest as bishops. The scribes were constantly in motion, gliding from one member to the next, recording the colloquy. The lamps were dim, as if to emphasize the obscurity of the proceedings, unintelligible to anyone not familiar with the matter at hand, an arcane parliamentary tongue as stylized as a sonnet. Axel was put in mind of the medieval holy fathers who published the Scriptures in Latin, a language the faithful could not read. The Mass was mysterious, the Bible more so. Ordinary Christians depended on the good faith and learning of their priests, the translators; and when they were disappointed, they turned to sorcery and witchcraft.

When the voices rose in legislative incantation, Axel could identify the various American regions, Mississippi and Louisiana, Maryland and Virginia, Massachusetts and Vermont. The accents had not changed since his father was in the Senate, and his father claimed that even then they had not changed since the Civil War. Illinois and Kentucky were easy enough, Cook County and its satellites, and downstate in the first; eastern and western in the second; and any state of the old Confederacy, thirteen varieties of molasses. The farther west you went, the more anonymous the accent — Arizona indistinguishable from New Mexico or Colorado, California — *Califarnya* — as bland as the Dakotas. Texas was monstrously distinct, however.

They were indoor men, drawn to enclosed spaces, whatever their private dreams of a day at the races, or on the golf course, or hip-deep in a trout stream, or in bed with a secretary. Their words rarely gave a hint of rivalry or petty jealousy, still less of the need for the windowless chamber and its many comforts and amenities, its consolations. His father told a story of a senator who had suddenly and most unexpectedly lost his wife, and in his grief and confusion rushed immediately to the floor to sit at his desk, grieving all day and all night, apologizing later for any disruption. But where else was he to go? Axel sat back and let the voices wash over him, a murmur like the sea in a soft breeze, the vessel barely making way. The sodden language of government had a beat and a rhythm to it if you knew the score. The lobbyists and their principals crowding the front rows had a rhythm also as they leaned forward in their seats trying to decipher whether a vote to move the previous question was a victory or not; and leaning far over the balcony's edge, they would search the face of the majority leader, who would wink or not, depending on the likely outcome. They listened for the great solos as attentively as any aficionado at Carnegie Hall and when the words died they would laugh or applaud, not raucously, because a certain decorum had to be maintained; their laughter recalled the crinkle of money.

Axel always sat in the rear row of the gallery, where he could watch the lawyers for the sugar producers, the man from the corn belt, the vice president of the railroad union, and the airplane manufacturer cup their hands to their ears when they heard something familiar — the quota, the price support, the tax break, the subsidy — and watch as the votes were tallied, ticking off the yeas and nays on their own scorecards and rising wearily at the conclusion, smiling or not, according to the vote, relinquishing their seats to the lobbyists whose legislation was still being marked up for the decisive vote. The moment had aspects of the bazaar and the auction block and the trading floor and the burlesque house, all business conducted in an arcane tongue with its special rules of grammar and syntax, assisted by a lifted eyebrow or a pointed finger. Axel knew the Senate chamber as well as he knew the garden room at Echo House. He knew the feel of the mahogany desks and the nap of the figured carpet, and knew also what the galleries looked like when a senator raised his eyes, the crowded rows filled with anxious men in rut. No wonder, in their crazier moments, senators wanted to be fitted for togas.

Axel sat alone by choice but occasionally one of the lobbyists would amble up the aisle for a chat, the latest gossip or headline. They were always interested in which item of legislation had brought him to the gallery and nodded skeptically when he said nothing special. He liked the spectacle; it reminded him of his schooldays, when his father allowed him to wander around the cloakroom during the final days of the session. He didn't know until later that he was wearing a leper's bell; the moment he appeared the whiskey bottles would be put to one side. The old senator was sending him around to spy, and more than once he was told to get his ass out of the private rooms, the senator not knowing who he was and apologizing later when he found out.

Axel was surprised one evening when he saw Ed Peralta making his way along the gallery aisle.

"Thought I'd find you here," Ed said. "What's going on?"

"Jimmy Longfellow's nomination to Lisbon. I got it this far; I thought I should be in the chamber for the vote."

"The nomination's not in trouble?"

"Not anymore. But I hear that Alfalfa Bob will have something to say about it. I sent down word that I'd be present so he could say it to my face. I want him to know I'm in the gallery."

Ed Peralta eased himself into the chair next to Axel. "Never cared for Congress. My father loved the House and always wanted me to come listen to the debates, but they never made any sense. Curly said that if you listened carefully enough you'd hear the nuance of the deal. Never appealed to me, all that open talk. Easy to get burned."

"Senate's different," Axel said.

Ed propped his feet on the seat in front and said, "Alec got in touch with Sylvia. She's not in London anymore. She moved back to New York last week. Do you know Willy Borowy? She's with Willy."

Axel craned his neck to watch the action on the floor.

"Wedding plans, too. I think."

Suddenly everyone around them was laughing, a colloquy that had turned unexpectedly droll. The president pro tem rapped for order.

"What's on your mind, Ed?"

"Money problems at the firm," Ed said. "I need your counsel."

"I heard you had some trouble."

"The things we're doing," Ed said. "They're ad hoc. We're improvising. It's a damned amateur hour, no fault of ours." Ed lowered his voice, peering down to the floor, where a member was unsuccessfully attempting to move the previous question. "It's our wallet, and they're behaving like it's a mercantile exchange, ten percent per transaction. They're eating us up. What did you hear?"

"Drums along the Potomac," Axel said.

"You're so helpful, Axel."

"Always at your service," Axel said.

"The problem we've got is the problem you'd least expect," Ed said.

"Transfers," Axel said.

Ed Peralta nodded. The money was transferred overseas, sometimes by courier, sometimes by pouch. And there had been some grotesque mistakes, fuck-ups really, embezzlement and theft being only the most embarrassing. The drawing account in Switzerland was safe but expensive and inconvenient in other ways, Geneva in the middle of everything but close to nothing. Swiss law was a briar patch. The banks still held Nazi assets.

Axel listened carefully, trying to see around the next corner.

"We even sent one of our people to visit with the old man up in Armonk. He's been helpful in the past and they're rolling in money and have the ways and means to transfer. But it came to nothing." Ed struggled with his cigarette lighter, zip zip zip zip. "The modalities, Axel."

Axel watched Alfalfa Bob, nonchalant in his chair; he was listening to his legislative assistant, who was speaking urgently into his ear, handing him an envelope. The senator opened it and sat up straight, looking into the gallery until he found Axel; his heavy eyebrows and scowl were reminiscent of Adolph Behl. The senator brusquely dismissed his aide, then wrote something on the back of the note and looked around for a page.

"Last month we had a crisis," Ed said. "One of the crises in which someone could've ended up dead or in Siberia, whichever's worse. Our man was in London. That bank in the City was closed because they were all off in Yorkshire, shooting grouse. Embassy funds weren't sufficient, and we've had problems with them in the past. They want everything in triplicate. So we had to go to our good friend in Curzon Street and ask him to give us a hundred thousand dollars at once, in greenbacks from his personal safe. Of course he was happy to oblige, as you would've obliged if the shoe had been on your foot. But it was embarrassing. It made us look like idiots. Our friend thought so, too, and let us know it."

"It's inefficient," Axel said.

"No problem with funding," Ed said. "We have funding. We're the drunk in the wine cellar, but we don't have a corkscrew."

"Yes," Axel said.

"We need something that's permanent, reliable, and private, always keeping the paperwork to a minimum. It isn't only them we're worried about; it's us. You know the foundations and philanthropies we've set up to meet the payroll. It's a nightmare to keep straight. Most of the people who are getting the money don't know where it's coming from, or pretending not to know. Reputation means a lot to our novelists, editors, and parliamentarians. And they're walking a tightrope, too. They like the things that money can buy but they don't like it known that the money's coming from Uncle Sam and Uncle Sam wants a return on his investment. We own them, but only so long as we're quiet about it. That's why we're holding this so close, do you see? But it's a time bomb, Axel. We need expertise from a man who knows how it's done, who knows how to keep his own counsel, someone who's been through the mill and knows the score. We need a treasurer *in place*."

Axel was silent a moment, remembering the story he had heard the week before. "What happened to the one we bought at Echo House last Christmas?"

"The philosopher?"

"No, the editor. Monsieur Straddle."

"He skipped."

"Where did he skip to?"

"Normandy. We know where he is. But what can you do? It was too much for him, poor bastard."

"He cost us, Ed."

"I know that, Axel. But it wasn't so much, and we learn from our mistakes."

Axel nodded sympathetically. Monsieur Straddle was a journalist who had spent the war in Paris maneuvering his newspaper around the Germans, Vichy, and the Resistance. He invented an icy prose of obfuscation and ambiguity and was so successful at it that when the war ended he was unable to adapt. He did not understand that the world had moved on. He had lived in his half-light for so long, he could not imagine another environment; and he was certain that one or another of the authorities he had annoyed would invade his apartment and seize his wife and children. He was recruited on a visit to Washington, invited for a drink at Echo House, and offered a subsidy for his newspaper. He agreed at once, all the while admiring Axel's art and the Persian carpets on the floors and the taste of the twelve-year-old Scotch. Of course he hated the Reds and would bring all his rhetorical powers to bear against them. His subsequent editorials were masterpieces of feint and wry indignation. He still feared the jackboot and the knock on the door at midnight, or the summons to the Conciergerie. Circulation fell and the subsidy went to a tiny property near Ivry; and one day the newspaper ceased publication and Monsieur Straddle and his wife and children fetched up at the farm, where the editor was now writing his memoirs of wartime Paris. Axel remembered him as an anorexic middle-aged Frenchman with a facial tic that grew more pronounced with each swallow of Scotch. He was an editor who had learned to live happily in no man's land, between the lines. His French was beautiful to listen to, as soothing as a lullaby.

"So we're in a little bit of trouble, Axel. We need a watchdog."

"An accountant to watch the accountants."

"An accountant with corkscrews," Ed said. "Maybe someone at Treasury."

Axel shook his head.

"Well, then," Ed said. "It's only a matter of time before we're blown. And then we get the works, a congressional investigation, political trouble. They'll put us out of business."

"You want a private banker," Axel said. "You want someone who can get your money from Washington or New York to Copenhagen or London and then to Málaga or Trieste with a minimum of fuss and delay. You want funds on hand in a dozen cities, greenbacks when you need them. You need a private bank and a banker who'll know the questions to ask, a banker who has connections abroad, meaning an organization in place. You'd take a piece of the bank as a silent partner. The books would be very carefully kept and cooked if need be, in the very unlikely event of an outside audit. But you'd always know the balance sheet. And there would be a section of that bank dealing with your interests and that section would be separate and staffed by your people with full security clearance. Each disbursement would require two signatures. I know the bank you want. You want Jimmy Longfellow's bank."

"The ambassador?"

"Our soon-to-be man in Lisbon."

"I didn't know he was a banker."

"His father was a great friend of my father and of Curly, too. You remember him, old David Longfellow. The Longfellows have owned the bank for a hundred years. Cousins and in-laws, nephews. There are probably a couple of godsons in their somewhere. They look after kin. They're honest but inattentive, so the bank's not profitable. They don't work hard at it. They're not *avid*. It's a bank filled with Sunday golfers and their stupid children." Axel shifted in his seat and began to massage the small of his back. "People have to look after themselves."

"I can see the advantages."

"Jimmy wants out," Axel said. "He has his new wife and his embassy. He wants to get Gladys out of New York. He thinks she knows too many people in New York."

"And you think he'd sell."

"He already has. I bought his stake."

"You own the bank?"

"A minority interest, so far."

"This is a creative idea, Axel. It solves all our problems. Trouble is, it's against the law. We can't own and operate a bank. We can buy airplanes but we can't buy an airline. We can buy an editor but we can't buy a newspaper. We can buy weapons but we can't buy Remington. The Treasury can print money and give us some of it but we can't buy a bank to put it in. We have to operate according to the established procedures. And this isn't an established procedure. This is outside our charter."

"Procedures can be changed," Axel said blandly.

"It's a beautiful idea," Ed said.

Axel watched a page enter the gallery and scan the spectators, a worried expression on his face. Axel snapped his fingers, and the boy nodded, relieved, and hurried to his side.

"Mr. Behl? The senator wanted me to give you this."

Axel took the folded piece of paper from the boy's hand, looked at it, and carefully wrote two words in block letters.

"Take this back to the senator with my compliments."

"Yes, sir," the boy said, and was gone.

"What was that about?" Ed asked.

"A note from Alfalfa Bob. The note said, 'Fuck you, Axel.' My note was shorter. Watch."

Ed Peralta heard an animal enthusiasm in Axel's voice and leaned forward to peer into the Senate chamber. The senator was sprawled in his chair, listening to the debate. He smiled when the page approached, but the smile vanished when he looked at Axel's note. He carefully tore it in halves and in quarters and moved to pitch the bits into the spittoon at his feet; then he changed his mind and put them in his pocket, all the while staring bleakly at the surface of his desk. When he touched the white handkerchief peeping from his breast pocket, Ed chuckled.

"That was quick. What was in your note?"

"A man's name," Axel said. "A man who's a great friend of Alfalfa Bob. He didn't know that I knew that. But now he does."

"An inconvenient friend," Ed said.

"Very inconvenient."

"No speech then," Ed said.

"No speech," Axel said. "We can go now."

"You make a bad enemy, Axel."

"I look after my friends," Axel said. "Jimmy Longfellow's a friend. The Man in the White House, he's a friend, too. So if I can make a difference by writing a note, I write the note."

"And they're grateful," Ed said.

"They'll never know. What they will know is that I said I'd help Jimmy and I did, no broken dishes, no commotion. No tie to *them*, do you see? That's the way to do things, if you can afford to."

"Like the bank," Ed said. "But we've never done anything like that."

"Fact is," Axel said, "you'd be saving the taxpayers money. If you set up the bank as a proprietary, and got serious people to run it, you'd make money as a matter of course. You'd make money the way Morgan's makes money. *You'd make a profit on the legitimate operations,* real estate in the beginning, other investments later. So we'd have our own funds, for the contingencies, the usual unforeseen emergencies, and so forth and so on. Given the uncertain and illiquid world we live in."

"It would be self-sustaining then," Ed said.

"More or less, yes. In part. In a manner of speaking. With serious people in charge, people who have your confidence. People who understand banking. And you've got them, too. You know who they are."

"Who are the other partners?"

"Various Longfellows."

"And you think they'd sell?"

"If the price was right," Axel said. "If we promised to keep the name."

Ed smiled. "Do we promise to keep the in-laws and the cousins and the nephews and the godsons also?"

"There are one or two that we would want to keep."

"The smart ones," Ed said.

"Not necessarily," Axel replied. "Do you want me to look into it?"

"Do," Ed said after a moment. "Of course — you'd want to keep your stake."

"Of course," Axel said.

"And there's no conflict there," Ed said.

"Why would there be a conflict? Where do my interests conflict with the government's interests? If I can be helpful to my government's intelligence service, why shouldn't I be helpful? It's symmetrical, Ed. There's no conflict."

"I imagine you have a man at Longfellow's. Someone who looks after your interest."

Axel said, "You know him. He worked for us in the old days. Carl Buzet."

"Carl Buzet," Ed said. "I know the name but I can't place it."

"He worked for Harold Grendall," Axel said. "He was Harold's paymaster. Carl Buzet managed the accounts and managed them well. They were difficult accounts. He's thorough and has a head for figures. Not for much else."

Ed Peralta was staring into the middle distance, his eyes half-closed. "Wasn't Carl Buzet in some trouble?"

"Nothing serious," Axel said.

"No, I remember distinctly. There was some trouble."

"He had a divorce," Axel said.

"An ugly one," Ed said. "His wife was unpleasant."

"She was Czech."

"She hated Carl because he was a Jew."

"Carl loved her," Axel said. "God knows why."

"She went with other men."

"That's right, Ed."

"I remember it now. He shot one of them."

"It was an accident," Axel said.

"He shot him in the face," Ed said.

"Drop it, Ed."

"And you're satisfied with Carl?"

"Very," Axel said.

"All right," Ed said. "He's your headache."

"That's correct," Axel said.

On the floor, the president pro tem banged his gavel. Ed said, "I've got to be getting back."

"I'll make the necessary inquiries into Longfellow's."

"Can we discuss it at lunch on Wednesday? I want Harold and Lloyd on board."

"Of course," Axel said. Then he put his hand on Ed's arm. "I think they're about to vote on Jimmy's nomination."

"Without a debate?"

"Looks like it," Axel said.

"Where's your man? I don't see him."

"Alfalfa Bob left the chamber a moment ago," Axel said. "He yielded back the balance of his time."

A moment later James T.C. Longfellow became ambassador to the Republic of Portugal, by a voice vote.

They were friends from OSS days now back in government and happy to assemble once a week at Echo House to discuss the situation in their beloved Europe, miserable and worsening. They gathered in the dining room below the forbidding portraits of Adolph Behl and his whiskered father, and Constance in an unlikely blue gown, a brooch at her throat, diamonds circling her wrists, an ardent smile on her powdered face. She could be said to preside at these weekly luncheons, peering severely over Axel's right shoulder; and "meeting" would be a more accurate word, since the food was indifferent and merely an accessory to the conversation. Carafes of wine rested here and there on the wide table. Axel used his best crystal and china and saw to it that each man had an ashtray and a silver cup of cigarettes. Various Cognacs and eaux de vie waited on a side table. If the day was warm, the windows were thrown open to the weather, bright belts of yellow sunlight lashing the table, the room redolent of Behlbaver roses and freshly mown grass. These arrangements never varied, except if the weather was foul, when the windows were closed and the sconces lit, making the room as faded and cheerless as a barracks.

Mrs. Johnson retreated as soon as lunch was served. Axel sat at the head of the wide table, flanked left and right by Ed Peralta and Harold Grendall. Lloyd Fisher was next to Harold and André Przyborski was next to Ed. André was one of the many Polish patriots who had emigrated to America rather than remain in London or return to the tortured continent, overrun with Reds and their surrogates. André received his paycheck from a Chicago congressman, on whose staff he was listed as legislative liaison.

The first part of the lunch was always concerned with person-alities, the latest rumors about the evenings of poker and bour-bon at the White House and who was up and who was down at the State Department and the various military services, and the implications for the budget. The weather was fine this noontime and the talk relaxed — until Axel made a remark about the *Iliad*, his current bedtime reading, war as a contagion, war begetting war, war so total and pervasive and strenuous and intoxicating that no combatant could remember how or why it began and could foresee no end. War was life's constant, as reliable as the tide tables. Peace was out of the question, not on the table, given the determination of the Adversary and the incomplete memo-ries of everyone else.

The men nodded grimly and agreed that the West was in for a long winter, one that would last for decades, a modern ice age. The trolls were gathering under the bridges of Europe, Ed Peralta said, remembering the story he had read to his six-year-old the previous evening. The old windbag Bernard Baruch had coined a useful term only the other day: Cold War. Cold War benefited the Reds because Cold War was war in the shadows, war under the skin, a war for souls, a war of feint and duplicity that suited a dictatorship, where there were no legislatures or courts of law, no free press, and if you spoke your mind they sent you to Siberia.

No public opinion, Harold Grendall said.

Plenty of public opinion, Ed Peralta corrected. You just can't say it out loud.

They want democracy, Harold said.

They like democracy, all right, Ed said. They're not opposed to it. They want the right to vote and the rule of law and the right to travel and speak up and read the books that interest them. They'd like a chicken in every pot. They'd like to own a car and watch a soccer match on Sundays and enjoy some vodka with their meals. They just don't like capitalism.

Ed Peralta observed that he had not read the *Iliad* since college and now he had no time to read anything at all, except reports from his men in the field. The reports made your hair stand on end, the organizational skills of the Kremlin were formidable, and terror had as much to do with it as money. They're disciplined people and they know what they want. There were Red cells in every government in Western Europe, with new ones added every day, led by some of the best educated men on that side of the ocean, men who *believed*. Some of them were like the early Christian mystics talking about the divinity of Christ and the Virgin and the pervasiveness of the spirit of God, an inescapable spirit that one day would transform the world. They've seen the socialist system, they know what it does, and still they believe.

Lloyd said, "Not entirely. They don't believe in that so much as they've lost faith in the other."

"Still," Ed said. "Some of these names —"

"Give us one of the names," Lloyd said.

Ed named a mutual acquaintance, a senior figure in the British defense ministry, a peer of the realm. "You remember him," Ed said. "Wore a dinky little toupee. Lived somewhere in Regent's Park. Had a good war. Great backgammon player, screwed everything in sight."

"I don't believe it," Harold Grendall said. "I knew him well. We used to go to the races together."

"Believe it," Ed said.

"You're watching him?"

"We are. Have done for some time."

Lloyd said, "The mother country thinks it's entitled to something, having stood alone for so long. They think they're entitled to the chicken in the pot and the car and so forth and so on and don't realize they're broke. Their banks don't have any money because all the money's over here. They think they're entitled to a reward and instead what they're getting is power shortages, strikes, unemployment, and condescension."

"He always won," Harold said.

"I never met him," Axel said.

"He lived somewhere near you," Ed said.

"Sylvia knew him," Axel said. "And his mistress."

"We don't know who to trust," Harold said.

"We'd better find out," Lloyd said.

"We don't know how to fight this kind of war," Harold went on. "They work in darkness and we work in daylight. We're learning, but it's slow work, and discouraging. We have to find our own shadows, to make our system work for us instead of against us. We only need a sliver of shadow here and there. The way it is now, all our trumps are face up and Ivan's aren't."

"Not all of them," Ed said.

"Most," Harold insisted. "And too many kibbitzers."

"I agree with that," Ed said.

"And the money," Harold said.

"We'll get to that later," Ed said.

André Przyborski was listening to them with growing alarm. He hated it when they began to doubt themselves. Doubt led to confusion and confusion led to a loss of purpose and resolve. The Red Army was formidable but not so formidable that it could not be undermined, given enough time, money, men, and resolve. The future of Poland depended on these men and others like them. André said, "My people know how to fight them."

"No one knows anything about Homer," Axel persisted. "You can't find him in the *Iliad*. He's the author of it but he's not present in it. You can't hear his voice as you can hear Tolstoy's or Carlyle's. Homer doesn't seem to be guiding the story. He's only the amanuensis, and war itself is telling the tale. Every war has its own personality, and our Cold War is a tyrant. Cold War is the novelist. We're only characters in the novel."

Ed shook his head. "Joe Stalin's the author of this one. He's the one who wants it and so far he's in charge of it."

"Then we'll lose," Axel said.

"And deserve to lose," Harold said.

"But what if I'm right?" Axel said.

André Przyborski moved uncomfortably in his chair, looking at the worried faces around the table. What was wrong with them? Djugashvili was just another ignorant peasant from Georgia, crueler than most, dumber than most, maintained by a system with so many inner contradictions that it was only a matter of time before it fell of its own weight. A system could bear the weight of only so many corpses before it became contaminated.

Of course you could help things along, worry them from time to time. You could never allow them an inch of room or an hour of peace. Poland would eat at Djugashvili's heart like a cancer. He would know no rest.

"We will not lose," André said.

"You have no idea of the people who are involved," Ed continued. "People who ought to know better, people who saw the last war at first hand. Educated people, serious people like us —"

"We got a report the other day," Harold said. "We think as many as five million people died in Siberia before the war. Five million Soviet citizens arrested on suspicion and sent to the labor camps in the East. Suspected of plots, everything from sabotage to cracking a bad joke. High treason. Poets, farmers, policemen, apparatchiks, soldiers, peasants, all dead. Stalin's whim."

Lloyd said, "It's not five million, Harold. It can't be. Five million's too high. Think about it a minute. They didn't have transport for five million souls from the cities to Siberia —"

"It was more than twenty million," André said softly.

The others were silent. Ed sighed and lit his cigarette, raising his eyebrows fractionally. André had an emotional Polish temperament and let his politics run away with him. His politics interfered with his judgment and damaged his own cause. He was irrational. His hatred of the Russians was such that he believed every atrocity, no matter how far-fetched. He saw unlucky Poland pressed between the fists of the Hun and the Bolsheviks, the Bolsheviks worse by far; his exaggerations served only to discourage the very intellectuals whose support was so essential to the struggle. André's twenty million was a fine round number to use in the newsletters and the congressman's speeches and in the private briefings he gave members of the Appropriations Committee when it was considering the supplemental. His general pessimism and bleak assessment of the Russian character, fortified as it was by his many grisly anecdotes, was much in favor on the Hill.

"Many, many more than twenty million," André said, glaring at them. "Maybe as many as thirty million, if you go back to the purges of the early 'thirties. And the Russian pigs didn't need trains or trucks. They marched them, west to east. They marched them across the time zones on foot." André leaned forward, angry, the veins in his neck bulging like ropes. Everyone said he had the face of a saint, perhaps El Greco's Jerome, long, thin, and tormented. Women found him especially attractive.

"At any event," Ed said after a pause, "Ivan's throwing money around, Swiss francs, escudos, dollars, you name it. They have as much money as they need because they have the keys to the treasury, thanks to Stalin. As Harold said, we need a sliver of shadow here and there. We need our own shadows to put our money in."

Harold Grendall cleared his throat. "Ed said he described the problem to you, Axel, and you had an idea."

"Axel thinks we should buy our own bank," Ed said.

Lloyd Fisher laughed. "What? Buy the Chemical Corn?"

"Jimmy Longfellow's bank," Ed said.

"Isn't he the one who married the Fifty-second Street quiff?"

"Lloyd," Axel said. "You're on thin ice."

"Let Axel explain it," Ed said.

Axel took them over the ground he had covered with Ed Peralta, adding a nuance here and a fresh detail there. He spoke for five minutes and when he stopped, the company was silent, each man assessing for himself the dangers and opportunities.

"Will they sell?" Lloyd asked.

"Yes," Axel said.

"We've never owned a bank before," Lloyd said.

Harold looked across the table at Ed, who was sitting back in his chair, imperturbable as Buddha. "Have you walked this up the line, Ed? Discussed it with the fellow in the corner office? Shown him the roots and the branches? Put him in the picture?"

"It's cleared," Ed said.

"He has no difficulties with it?"

"None he expressed to me."

"Hard to believe," Harold said.

"He was satisfied that Axel was involved. He wanted to talk to Axel."

"And has he?"

"Yes," Axel said.

"You explained everything to him?" Harold asked.

"I answered his every question," Axel said.

"I'm worried about the security of it," Harold said.

"So was he," Axel replied. "But I've reassured him."

"And the nature of your reassurance?"

"That's my end," Axel said. "Don't worry about that part."

"I don't know," Harold said doubtfully.

"I'm in," Lloyd said. "How soon can you do it?"

"I've done it," Axel said.

"Whoa," Harold said.

"I own Longfellow's, as of Monday. Amazing how eager the cousins and the in-laws were to sell. And after we signed paper, they told me I'd taken a risk because of the certainty of a world-wide depression, now that the war was over. The banks would be the first to fall." Axel lifted his eyebrows. "If you want a piece of this bank, I'm inviting you in. If you don't want a piece, that's fine, too. It's a superb investment for me."

Ed said, "They're idiots."

"What's our next step, then?" Harold asked.

"You and Ed meet with Carl Buzet. Lloyd, too. Lloyd can handle the paper. We'll need papers of incorporation and so forth and so on. We'll need to allocate the stock, set up a board of directors. Carl handles my interest, so you'll be dealing with him."

"I never trusted Carl Buzet," Harold said.

"He doesn't trust you, either."

"I like Carl," Ed said. "I'll handle Carl."

"No one 'handles' Carl," Axel said. "You talk to Carl as you'd talk to me."

"What's our stake?" Ed asked.

"Forty percent," Axel said. "I keep sixty."

Now Lloyd Fisher cleared his throat and the others turned toward him. His pale face twitched. He said nothing for a moment, then announced he had bad news. Next Wednesday would be his farewell lunch at Echo House, because he was resigning from the government. He was leaving to return to Chicago to take over the family firm, almost bankrupt. Fisher, Gwilt had been very, very good to kin for generations, since before the turn of the century. They, too, had been inattentive, but when you're inattentive in court, you lose the case, and then you lose the client. The firm's affairs were a mess and someone had to take charge.

"My father begged me, and I couldn't refuse him. I wanted you fellows to know first. Christ, I hate it. I don't want to leave Washington but I've got no choice. My grandfather founded the firm, you see."

There were expressions of sympathy all around and then Ed Peralta asked how long it was since Lloyd had opened a law book.

"Since 'thirty-nine," Lloyd said. "But there's more than one way to practice law. Some of the ways don't require a law library. You have to call yourself something, so you call yourself a lawyer." He went on to explain the life he imagined for himself in Chicago, the city that crackled with the sound of banknotes; and the banknotes could buy you anything you wanted, except a life inside the federal government working with your closest friends. Golf on the weekends, same foursome every weekend, and dinner every Saturday night at the Club with Republican *Dummkopfen* complaining about Truman and the Jews and the socialists in the government and high taxes and labor unions and the rest. "Be sure to let me know how the Cold War turns out, and if the Jews win it."

Ed said, "Get the firm on its feet and come back. There's always a place for you here, Lloyd."

"It'll take years," Lloyd said.

"So will the Cold War," Ed said.

"Maybe we'll need some help in Chicago," Harold said.

"I can get you Republicans and mobsters, nothing in between."

"I have friends in Chicago," André said.

"Sorry, old boy," Lloyd said. "They wouldn't be admitted into the Club. They'd be turned away, Polish riffraff."

"One of them's a count," André said.

"That's different," Lloyd said. "If he isn't married I can fix him up with a divorcée or a debutante from the North Shore. Maybe he wouldn't mind changing his name to Devonshire or Salisbury. Romanoff, even. The debs are partial to English lords and White Russians."

"I'll give your name to the congressman," André offered. "He has many business interests in Chicago. Often he needs legal counsel."

"I'd appreciate that, André."

"It helps to know people in Chicago," André said. "I also know an alderman and the sheriff."

"And I'd like to meet them," Lloyd said.

"Chicago can't be as bad as you say it is," Harold said. "Why, that's where we developed the atomic bomb."

Lloyd mustered a lethargic smile and allowed his gaze to drift around the dining room, the dark walls and the portraits, Adolph so gruff, Constance so unforgiving. He had spent many reward-ing hours in Echo House, but he wondered how Axel stood it night after night. Lloyd Fisher couldn't imagine dining alone in such a place, the family ghosts gathered round; the previous century seemed close enough to touch and the modern world invisible in its shadows. In this house the *Iliad* was contemporary fiction. The room oozed conspiracy, secrets given and secrets received in a language as subtle as a hangman's smile. He knew that this would be the last time he would lunch at Echo House on Wednesdays. Private citizens were not welcome where gov-ernment business was discussed. He wondered if he would ever know the fate of Longfellow's bank.

He said bitterly, "I wish you luck. I'm cornered. I feel as if my life is over," and was delighted and surprised when Axel said he'd like to consult with him from time to time; the circumstances were such that outside counsel was often helpful.

"Of course," Lloyd said.

Axel rose and raised his glass. "We can't have all our apples close to the tree," he said.

As he always did after everyone left, Axel took a stroll on the back lawn, one awkward step after another, painful exercise insisted upon by his doctors. The rain had slipped under a fat thunderhead that had rolled in from the Southwest. Rain was in the air, a lot of it, from the smell of things. He watched the songbirds as they moved here and there, seemingly without effort or forethought; but if they were careless they were pounced upon by the fat gray cat next door.

Axel leaned on his cane, feet firmly planted on the ground. He loved birds. He envied them their freedom of the city, so unlike spiders bound to the webs of their own making or ants to their anthills or men to the tasks they set for themselves or had set for them. It was always worthwhile watching the birds migrate. When the seasons changed, they were happy to build another nest in a warmer, more appealing climate. Probably they were like American corporations, with a home office and branch offices to service the territory; commercial banks, for example. They had loyalty to headquarters but investigated opportunities in other habitats, many of them far afield. Certainly the birds were unpredictable, not to one another but to the uninitiated or the predatory; the fat gray cat, for example.

Axel sat in the Adirondack chair under the big elm, tapping his cane on the toe of his shoe and watching two robins chase each other on the croquet court; and while he sweated in the humid electrical atmosphere and watched the birds cavort he thought about what had been said over the vichyssoise and cold chicken — Ed Peralta's enthusiasm, Harold Grendall's caution, André Przyborski's passion, Lloyd Fisher's cynicism. In their personalities they resembled the nations of Western Europe and were just as competitive, except for Lloyd, who was on the margin now and knew it. Lloyd was Switzerland, an inconvenient country that no one would think to visit, but a country with certain advantages of distance and discretion. Lloyd wanted to stay in the game and would meet any ante required, even as he knew that the deck would be cooked and the deal irregular; that was part of its appeal. Lloyd was very brave and very able, and one of the best interrogators they had; a shame to lose such a man to a city as transparent as Chicago. But there were ways and means to keep Lloyd active.

Axel removed his coat and loosened his tie and lit a cigar, blowing a thick smoke ring in the direction of the robins. The heavy air carried it away intact and then it slowly broke apart. The city was lethargic, owing to its Southern climate, its torpor reflected in the Senate and elsewhere. The country would be a different country if its capital were located in Boston, San Francisco, or Chicago, brawling immigrant cities quick to lose patience, quick to anger, quick to act, quick to claim credit and demand their rightful place in the scheme of things. In Washington a man was wise to seek the shade, to dwell in the dark seven-eighths that supported the sunny eighth. The hard, dangerous work went on in the shadows. That was where it belonged, away from public view, because so much could be misunderstood. Europeans knew this instinctively, ingeniously concealing their fortunes and the influence that went with them. Your reward and consolation was knowing that the work was thrilling and of consequence. The darker the shadows, the more consoling and rewarding it was.

The United States faced an emergency. That was the simple fact, and Axel was prepared to intervene as the Rothschilds had done in Denmark and France and Britain and Austria and Italy, at various times and for various reasons. Fundamental to all the reasons was equilibrium, statecraft's golden mean. Naturally this assistance could never be eleemosynary; you made a profit so that you could live to intervene again. You could collect wine or old masters or butterflies or women, but your reputation would rest on your service to the nation. This much was also true: you bought yourself a measure of safety.

Axel and Carl Buzet moved rapidly and by the end of the year Longfellow's had doubled its assets and expanded rapidly overseas. Axel's lawyers had devised a corporate structure with one board of directors and one set of books for the American bank and another board of directors and another set of books for its European subsidiary. An asset on one set of books might be a liability on the other. It was not clear whether the American bank owned the European bank or vice versa; it was very clear that the

European bank acted on behalf of private clients whose identities could not be disclosed for reasons of confidentiality. A dedicated investigator with subpoena power, unlimited funds, and a sly turn of mind could follow a paper trail to a Delaware concern, American Summit, Incorporated, which listed as its assets a portfolio of blue chip securities along with a partnership, Group ABCB, Axel Behl chairman, Carl Buzet president.

Axel now had four rooms on the top floor of the building at Farragut Square. He was careful to stay current with the bank's many footings but took no part in operations except to answer an occasional inquiry from the Treasury and (once) from the Internal Revenue Service. Now and then he personally undertook missions of particular subtlety, payments to a finance minister, army general, parliamentarian, trade union official, or newspaper publisher. Axel was in no way formally affiliated with the American government, merely a knowledgeable and public-spirited citizen troubled by the issues of collective security — he called it "equilibrium." And weren't the scales balanced by a kind of benign socialism, indistinguishable in important respects from American capitalism? In other words, European wine in American bottles.

So it was only a matter of time before the wretched Committee on Un-American Activities was looking into his affairs: who was Axel Behl anyway, and who were his sponsors? He ran in the same Georgetown crowd that included Alger Hiss. His former wife was a nutcase; and her father gave money to dubious causes. When you asked Axel Behl what he did, he said "investor" and dared you to contradict him . . . This was one of the unfortunate consequences of exaggerating the enemy's evil. You were obliged to exaggerate your own virtues as well. To counter the enemy's fiendish subversion, you wielded a blunt instrument of righteousness. And then you got a congressional committee of yahoos with subpoena power and God on their side. Too bad you couldn't leave it in the hands of professionals, but that wasn't the way the system worked; you needed money, so you went through the appropriations process, and testimony leaked in unpredictable ways. If only, Axel thought. If only they weren't so god damned dumb. They weren't dumb in his father's day.

Returning to his office each day after lunch, Axel placed a telephone call to Carl Buzet, then leafed through his messages. They were his link to the world and he always returned them in order of receipt; no exceptions, not even the President. He swiveled his chair so that he could see out the big window into Farragut Square, talking into the telephone while he watched people go about their ordinary business, hurrying to a doctor's appointment, waiting for a bus, buying a hat. His conversations on the telephone affected them mightily, usually in ways they would never understand. So Axel observed them carefully as they hurried or strolled, looking into store windows while they waited for the light to change. At these moments, seated behind his father's old desk, disposing of the messages, Axel thought of himself as a builder of bridges.

He saw his chores literally as bridges, elaborate spans of iron and cable soaring into the sky as gracefully as a hawk in flight. A bridge took you from one frontier to another. Axel identified with the agile and imperturbable New York Indians, the Mohawk who balanced on the footwide beams, a thousand feet to the treacherous river below, ambling with perfect equilibrium or swinging lazily in the iron basket held by ropes and pulleys, placing the rivets just so, welding them into place, scratching your own signature on the underside of the beam where no one would ever see it. Such work called for more than brawn and an inactive imagination. It called for strength of character and the sort of nerves that were wired into the genes, not learned or acquired but present from birth. Such men were not afraid to look down but seldom bothered, because their eyes were fixed on the work at hand and when their attention wandered they looked skyward to the heavens. *Ad astra per aspera.*

Their work was done in the clouds, hidden from view. Who noticed the Mohawk balanced on the topmost beam, his hands at his side and his face washed of all expression? No one. No one on the ground could see him, and if by the merest chance they caught a fleeting glimpse, looked up from the traffic light or the hats in the store window, they turned away terrified and faint-hearted at the prospect of an accident owing to the wind or a sudden tremor or a misstep or moment of confusion. If you were successful, your labor and the elegance with which you went about it were noticed only by your fellow aerialists, those who shared the heights. The danger was a given. And the danger was not the point. The bridge was the point, and the applause, when it came, would never be heard by the spectators below. That was its value.

4

Springfield,
November 4, 1952

∽

ELECTION NIGHT in the governor's mansion. Each campaign was unique, and each died on election night. Axel prowled listlessly from room to room, observing the last hours of their civilization. Phoenicia or Pompeii before the eruption. He had been on the telephone all day, calling friends in a dozen states, the question always the same: What do you know? And the excited answer: the vote was heavy everywhere, all states, all regions. The mood in the mansion was cautious, everyone prepared for defeat, accepting and allowing for it while retaining the knowledge that the country was very large and often erratic. No one knew what voters would do in the privacy of the booth because voting was never truly private. People walked into their polling places with a multitude of voices competing for attention. Vote your heart, vote your wallet, vote your hopes, vote your fears, honor thy father.

Confounding experts is the national sport, Lloyd Fisher was saying. Let's wait for the hard numbers. Remember 1948. "What do you think, Axel?"

They turned to him, the scarred square-faced man in the double-breasted suit, the deep-voiced one who was always so direct, dark eyes unreadable under black brows, huge hands resting atop his cane. Everyone knew stories about Axel Behl, but Axel was silent now because his thoughts were private. He wanted to remind them that they were all fish swept along in the same current. The current came from the past and flowed into the future. You did not choose the current. Adlai was unlucky because he was forced to struggle against it, while the general was able to give himself over to it until at last they were indistinguishable, the general and the current.

"I don't believe in experts," a young woman threw in.

"Very sensible," Lloyd said. "What do you believe in?"

"That it will be a long night and the Guv will win because — he has to. He must. Do you think it will be a long night, Mr. Behl?"

"No," Axel said. "I don't think I do."

"Axel's our Gloomy Gus," Lloyd said. "It's because he lives in Washington and doesn't get around the country much. He can't listen to the heartbeat of the nation. We'll see about it, when the hard numbers come in. Connecticut should be any time now."

Axel listened to Lloyd a moment longer, then turned away. Nervous chatter bored him and he could not shake the blues. The girl was exceptionally pretty, though, with a complexion by Renoir and a body to match. She did not seem attached to anyone but was entirely at ease in their company, leaning forward now and laughing at something Lloyd said; so perhaps she belonged to him. Leaning heavily on his cane, Axel limped into the empty study off the living room and eased himself into the big armchair by the window. The Lincoln Hotel was only a block away, and he sourly imagined the scene in the bar, Republicans celebrating twice over — Ike would be in Washington and Adlai out of Springfield.

He watched a car pause in the street, the occupants peering up at the mansion. And then a hound began to howl outside, a specific domestic interruption signaling that ordinary life went on after all; it went on willy-nilly despite a presidential election. The howling ceased abruptly and then, faintly from the next room, Axel heard a commotion and the young woman's nasal Racquet Club voice, *Oh my Chroist.* Hard numbers at last, Axel thought, and from the sound of things they were not encouraging.

He was content waiting in the study for Alec, due any moment from the airport. The boy hadn't wanted to come, pleading football practice, pleading overdue papers and general midterm funk, but Axel insisted. One day this would be his son's world, too, and it was necessary that he know the moral architecture of things, Washington and Springfield along with Pompeii and Phoenicia. This was knowledge that did not come from books. On the whole, defeat taught harder and more durable lessons than victory — no matter how fond you were of the loser, and he loved Adlai Stevenson like a brother. But that was personal and you had to put it to one side in order to see things whole, the volcano, the drought, the plague, the mystery of the current. The most he could do for his son was introduce him to public life so that he could see things at first hand. You had to know what was real before you could identify the propaganda. You had to know how men talked to one another, and then you could begin to understand why one man reacted one way and another man another way to good news or bad. You tested a wooden nickel with your teeth, and character the same way. So he had arranged for the Cessna and told Alec to be on it.

Axel watched his son alight from the cab and reach in to pay the driver, explaining something with an embarrassed turn of his shoulders; no doubt an explanation why he was visiting the governor this night of all nights. Alec was tall, all sinewy arms and legs, dressed in gray flannel trousers and a tweed sports jacket, no topcoat even though it was cold. His face was as transparent as glass, his emotions instantly readable — boredom, anger, elation. The hound had begun to howl again, and Alec looked around him, patting his knee. When the dog didn't come, he gave it the finger, picked up his duffel, and walked up the sloping driveway to the entrance of the mansion. Axel heaved himself to his feet and walked to the top of the stairs.

He said, "Nothing solid yet."

"Is he going to win?"

"I don't know," Axel said. "I don't think so. How was your flight?"

"All right," Alec said. But he had found it unsettling, trying to read his history text and looking down every few minutes to watch America slip past, the land in places so worn and monotonous that it seemed stationary. Once past the Hudson River there were no landmarks and he realized he could be flying anywhere. He had no interest in this part of the country and did not imagine it as different from any other part. The terrain resembled the average middle-aged face, wrinkled rivers here, knobs and bald spots there, eye-shaped ponds. Alec had no interest in travel, believing that his parents had done all the traveling that needed to be done in one American family.

"How did you like the plane?"

"It bounced around a lot."

Then the governor was in the room, smiling, shaking hands, accepting praise for the campaign he had waged. The news from Hartford was bad, but Bridgeport was still to come. Be of good spirit. The governor made his slow transit of the room, exuding a host's warmth. His bald head reflected the glare of the electric lights and he looked much older than his pictures. He had a private word with Axel, speaking in a voice so low it could not be heard two feet away, giving a little weary shrug at the end of it. Axel gripped the governor's elbow in a rush of emotion. Tears jumped to his eyes and his voice was gruff as he introduced Alec. The governor asked after Sylvia, remarking that he had not seen her in many years. Alec thought the governor had an actor's mobile face, soft now from exhaustion. Give her my best when you see her, the governor said. Is she still writing? He took time to ask Alec what he was studying in college and what he intended to do when he graduated.

Avoid politics, the governor said with a sharp laugh and a wink to take the edge off. In his affability and nonchalance the governor seemed relieved that the campaign was over and the outcome still in doubt. No doubt he was one of those who saw the great office of the presidency as a mighty burden and a splendid misery, so relief would not be the word, after the heroic effort he had made. Alec knew at once that the rumpled overweight man in front of him was not the man he had seen and read about; they were obviously two men, one for the public and the other for his friends. No doubt there was a third one also, and he wondered how the governor kept them straight. One of the three would be as false as his father's tears.

Men and a few women crowded around to say hello and shake hands. Someone handed the governor a glass of Champagne. They were reminiscing about the things that had gone wrong, incidents in Trenton and Boston, even Chicago, a speech that had been misplaced or a hall the advance man had forgotten to book, the Southern congressman who was so drenched in bourbon that he could not make the introduction and somehow thought that Adlai was Mr. Truman. The men were loose and friendly, rumpled from their long day. A few of them were tight from drinking, laughing louder than they needed to, making broad gestures with their arms. They obviously held the governor in great affection and wanted only to be near him at this — Alec supposed it was the decisive moment, the roulette wheel turning slowly and the ivory ball poised to fall. Alec noticed that his father smiled wanly at their jokes, making an effort; his focus seemed to be elsewhere.

Alec understood little of what was said. They were speaking a language of familiar words and obscure syntax. It was like listening to Shakespeare, and the ambiance was Shakespearean as well, not the scenes of high emotion but the casual moments that prepared the way. As in any drama, only one actor was the focus at any given moment and the governor had everyone's attention whether he was speaking or not; and Axel, too, was conspicuous, though he said little and seemed preoccupied.

My feet are killing me, the governor said, and those standing around him looked at his shoes as if they had taken arms against him.

"Do you want to sit?" someone asked.

"A killing day, Guv. And it's not over yet —"

"A day that will live in infamy," the first one said, but no one laughed because the remark was in such questionable taste. Why, in the West the polls hadn't even closed.

Alec drifted off and stood at the bay window. He touched his forehead to the cold glass, hoping that his father would want to leave soon. He was still disoriented and in motion from the long plane ride. Illinois was the end of the earth; and then you reached the Mississippi. He tapped the glass with his fingernail. Now and then a car drifted by, the driver dipping his headlights or honking. Behind him he heard a collective groan, and then the ring of a telephone and a woman answering.

"You," she said. "You bastard, why should I have anything to say to you?" Alec listened hard, because he rarely heard women use rough language, only Sylvia when she was very angry or elated. He heard the woman laugh and lower her voice. "Bridgeport's lost, and if we lose Bridgeport we lose everywhere." She paused, giving a drawn-out sigh. "The usual," she said. "It's the rising divorce rate. People want a new head of household, a military man who'll bring home a fat pay packet and keep the Reds from our door and not trouble our sleep during the long winter nights. They want a hero instead of a wiseacre. I don't know what Adlai thought he was running for, maybe president of the Triangle Club. Everyone told him that Americans like their politics sober and every time he cracked a joke he lost ten thousand votes, and he knew it, too, but couldn't help himself. The man has no discipline, so it was obvious from the beginning that we'd lose and lose big. Of course it would've helped if we'd had more money. It would have helped if the bastard newspaper publishers had given us a fair shake. And yours was the worst. Don't you feel like a weasel every time you cash your paycheck?" After a little silence she continued, "The usual gang; everyone's being cheerful, except Axel Behl. You could measure Axel for a shroud. Thing about Adlai is, people like him. They're real fond of him, except the millions and millions who didn't vote for him. Trouble was, we ran a one-legged race. That's off the record. Everything I've said is off the record," she concluded and rang off.

The woman said, "Who are you?"

Alec turned from the window. "Alec Behl."

"Yes, of course," she said brightly. "Axel's boy. I've heard quite a lot about you. I'm Leila Berggren. I know your father."

When she left to join the others, Alec turned back to the window. Leila Berggren seemed young to be part of a political campaign, and much too young to have so sharp a tongue. She was attractive in a Bohemian way, dark eyes, long dark hair, black turtleneck sweater; chain-smoking cigarettes and drinking beer from the bottle. She looked as if she had just arrived from some basement bar in Greenwich Village, flushed with revolution or blank verse. She did not explain how she knew his father but it wasn't necessary. Axel knew everyone. Then Alec heard the tap-tap of his father's cane and his weary voice, its tone just this side of sarcasm.

"I see you met Leila."

"Who is she?"

"One of the Helpfuls," Axel said. "I know it's boring for you. I felt the same way at your age. Politics and government, government and politics. They'd talk and I'd pretend to listen, until the night I told you about a few years ago, your grandfather and his friends in the Observatory at Echo House. And that night I learned some valuable lessons and you will, too, if you listen hard and keep an open mind." Axel drew a chair close to the window, nodding at his son to sit. They sat together in a zone of incompatible silence and then Axel said, "All high emotion lives on the margins of chaos, and chaos is the enemy of judgment."

Outside, a driver honked his horn, shave-and-a-haircut-two-bits.

"What does she do besides live on the margins of chaos?"

Axel sighed impatiently. "I told you. She's a campaigner, like most everyone else here tonight. They're speechwriters, issues men, money men, advance men, men we call the Helpfuls. They're helpful people who know other helpful people. They have telephone numbers, the sheriff of Dade County, a banker in Austin, or a union leader in Kansas City. They know who'll lend you an airplane and a pilot to fly it. They're people who can

hire a hall and an attractive crowd to fill the hall and police
protection and the meals and refreshments later and the telephone and Telex machines for the press and cars to get everyone
around in comfort and safety and do it all on twenty-four hours'
notice, meanwhile arranging credit if the campaign's flat. They
know an advertising man who'll write you a spot in his spare
time gratis. They're people who walk into town with a bag full
of nickels and make fifty phone calls in an hour, locating dance
bands or latrines or a beer truck. Leila's one of the best. She
organizes the press when she's not fooling around with her numbers." Axel began to talk of continuity, sounding now like a
biologist discussing the great chain of being, conventions linked
to one another, elections linked, candidates linked, Helpfuls
linked, passing the tricks of the trade from one generation to the
next. Why, the son of a man who was helpful to Adolph Behl
was doing the same work for Adlai in Milwaukee or was it Min-
neapolis . . .

Alec's attention wandered, to Leila Berggren and the weasel
who worked for the bastard and the undisciplined one-legged
campaign. What a cast of characters! And this was his family's
milieu. He remembered his mother's description of the old senator, Senator Misogynist, she called him behind Axel's back, his
days spent on the floor of the Senate and his nights in the card
room of the Metropolitan Club. Summers he traveled in Europe
with Sir Charles Rath. April and May he spent in the State with
John Baver, cultivating roses and visiting American Legion halls
and Rotary Clubs so that he could say he kept in touch with his
"people." Dead three years after you were born, Alec, widely
mourned at the Metropolitan Club, not mourned at all in the
Senate, where they drew lots to select the eulogist; and the loser
paid the old man's administrative assistant to write the appropri-
ate encomium, "We shall not see his like again . . ." And that
drew a smile: God willing. Not mourned by Constance. Deeply
mourned by your father, Sylvia said, because the Behls were a
patriotic family. Testosterone is an addictive chemical, men get
bewitched by it, and in the ensuing masculine rapture exclude
and degrade women.

Axel said, "You can draw a line back from this election to FDR's to the election when your grandfather should have been the nominee but wasn't. I know Sylvia didn't like him." Alec nodded; the old man reading his mind again. "They didn't get on from the first minute, and for a while I found that amusing and then I didn't. I don't like disharmony at home." Axel suddenly lifted his head and put a finger to his lips.

In the living room Lloyd Fisher turned up the volume of the television set. Connecticut was lost and then, in succession, Massachusetts and New Jersey. Ohio looked very bad and even Illinois was doubtful. As the tide rolled westward the Republicans claimed landslide. Many of the men in the room were pleading with the governor not to concede. The polls were still open in the West. If the South held — and then someone looked in with the news that Mobile had gone Republican.

"Worse than I thought," Axel said.

"Will he concede now?" Alec asked.

"Not yet," Axel said. "You have to choose the moment, then say exactly the right thing. We'll see. Adlai's grown up in this world; he'll do things the right way, not the way my father did them. He couldn't let go of his ambition, didn't understand that what you lose today you can win tomorrow." Axel peered into the interior of the room, where the others were, and dropped his voice. "The vice presidency would have changed your grandfather's life and, maybe, the life of the nation. Instead, he became embittered and the last bad years canceled out the early good ones. And his election would have changed my life beyond imagining. I would have had a different war because my circumstances would have been different. I would have practiced diplomacy in Moscow or London. I would not have been behind the lines in France, chasing after George Patton, blown up on a road you can't find on any map."

Axel's voice had risen. His son touched his arm.

Axel said quietly, "And it would have changed your life, too, because it would have changed my life. My circumstances would have changed your circumstances because right now we wouldn't be at Adlai's Election Night party. We'd be at mine.

Senate, governor, House, one of those three, because I would have believed in promises and mumbo-jumbo. I would have made a different marriage, not a Bohemian with a sharp tongue. Not a woman who thought of government as a spittoon and a stuffed ballot box."

"That's not fair," Alec said stoutly.

Axel laughed unpleasantly.

"I don't want to talk about it," Alec said and looked again out the window.

"Having a President or vice president in the family is like having a suicide. It's always an option."

"Jesus," Alec said under his breath.

"Ask Henry Adams. When he was a young boy he thought the presidency was the family business and that was what you did when you grew up. Ask Adlai," Axel said, pointing at the governor, tête-à-tête with an older woman, who seemed to be explaining something to him, because he was looking at his shoes and nodding. They were standing under a huge oil portrait of a heavy-lidded Abraham Lincoln.

"Adlai's grandfather was one of Cleveland's vice presidents, forgotten now except, naturally, by the family. All he did in four years was to fire forty thousand Republican postmasters. That's history's verdict on Vice President Stevenson's four long years. But you can bet that wasn't what he remembered as he recollected it later. He remembered the Pullman strike and congressional intrigue and stories about the President. So what the curious public knows from history books, the Stevenson family knew from the old man himself. His family listened to him as one day another generation will listen to Adlai, and when he's forgotten except by a few students of American politics, he'll still be remembered inside the family, if only as an option."

Axel paused then, self-consciously shifting in his chair, tapping his cane on the toe of his shoe. In the big room the governor was telling a story and people were laughing, crowding around him. The company had become disheveled, men in their shirtsleeves and women in their stocking feet, everyone smoking cigarettes except for an elderly man sitting alone in a corner of the room, quietly pulling on his pipe. Somewhere a telephone was ringing.

"Get that phone!" the elderly man cried. "Ike can't read the numbers; he's conceding!" And everyone laughed as the phone continued to ring.

Axel paid no attention. "What's done's done. You can't walk back the cat."

"Seems to me a small ambition," Alec said. "Vice president of the United States, vice president of the junior class. It's ceremonial. Who needs it?"

Axel waited a moment before replying. "The official version was that Adolph wanted it out of vanity. But what he really wanted was to use his influence to establish museums in every region of the United States. He wanted to do for museums what Carnegie did for libraries and he was prepared to use the family money to help it along. He wanted to put them everywhere, art museums, natural history museums, museums of science, museums of Americana, whaling, farming, sport, the frontier, commerce, politics. You would think it quixotic and you would be right. But it wasn't a stupid idea and it wasn't vain. It wasn't a small ambition. And he didn't care what you thought. Or anybody."

Axel fluttered a hand at the governor, who smiled wanly. He was listening to a middle-aged woman who twisted the pearls at her throat as she talked. The atmosphere was suddenly swollen with frustrated desire, everyone realizing that the campaign was finished; America had looked at them and turned thumbs down. The woman with the pearls leaned on the governor's arm. She seemed near tears, her voice loud in the now-quiet room. She was telling the governor how sorry she was that he would not be President after all. We love you, Guv. What fun we could have had in Washington.

"One of Adlai's socialite friends," Axel said sourly.

She did not look like a socialite to Alec. She looked like someone's distraught aunt.

"Adlai's biggest problem," Axel said. "He's not a prick. You've got to be a prick in this business and he's not. He won't tell her to get lost. He knows she contributed a magnificent twenty-five dollars to the campaign and her husband handsomely matched it, dollar for dollar. He knows because I told him. The socialites just love the Guv, love him to death. They think campaigns are run on love. First campaign I've seen where socialites were involved and at first I didn't see the attraction for them. They hate the government because it's the government that collects their taxes. But the government isn't the point. The White House is the point. They think the campaign's a kind of national coming-out party or race meeting at Saratoga. It's a fashionable place to be. It excites them, being in the receiving line or in the paddock; they don't care much for the stables, though. They love hanging around and giving advice to the professionals but they don't like to give money. If they gave money, someone might think they had something to gain. Someone might think they wanted something, perhaps an ambassadorship, some pleasant Old World country in a temperate zone." Axel grunted, glancing sideways at his son. "This is the first socialite campaign I've seen but I have a feeling it's not the last."

The governor was helping the woman with her coat, murmuring words of consolation.

"Parasites," Axel said. "He's not prick enough to tell her to get lost. It's pathetic. And she voted for Eisenhower. In the privacy of the voting booth she looked up and her dear father's hand was on her wrist and guiding her fingers to the box that said Ike and Dick. I'd stake my life on it."

Alec sighed. Listening to his father was like listening to an insistent drizzle, the words falling and puddling, slick under foot. For this he had left a barefoot sophomore with a ribbon in her hair and a cashmere scarf around her neck, a drowsy golden-haired girl with a garden-of-earthly-delights smile and an uninhibited attitude, a devotee of Blake. Yes, he'd said with no little self-importance, I'm off to meet Adlai Stevenson — and she had laughed and laughed.

"When you get involved yourself some day you'll know what I mean. Campaigns are xenophobic, like nations. We don't like tourists in our country. They don't understand our customs and they don't speak our language. We think they're a distraction to our sovereign, who must be focused every hour of every day. So we don't like them. And they don't like us." Smiling falsely, Axel waved goodbye to the woman with the pearls. She did not wave back.

Axel continued to drizzle. From somewhere nearby Alec heard Leila Berggren's brass laugh, filled with sarcasm and mischief. He tried to imagine her in the cashmere scarf and couldn't. She belonged in a crowd. He wished he had refused to come; there was nothing for him here. The room seemed to him isolated from the world and the governor isolated in the room. He did not look like a sovereign, a tired middle-aged man with scuffed shoes, no hair on his head and a fleshy nose. Now he stood alone sipping from a glass of Champagne and looking at the Lincoln portrait, apparently unaware that he was being observed. Alec felt a sudden sympathy for him. He was alone with himself and perhaps that was not where he wanted to be on a night of defeat. Probably he had enjoyed the floodlit union halls and auditoriums, the orchestras and microphones, speaking a smart sentence and listening to the applause. If you were in politics, that was where you belonged, even on a night of landslide, the terrain changing before your eyes; and you were the cause of the changes. But looking at the governor now, it was evident that his thoughts were unknowable. Even the Champagne might have been soda water.

Axel went on and on. People milled about, collecting in front of the door, then backing away, uncertain where to go or what to do when they got there. The atmosphere in the room was still heavy, as if they were all below sea level. Alec wondered whether these were tomorrow's men after all, or remnants of a dying civilization as out of date as the old senator planting roses and investigating the life of Goethe or Axel's dislike of socialites. The room was purposeless and stale, the men plodding around it. He thought of cattle in a corral. Yet the governor was composed and at ease, staring at the Lincoln portrait, humming to himself. Lincoln's expression was one of great unquiet grief. With sudden certainty Alec realized he had no idea what the governor was thinking or feeling. Perhaps his mind was a blank, the only sensation the effervescence of wine on his tongue. Probably all he wanted to do was go to bed. The telephone began to ring again.

Alec wondered if Leila Berggren was staying at the mansion or in a hotel somewhere, and if she was alone or with someone. He looked up when a red-faced man touched his father on the shoulder.

"It's good to see you here, Axel," the red-faced man said, smiling tentatively.

"A disappointing night," Axel said sadly, extending his left hand.

"We lost Mobile. Can you believe it?"

"I want you to meet my son. I was just telling him some family history, some stories from the old days. Alec, this is Lloyd Fisher. We were friends in the war."

Lloyd Fisher smiled and shook hands, his grip hard as iron, and returned to the matter at hand. "Mobile, can you believe it? My wife's family comes from Mobile and they assured me it was safe, we didn't have to worry. And I believed them. *Mobile,* it doesn't seem possible. First time in history, Mobile goes to the Republicans."

"Grant won it in 1872."

"You're joking," Lloyd said.

"General Grant," Axel said, raising his eyebrows.

"That explains it then. They're unreliable in Mobile. They're idiots. You can't trust people who'd vote for a man who defeated their army in a war and generally fucked them over, excuse me, Alec."

"An omen for the future," Axel said.

"We can be proud of our campaign, though." Lloyd smiled sarcastically.

"Adlai can. I don't know if we can."

"The historians'll like us even if the people didn't."

"Too bad there aren't more historians in Mobile, Lloyd."

"What the hell, you do what you can. Sometimes it's beyond your control; people believe what they want to believe. Racial, ancestral, whatever you want to call it. We lost too many Chicago Poles this time around. We had their wallet but Ike had their heart. The Poles approve of generals running things. They're a romantic people. They liked the Sikorskis and the Pilsudskis and now they like Ike. I'm damned if I know what they think he intends to do. Listen to them and you'll get the idea that he'll throw a nuke into the Kremlin and send the Marines to declare the restoration of Great Poland, free, strong, and Catholic once again. And stop the sideshow in Korea so that we can get on with the real war, the one against the Soviets. I always thought a man voted his wallet, but sometimes he doesn't. Sometimes he votes his genes or his adolescent memories, Mass at Saint Stanislaus, trolling for perch in the Warta, a Chopin sonata, or his grandmother's noodles, not forgetting his permanent state of grievance."

Axel began to laugh. Alec was mesmerized.

"Democrats are soft on communism, it's well known. The shit from Wisconsin has done more damage than Fuchs, Hiss, and the Rosenbergs put together. He's a greater menace than Stalin, though I don't have to tell you about that, do I?"

"No, you don't," Axel said sharply.

"So our Chicago Poles forgot about the New Deal and the Fair Deal and talking sense to the American people. They left their union cards in their lunch buckets when they went to vote, because Ike's going to liberate their homeland. And I'll tell you something else. We've lost them for a generation. André agrees with me."

"I have no doubt," Axel said.

Lloyd looked at Alec, then back at Axel. "Emma left me."

Axel said, "I heard."

"Hated it in Chicago. Hated the weather. She thought all anyone was interested in was money, which is true but that's what Chicago *is,* a money foundry. If you want to sniff flowers, move to Mobile, which she did for a while. She's with someone, I don't know who." He rubbed his knuckles and frowned. "She was in a permanent state of grievance, like our Chicago Poles. Aren't women unpredictable?" Alec saw the sadness in Lloyd Fisher's eyes and his father's evident embarrassment. They stood quietly a moment, lacking words to illuminate either grievance or unpredictability. Alec thought both men were masters of disguise.

"Forget it," Lloyd said. "You should come back to Chicago with me tomorrow. We can survey the battlefield, count our casualties, see where we are and where we're going and who we're going with, next time around. Adlai might try again."

"Might," Axel said.

"Depends on how much he liked it. What he felt like when he went to bed at night and what he thought when he woke up in the morning. If he can remember the good shots and forget the bad. Politics is like tournament golf; you have to believe the ball will go in the hole and if it doesn't it's not your fault, it's the fault of the weather or the groundskeeper or the spike marks on the green. And he'll have a better chance, next time around. The Republicans don't know how to govern, never did. They'll screw up. So Adlai's our man if he remembers the putt that went in the hole instead of the four shots it took him to get out of the bunker." Lloyd paused then and put his hand on Axel's shoulder, squeezing. "I'm sorry about your trouble."

Axel nodded, glancing warily at his son.

Lloyd didn't miss Axel's caution. "And I'm glad to see you dodged the bullet."

"It wasn't close," Axel said.

"We've all got to be careful." Lloyd sighed and lowered his voice, though no one was within earshot. "That committee, they've got investigators everywhere and informers. Damned gumshoes. Vigilantes. I heard they were looking into your European operations."

"I have some charities in Europe. They didn't care for some of the people who were running the charities."

"I had a feeling, Axel. Longfellow's bank was an accident waiting to happen."

"It wasn't anything to do with Longfellow's," Axel said. "They thought it was, but it wasn't."

"Yessss," Lloyd said, smiling.

"It was a fishing expedition."

"Where did they get their information?"

"He's no longer with us."

"Not Carl?"

"No, not Carl," Axel said.

"Who was the real target? Ed?"

"They want you to grovel," Axel said suddenly.

"It's either that or a contempt citation."

"I didn't grovel."

"That's what I heard," Lloyd said.

"What else did you hear, Lloyd?"

"That you got an apology from Tail-Gunner Joe himself."

"Not quite an apology," Axel said.

"And Cohn, too."

"It wasn't Cohn. Cohn's never made an apology in his life. Never will. McCarthy said, 'I have no further use for this witness.' If you want to call that an apology, that's what he said."

"He ask you if you were a Red?"

"He asked me how much time I'd spent in 'that France.' Then he asked me if I was or if I'd ever been. I said I wasn't now but had no memory of then."

"Jesus," Lloyd said.

"I didn't like it," Axel said. "However, it's a great opportunity to find out who your friends are."

"I found that out a long time ago," Lloyd Fisher said, turning to Alec and telling him how lucky he was to have a chance to watch Election Night at ground zero, like a box seat at the World Series, ha-ha, except your team's getting the shit kicked out of it with no chance for ninth-inning heroics. Still, the important thing was being there. Taking part. Getting to know the people involved. You get your father to bring you to Chicago; we'll have a night on the town, I'll introduce you to some wiseguys. Lloyd nodded vigorously, opening his mouth to say something more — but touched Axel on the arm, and wandered off in the direction of the bar.

"So," Axel said to his son. "Do you like it at ground zero?"

"No," Alec said. "And it would've helped if you'd said something about McCarthy's committee. So that I'd have some warning in the event my name shows up in the newspaper. What's it about, anyway? Or is it another secret?" ·

"I should have put you in the picture. McCarthy thought I was part of the twenty years of treason, and when he decided I wasn't, he let me go. I give money to certain people in Europe. Some of them are socialists, social democrats they call themselves. Washington doesn't get the distinction. McCarthy thought I was Stalin's banker. I have friends who helped out, made telephone calls. Hard to know what would have happened without the friends and their phone calls. I got to people who got to him. I should have told you. But I was busy day and night. And I only did just dodge the bullet."

"Is it over now?"

"It's never over," Axel said. "That committee throws mud and it sticks, nothing to be done about it. Means: in the holy war you were friendly with the antichrist. No one ever forgets. I suppose you've noticed." Axel raised his head and looked around. "That I'm not the most popular man in the room."

But it seemed to Alec that his father was neither more nor less popular than usual. People always treated Axel Behl with caution. "Popular" was not a word he associated with his father.

"It got into the newspapers then?"

"No, but it's out. Some version of the hearing, what Senator Joe said and what I said and what Cohn said." He said, singsong, "Axel Behl, that prick. What did they have on him? I heard he got it quashed. I heard he had something on Joe and got a man to make a phone call to make certain Joe knew. What do you suppose it was, the evidence that Axel had? Something to do with money. Money or women. Axel Behl's rich as sin and's not afraid to pay for information . . ."

"And that was what you did?"

Axel shrugged.

"Who are they? The people you helped."

"They're good people," Axel said after a moment. "They're excitable. They worry about the future. Us and the Soviets, we're so big and so very thoughtless. They worry about the future because they've lived in darkness and their eyes aren't accustomed to the light. They only want to avoid the giants. They want to cross the bridge safely, avoiding the trolls underneath. They want their privacy back, Alec." Axel smiled, but his son looked at him coldly. "So I help them out. I give them money. I make it possible for others to give them money."

"Bribe money," Alec said.

Axel looked at his son as an appraiser would look at a portrait of dubious provenance, something not quite genuine in the shape of the eyes and the suggestion of a sneer around the mouth. He was not drawn by a single hand. Alec was the product of an atelier, careless artisans working on deadline. He had so much to learn and his appearance was against him. "Don't be a moron," Axel said.

Alec smiled then. "And in return you get —"

"Loyalty," his father said.

The governor drove downtown to make his concession speech. The room was silent, everyone watching him speak; and then they turned away. The television set remained on, but no one watched it except Axel and the men who had been working the telephones; they had discovered that the television was quicker and more reliable than their informants in the precincts. Axel moved closer until he was only a few feet away, the electric glow of the screen reflected on his forehead. The air was thick with cigarette smoke. Alec stood in the doorway watching his father bend forward toward the soft shadows. An announcer was reading from a piece of flimsy paper, nothing but bad news everywhere. Axel did not seem to be listening, intent only on the watery surface of the screen, rippling now as if a breeze had disturbed it. Axel muttered something to himself. They did not own a television set, yet his father was staring at this one with the most open fascination. He turned to one of the men beside him and said, "It's like watching the invention of gunpowder."

The exodus had begun. The room was nearly quiet except for four men in coats talking earnestly in whispers near the door, the coats loose on their shoulders like capes. Lloyd Fisher was in a corner of the room with Leila Berggren. The room had the forlorn look of a hotel lobby at midnight. A servant was collecting empty glasses and dirty ashtrays. The governor was nowhere to be seen. Axel sighed, fumbling in his coat pocket. He took out a vial, shook a pill into his palm, and swallowed it dry.

"Isn't it time to go now?" Alec said.

"In a minute."

Axel caught bits and pieces of the conversation near the door. They were making book on the new faces of 1953, Cabinet officers, White House staff, agency heads, ambassadors, assistants beyond count. Axel listened carefully, amused at their neglect of the obvious, the appointments that were never announced formally though word got around quickly enough — the friends, who was coming to drinks or dinner and who was in the foursome at Burning Tree or spending the weekend in the private quarters of the White House or on the fantail of the *Sequoia* at dusk, and not all the friends were men. Friends of Franklin, friends of Harry, and, as of tonight, friends of Ike. And with a few conspicuous and obvious exceptions they were different friends; and, of course, *they* had friends who'd enjoy meeting the chief executive, have a cocktail, maybe play some bridge and talk business on the side, suggesting perhaps the ideal choice for chairman of the Securities and Exchange Commission or Secretary of the Treasury. When the White House changed hands a whole new set of keys were handed out. The old ones were useless because the locks had been changed.

The servant opened one of the windows, causing a blast of cold night air to fill the room. With the cold air, inside it and surrounding it, came the sound of traffic and faraway laughter. Axel glanced at the window, shivering, and his son quickly took off his own coat and put it around his father's shoulders.

"Will you close that god damned window?"

Alec did as he was told and the sounds of the outside world vanished.

"What are you two doing, sitting over here alone? The party's over." Leila Berggren reached down to touch Axel on the arm.

She carried two bottles of beer and handed one to Alec. Axel smiled up at her. He said, "Surprised?"

She said, "No."

"Memphis?"

"Maybe Memphis," she said.

"Leila does her homework, keeps an open mind," Axel said. "Knows the numbers. Knows the people who make the numbers. Leila's a professional in a basket full of amateurs, gave up a fine career on Wall Street to work in government. Leila's a mathematician."

"Statistics," Leila said.

"What she doesn't know about capitalism isn't worth knowing."

"Don't listen to him, Alec. You have no idea how much isn't known."

Alec laughed. "All I do is listen to him."

"Axel," Leila said. "You were not lecturing this man?"

"He's still in school, Leila."

"He used to lecture me, too," Leila said to Alec. She smiled and brushed a stray curl from her forehead. "But he doesn't anymore."

"Leila's interested in bias theory," Axel said.

"Voters' biases?" Alec asked.

"In the statistics," she said. When he looked at her blankly, she added, "The numbers lie."

"Leila's not your ordinary statistician," Axel said.

"That's what they thought on Wall Street," Leila said.

"Republicans," Axel said. "What can you expect?"

"More than I got," she said. "And the Democrats aren't any better. They talk better. They're great with talking. Not so great when it comes to doing, and even worse when it comes to paying."

"You have to be patient," Axel said.

"Bull," she said. "You've always been square, though."

"Leila did some work for me," Axel said.

"I love my numbers," she said to Alec. "The uglier the better. But sometimes they're unfaithful. They tell you they love you

but they don't, really. They're alley cats, following their own instincts, in and out of every bed in the neighborhood. They're promiscuous."

She was drinking beer while she talked, raising the neck of the
bottle with two fingers, sipping and swallowing. Alec watched
her neck muscles work. She and Axel seemed to occupy the same
rung on the ladder; she was almost playful with him. Alec said,
"I never thought of them as having personalities. I never thought
of loyalty as a characteristic of numbers."

"Believe it," she said.

"If you say so."

"Numbers were invented by human beings. Error inherent.
Error predictable. Error fundamental."

"And unfaithful," Alec said.

"That most of all."

"Yet you love them."

"More than anything. I love their instability."

"Their distance," he said.

"Not that, no. I want my fingers on the plow," she said, backing away. She winked at Alec and waved at Axel, then disappeared down the stairs, swinging the beer bottle by its neck. Alec
watched her go, watched her hips move, watched her hand
smooth her dark hair, and listened to the commotion when she
arrived on the first floor, and then the door opening and closing.
And then silence. They seemed to be alone now. The telephone
began to ring again but no one answered it.

Alec said, "What did she mean about the plow?"

"She's given to mystification," Axel said. "But I believe the
expression is Lenin's. Maybe Lenin's wife. At any event, a Russian."

"How do you know her?"

"She did some work for me."

"That's what she said. What kind of work?"

"This and that," Axel said. "The markets. Customer confidence in a product as it relates to price, packaging, and so forth.
She thought there was a way to compare that to a political
campaign. But there isn't. Or if there is, she didn't find it."

"She was doing this for you?"

"I put up the money. If she'd been right, her results would've been worth knowing. It didn't cost so much. She's a bright girl."

Alec sneaked a look at his wristwatch. It was after midnight.

"We can go now," Axel said. His voice had acquired a familiar edge and he was working again at his scar. Two men emerged from a side room, talking quietly, pausing under the Lincoln portrait. One of them made a brusque motion with his hand and stepped to the door, the other following, apparently explaining something. When one of the men raised his voice Alec heard Leila's name; nothing complimentary, from the look on their faces.

Axel sighed and said, "She made a mistake in her numbers. Leila did. One important mistake but that's all you get, one. The Helpfuls didn't like it and now they're on her back. Women are unreliable, too emotional to work with numbers, et cetera. Phases of the moon and so forth and so on. But that isn't the problem. The problem is that Leila doesn't like certainty, doesn't believe in it. She believes the numbers are always unfaithful and her task is to discover the nature of the faithlessness. In any set of figures one number is having an illicit relationship with another; she calls it the F Factor. A complicated concept, too complicated for the derby hats." Axel smiled blandly. "Of course they've got her all wrong. They think she's a bubblehead. They think she's not serious, ruled as she is by the phases of the moon. But it's the opposite. She's a theoretical mathematician in a business that calls for simple arithmetic." Axel grunted, not unkindly. "Stay away from her, Alec. She plays around."

Alec stared out the window. Leila and an older man were leaning against a car, talking. Suddenly the man put his arm around her, holding her close. They stood like that a moment, Leila's head bent in an attitude of defeat. He was talking to her and she began to nod her head.

"What's your connection to her?"

"None of your damned business," Axel said. Then, "She's finished in New York. She made a mistake there, too, and then took up with the wrong man. Two mistakes. She's undisciplined."

"Something you know about," Alec said.

"A damn sight more than you," Axel said. "They don't forgive in New York. New York's tribal, it never changes. As long as you belong to the tribe you're at the top of the tree. You're there today and there tomorrow unless you go broke or go to jail. And your parents are there and your cousins and someone new comes to town and it takes a generation before their foot fits the slipper. The New York squires don't like Southerners, Westerners, or Jews. They particularly don't like Washingtonians, because we're the competition and anyone can play. Win an election, get nominated to a Cabinet post — and there you are; you're in the game. We don't care who you are or where you come from because we're a city in motion." He paused then and drew Alec's jacket more tightly around his shoulders. New York was a spoiled, conceited city run by gangsters and the plutocracy; and its offspring, Chicago and Los Angeles, were no better. Chicago was much worse. He said, "An outsider makes a mistake in New York and they cut his nuts off. That's what they did to Leila, because she threatened them and the cozy world they've made for themselves. So she doesn't belong there. She belongs in Washington. We don't practice nepotism, the bank vice presidency or the seat on the Stock Exchange or the partnership in the law firm. You can't hand down political power. If you're a senator or a Secretary of the Treasury you can't leave that to your son in your will. He has to make it on his own. And he will, if he's careful in his choice of friends."

Alec remained silent, still watching Leila and the older man.

"Now she's in Chicago, worst god damned place in the world. She's not patient. The derby hats are on their way out. There'll be a whole new generation of Helpfuls and they'll be comfortable with uncertainty. Instability, even. Leila can be one of them, but she won't be patient." Axel said softly, "You, too. It's important you make up your mind; you're graduating next year —"

Leila and the older man had vanished and the street was

empty. An empty beer bottle glittered in the light of a street-
lamp.

"— so you should think carefully about what you want.
Washington's a meritocracy, but there's a paradox, for those of
us who've lived in the village for a generation or more and whose
families have achieved a certain standing. You begin as your
father's son. That's your identity and you live with it. But in time,
if you're successful, the world shifts its opinion and he becomes
your father. And then, if things work out, in the eyes of the
world you become your son's father."

Alec waited for the payoff, the homily that would end the
sermon. The men near the door walked through it, still discussing Leila. She would have to pay a penalty and he wondered
what it would be and if she had the patience to wait them out in
Chicago. Now the room was silent except for Axel's breathing.
He took Alec's hand, rubbing his thumb along the boyish knuckles, pressing hard.

"That's what worries me, you see. Do you think things will
work out for me, son?"

Downstairs Lloyd Fisher was nose to nose with the girl with the
Renoir complexion. She was obviously tight, squinting as she
listened to Lloyd, her bow lips parted in an itchy half-smile. She
barked a laugh, tossing her head, moving in closer. Alec wondered what it was about politicians that attracted footloose wom-
en, first Leila, now this one. They seemed powerfully drawn to
the disheveled old men who smelled of tobacco and whiskey;
and perhaps it was not them but the milieu, the atmosphere of
authority and brutality, the emotions that went with high drama.
Lloyd introduced her as Flo, everyone's favorite, a girl with a noble ambition. One day she intended to occupy the White House
and transform it utterly.

"A jazz band every Friday night," Flo said. "Lester Lanin on
Saturdays. Open house every Sunday with a beautiful buffet and
bloody marys. Throw open the old mausoleum, let the air in,
hear some laughter. Don't you love the idea? 'Course, first I have

to marry the man who'll be President. But Dolley Madison did it. So can I."

Alec began to laugh at her vision of the weekend White House.

"Politics is sexy, don't you agree? All that fear and trembling. All that pressure and frustration and not knowing what's going to happen tomorrow. The entire world crowded into that one small district, Washington. But of course you know that. You live there."

Alec said, "It's boring, Flo. Boring beyond words."

"It won't be when I get there. Trouble is, I need a candidate and I haven't found him. It's only a matter of time and some chemistry. And luck. The boys I know hate government. They think it's an old man's sport, like golf. But golf's got a lot to recommend it when you know how to play." With that, she gave a little military salute and walked off.

Lloyd thoughtfully sipped his drink as he watched her go. "She's a character. Fun-loving I suppose you'd call her. She's got a big heart. Her father's a lawyer in Oak Park and her name isn't Flo. That's what everyone calls her because she wants so badly to be First Lady of the United States. She's smart about politics."

"You could have fooled me," Axel said.

"Likes to conceal it. Flo says things go easier that way, as opposed to Leila Berggren, who's indiscreet. Who can't keep her mouth shut and makes enemies she doesn't need because she's got a fresh mouth she can't keep shut. Flo knows you need friends." Then Lloyd turned to Alec and said how glad he was to see him again; the last time was at Echo House years ago. He had heard wonderful things. Of course he'd head back to Washington when he finished college.

"No," Alec said.

Lloyd brightened. Alec should think about law school then. Law, along with automobiles and steel, was the great growth industry of the United States. To be a lawyer now was like being a religious in the Middle Ages; it opened any door.

"I've thought about it," Alec said, the words escaping before he knew they were there. Lloyd looked at him approvingly and said that when he had his law degree he should come to Chicago because it had a livelier atmosphere than Washington. It was welcoming to outsiders. Ask Leila Berggren, who had had her fill of New York and Washington and now loved Chicago.

"I didn't know anything about law school," Axel said. "I never heard you mention law school. Where did you get that idea? It's a crazy idea. Is it Sylvia's idea?"

"It's been decided," Alec said. "I decided tonight because Chicago's so attractive and livelier than Washington."

"I don't know why anyone would want to work in Chicago, but I'll call Dick Daley —"

"Dick's a friend of mine, Axel," Lloyd said.

"It'll be a few years," Alec said.

"I'll be here," Lloyd said.

"Sometimes these things decide themselves, don't they?" Alec said.

"'Deed they do," Lloyd said.

Axel said, "It's stupid."

"I'll call," Alec said. "That's a promise."

"I like enthusiasm," Lloyd said. "That's why I like Leila, her enthusiasm. And you'll like her too, once you get to know her."

They watched Axel march back up the stairs.

Lloyd said, "Where are you going?"

"To wish Adlai a good night," Axel said. "Because he's entitled to one."

PART II

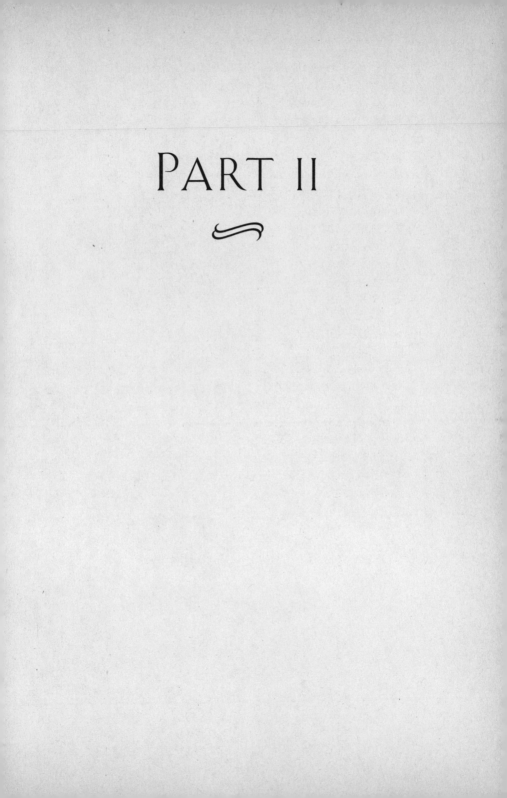

5

Camelot

~

$\mathbf{B}$Y THE AUTUMN of 1962 Washington was no longer just another glum city of government, like Albany or Sacramento. Instead, it was fabulous — though not yet fabulous on the scale Constance had envisioned, maritime Venice at the end of the fifteenth century or brainy Vienna on the eve of World War One. Any nation's golden age was most vivid at the moment of irreversible political decline, and in late 1962 Washington was at its most muscular and confident. The Russians had been humiliated in Cuba, and the young President was now seen not as a novice out of his depth but as a statesman of charm, subtlety, integrity, and tact. In private moments he spoke alarmingly of a long twilight struggle with the Bolsheviks; but that was seen not as evidence of pessimism or exhaustion but of an attractive worldliness, a newly mature American statecraft on the model of Whitehall or the Quai d'Orsay. Certainly there was no evidence of decline; quite the reverse. In such fine weather no one would think to listen for the scrape of the keel on the shoals.

Eisenhower's Babbitts had been expelled and discredited, even Nixon gone for good, disappeared somewhere in the California wasteland. Suddenly every Democrat wanted to be in Washington, indisputably the epicenter of American life. Civic-minded industrialists, university professors, foundation executives, writers, provincial politicians, lawyers beyond count, settled in so-

ciable Georgetown or Cleveland Park as the American émigrés
to Paris forty years before gathered in the quarters of the Left
Bank, charmed by the natives, avid to absorb the culture. They
arrived in station wagons from Cambridge or Ann Arbor with
their wives and children, settling in as if they never intended to
leave — a logical assumption, since there was every prospect of
a sixteen- or twenty-four-year dynasty, so long as they did their
work with competence and élan, and learned the language of
government, indeed married the language of government to the
language of the boardroom, the courtroom, the faculty lounge,
and the newsroom. They thought of themselves as the permanent civil service that would supervise the long twilight struggle.
There came to be a kind of syncopation to the capital, jazz
rhythms to the press conferences and glittering White House
evenings, as the big cats pranced and prowled and did their business, and then went reluctantly home.

Echo House had been refreshed as well. A coat of paint and a
landscapist's attentions gave the back yard the look of a country
estate. The English garden so despised by the old senator was
gone, replaced by Kentucky bluegrass. The croquet court had
not been used in many years, yet it was in place, the court
carefully graded and shaded by trees and beautifully groomed,
white wickets and stakes placed just so, a little bit of pretty East
Anglia in Rock Creek Park. Axel's neighborhood was changed,
old people dying and moving to smaller quarters. Harriet Bilbauer, ninety-two and a widow for thirty years, moved to a suite
in the Shoreham after selling her house to a young senator from
the West. George Steppe's son sold his father's place for an un-
believable six-figure sum and retired at once to Cape Cod. The
new owners were a journalist and his wife, friends of the First
Lady. Many of the new people were alarmingly young. Baby
carriages sprouted on the sidewalks, as often as not wheeled by
nannies in crisp white uniforms. On warm nights Axel could
hear the commotion of cocktail parties in nearby gardens, a
lively atmosphere on the staid old street. He always received
invitations but went only occasionally because he did not like to
stand for long periods, and there were so many unfamiliar faces.

Always the host and hostess were solicitous, taking him around to meet everyone. Guests were introduced by name and title. It was surprising how many of them worked for newspapers or magazines, and how au courant they seemed, and how eager for information. They were attractive people but aggressive. They seemed to think he knew everything and what he didn't know he could find out. Axel had an idea they kept files on people; in any case they were vacuum cleaners of information. He rarely saw friends of his own generation at these gatherings, and so much the better.

Axel enjoyed reporting back, Margaret Mead returning from a summer in Samoa. He always saved an especially presumptuous item for Ed Peralta, Harold Grendall, and André Przyborski at Wednesday lunch. Do you know what one of the Hoovers asked me? It's outrageous. He asked me if I would confirm that Jackie had a bidet at their place in Virginia. An anecdote for his magazine, he said. The editor's personal request. I told him I wouldn't discuss the First Lady's plumbing, for God's sake.

Nothing's out of bounds for them. Nothing's private.

Still, it was valuable, meeting the younger crowd.

They were the future of the government, even the journalists.

Axel was always happy to return to Echo House, the first-floor lights ablaze and welcoming in contrast to the dark neighborhood. Washington had become an early-to-bed-and-early-to-rise community, evidence of vigor in the conduct of the nation's business. The old mansion gave him comfort, the somber Soldiers Cemetery across the street with its many Civil War dead lent it an air of purpose. A stand of startling magnolias concealed the porte-cochère as a sextet of giant elms concealed the magnolias. Tucked off to one side was a Prussian blue gazebo and inside the gazebo a bronze bust of a glowering Wolfgang von Goethe, Germany's greatest soul forever bolted to an iron plinth, according to instructions contained in the last will and testament of the old senator — who, failing to control the sprawl of the English garden, would at least have the last word on the occupant of the gazebo. It was shaded by a thick-waisted beech. A heavy wrought-iron fence protected the property from the street, but that did not discourage tourists from stopping and peering through the bars, admiring the gazebo and the landscaping and wondering at the identity of the owner, obviously a Washington grandee. That was the way they lived, protected from things, their doors always closed to outsiders. Probably his face would be familiar, one of Washington's unelected elite; and if you asked him a question he'd turn a deaf ear or have you arrested or run out of town. But he had done very well for himself in the capital. Politics paid well, no question. Moreover — who wanted to live in a country where you couldn't fix a traffic ticket?

On an overcast Saturday afternoon in late November 1962, the iron gate stood ajar. A dusty MG swung in from the street, hesitated a moment, then wound up the driveway past Goethe's bust and the grove of elms, and stopped under the porte-cochère. The car's top was down, though the day was chilly and threatening rain. Sylvia Walren Behl Borowy did not open the car door but sat relaxed at the wheel, finishing her cigarette, listening to the radio. She undid her scarf and shook her head, running her fingers through her hair, all the while glaring at the miniature stone lions that sat either side of the front door. Nothing had changed, not one single thing, except that the lions had acquired a greenish tint.

She had been in Washington only twice in the last decade and was there now only to discuss personal business with her son. She had not seen him since the summer, when he came to New York for a lawyers' conference. He lived in Chicago but was in Washington on business, staying at Echo House. Dirty business, no doubt, business manipulating the government in some unwholesome way. And what better theater of operations? She was not surprised that Echo House looked exactly as she remembered it, impregnable as a fortress and as hostile. The cemetery across the street, the gate, Goethe, the beech tree, the lions, the godawful Teutonic pretentiousness of it. Living at Echo House was like living in the Reichstag. The place gave her the creeps, as she had complained more than once, not that anyone ever listened. Listening was not one of the things they were good at in Washington. Sylvia pitched her cigarette over the windshield, watching it fall and die in a shower of sparks; and then she noticed the iron weather vane atop the gazebo.

Alec watched her from the vestibule window, seeing her eyes narrow and her lips move, her face a catalogue of torts. She looked windblown but generally composed, despite the scowl. He was amused that she had taken the antique MG, a roadster suitable for a coed; but he had to admit she almost looked like one, in her scarf and sweater and short hair, her cheeks bright from the wind. It was either the wind or anger at being at Echo House once again. She was staring at the weather vane as though it were a swastika; and now she lit another cigarette, still declining to open the door of the car. He heard music then, something classical. She tapped her fingers on the steering wheel and smiled suddenly, her smile brilliant and without guile or affectation. *La Bohème,* no doubt. *La Bohème,* certainly. Alec wondered where her own barricades were now.

When they embraced, she had tears in her eyes. The music, she explained. It always gets to me. I try not to let it and then I say, Why not? Where's the harm? If you don't cry, you can't live.

He said, "You've cut your hair."

She daubed at her eyes and said, "Like it?"

"It's different," he said. The haircut reminded him of Leila Berggren's, but that was a thought that would go unsaid.

"You should let yours grow, Alec. You look like a Marine. But of course Kennedy wears his short, too. Is it a fashion statement or a political statement, or what?"

"Semper fi," Alec said.

"Honestly," she said.

"Does Willy like it?" Willy Borowy was her husband.

"Says he does," she said.

"That's what counts."

She looked at him and nodded; time for that later.

Alec opened the car door and offered his hand, but Sylvia was looking elsewhere, over his shoulder in the direction of the gazebo.

"What's that?" she asked.

"What's what?"

"That thing on top of the gazebo. That installation that looks like a human head surrounded by barbed wire. It wasn't there in my time."

"His weather vane," Alec said. "Someone gave it to him. It's German. It's supposed to be a grasshopper."

"God, yes. It's German, all right. It's straight from Buchen-wald."

"It's from a castle on the Rhine," Alec said.

She snorted, not unkindly. "Your father never needed a *weather vane* to tell him which way the wind was blowing."

"I think he likes the way it looks," Alec said.

"I'll bet he does," she said.

"Sylvia," he said. "Lay off." Then, "How was your trip?"

"Lay off what?" Innocently. "It struck me as the slightest bit *odd,* an iron grasshopper on top of the gazebo, but now that you tell me it's from a schloss on the Rhine, I understand perfectly. Ghastly, the trip."

"It must have been cold," Alec said, tapping the windshield. *La Bohème* was ended and now the announcer was talking about Texaco.

"Brisk," she said. "Traffic all the way down from the city, but I picked up the opera in Baltimore and that kept me company. And then when I was driving down Mass. Avenue trying to re-member the way, it's been so long, I was stopped for hours and hours by a motorcade, some characters flying flags from their limousines, tinpot despots from Central America or Southeast Asia tying up traffic. I should have flown, but it was such a nice day in New York that I thought I might as well drive the MG just for the hell of it."

"I'm glad you're here," Alec said.

"I know you're out on a limb," she said. "Me in Echo House."

"I'm not out on a limb," he said.

"Where is he anyway?"

"In Florida."

"Palm Beach, I suppose."

"Beats me. I have a phone number, in case you want to reach him."

"Sarcasm does not become you, Alec," she said primly. "When I hear your sarcasm, I hear Axel's voice. I was only curious because I heard somewhere or read that he was advising — 'summoned,' I believe the word was, to Palm Beach to work on some crisis. Isn't that where they are, working on the crisis, Palm Beach? Do you know what crisis it is? And wouldn't it be a good idea just to leave it there, sweltering in the sun? Solving a crisis in Palm Beach would be like organizing a poets' conference at Ephesus, and why not, everyone speaking a dead language in a dead city once populated by Amazons and now surrounded by the villas of the filthy rich."

Alec laughed. "Come on inside. I'll fix us some tea."

"I'm surprised someone hasn't written a poem about them, gathered amongst the yacht basins and golf courses, drinking daiquiris at sundown. Archie MacLeish could do it, unless of course he wants a job. So many do, you know."

"It's about to rain," Alec said.

"I wanted to see the old place again," Sylvia said. "I don't know why, but I've been thinking about it lately."

Alec said nothing to that, but he was instantly on guard. He continued to hold the car door, though she showed no signs of moving. She blew a smoke ring and watched it collapse in the breeze.

"I've been working on some poems," she said. "Some new things, interesting things. Disturbing, autobiographical things. I don't know where they're coming from, but I think of them as my Cold War poems. I have an idea that the Cold War is to us what the subconscious was to the Viennese, a kind of basic organizing principle of modern times, explanation and dogma in time of personal crisis. Cold War explains your fear of being blown to smithereens by a nuclear weapon. Cold War is a trauma no less than repressed infantile longings, wouldn't you say? I'll bet Freud would. Your father had a Polish friend, André Przyborski, we used to see him around at parties, some sort of superspook who was supposed to know everything there was to know about Stalin's terror. There was no doubt in my mind that if André was given a bomb he'd use it at once on the Soviets. A frightening man, magnetic in his way. I wonder where he is." She smiled enigmatically at Alec, who was listening to her without comprehension. "Anyway, I work on them every day and long into the night and Echo House keeps coming up and I thought that if I saw it again, went inside, nosed around, prowled the premises, I'd figure out what it is that's nagging at me. Something is. I'm seeing Echo House in my dreams."

While Alec boiled the water and set out the tea service, Sylvia began her reconnaissance through the Chinese boxes, beginning in the foyer, scene of so many comings and goings. She moved circumspectly, unnerved at the vast opulent solemnity of the place, the pictures, the carpets, the wall hangings from Persia and China and India and Austria. She had an idea that she would meet her younger self coming around a corner and recognize her at once; but the reverse would not be true, because young Sylvia had no idea what surprises life held and the effect of those surprises on her future looks and bearing, everything from the lines in her face to the length of her stride. The room seemed to echo with the rumble of men's voices, as if it remembered the many masculine evenings of cards, whiskey, and political conversation. The room vibrated with the voices of authority and experience, monotonous as drums.

She turned her back and stepped into the living room, its ceiling higher than she remembered it. Only one of her additions remained, the art deco mirror bought at a shop in the Portobello Road in 1943, an extravagance but a necessity also, because looking into it was like looking into the present century, the one that began in 1914. Axel had changed its location so that the mirror reflected back through the room, where it found another mirror, and so on echoing to infinity. In that way you could look into the mirror and see around corners, all the way back to Bismarck. One century was never enough for Axel. She had seen the mirror in her dreams but saw it where she had hung it originally, in the foyer near the staircase. Its curves reminded her of Klimt and Schiele, degenerates in the Teutonic scheme of things.

She devoted a few moments to the Behl portraits in the dining room, noting the long foreheads, a family signature no less than lobeless ears or a club foot; and Axel's preposterous Barkin lip. Alec resembled them, though there was something of her in him, too. Her own good English stock had been overrun by the Hun but not annihilated. The portraits had not been part of her dreams, and she realized now that she had forgotten them. When she was seated at table in the old days, they were unavoidable as she faced Axel across the expanse of polished hardwood, as cold and hostile as the north German plain, Adolph and Constance bearing down from the wall behind him. She thought of them as hanging judges.

She moved into the garden room, pausing here and there like a visitor in a museum, and looked into Axel's study, appointed exactly as she remembered it, books floor to ceiling, a single framed etching in the shelf behind his desk. Some OSS comrade had given it to him, number thirty-seven in Goya's Horrors of War series, six figures in various stages of distress overseen by a complacent officer in tricorn; the officer might have been callow Corporal Bonaparte. Goya called the piece *Lo Peor Es Pedir* — "The Worst Thing Is to Beg." On the desk were the same three photographs, one of Alec suited up for rugby, one of Axel and Fred Greene, and one of a brightly lit old-fashioned airplane hangar, five men straining at a trolley containing a heavy shrouded object; and no need to ask what the object was, for the bomber in the background had a name, Enola Gay. There were signatures at the bottom of the photograph, the plane's pilot and navigator and, in characteristically clear, Palmer-method script, Harry S Truman. She decided that in this bleak study the world had not changed since about 1947, Alec an adolescent, Fred very much alive in Axel's memory, the ghastly bomb a presence now as it was then. Of course in 1947 there had been a fourth photograph, but it was long since discarded, perhaps destroyed — her own lissome self at a café table somewhere in the St. Germain-des-Prés, June 1940. A German officer was visible in the background, openly admiring. Sylvia remembered, she was smiling to beat the band, presenting her bravest face to the world because Germans terrified her and she and Axel were not due to leave for another week. They were practically the last Americans in Paris, though when anyone asked, and many did, they were Swiss nationals and had the passports to prove it. The smell of defeat was everywhere in Paris and she longed to be in warm-hearted England, yet Axel seemed exhilarated, almost boyish, now that the European war had begun at last. Roosevelt would be unable to delay much longer; and then Axel could go to work. He had always been able to carry her along in his enthusiasm, but he could not carry her along in this, a European war.

Then the war ended and they were back in Washington, occupying Echo House. She remembered that it was very warm that afternoon in early August when she entered the study, unannounced, around cocktail time, sitting in the leather chair in the corner, watching Axel as he talked on the phone. It was an overseas call and the connection was bad. He was shouting. The window was open, admitting the thick Washington heat, so heavy and damp that no birds sang. She sat quietly and listened carefully and did not understand one word. At first she thought he was discussing the Marshall Plan, something to do with the German mark. Then she realized that the subject was a man named Mark, who had lived in Germany before emigrating to Canada. Whoever he was, he was important to Axel. She listened to Axel's side of the conversation, breaking it into phrases, and rearranging the phrases in her own mind to resemble verse. It was verse such as a perverse playwright might render it, portentous, suggestive, without context.

> How certain are you
> of his record?
> But where was he then?
> I can find out.
> Let me do it.
> We can get the money.
> Uh-uh.
> Don't worry about money.

It's only money.
I said IT'S ONLY MONEY.
We have to pin him down.
We have to know his provenance.
Where he's been and
With whom.
Who's *owned* him
The way we'd do with a Vermeer.
Right.
Alleged Vermeer.
Huh-huh.

Sylvia left and returned with a drink, sitting quietly, and watching him speak into the receiver, his voice rising and falling with an intensity that fascinated her, his swivel chair creaking as it moved minutely to and fro. When he finished, he replaced the receiver and faced straight ahead, his eyes closed, apparently still thinking about the German who had to be pinned down in order to establish his provenance, meaning who owned him. She was certain that Axel had forgotten she was in the room when he suddenly looked at her and smiled warily, asking her how her day had gone. Who was that? she asked. Who were you talking to on the telephone? The usual business, he replied, boring overseas business to do with a man who won't cooperate; it's not a big thing but we have to do it, you see. His right hand went to his scar as he continued to smile tightly at her. But he volunteered nothing further.

There was a time when, with his great charm and energy, he could make her do anything, go anywhere, Helsinki in winter, Calcutta in summer, Paris on the eve of invasion; not to go with him was to miss out. He seemed invulnerable then, happy all day long. Axel Behl drew people to him like a magnet. He had such gaiety and sincerity, and grace. He attracted men as well as women and why not — he wore ardor on his sleeve. Men admired him and women sent him flowers. But that was in Europe before the war. That was before the OSS. That was before he left her in England to go play soldier with wretched Fred Greene, with disastrous results.

She remembered that he wearily proposed a drink, pushing back from his desk, waiting for her to precede him into the garden room, where the drinks paraphernalia was laid out. He looked at her curiously when she did not move, except to place her highball carefully on the edge of the desk and begin to speak to him, so rapidly that the words tumbled over themselves. She was so eager to get it over with.

She demanded a sincere apology from him for the previous evening, and a promise that he would never again hit her, ever, for whatever reason. It would be difficult to begin again, but impossible without the apology. When he remained silent, she told him she was leaving. Any idiot could see that their marriage was a misalliance. They both wore false faces. She'd thought she could make a go of it but couldn't no matter how hard she tried, and she had tried; give her that. They were not suited to each other. They did not believe in the same things. People changed whether they wanted to or not and suddenly black was white. She had not wanted anything to happen but something had happened and she was leaving at once to join Willy Borowy in New York. I'm sorry about it, she said. Forgive me, she added, as she moved to hurry from the room and out the front door to her car, already loaded with her luggage. She remembered that Axel had not moved as she spoke to him except to narrow his eyes when she said, "Forgive me." She had meant the remark as a concession, but Axel did not look pacified.

She paused briefly, waiting for anything he might say — in anger, in sorrow, in spite, in apology. But he remained silent and his eyes clear, staring at a point just over her right shoulder. No doubt he would have a word or two concerning Mrs. Pfister. But the silence lengthened, and when she turned at last she saw what was in his line of sight, a white-bordered photograph in a plain glass frame, a young girl in a beret. It had not been there the day before. She had never seen it in her life. But Sylvia knew who she was.

She wheeled when she heard a floorboard creak behind her. She was still thinking of that August afternoon fifteen years ago, and wondered if Axel had returned unexpectedly. She lowered her eyes.

Alec stepped from the shadows carrying the heavy tray. It had taken him a minute to find her, though he expected she would make for the study, Axel's sanctum now as it had been then. If she was looking for his spirit, that was where she would find it. And indeed she was standing just inside the door, her head bowed as if she were at graveside. From the rear, in her cashmere sweater and corduroy trousers and short hair, she had the vivacious float of a well-bred college senior. Alec said nothing for a moment, watching his mother stand quietly, her fingers touching the edge of Axel's desk. He could only guess at her thoughts after so many years and so much discussion — but her organizing principle had always been *Lo peor es pedir*. And she thrived on mystery. He knew his father would not be pleased if he discovered her there, "nosing around," as she put it, prowling the premises. God alone knew what she wanted really, but it had nothing to do with the Cold War or Echo House in her dreams. Sylvia had the bad habit of turning up at unexpected times and places, always at her own convenience, usually with only a few hours' notice. If you had plans, you were expected to drop them or revise them or include her in them.

So when she called that morning announcing her imminent arrival, Alec was not surprised, in part because the moment was awkward. He had arrived on Thursday from Chicago, had met with the senator in the afternoon and the publisher all day Friday, a delicate matter involving a license for a television station; the young publisher wanted it, and the senator wanted to help him get it, but the owner of the license didn't want to give it up. Negotiations were stalled and were likely to remain stalled until Lloyd Fisher himself arrived from Chicago, the aging veteran replacing the rookie who couldn't quite manage a squeeze play. Alec hated calling Lloyd and was lying in bed thinking about it when Sylvia called, causing Leila Berggren to sit up straight, alarmed when Alec mouthed "my mother" and began the usual decathlon, fine, how are you, yes that would be a wonderful surprise, grand, when do you think you'll be hoving into view? Sylvia did not care for that locution, interpreting it as sarcasm. She said, I'll be hoving into view when I damn well feel like it, not before four, not after six, depending on whether I fly or drive. Your darling secretary said you'd be staying alone at your father's, so I'll meet you there.

Leila was put out, because Alec had promised to come to her dinner, a fund-raiser in a private room in a restaurant downtown. She and her partner were raising money to establish their own research institute. They were selling ideas and trying to estimate the market. Leila wanted Alec on hand because she was nervous and he was a calming influence, never obtrusive or insistent but always reliable and shrewd about money; he knew Washington so well, and he was Axel Behl's son. She thought it would be good for him, too, meeting fat cats as opposed to the usual alley cats. It would help me if you were around, she said, and naturally he agreed because he loved her and wanted her to succeed in Washington. They had been apart now for a year and he could sense that she was moving into a new phase of her life, one with much opportunity but some danger also. Moreover, he enjoyed her fat cats.

Alec explained that Sylvia had not visited Echo House in many years and that her arrival now meant she was in a crisis of some kind and needed him. But what about me? Leila said. I have the most important dinner of my life and I want you there and you want to be with your loony mother instead. What did she ever do for you? Leila demanded and threw a pillow at the wall. Alec promised to cut off the meal with Sylvia as quickly as he decently could and go directly to Leila's dinner. I'll be there before ten, Alec said, but Leila wasn't buying. I won't forget this, she said, a threat that sounded like a prophecy.

He moved forward with the tea tray, hearing the floor creak, and watching Sylvia stiffen.

"Tea's on," he said.

"You startled me." Then, "This room gives me the creeps."

"Is it the Goya?" Alec asked, knowing it was not the Goya.

She looked at him sideways. "The Goya's all right; it's an ordinary appalling Goya. But years ago there used to be a picture of a *jeune fille,* a pretty little peasant in a beret. Where's she?"

"His bedroom," Alec said.

"How adorable," Sylvia said, but she was smiling as she said it. She wondered what story Axel told the occasional visitor to that bedroom, or if on such an occasion he turned the picture to the wall. "I heard the most fantastic story the other day, Axel arriving at a benefit with that Italian actress on his arm. Lovey-dovey was the way they were described, though surely the age difference was conspicuous." Alec was looking at her with a half-smile and she knew she would get nothing from him, even if there was anything to get. The Chinese boxes of Axel's life were closed, and admittance to one did not mean admittance to the others. Months would pass without a sighting of any kind; then his name would show up as one of those present at a White House ceremony or international conference or benefit for some obscure cause, always worthy and neglected. Her stepmother had seen him and the Italian actress — she had a nickname, Belladonna or some such — at a benefit for refugees of the Spanish Civil War. They were holding hands, according to Grace, who described the actress as *really cute,* nuzzling Axel. Axel laughing, Axel nuzzling back, Axel feeling like a boy again.

"Let's have the tea," Alec said.

They sat in the garden room; Alec poured. They talked for a moment of this and that, Sylvia trying mightily to work the conversation back to Axel; and when that failed, she inquired about Alec's work at Fisher, Gwilt, and what it was precisely that he *did* and for *whom,* Alec stubbornly leading her back into her own life. When he asked if she had discovered what was nagging at her, she said she hadn't and hadn't expected to, really. It was a long shot, like a hunch bet at the racetrack, but you never knew when you'd come up winners. It was strange that Echo House was at the center of her thoughts, asleep and awake, and some part of it present in all the poems she had written lately, the dense Cold War poems that were so disturbing and autobiographical. No muse ever lived at Echo House, she said. Echo

House was a climate. You wrote into the climate whether you wanted to or not, yet it was important to understand that beyond the storms, the thunder and electricity, lay a vast and pregnant silence, and it was the silence that beckoned. You had to discover a way to give voice to the silence between explosions. This subconscious was her true subject, but so far she was groping in heavy weather, unable to achieve the radiance she desired. She listened for the poem's heartbeat. She was listening hard for the silence that eluded her. She had always possessed a third ear that came alive at moments of high emotion, and she thought that Echo House would inspire her. If it represented the grammar of Cold War, it seemed also to represent the marriage that had failed in the city she despised, and no doubt there was a direct link between them. Or conceivably they were the same thing.

"But there it is in my dreams," she said, reaching for the sugar, selecting two lumps, and slipping them into her teacup, stirring idly. "So what do you think, darling? You're a lawyer, trained in observation. You're supposed to have ideas about these things and be able to explain them, or at least weigh the equities. Assess what lies beneath. When I'm in Echo House in my dreams I feel as if I'm about to fall from a great height."

Alec was tempted to reply, "Repressed infantile longings," but did not. Sylvia's sense of irony seldom extended to herself. He thought it likely that her dream Echo House was a surrogate for the house she had grown up in, a Gramercy Park fortress no less opulent, no less forbidding, and no less populated by ghosts. Her father was a sportsman as obsessed with horse racing as Axel was with statecraft. He was quick to leave her mother for a showgirl — "chorine" the word was then — and move to Saratoga and never look back. He lived there still with his showgirl, splendidly fit in his seventies, appearing younger than his wife, whose china doll beauty did not survive the hot summers and brutal winters and extended cocktail hours in all seasons. Sylvia had written poems about him and her, too, witty poems, if you could overlook the condescension.

Grace's daily double
turned you inside out
Old War Admiral
Winning by a neck

Every Christmas Alec received a tie from Charvet and a check drawn on a bank he never heard of. What kept the old man from being a cliché — another rich dimwit taking the usual revenge — was his conversion, late in life, to liberal politics. He hated Republicans with the passion of a Tammany Hall boss. Sylvia maintained that it wasn't really Republican politics he hated but his Saratoga neighbors, who snubbed him in the paddock and refused to attend his Sunday lunches or include him and the showgirl at theirs. And so in 1952 and again in 1956 he gave conspicuously large sums to Adlai Stevenson and was among the sponsors of causes ranging from Israel to the NAACP and the closed union shop. David Dubinsky was one of his favorites, and any advertisement placed by the ILGWU was certain to have among its signees Harry and Grace Walren, Saratoga Springs, New York. In 1960 he had a crisis of conscience because Joseph P. Kennedy had failed to recognize him at a party, a lapse he interpreted as a cold shoulder — Curly patronizing Moe, he called it — and sent a large check to the American Labor Party.

Alec said, "Pay attention to the details. Write them down."

"I don't have to write them down. I remember them. André Przyborski showed up in one last week. And Lloyd Fisher. I'm in my house. The lights are turned up full and there's traffic in the street. It's nighttime. Axel's away and so are you. Lloyd and André are in the study talking about some operation. I can't hear them but I know that it has to do with the next war. Because Lloyd is there, I think you're involved in some way. Are you involved with André Przyborski?"

"Lloyd knows him," Alec said.

"They all had lunch here, every Wednesday. All the spooks. And I suppose they still do."

Alec said nothing to that.

"Of course Lloyd left Washington about the time your father bought that bank."

Alec said nothing to that, either.

She looked at him and shrugged, an apology of sorts. "You know how it is with poets. No regular hours, so much mischief."

"Sometimes a headshrinker can help with dreams."

"I prefer clairvoyants. I knew one once here and she was a tremendous help. She saw to the heart of things, though she was better on the past than the future. I have no use for headshrinkers. You start letting people tinker with your memories, you're through as a writer." She lit a cigarette and leaned close to him, the prelude to a confidence. "It's true about my friend they've got in the bin in Hartford now. They've ruined her memory. They've given her shock and God knows what else. You know who I'm talking about."

Alec opened his mouth to say something, then didn't. He had no idea who was in the Hartford Retreat.

"She's a dear friend and a fine writer."

Alec carefully held his face in neutral.

"I hear she's a mess and all I want to know is, how much of a mess. And can I help out. But they won't let me in to see her."

He looked at her a long moment and inquired, "Why are you here really?"

"Willy and I are quits," she said in a clear voice, her head high.

She thought she would have a drink, if he didn't mind. There wasn't much story to tell but what story there was went down easier with a drink. Alec served her and they sat quietly a moment, looking into the damp darkness. Lights from the garden room cast long shadows on the croquet court. She noticed that and smiled crookedly, saying that she was surprised it was still there, intact and unspoiled. Axel always hated croquet.

"I'm not saying it was the greatest marriage in the world, because it wasn't," she said after a pause, still looking out the window at the wickets and the stakes. "But we had good times together and loved each other and got along pretty well most of the time, which is more than I can say of the marriages of ninety percent of my friends, although maybe I have the wrong friends. But Willy's gone."

"I'm sorry," Alec said. "I'm very sorry."

"I haven't begun to miss him yet, but I will. We were used to each other."

Alec nodded, uncomfortable listening to this news in the room where they had often gathered as a family in the years just after the war, Sylvia in the wing chair next to the window and his father facing her, the air redolent of flowers. On Saturday afternoons they listened to the opera. But now Willy Borowy was in the room, too.

"I can't imagine New York without Willy. You liked him, didn't you?"

"Very much," Alec said.

"He likes you," she said. "He always liked it when you came to visit."

"I had no idea," Alec said.

"Oh, he did," Sylvia protested. "You were one of his favorites."

"No," Alec said. "I meant that things weren't all right between you. I had no idea there was trouble."

"Willy was naughty," she said. She stared at her drink and again at the croquet court. She was holding the drink with both hands, and when she lifted it her rings clicked hollowly against the glass. "The croquet court looks so forlorn."

Alec looked out the window and nodded.

"Does he actually use it?"

"I can't remember the last time," Alec said.

"We were together fifteen years; it's hard to believe."

"Fifteen years both times," Alec said.

"Willy forced my hand," she said. "He left me no choice."

Alec looked up as if he understood; she was leaving so much unsaid and that was unlike her. He was grateful for her tact, having no wish to hear the details of Willy's transgressions, whatever they were. He had not seen Willy in months and the last time was at a restaurant in New York. He had seemed preoccupied then, almost morose, without his usual supply of jokes.

He and Sylvia had a complicated argument over where they would spend August. She wanted to rent a house on Long Island and he wanted Nantucket. She insisted that first they visit her father and Grace at Saratoga, a plan Willy vetoed. The only thing worse than horse players were trust-fund liberals and with Harry and Grace you got both at once. He was tired of being lectured to about the many virtues of the plucky little state of Israel and the organizational genius of David Dubinsky, with the usual side references to the vigor and tenacity of "the Mediterranean races," by which Harry seemed to mean the Jews, forgetting that Willy's family had flourished in New York since the eighteenth century, having emigrated from Holland on a family-owned vessel; and if there was any tenacity and vigor in the Borowy clan, it had escaped Willy's notice. They were hanging on by their fingernails. It was a burden, being rich for three centuries, and now the family was as desiccated as Harry's, though for the opposite reason. Borowy *père* believed there had been too much intermarriage in his family, while in Harry's there had been none at all, until Willy. But at least the Borowys didn't talk sentimental claptrap about Israel, or the ILGWU either. The Borowys were traders and indifferent to national boundaries. National pride was a calamity, even in the Mediterranean. Besides, Willy said, in Saratoga they drank all the time, beginning in the morning with bloody marys and by evening they were talking claptrap. Your problem is, you never win at the track, Sylvia said; you pick by hunch and it never works out. That's only the most obvious problem, Willy said. He could be very droll. Sylvia settled the argument by saying she would go by herself to Saratoga, spend a week at Yaddo and three days with her father and Grace, and then meet Willy at Nantucket if the fog lifted long enough for the airplane to land.

"This is between us," Sylvia said with a sharp look at her son. "I don't want Axel to know. I won't have it."

"He usually — finds things out."

"I know that," she said. "The news will find its way to Palm Beach. Bad news travels with the speed of light to Palm Beach. But not for a while yet. Axel —" She went on to complain about

Axel, a sponge where gossip was concerned, no item too small to escape his attention or merit his comment. Alec listened with a show of polite interest to this speech he had heard many times.

"Willy has no pride," she said suddenly.

Alec looked at her, startled.

"Axel's up to here with it and Willy doesn't have any at all. Willy's ashamed of who he is and where he comes from."

Alec managed, *"Willy?"* He thought Willy Borowy the most civilized man he knew.

"Willy doesn't like being a Jew."

"Willy loves being a Jew!" Alec almost shouted. "A Jew at the end of the line. A Jew living on an inheritance, just like your father, except it's a smaller inheritance and getting smaller each day. Willy" — he remembered something Leila Berggren had said to him that morning, a comment on John F. Kennedy's ambassadorial appointments — "likes to cast against type. Who did he vote for? Nixon. Who's his favorite movie actor? David Niven. His favorite city? Berlin. His favorite poet?" He let the question hang.

"You seem to have given quite a lot of thought to my Willy," Sylvia said. "I never would have guessed. So who's his favorite poet?"

"You," Alec said.

"As a matter of fact, it's Delmore Schwartz," Sylvia said dryly.

"And Auden," Alec said.

Sylvia shook her head. Poor Alec, so ignorant of the wider American world, so bewitched by Willy's well-known charm. But the charm was a mask to hide his true soul. He lived always in Washington's shadow. His father worked for FDR, so he grew up in Washington and for the longest time didn't think of himself as a Jew. Jew didn't come into it because his family was not religious and no one else cared. In Washington the New Deal was a secular religion, and Willy and his family were Feds just like the neighbors. He discovered anti-Semitism later and was surprised by it. Anti-Semitism was new to him and it was disgusting. Growing up in Washington, you weren't Irish or Italian or German or Jewish; you were a Fed. Willy grew up deracinated, even the name, Willy Borowy. And when he found out that Washington was a special island of ethnic agreement — "broad-mindedness," they called it — it bothered him. It drove him crazy. He decided that Washington in its American way resembled Moscow under the Reds, communal hatreds suppressed in the name of patriotism or morale or public relations or setting a good example. And instead of admiring Washington for its tolerance and good sense, he despised it for its deceptions. There was a kind of snobbery among worldly Washingtonians, who believed they were above the coarse prejudices of the mob. In one sense, of course, they were — until there was a crisis, an election, or a sweet piece of legislation or a nominee to the Court, a place at the trough, in other words, and then their elbows were as sharp as axes. Willy grew up living in an illusion and he thought he had been cheated. No one had ever told him the way the world worked really, so he was twenty years old before he heard the word "kike." No one had ever used that word or its many synonyms in polite and civilized Washington and snickered at its use elsewhere, as French-speaking Muscovites belittled the earthy language of the peasant masses. Axel would have slit his throat before using that word or permitting it to be used in his presence . . .

"Willy thought that growing up in Washington was not a good preparation for life," Sylvia said mildly.

"It doesn't sound like shame to me," Alec said.

"Shame takes many forms," she said imperiously.

"He never seemed to me *ashamed* of who he was. Shame's not a word I associate with Willy. Willy's attitude toward life is ironic. Willy lives by irony."

"Sometimes it's the same thing."

Alec looked up at that.

"Willy likes to undermine himself," she added.

"He never took himself seriously, if that's what you mean."

"Oh, no," she said. "You're wrong there. He took himself very seriously. That was the trouble. Not on the surface, though. Never on the surface. That's one of the things that attracted me to him right away; you could see his mind go in one direction while his mouth went in another. Nine-tenths of Willy was between the lines, like a good poem. It took time and effort to appreciate Willy, who never understood where he fit in or whether he was supposed to."

Alec was silent, suspecting that a comparison with Axel was at hand.

She fluttered her fingers, smiling brightly. "And one thing I knew for sure, the moment I met him. Willy hated Washington even more than I did."

"Another bond," Alec said.

"That's why he voted for Nixon. He thought Richard Nixon was Washington's exemplary specimen. Washington created him, Washington should have to live with him. Willy believed that Nixon was a creature of his environment no less than a clam in the mud. He was heartbroken when Nixon lost; an opportunity like that only comes along once in a lifetime. He believed that Washington wanted Kennedy to win so that it could think better of itself, an appalling prospect. So he got me to vote for Nixon, too. A Nixon victory would bring Washington to its knees in disgust and self-loathing, though that was probably too much to hope for."

"Much too much," Alec said.

"They'd blame the country."

"Probably they would. Blame the people who voted for him."

"I don't know why things never work out," Sylvia said quietly. "If only men were consistent. If they didn't have one personality for the inside and another for the outside. If they didn't spend so much time prowling. If only they'd stop and think." Sylvia turned to look out the window. The rain had stopped and the moon was visible over the giant elm. The croquet court was very bright and frozen as if caught by an artist. Nothing moved; even the trees were still. She was staring intently at the croquet court the way she would stare at a picture in a gallery. If she stared long enough, it would speak and tell her something important. Alec stole a look at his watch and was alarmed to discover that the time was almost seven. Leila's dinner was due to begin in thirty minutes. Sylvia continued to stare out the window, her glass dry.

"Can I make you another drink?"

When she shook her head, Alec thought to ask, "Where are you staying?"

"Some people in Bethesda," she said wearily. "Friends of Willy's."

He was suddenly afraid that she would fall to pieces without Willy Borowy, nine-tenths between the lines. They had always looked after each other, and Sylvia was not the sort of person who easily lived alone; at least she never had. She had never paid attention to the mundane details of life; that was Willy's job. Alec looked at the ceiling, calculating the time it would take to get to the restaurant.

She said, "I suppose I'll go back to New York tomorrow."

He said quickly, "Stay a few days. We can go to the National Gallery tomorrow."

She turned from the window and looked directly at him. "I wanted to tell you about this myself, my own words, and now I can go back to New York. When Willy left he took only his library and his dog; can you believe it? I don't even know where he is."

He said, "Is there anything I can do for you?"

"Yes," she said promptly. "There is. You can take me to dinner. We can have a little dinner together, just us two, like the old days."

When were they? He could not remember dining alone with her in the old days, unless she meant London during the war. She was grinning broadly, delighted with this thought. In the sudden silence that followed, Alec moved his shoulders indecisively and gave an unwilling sigh. For the last ten minutes he had been thinking about Leila, her long legs and the down on her belly, and her purr when she was excited. He heard her voice in his ear saying how important it was, how *crucial* and *urgent*, that he be at dinner to romance her fat cats —

Sylvia carefully put her glass on the table and prepared to rise.

"Of course," he said.

"Oh, goody," she cried. "Sure it's all right? Did I hear some hesitation? I'm not disappointing some adorable girl?" She smiled brilliantly. "I'll tell you something; it'll come as a surprise. I never liked being a mother. That's the truth. I love you, God knows, but the details of maternity always baffled me. It was like trying to learn French, too many verb declensions and they were always criticizing your accent. I never knew what to say or do. I never knew how much to tell and how much not to tell and what a child ought to know. I knew a lot, but I wasn't sure that the things I knew had any — relevance. Small children frightened me; they seemed so insistent and demanding and so fragile and incapable. God, what a nightmare. The laundry! I couldn't wait until you were grown up. And now you are!"

It was almost ten when he turned the corner of the Treasury, driving Axel's black sedan. He guessed that dinner was ended, though when he'd spoken to the maître d' fifteen minutes before, he was told that the party was still at table. Probably they were finishing their coffee, but it made a late night for the up-with-the-birdies Washingtonians.

The maître d', leaning on his lectern reading a newspaper, sullenly pointed to a staircase. Alec could hear voices upstairs, one voice rising above the others. He opened the door to the private room, pausing just beyond the cone of light to listen to the speaker, her voice rising like a drill sergeant's.

"It's a bad plan, gentleman. It's flawed. It is not *stürmisch*. It lacks *verordnung*. It has no organizing principle. Where it should be *angestrengt*, it is *schwach*. And where it should be *schwach*, it is *angestrengt*. So we are faced with a disaster unless steps are taken." She glowered fiercely. "Leave this to me. I know what must be done. I will inspissate this plan, and we can move forward."

This seemed to be a private joke of some kind, for there was laughter from the two men who sat with their backs to Alec.

"I will take it to the Attorney General," the drill sergeant said.

"He didn't like your last plan."

"His people didn't like it. His gofers didn't understand it. Gofers are rats devouring the casualties. I am not taken in by rats. Rats hold no interest for me. Fuck rats!"

Alec was watching Leila, who was sitting next to the drill sergeant, a lazy smile on her face. She knew a performance when she saw one. Perhaps that was what you gained from proficiency in higher mathematics, her unfaithful numbers, her F Factor; everything was a performance.

When Alec stepped from the shadows, she looked up but seemed not to recognize him. He thought that she had never looked more alive, her skin glowing, her eyes luminous; and then she winked. The hairs on the back of his neck began to rise when she grinned broadly and motioned for him to sit beside her.

"Our foot's in the door," she whispered when he was at eye level. "And it's there to stay."

And when he glanced around the table he knew why. To his surprise, Lloyd Fisher was directly across the table, sitting with André Przyborski. Leila's partner, Hugo Borne, was next to Lloyd, and a wiry young Negro was next to Hugo. That would be Wilson Slyde, Leila had mentioned him often, a defense expert from MIT, a protégé of one of the vice president's people. A stranger completed the table. There were two empty chairs and crumpled napkins carelessly thrown beside empty wine glasses. So there had been two others present, and they had been the ones with the money; unless Lloyd was the one with the money.

Alec recognized the stranger but could not put a name to the face. Lean and saturnine, he had the ranginess of a cowboy, but he did not look like a cowboy, in his tailored suit and striped tie and polished shoes, indolently leaning back in his chair, thumbs hooked on a pair of bright red suspenders, grinning maliciously. He had what appeared to be a solid gold PT-109 tie clasp, conspicuous as a headlight. He looked vaguely out of place, and Alec wondered if he was one of Leila's inventory of specialists — weapons, the Soviet rail system, Third World, Swiss banks.

But "specialist" was not the word that came to mind as he looked at the cowboy. Alec was certain that he had something to do with Democratic politics, a perennial Washington helpful, university division.

"There will be two areas of concern," the drill sergeant said. "Southeast Asia and the Caribbean."

Alec saw André roll his eyes and pour an inch of the wine into his glass.

"And that is where we should concentrate," she said.

"A sideshow," André said, stifling a yawn.

"It is where the contracts are, my dear André."

"Our two friends will have something to say about that," André said.

"I agree they are serious people," she said.

André muttered something in Polish, and the company fell silent.

"Well," Hugo said. "This is a fine beginning."

Lloyd looked at Alec, nodding fractionally, a finger on his upper lip.

"What are your thoughts, Lloyd?"

"I'll have to take this up with my principals, of course. In all its details. But I do believe we've made real progress tonight, even though there're some rough edges. Do you have a thought, André?"

"I like the rough edges," André said.

Hugo and the cowboy laughed, and then the drill sergeant spoke up again, staring directly at André; the others listened politely, but it was obvious the evening was almost over.

"You are late," Leila said out of the corner of her mouth.

"She wouldn't let me go. Am I forgiven?"

"You're forgiven. What did she want?"

"Family business," Alec said.

"We're done here. If Jo will just shut up."

"Why is she speaking German?"

"Her native language," Leila said. "Her name is Josephine Broch. She uses it when she wants to mystify, which is most of the time. She never uses it around me, because she knows I understand it. She's very good, really. Interpol background. God knows what else."

"I'll have some papers drawn up," Lloyd said, leaning across the table to say something privately to Hugo. The others sipped their coffee, except André, who was drinking wine. The air was dead, as if the oxygen had been drawn from it. Only Leila gave off any vitality, and now she moved closer to him, her fingers reaching. Alec looked up to see the cowboy staring at him with an indolent smile.

"My name's Red," he said. "I know your father."

His voice was low and round, with a vibrato that suggested he had been trained as a radio announcer. Alec recognized him now from a newspaper photograph, Red Lambardo, one of the many young advisers, formal and informal, in splendid orbit now that the new administration had found its feet at last. Alec remembered that he was an economist.

"Your father and I are in the same business, more or less. Remarkable man."

"Business?" Alec asked innocently. All his life people had confided that they knew his father, pronouncing the words solemnly, *your father,* never *Axel.* And they grinned when they said them, as if acquaintance with this remarkable man made them both remarkable men, with shared values, such as absolute discretion and hard-won knowledge of the way the world worked.

"Politics," Red Lambardo said easily. "And lending whatever support and expertise we can to the fine new team at bat. I saw him in Palm Beach yesterday. Sitting in the warm sun with the President, everyone in shorts and polo shirts and your father in his dark suit and white shirt, bow tie, black shoes. Jack says, 'Axel, don't you ever relax?' And your father takes off his wristwatch and puts it on the table. Jack laughed like hell. We all did."

Alec admired the opening gambit, Red Lambardo establishing his bona fides; it was the sort of remark the President might make, if he had said anything at all and if Lambardo had actually been there to hear it. You listened to stories about "Jack" all the time, what he liked to eat and drink, witty remarks that he made, his prowess on the golf course, his aches and pains; and other stories, none of them verifiable. Probably the same thing was true of the Pope or Chairman Mao, mysterious personalities whose offhand remarks proved that they were only human after all, with good close friends to prove it. Red was smiling and shaking his head, all the time looking inquisitively at Alec, apparently expecting a reply of some kind, perhaps an anecdote in return, a lively anecdote that might up the ante. But Alec only turned to Leila and raised his eyebrows. Isn't it time to go? Shall we get out of here? Lloyd was still conferring earnestly with Hugo Borne. André was staring into the middle distance, sipping wine. Wilson Slyde was casually eavesdropping.

"Jo said you were a friend of Leila's and might be along after dinner. So I'm glad we have a chance to meet and say hello."

"Red, darling," Josephine said. "It's late."

"In a minute," Red said, leaning forward and flexing his fingers like a pianist. "You would have liked it in Palm Beach, Alec. The weather was superb and everyone was friendly and relaxed. Lots of pretty girls around. The enthusiasm was infectious. La Bella Figura was there with your father and she had brought her sister. She's an actress also; isn't that right? They look so much alike we called them Una and Due. Hard to keep our minds on business with those two going through their paces, Una on the high board and Due on the low. Even so, Allen's threat assessments were sobering. We're playing a hot hand right now but the enemy hasn't gone away. He's only underground, planning some crisis we can't even imagine. What do you do, Alec?"

"Lawyer," Alec said. Paulina went everywhere with Axel, but surely he would have drawn the line at Palm Beach, if not with Paulina at least with her sister. Axel did as he damn well pleased, but this was hard to believe.

"Only the other day the President was saying we need some fresh blood, people who know where their loyalties lie. The Attorney General was emphatic on that point also. Folks like Leila here, and Jo and Hugo and our new friend, Wilson. Foreign policy's the key, of course, and we still have too many square pegs in round holes. It's such a simple thing, loyalty, but you'd be

surprised how quickly people forget the simple things. The campaign'll be hard fought and fortunately we won't have that bastard Nixon to worry about. Of course we're looking for the best
people, loyal people with brains and initiative, people who can
be trusted, tough people, can-do people who enjoy their work.
You'd've loved Palm Beach, so groovy." He smiled wistfully. "So
you're a lawyer. Ever think about politics?"

"My father takes care of the politics in our family."

Red Lambardo chuckled; of course he understood about the
father. "The great thing about the law is that it's fungible and
you can practice it anywhere. It's fine training. It rewards precision and thorough preparation. And of course discretion."

"He works for me," Lloyd said suddenly.

"My God," Red said. "Of course that's right! Axel mentioned
it when Jack asked after young Alec here. Jack knew he'd been to
the law school and done well, and it was only a matter of time
before he went into the family business, ha-ha. Axel said you've
got quite a firm on that La Salle Street there — "

"Red," Jo said.

"Later," Red said without looking at her. "So you've got Alec
here as a partner."

"Not a partner quite yet," Lloyd said.

"Ah," Red said, turning again to Alec. "All in good time, I
would imagine."

"So would I," Lloyd said.

Alec listened to this with growing disbelief, wondering how
much was fact and how much fiction and how much fantasy. He
reckoned it worked out in thirds. Red Lambardo was making
quite an effort, and he did not look like a man who often made
efforts, at least to thirty-year-old Chicago lawyers. He wondered
again if Lambardo had actually been to Palm Beach; and if he
was as loose as he sounded or if this was the satiric first act of
his own two-act play, the tragedy arriving in act two.

"Thing is, with private law, it's a hell of a long apprenticeship
and you're as old as Gepetto before you're making the shoes; do
you see what I'm saying here? It's the wills and the trusts that get
a man down, the title searches and so forth and so on, while so

many young men — and women, too! — have come to Washington to work for our administration. Public service, that's the thing. But of course you know all that."

"You were an economist," Alec said.

"Am," Red said. "Still am."

"Working then at Treasury?"

"No, they're monetary over there. I'm fiscal."

"I see," Alec said. "The House Ways and Means Committee?"

"The House of Representatives? No, they're slow on the Hill. They're tortoises; no place for a man who likes to get things done lickety-split, no fuss, no broken dishes. No, I'm in another activity altogether —"

Act two, Alec thought.

"— Fact is, I'm over at State heading up a working group on the Caribbean. Me and three others and a small staff to push the paper around, cryptology and so forth and so on, procurement . . ." Alec noticed that Lloyd had begun another conversation with André and Hugo Borne, and Leila was preoccupied with Jo. Wilson Slyde was listening hard to Red, and from the expression on his face he did not like what he was hearing. Red motioned for Alec to lean close so that he could talk without being overheard. "And we have need for an outside man, someone who can speak with authority, someone who can brief the reporters, Diplomatic Correspondents they call themselves" — Red looked up and grinned wolfishly — "and this man must be absolutely trustworthy, a man who knows the score, wasn't born yesterday, and's been around Washington for more than a minute and a half. Knows who counts and not only because he can read newspapers. He knows who counts because he knows them personally, has been inside their homes, knows their wives and children. This calls for a man who knows that in Washington even the skeletons have skeletons; and he's made their acquaintance, rattled their bones. Are you in the picture? This isn't something that's going to last forever, at least I hope to God it isn't going to last forever, because I hope to move on in a year. A reform of the tax code leading to a redistribution of wealth is my special interest, and I know it's yours as well, and when I move on my team will move with me. And I'm reporting to Highest Levels, Alec, not some la-di-da flunky in the State Department. See, we all have to get our feet wet sometime, don't we?"

"You want a press spokesman."

"That's correct, Alec."

"Without any experience," Alec said. "At all. Nil."

"Without the wrong kind of experience," Red said. "The trouble with most spokesmen is that they have too much experience, none of it pertinent. Most of them are retreads with drinking problems and too many friendships, and the kind of cynicism that comes from sitting in the bleachers too far from the field. They're sun-struck. They've been looking at things in the glare for too long, and don't know how it is up close, six or seven decent hard-working men sitting around a table trying to get something done, move the country forward. It's *our turn* and the old farts have got to step aside. We need people who understand the modern world and aren't afraid of it. Who understand also the world beneath the bleachers, where things aren't so pretty, and where the sun never shines."

Red sighed heavily and pinched his nose, closing his eyes; what a long day it had been, doing the nation's business. "They're old," he went on. "They don't like to work on Sunday or their wife's birthday or the long Labor Day weekend or when their kid has a piano recital, and they don't know how to function as a team with a single objective: help the man the American people elected President. They've been stenographers for so long they don't know how to *think*. They're still worrying about the evening deadline and the lead of the story and what kind of fancy splash they can make if it's on page one with their by-line front and center. Thing is, Alec. Loyalty's not their long suit. But it's my long suit. And it's the President's and the Attorney General's long suit. And I'm betting that it's your long suit."

Alec looked at him, allowing the silence to lengthen. "Did you speak to Axel about this?"

"No," Red said, looking offended. "Of course not. Would it make a difference if I had?"

"What's in the Caribbean?" He wanted to hear Red's version.

"A dictator, worse than Stalin. Who's defying the President of the United States."

"And your 'working group' —"

Red Lambardo shook his head, no details on that; he pushed his fists together, meaning that the facts, whatever they were, were tightly held. "I can tell you that Wilson has been acting as our press spokesman, doing a fine job, although there hasn't been much to say so far. As you can see, Wilson's young and we need someone with more experience or, as I've said, the right kind of experience. Everything depends on the presentation. That's the *test,* you see." He glanced at Wilson Slyde, who was staring sullenly at his empty wine glass. "Sometimes you need merely a wink and a nod, especially now that things are going to get complicated. Controversial, even. Sometimes just one word does the job, if it's the right word in the right ear. So that's where we are. Interested?"

"Not really," Alec said, looking sideways at Wilson Slyde, whose expression had not changed, except that Alec had mistaken sullenness for fury. God alone knew what effort it had taken Wilson Slyde to make a place for himself at the table, and now it was about to be snatched away. "It's Wilson's job. Let him do it."

"Mistake," Red Lambardo said coldly. "Big mistake; you don't know what you're missing."

"Yes, he does," Wilson said. "He knows what it is. It's a field hand's work. Leave it to the field hand. Leave it to the nigger."

Red smashed his fist on the table and snarled, "Never use that word again in my presence, Wilson." Red flicked an imaginary ash from the lapel of his jacket, stretched, and got up stiffly, shaking the creases from his trousers. On his feet he looked nothing like a cowboy. He was stoop-shouldered and uncoordinated, with the beginnings of a pot belly. Jo rose at once and Lambardo went directly to her, pausing to lay a brotherly hand on Wilson's shoulder, squeezing harder than he needed to. He whispered something in Jo's ear. She laughed and executed a little shimmy, turning to say goodbye to Leila and Hugo, nodding at Lloyd and André. She did not look at Wilson or Alec. She seemed suddenly very young and vivacious, not at all *stürmisch*. When he first saw Jo, Alec thought of a drill sergeant. Now she looked like a starlet. Red Lambardo took her by the arm and they swept from the room.

Alec said to Wilson, "Isn't he a peach?"

"Mr. Red is a man with many friends and convictions to match," Wilson said.

"What is he doing here?" Alec said to Leila.

"He represents some people who have an interest in our work. Jo brought him."

"What's he offering? An invitation to Palm Beach?"

Leila smiled demurely. "That's not the half of it."

"Time to pack it in," Lloyd said. "If I could have a minute alone with Alec?"

They stood in a corner of the room and Alec explained that the negotiations were stalled, the young publisher in a panic and the senator only slightly less so. They wanted Lloyd Fisher in person, not Lloyd Fisher's assistant. I was going to call you, Alec said. When Lloyd raised his eyebrows, Alec added that the matter of the television license was more complicated than he thought, meaning more political; and he felt he was not fully in the picture. Lloyd nodded; that was true and he apologized for it. In fact the senator felt that Alec had not been adequately briefed on the importance of the case. No complaints about your lawyering, Lloyd said; no complaints about your grasp of the facts of the case. Question here of getting a piece of paper from an in-box to an out-box, and lawyering doesn't come into it. There were subtleties involving two members and some staff of the commission, where the matter would eventually be decided. Private discussions were necessary. As you know, Lloyd said, it was an absolute must that the television license be awarded to the publisher, because the publisher was the senator's ally and around election time put all his resources, financial and editorial, to work for the senator. A television license added mightily to the resources, guaranteed them, as it were. And it all came down to moving a piece of paper from an in-box to an out-box.

Damnedest thing. Television's like the Hearst press in the old days. You make money faster than you can count it, and then you elect a man to make sure you keep it.

You've done a good job, Lloyd said. Don't worry about it. But for the next week or so the negotiations would get contentious, and he, Lloyd, would handle that end himself. He smiled and threw a fatherly arm around Alec's shoulder. You need a linguist's knowledge of the subjunctive voice and full command of the many verbs that march up to a subject without quite surrounding it, a different climate altogether than Chicago's, less raw, less windy, more humid. They'll do anything in this town; they just don't like to admit they're doing it. You'd say it's a simple matter of not wanting to get caught and of course that's true. But it was also true that if you explored a matter with subtlety, a sort of formal reconnaissance in force such as the Chinese are so fond of, then one plain fact could assume many identities — a bribe became an impropriety, the impropriety an irregularity, and the irregularity a misunderstanding. Many suits of armor, as it were, depending always on the verb that doesn't quite surround the subject. In any case the clients demanded his personal intervention. Principals only, he added pointedly. I'll give you an oral report, he said. I'll fill you in on all the grammar, since you'll be doing it yourself soon.

Odd, he said. These things come and go and for a day or a week you're obsessed by it. Then it's settled one way or another and you forget about it as if it never existed, as in a way it never did.

"You handled Lambardo well, Alec."

"Thanks," Alec said. "He's an idiot."

"No, he isn't. And stay in touch with him. Mister Red Lambardo's going to get into a lot of trouble one of these days or, more likely, get someone else into a lot of trouble. He talks too much, about the wrong subjects to the wrong company. He underestimates people. He underestimated you. But I like his friends, and when Red lands in the hot water I'd like to be in a position to help out. That makes his friends our friends."

Leila was suddenly between them, saying that the party was over, it was time to go home.

"I was just telling Alec," Lloyd said. He put his other hand lightly on her arm, moving his fingers, smiling blandly. "I think it'd be a good idea if Alec came aboard with you and Hugo and Jo as general counsel. You're going to need someone to examine the contracts, give advice when you ask for it. More important, not be shy to listen to advice when you don't ask for it. Alec's in the picture."

"I'll buy that," Leila said. "I know Hugo and Jo will, too."

"Small detail," Alec said. "How do I advise from Chicago?"

"That's the other thing," Lloyd said. He was talking to Alec but looking at Leila. "I've been thinking about it a while. I'm selling my stake in Fisher, Gwilt. Let's leave Chicago to the true-blue Chicagoans. I'm itching to return to our national capital and establish a new firm altogether. And I will call that firm Fisher and Behl. Congratulations." He winked at Leila.

"What a wonderful surprise!" Leila cried.

"And I know you won't mind coming back home," Lloyd said.

Then they were all talking at once, Alec and Leila laughing, Lloyd looking on paternally. There was enough wine for a single glass, and they each sipped from it. Lloyd offered a final toast. Leila looked around her, puzzled. Where was Wilson? He was there a moment ago, and now he'd vanished without a trace. Did anyone see him go? He was sitting right *there,* Leila said. And now he was gone like a thief in the night.

"That boy has got to watch his tongue," Lloyd said.

Late that night, in bed at Echo House, Alec asked Leila if Lloyd had already told her about selling Fisher, Gwilt and moving to Washington. He'd mentioned something about it, she said vaguely; no details. She was sworn to secrecy. It's wonderful, isn't it? And even better that you'll be working with us, Hugo and me and the others. We don't know anything about organizing a business that'll be part private, part government. It's uncharted territory, she said, sort of like the Tennessee Valley Authority, except what we're selling is ideas. She went on to talk about the evening, how well it had gone despite Jo Broch's filibuster and Wilson's unfortunate remark at the end. What got into him? He doesn't know how lucky he is. But thanks to Red Lambardo there was a serious commitment from the federal government, two studies right away, with more to come. Wilson's handling one of them, an analysis of the Cuban army's order of battle. He's absolutely first-rate, you know, ran away with all the honors at MIT and he's in very tight with the administration. Do you know someone called Ed Peralta? From the Defense Department, supposedly.

Yes, Alec knew Ed Peralta.

Is his word good?

Good as gold, Alec said.

We'll be reporting to him, Leila said.

She continued to reprise the dinner. Alec listened half-heartedly. He was pondering his return to Washington, working with a man he had known intimately for ten years, in the office and after hours in the Loop. At times Lloyd treated him like a son, at other times like anything but. Alec knew about Lloyd's father's mismanagement of the firm and Lloyd's struggles to save it, including the corners that had to be cut. He knew that Lloyd's voice thickened after the second martini, and at those times he liked to talk about his days in Berlin after the war; besides that, Chicago wasn't so much. It was only a place to make money and he had no children to give the money to, so what was the point? He was not popular with the five other lawyers in the firm or with the elite of the Chicago bar, because he had no interest in bar politics and rarely socialized at the Chicago Club or the Tavern, preferring instead the raucous dining room of the Morrison Hotel with an alderman, or the old world west-side Polish restaurant with André Przyborski.

Lloyd Fisher never belonged in Chicago despite the ancestral offices on La Salle Street and the fine apartment on the near North Side, the cottage in Door County, the country club memberships, and all the rest. Of course he grew rich, practicing law and marking time, always happiest when preparing his monthly visits to Washington, his business always vague, except he was now welcome again at Echo House for Wednesday lunch. Back in the game, Lloyd said.

He would return from the capital with a morning's worth of

involved anecdotes signaling change in the way business was done. He hadn't worked out the implications, but it was obvious that the American government and American business were no longer enemies, despite Kennedy's angry rhetoric. In some ways there was very little difference between government and business, and the universities, too. You could call it a partnership or you could call it a cartel; the new relationship had aspects of both. Managing the transition would be the lawyers, now emigrating to Washington in huge numbers. I don't know what it means, Lloyd said, except that we're all going to be much, much richer than we are, thanks to the Cold War.

And what will you be leaving behind in Chicago? Leila asked.

But he didn't answer her question because he wasn't sure what he was leaving behind or if he was leaving anything. They had been together for five years, inseparable insofar as their work allowed. Leila was often absent, performing chores for Lloyd or for the Democratic National Committee. Then, the year before, Hugo Borne had offered her a job in the boring Bureau of the Budget and she had accepted at once, because it was a chance to return to the capital on her own terms; she and Hugo had talked for years about forming their own consulting company. Leila said she was the happiest she'd been and pleaded with Alec to join her in Washington. There isn't anything for you in Chicago, she'd said. And you could help me out. Do you have any idea how hard it is for a woman in this town just trying to get her foot in the door. It isn't Flo, is it?

Once a month he had dinner with Flo and her dull husband, Flo as animated as ever and single-minded about the White House, some day, some way. She and Leila had never gotten on and now with Leila gone Flo was candid about exactly what she intended to do. Jackie Kennedy had proven that you could seduce the public but there was much more to be done than musical evenings and shopping for antiques. Flo bullied her husband into a congressional race he had no chance of winning; and in due course she found her way to Alec's apartment, seeking advice on how to talk to Chicago newspaper reporters. Instead, they talked about Leila.

Why doesn't she like me? Flo asked. Leila's a little bit of an outlaw and she thinks you're the sheriff, Alec said. She thinks you're smarter than you let on and she wonders why you don't let on. Are you afraid of them? And she drinks beer from the bottle and you don't, Alec added, and at that Flo laughed and laughed. She said, Leila has to learn that there are two ways to skin the cats, an axe or a scalpel. I prefer the scalpel. The scalpel suits me. But I know how to use the axe, too.

She stayed for a drink and one thing led to another, as it was bound to do. Flo resisted a little and then she didn't resist at all. Life is full of surprises, she called from the shower. What fun! I never would've guessed. Don't you sometimes feel like just letting go? At heart I'm a bourgeoise, a suburban wife and mother of two with an unusual ambition. I'm supposed to be considerate and tactful and tentative, and that's not me at all. At least it isn't me when it counts. This was just stu—

He started, expecting the rebuke.

—pendous, she concluded.

Then she appeared from the shower, dripping wet, still talking. Her skin glowed; she gathered a towel around her middle. She stood in the half light, bending to towel off, laughing again, looking as if she was posing for Renoir himself. Looking at her, Alec thought that in another life they might have been ideal for each other. At heart he was a bourgeois, too. And he preferred the scalpel to the axe.

To everyone's surprise the dull husband enjoyed campaigning and won his seat — thanks in part to Flo, who proved a superb speaker in small gatherings, her tiny twin daughters seated on her lap, saying that politics was an effort to secure the future for children, these children, your children, children everywhere. The girls were good as gold and always clapped adorably when their mother had finished. When Alec sent a bottle of Champagne on Election Night — he was conveniently in Washington — she replied with a box of golf balls.

Chicago was attractive, all right. He liked his apartment and the jazz club under the El station four blocks away. He especially liked it when mail came to him misspelled, Alec Bell. That never happened in Washington. Really, he didn't know what to think about Chicago, Flo, the firm, and their places in the general scheme of things. Probably this time was a parenthesis in the middle of a long-running sentence that would begin and end in the capital. He had to learn about Washington again, Leila's world as well as his father's world. Perhaps there would be Palm Beach weekends in the future, the President and the First Lady and Axel and La Bella Figura, with Red Lambardo to mix the drinks and record the conversation. Surely it was only a matter of time before Flo found her way to the White House, initially a state dinner, later the quiet evenings of French food and witty conversation. He could hardly believe that Axel had taken Paulina to meet the President, though Sylvia was not far wrong in suggesting that he was feeling like a boy again; acting like one, anyway, where Paulina was concerned. So if he saw more of Axel, he would see more of Paulina also; and no one would ever misspell his name again.

Alec had no particular affection for the law, and in fact what he did had little to do with law. It had to do with regulations and procedures. It had to do with disputes between one man and another, the disputes arising from ego as much as from equity. He introduced one man to another man and handled the marriage ceremony if it worked out and the divorce if it didn't. From Lloyd he was learning to march his verbs up the hill and down again, feinting, thrusting, maneuvering, never quite surrounding. He remembered the cases because of the amusement they afforded, and the fee at the end of the day; but he had never cared much about money, and in that way he was his father's son. He did have a leather book filled with clippings from the *Tribune* and the *Daily News*. But he could as easily have been in medicine or business or diplomacy or journalism or films; he admitted a certain attraction to bright lights, perhaps his name in bright lights, but that never happened outside the criminal law. Alec supposed that, like Lloyd Fisher and his father, he belonged in the federal triangle, internist to the nation's metabolism. A famous internist, he thought suddenly, an internist who performed miracles. Axel always believed that all serious work was done in the shadows; but Axel had been wrong before.

Nothing at all? Leila said after a moment.

Some good friends, Alec said.

No matter, Leila said. You belong here.

Why do you say that?

Because this is where the edge is. It used to be in New York but it's here now.

I suppose it is, Alec said.

I thought Red Lambardo was having an orgasm, meeting you. You fit in, Alec. The President knows who you are. The President! You already have your foot in the door, and now mine's there, too.

6

Washington's Jew

❧

Bʏ 1973 Sylvia was back in Washington with Willy Borowy. A chance meeting on Fifth Avenue had led to lunch and lunch to a long weekend on Nantucket. Willy had come into some money and had bought a cottage by the sea. The weekend became a year and then five years. The move to Washington was Sylvia's idea, though Willy did not object. He wanted to test his perverse theory of Richard Nixon as the capital's true son and heir, and Sylvia wanted to see more of Alec and her grandchildren. She had been away almost a quarter-century.

And she returned in triumph. Nantucket — so distant, so silent, so spare, so cold — had forced her to begin to write again. After a long fallow period Sylvia had published two books in two years, and these had brought her prizes and praise from her contemporaries. She was frequently in the news because she gave such marvelous readings. She was in her early sixties and looked it, her hair gray and her Modigliani face filled out. She had dimples in her cheeks. But her voice had the range and timbre of a youngster. Sylvia was an irresistible performer in her jeans and signature black cardigan, gold medallion at her throat — Aries, the Ram — peering myopically over half-glasses, either reading from her own work or appearing on the conference circuit, giving studied answers to Simone Weil's great question, What are you going through right now?

It's a wonder what boredom can do, she said. Boredom is the ur-inspiration of poets, better than Scotch, better than sex — so long as it isn't allowed to go on forever. Her work needed a new twist, something beyond Cold War and feminism. She wondered whether she could smell the corruption in Washington, actually *smell* it, like onions or sweat or brimstone. As for Willy Borowy, he was happy to go along. He believed that calamity was at hand and wanted to see for himself how the capital would comport itself. Who would supervise the running of the tumbrils on Pennsylvania Avenue? And if it turned out to be another carnival act — well, Nantucket was only a few hours away.

At first Sylvia was disconcerted. She had forgotten how pretty the city was, how spacious and composed its vistas. The autumn of 1973 was a masterpiece, long golden afternoons that seemed to last forever. The streets smelled of leaves and fresh-baked bread. Each day she took meandering walks to reacquaint herself, strolling along the towpath and in Rock Creek Park, up M Street and Pennsylvania Avenue to Lafayette Square, along Embassy Row to the National Cathedral, and at last to Soldiers Cemetery opposite Echo House. She took a turn around the winding footpaths, stopping at the Behl plot and obscurely pleased to find it beautifully manicured. The old senator's stone was shrouded by Behlbaver roses. Then Sylvia turned to look at Echo House, the mansion grander and surlier than ever behind its high iron gates. Axel was not at home.

She realized that the city was much changed from the leisurely capital of the prewar and postwar years, busier, larger, and somehow more settled, certainly more aware of itself and much, much richer. Georgetown was the neighborhood of choice now, as it had been since the late nineteen-fifties, and it was easy to see why, the redbrick and clapboard Federal architecture so solemn and formal, the cobblestone streets and narrow sidewalks and stately shade trees a superb environment for the newly prosperous and very public Washingtonians. Easy to cast back in time. Someone told her he almost had a heart attack one day on N Street when he saw a forty-year-old Jack Kennedy tool by in a powder blue Pontiac convertible, his arm around a spectacular honey blonde in red sunglasses — and then he saw the truck with the cameras and realized it was a television movie.

I knew Jack Kennedy well, he said. Jack was my buddy.

God, it gave me a start. I thought it was 1960.

And everything since had been a nightmare.

Sylvia picked up the paper one morning to find a grumpy statement from Axel complaining about the moral tone of the administration, appalling and disgraceful. He compared the Nixon administration to Rome in its decadence. She almost laughed out loud; scratch Axel and you found Cotton Mather. Axel proposed that the senior staff of the White House resign over the squalid Watergate affair. She had yet to grasp the details of the crime; it seemed fundamentally French in its subtlety and complexity; but each day it grew, now a puddle, now a pool. No one could keep the details straight, but it was obvious that something somewhere was fishy, and that Nixon was responsible; and then the tapes came to light. Willy Borowy could not contain his enthusiasm.

They've got him now, Willy said. They've got his actual language, the language of a race-baiting roughneck. And that will become the issue. He's finished. Washington cannot abide the common speech, the words that people actually use, the petty evasions and nuance and exaggeration and resentment and hatred of the other. They want all Presidents to talk like Lincoln or FDR. They want words you can chisel in marble.

He's let them down, you see.

Just as they knew he always would.

Poor bastard; they'll ride him out of town on a rail.

It's a matter of revenge, Willy said.

So they can think better of themselves.

Sylvia remembered years back, the summer she left Axel, there was a scandal in the Truman White House. She couldn't remember what it was, but it, too, was appalling and disgraceful and suggestive, if not of Rome then of Kansas City. Whole evenings were devoted to worried conversations about the accidental President and his entourage, cronies from Missouri and worse. Hawaiian shirts, poker and bourbon, coarse language.

She listened one night until she thought she would lose her mind
from boredom and then brought the table to a full stop with an
impromptu monologue describing her hydraulic theory of gossip in the capital, the first draft of scandal tasted on the higher
slopes of northwest Washington, a leak of the purest spring
water, only a few drops but sufficient to inspire a mighty thirst.
The source was impeccable, so the water was allowed to flow
unimpeded, and as it meandered downhill it gathered force,
joined here and there by other streams more agitated and less
pristine, streams whose sources were obscure and therefore be-
witching, the sort of fountain sought by explorers for centuries. In Washington, provenance was all; and if the provenance
was suspicious or disreputable, it was at least within possibility's
realm that one was tasting — nectar. Meaning: spillover into the
Oval Office itself.

Axel said, Sylvia, shut up.

I like it, Ed Peralta said. It's ingenious —

People folded their napkins and rolled their eyes as she continued, leak to freshet, freshet to torrent, carving an ever-deeper
channel and at last slipping its banks, muddy now and eddying,
thick with debris, a furious Amazon of rumor and speculation
and innuendo — and at about that point it overflowed into the
newspapers. A reporter dipped his cup into the flood and shared
its miscellaneous contents, by then so corrupted that it was impossible to separate the leak from the trickle and the stream from
the freshet and the freshet from the torrent. All the sources were
given equal weight, because they were indivisible and fungible as
well, so many blue serge suits hanging on a plain pipe rack,
declining to be identified by name. And at last, the scandal fea-
tured on the evening news and again and again on page one of
the newspaper; people would gasp audibly and observe, "If you
made that up, no one would believe it."

For the very good reason — Sylvia in full voice now as she
flew into her concluding aria — that it was made up, most of it,
a yarn woven from the blue serge suits. Washingtonians were the
last Americans who actually believed what they read, and the
more bizarre the story, the more timely and reliable it seemed;

in any case, impossible to ignore. Are you still with me? Sylvia inquired mischievously as the company shifted uncomfortably and someone muttered, Gramercy Park gibberish. So they stood nervously on the beach and watched the boat sink and the sharks begin to gather.

The difference between then and now: much was withheld in the old days when there were only a hundred people in the world and they all knew one another. Inside information was similar to a precious stone; its value depended on its purity and scarcity. It was obvious that where there was smoke there was fire, and the ones at the highest elevations of the city disregarded the smoke and investigated the fire in order to extinguish it. It seemed to Sylvia thirty years later that it was the smoke that mattered, the fire be damned; and in the clumsy efforts to scatter the smoke, the fire raged out of control. As pandemonium became general she listened to people complain that they had never expected things to go so haywire. Watergate seemed such a simple matter and suddenly it wasn't simple. One scandal followed another. Courageous, brilliant reporting and disinterested, creative editing would bring down Nixon at last. The presidency itself was in the balance — yet the commotion was threatening the stability of the government, straining the fragile threads that bound the leaders to the led. This was an unintended consequence, Washington itself on trial. Someone had to put a stop to it; otherwise —

He is destroying himself, they said. Will he destroy us as well? Nixon himself was a cancer on the community.

In early December Sylvia encountered Ed Peralta on Wisconsin Avenue. His hair was white and thin and he walked in a kind of belligerent crouch. She almost missed him in the crowd of shoppers, but something about the set of his shoulders caused her to look twice, and when he smiled at something he saw in the window of the bookstore, she knew it was Ed. She followed him as he checked his watch and continued his slow stroll. She wondered if he was meeting someone, but she decided from his manner that he was only out for a walk; strange, since it was a chilly weekday, early in the afternoon. She followed him past the jewelry store, reluctant to disturb him. Ed looked so private, hands plunged into the pockets of his Burberry, head down, hatless. She came up to touch him on the shoulder, when suddenly he wheeled to face her, his face red and contorted with rage, his blue eyes blazing, though without force. Alarmed, she took a step backward; and then she winked at him.

"You've been on my back for ten minutes and I don't like it. Get away from me. Go back where you came from. I have nothing to say to you people now or in the future, God damned vultures —"

"Ed, it's Sylvia Behl."

He blinked. "Sylvia?"

"I didn't mean to startle you."

"My God, it's you," he said, and gave a little half-laugh. "I thought you were a reporter. I thought you were one of Slyde's people."

"No, just me."

"I apologize, talking to you like that, but they're all over the place. Bastards won't let me alone."

"Ed, what's going on?"

"Sylvia, where have you been?"

"An island," she said. "I've been living on Nantucket."

Ed Peralta laughed, shaking his head. That explained it. Still, they had newspapers in Nantucket.

She said, "So? Who's Slyde?"

"Bastard newspaper columnist who thinks he's my biographer. I'll tell you about it later."

Over coffee, they caught up. Of course he had seen her name here and there over the years and congratulated her on her success. He admitted that he had no time for poetry himself but Billie had faithfully bought all her books and read them and admired them, really. I'm happy for you, he said. It's good to have recognition late in life. Better late than early, because you can take time to enjoy it. He gazed at her fondly and said she looked like a million dollars. She thought she heard insincerity. She told him about Nantucket and persuading Willy to move to

Washington for a while; it had been so long, and she wanted to reacquaint herself, see what had changed and what hadn't changed. She hadn't been in touch with any of the old crowd, and Alec was away on business. She thought she might even buy a house. It's Willy who looks like a million dollars, she added.

Nothing much has changed here, Ed said.

Or I'm so close to it I haven't noticed.

When she asked him if Axel still provided lunch on Wednesdays, Ed said that he did, always the same menu, always the same crowd, Harold Grendall, André Przyborski, and Lloyd Fisher. Sometimes Red Lambardo showed up. Red was a younger fellow, in the thick of things. Harold was still working for the old outfit and naturally André continued to agitate for the liberation of Poland. Lloyd was into this and that. And Alec joined them occasionally when he was free. It was always helpful to get a younger perspective on the situation, and Alec was very well connected on the Hill and downtown. His practice was thriving now that he was doing Lloyd's heavy lifting, Lloyd so often out of town. Alec's a fine young man, Sylvia. You should be proud.

"I am," she said. "Is Axel?"

"Now, Sylvia," Ed said.

"Are they speaking?"

"Of course they're speaking. Axel has high regard for Alec, who he is, what he does."

"Huh-uh," she said.

"Axel doesn't go overboard, but that's his way."

"No kidding," she said.

"Alec represented me in the late unpleasantness," Ed said, looking at Sylvia closely for a reaction, and when there was none he concluded that she had been telling the truth moments before, when she said she did not know of his trouble. They were crowded together at a small table at Arthur's Café, only the two of them in a corner of the room. "Axel asked him to do it. He did a fine job, too, with a difficult brief. At least I'm not in jail. But I'm not employed, either. Someone had to go, and it was me. They put a bullet in the chamber, spun the chamber, and fired.

The bullet missed Harold but it got me on ricochet. A lucky shot, not Alec's fault."

"What was it all about?" she asked.

Ed mumbled something and turned his head this way and that, as if to ease a stiff neck. She knew he was scrutinizing the room, assembling his thoughts, collecting bits and pieces from the various locked drawers of his mind, deciding what was worth showing and what wasn't.

"Axel's bank," he said, and that was all he said for a long moment, allowing the silence to gather. "Longfellow's bank, the one Axel bought and the government used when it was necessary that there be absolute secrecy, private transactions that were in the national interest and for the national security. When you had to get money to someone very quickly and without red tape and fifty pieces of paper." He sighed and lowered his voice, although there was no one within earshot. "Fully audited."

"Of course," Sylvia said when he paused again and she feared he would not go on, because he may have said too much. She had only the dimmest idea of what he was trying to tell her.

"The fool taxpayers didn't lose a single penny. As a matter of fact, the bank made money. *Everyone* made money, including the taxpayers. Carl Buzet ran a tight ship, and our section was more efficient than Chase Manhattan." He was looking off into the middle distance, a dreamy look on his face. "But that wasn't the way it looked to the Senate Committee. It looked to the Senate Committee as if we had set up a proprietary, stuffed it with government funds, and skimmed the profits for ourselves, all the while hiding behind the statutes that protect the national security. They accused us of profiteering with public money. And we never did, I swear it. Naturally we lost some funds; you always do. It's spillage and part of the cost of doing business with dubious characters. We're not Boy Scouts, and the people we dealt with aren't Boy Scouts. So we'd make a bad investment, put our faith and trust in the wrong man, buy long when we should have sold short. It's obvious that some of the accounts were irregular. They had to be, for Christ's sake, the people we were paying off —"

"Ed," Sylvia said, and put a finger to her lips.

"— were taking mortal risks," his voice now a whisper, "so the accounts were set up in the name of aliases, dummy corporations, and so forth."

She nodded, getting a little closer now to the heart of the matter.

"The bullet nicked me and young Alec stepped in to stop the bleeding. It was a god damned witch hunt, you want to know the truth, and it's not ended yet. We got a little careless, no question. Not with the accounts themselves but with the disbursements. Success went to our heads; we'd been doing it for twenty-five years with no headaches. It's the crumbs that'll trip you up every time, stuff you don't worry about because it's so god damned small. The residue of design, if you get my meaning. After a perfect little gem of an operation in Munich, André, another chap, and I had an evening at Kempinski's and somehow the bank picked up the tab and paid it from an open account, just a simple mistake, almost a clerical error. We decided to have a nice dinner to celebrate our success. And that was what the investigator from the Senate Committee discovered. Piddling little supper after one of the most brilliant coups in the history of our intelligence service, worthy of a night out."

"A scandal," she said.

"Big scandal," Ed said. "Red Lambardo's work. Alec's known him for years. He moonlights here and there, always free lance, always per diem, you know the type; sweeps up more dirt than a vacuum cleaner, doesn't care who he works for. Lambardo somehow got the itemized bill from Kempinski's, the cocktails, the caviar, the sea bass, the Sacher tortes, the Mumm's, the Cognac and the cigars, and of course the car and driver we hired. Spies' Night Out, he called it and leaked the memo to one of the papers, and I go up to the Hill to testify because the director asks me to. 'Explain to them what you were doing but not why you were doing it,' the director said, and I replied, 'Aye, aye,' and did what I was told. And I got hung out to dry." He drummed his fingers on the table and took out a cigarette, holding it lengthwise under his nose. "It was a good thing that Alec knew this Lambardo, because the affair could have been much, much worse than it turned out to be."

"What did Alec do?"

"Probably there was something that Lambardo wanted, and Alec got it for him."

Sylvia said, "Was it money?"

Ed said, "Probably not. It would lead to money but it wouldn't *be* money. Maybe it would lead to something else, and the something else would lead to money."

Sylvia was silent a moment. Then she said, "Is that what Alec does? Get things for people?"

"He's a lawyer. That's what lawyers do."

Sylvia managed a smile and shook her head. "Elizabeth Bishop says that this is our worst century so far, and I think I agree with her."

"Bishop. Isn't she over at the Democratic National Committee?"

"She's a poet, Ed."

"And she doesn't know squat. You think this century is bad, try the fourteenth."

"Isn't it great how things have improved?"

"Alec and Lambardo were friends back in the Kennedy administration. That was quite a bond for people who were in government for the first time; they never forgot it. The friendships were forever and they took the assassination personally, like a death in the family, and never forgave poor Lyndon. It was like being comrades in the war except that the war ended in triumph and the Kennedy administration didn't and later when they thought about it — I think it gave them an excuse for their own inattention. And it was all so public, you see, on television day and night, their grief so palpable and exposed." Ed lit his cigarette with a brass lighter, then slid the lighter across the table to Sylvia. It bore an unfamiliar insignia and the inscription *To E.P. from A.B.,* the letters almost effaced now from years of use. "Maybe it gave them a regard for publicity that the rest of us don't have."

"Alec was never in the government," Sylvia said.

"When you live in Washington, you're in the government."

"He's a lawyer," Sylvia said.

"A lawyer who charged me a hell of a fee."

"Well," she said, and began to laugh.

"I didn't have to pay it. Others paid it and God knows he earned it, but, Jesus, it was a hell of a fee." He looked away, and then back at her. "Actually it was Axel's idea to get Alec involved, because Alec and Lambardo knew each other and could talk without finishing their sentences, as Axel put it. It's a kind of code they have. You know how these things work."

Sylvia turned the lighter over, the brass soft beneath her fingers. She murmured, "Not really."

"I have a code in my business, too. We all do in this city, and each code's different so you need all the ciphers."

"Axel," she began.

"Was quite insistent," he said. "And no question, it's always better if there's a relationship between adversaries, some sort of shared past. Water seeks its own level. The point's to reach an agreement without breaking too much crockery. You have to know where the fault lines are and when to use smoke and when to use mirrors, and when a simple *yes* or *no* suffices, and what those words mean beyond what they say. Meaning: *what they lead to.* Alec calls it the art of testimony, and you need as many colors on your paintboard as Sandro Botticelli. Believe me, Sylvia, you concentrate and you concentrate hard."

Ed remembered the immense near-empty hearing room, with its high ceilings and wainscot paneling, indirect lighting too dim to read by, Lambardo at one end of the curved dais, speaking quietly into the microphone, staring all the while at Alec even though his questions were not directed at Alec, speaking through a little curl of a smile. He felt an oppressive sense of occasion, something momentous, as if the ghosts from hearings past had begun to gather round, McCarthy and Welch, Hoffa and Bobby Kennedy, vicious little indoor duels conducted under klieg lights. He thought he could hear them whispering in the corners of the room, a sound like the rustle of leaves; and then he understood that it was only the hum of the air conditioner. Lambardo was superbly relaxed, wearing a red tie and red suspenders and speaking in an unidentifiable drawl, part Bronx, part Boston, with Richmond there somewhere. He habitually dropped his *g*'s. Five senators, three from the majority and two from the minority, lounged back in their chairs while Lambardo interrogated. Occasionally they shook their heads or lit a cigarette but said nothing, because the hearing was closed, no press and no spectators, and Lambardo was the designated inquisitor. It was his investigation. He was following the paper trail piece by piece, and when he approached the bank itself and the use the government had made of it, his questions became longer and vaguer and — off the point. Lambardo concentrated on the one open account, and the committee members drifted away. Ohio began to doze, and Michigan and Idaho to read documents from their briefcases. No aides were allowed, because the hearing was operating under the strictest security procedures. He remembered receiving a nudge from Alec, the signal to enter into the *yes* and *no* phase of the dialogue, the moment of maximum danger, each answer leading him farther into the swamp. He concentrated fiercely, considering each question for a few moments before replying, often adding "to my knowledge" or "to the best of my recollection." That was the art of testimony, crafting simple answers to complex questions; you had to decide which part of the question you were answering. As the questions became increasingly ambiguous, he felt Alec relax. All the time he sat at the long table, sweat dribbling down his back, leaning forward to speak clearly and to give an impression of forthrightness, although his memory was necessarily limited owing to the passage of time. He thought of himself hanging from a limb, the noose tightening, the stallion beneath him rearing. And abruptly they were back in the pleasant ambiance of Kempinski's, the banquettes and the chandeliers, the Champagne, the *Brunnenkresse Salat mit Kalbsbries und Trüffel,* the *Seebarsch mit Sauerampfer,* the *Kaffee,* and Cognac later.

"And that wasn't the only time you dined lavishly at the expense of the taxpayers, was it?"

Hard to keep a straight face now, but he answered in the same monotone. No, it wasn't. And he gave the opposite answer when asked if the open account at Longfellow's was for the exclusive use of senior officers on duty in Europe, the question that went to the heart of the matter, though its phrasing was clumsy.

"What was the nature of the relationship between your agency and the Longfellow bank?"

And he had replied, "The usual relationship. It was reciprocal."

"You mean, between a bank and its customer?"

"That's correct," he'd said.

"So your agency had an interest in Longfellow's bank."

This was statement, not question, and he had paused again, looking at Lambardo, remembering Alec's observation that verbs were not always the weak links in the enemy order of battle; nouns were cowardly as well, and now he focused on the noun *interest*, a word that could mean either *curiosity* or *stake*, and chose a Schweik-word of his own in reply.

"Certainly," he'd said.

Lambardo spoke softly into the microphone. "Isn't it true then that, strictly speaking, your agency was operating outside its own guidelines in" — and here Lambardo hesitated, having become mired in his own trench — "maintaining this unusual interest, wouldn't you agree?"

"Strictly speaking," he replied. "Yes."

"And you were the responsible officer?"

Now the answer that he had rehearsed with Alec, an answer that was both true and false. The senators were alert, Ohio and Michigan lighting fresh cigarettes, Idaho tapping his pencil impatiently, the three of them frowning at him from their great height; he remembered the American flag hanging limply from its standard behind them. Lambardo waited.

He said, "I was the responsible officer, yes," adding, as if to ensure precision in the effort to be entirely candid, "at that time."

Lambardo said quickly, "And could this be characterized as a rogue operation?" Perhaps he did not realize that there was no antecedent to "this." "This" what? But Ed was able to answer no. It was perhaps unwise. Certainly mistakes had been made. But, no, it was not a rogue operation. He would give them most of what they wanted, but he would not give them that. And when Lambardo asked him whether he was aware of the penalties for perjury, he replied that he was.

"Would you then reconsider your answer?"

Alec nudged him again but he was calm in his answer, a simple no.

Ed realized now that he had been silent. What had she said to him? It was something about Axel.

He smiled. "So when you enter the swamp, you need a friendly guide. Not that every little bit of quicksand is marked. Sometimes the guide knows only one trail in a swamp of many trails."

Sylvia smiled back, nodding as if she understood. She was trying to pick her way through the thicket of water levels, shared pasts, fault lines, and swamps. Ed had quite a way with a metaphor, except that his metaphors tended to cancel each other out. But he was talking to her as an equal or near-equal, and she knew that if she listened carefully, somewhere beneath the fleshy folds of his language she would hear a heartbeat, the soul of some living thing. She said mildly, "So it was Axel's idea to bring my son into it, for his friendships, and for his smoke and his mirrors."

Ed nodded. "I was of two minds," he said.

"And what was the other one?"

"I thought it would be better to have someone more visible, someone who'd make the senators sit up a little straighter, pay attention to the proceedings, treat you with respect, because maybe, sometime in the future, *they'd* need help from Mr. Visible. A dubious campaign contribution, sexual mischief, a grand jury summons, malfeasance or misconduct, the usual petty blackmail or extortion. At that time it's mighty handy to have Mr. Clifford or Mr. Williams on your side, explaining things. I thought I could use someone of that distinction and weight. But Axel argued that that was precisely the wrong approach, because the Washington Visibles come with a reputation and an entourage. Word gets around that they've been retained; it's a bullhorn to the god damned press. Wait a minute, this is serious, there's something nasty afoot, something embarrassing to the government, perhaps to the President. Clifford or Williams guarantees publicity and sometimes that's what the client needs. Sometimes you want to try the case in the press because you sure as hell don't want to try it in front of a jury or judge, or the Select Committee on Intelligence. But that wasn't what we wanted. Axel didn't want it and I guess I didn't want it, either. My superiors didn't want it. The habits of a lifetime die hard, Sylvia. People in my business live comfortably in the shadows. We do not care for daylight. Moreover, it was obvious that Lambardo was the key. He was running the investigation. So when Axel pointed out that he and Alec had the kind of relationship where they didn't have to use verbs in their sentences, et cetera, I went along. We put the case in Alec's hands."

"Yes," she said slowly. "I see."

"And the truth is, you can always rent a Visible for an hour to make a telephone call and explain what the situation really is as opposed to what it appears to be. These proceedings are always political and therefore it's a question of point of view. It has nothing to do with law and nothing to do with ethics. It has to do with optics. The lawyer's job is to make absolutely certain that everyone understands that there's more than one point of view, each with its own primary colors. The Visibles are experts at building up one and tearing down the other. My Botticelli is superior to your Picasso, that figure with two noses and three eyes and a hole in her stomach. They aren't lawyers, really. They're opticians, each with his own eye chart."

She said, "I suppose Alec wouldn't be good at that."

He looked at her strangely. "He's very good at it. And he'll be better still when he has some age, gray in his hair, and can stand with them on an equal footing. Washington's a hierarchy; everyone knows that. He needs a shared past with Senator X or Congressman Y, so he can call them on the telephone and invite them to the Metropolitan Club and say, Bill, let me tell you what this is about really. Let me show you the skeletons in these closets. When he can do that, he'll become a Visible. Until then he has Lambardo and I suppose other Lambardos here and there. And pretty soon he'll move on from Red Lambardo to the chairman of the Senate Judiciary Committee. When he has that, he can expect calls from the White House asking his advice on matters of some sensitivity."

"In all this," she said hurriedly, "the hearing and the preparation for the hearing and so forth and so on" — she caught herself, realizing suddenly that she was beginning to sound like him — "where was Axel?"

Ed leaned across the table and laughed his half-laugh, more grunt than laugh. "Where was Harold Grendall?"

"No, really," she said.

"Yes, *really*," he mimicked, not unkindly but amused that he was obliged to explain Axel to Sylvia, of all people. Sylvia had the usual female blind spots, but she wrote the book on Axel. "When the hearing began, Axel was out of town. He was in Spezia with La Bella Figura. She was filming."

"You were in the witness chair while he was on a yacht?"

"Be realistic, Sylvia. He couldn't've done anything if he was here. Everyone thought it best that he get out of town, though there was some discussion that in the unlikely event that they'd subpoena him, he could show up with Paulina in her sunglasses and minidress to distract the committee. They're easily distracted, believe me. Paulina was all for it. I think she thought she'd win an Academy Award." Ed laughed, remembering that Alec hadn't thought it funny. And from the look on her face, Sylvia didn't either. "He telephoned every day."

"That was big of him."

"It wasn't his fight," Ed said.

"So they never touched him," Sylvia said.

"Axel," he said patiently. "Axel's a force of nature. No one laid a glove on Axel. They never do. Axel's always way, way back in the woodwork, wearing his usual camouflage. That's where he lives, heard but not seen. Axel's bulletproof. The bullet hasn't been invented that could wound Axel Behl. You know that, Sylvia. You know that better than anyone. Axel's the one who makes things happen, never takes credit, never shares blame. He's my oldest friend."

She looked at him in disbelief, opening her mouth to reply; and then she noticed that his hands were trembling.

"We've been through the mill together."

"Yes," she said.

"Here and overseas. More than forty years now."

"Yes," she said.

"I don't know what I'd do without him," Ed said.

"But it's Axel's bank," she said softly. "Doesn't that mean he's responsible, too?"

Ed Peralta smiled. Something was nagging at his memory. Sylvia Behl had an unpredictable effect on him. In her company he always had an urge to perform. He had told her things — hinted at them, anyway — that he had not even told Billie. That was because Sylvia was a subtle woman who liked to listen for the thing unsaid. You didn't have to cross every *t* and dot every *i* with Sylvia, even though in the old days she had been an outsider in their community, distrusted by the other women. Everyone wanted to protect Axel, so beaten up in the war. The community's sympathy went to Axel; and that was true today.

"He owns Longfellow's," she added. "It's *his.*"

"Yes, of course," Ed said patiently. "Up to a point, it is. His idea, his man in overall charge. He owns the majority stock. He's chairman. There's no question that Axel made a bundle of money — but why not? Axel doesn't care anything about money, never did, so it's not greed, only a natural consequence of foresight and good management."

She looked at her fingers, listening for sarcasm and not finding it.

Ed shook his head. "You know what I'm saying is true. It's one of Axel's great strengths. Not caring about money."

"There's more to greed than money," she said, knowing that in some abstract way Ed was correct.

"The bank had several divisions," he explained. "In fact it had two divisions, each distinct from the other. One of the divisions was ours even though the bank was Axel's. They could never connect Axel personally to us, not that they tried very hard. They were on a treasure hunt and Axel didn't figure in the treasure. He was not a target. The idea was, Axel was doing his friends in the government a favor and the way the favor was managed was the government's responsibility. Axel's umbrella, our leak. No one wanted Axel to get burned. When Lambardo pressed the matter, the chairman told him to forget it and move along. And that testimony, what testimony there was, was in closed session and so sensitive that it never leaked. An aura surrounds these affairs. There's a specific context, the inquiry is pointed in a certain direction, and it does not waver, unless someone makes a childish mistake, goes beyond his brief, gets too cute . . ." That had happened more than once, to everyone's disadvantage and embarrassment. You had to keep the thing within a closed circle, the action as stylized as a bullfight. He said to her, "The fact that Axel was involved at all gave the operation a sweeter smell than it otherwise might've. I mean legitimacy. Axel's reputation is true blue, and he never refuses a man a favor. He's as close to untouchable as you can get in Washington, unless they change the rules of the bullfight. Maybe some day they'll put the *toro* in the *traje de luces* and make the man fight naked, without a sword." Ed chuckled at that thought, the bull done up like a Madrid grandee and the man bare as the day he was born, the critics cheering the bull, the critics having the final say, the president of the arena as helpless as an usher.

"So there has to be a story," he concluded. "A narrative. They have to connect the dots in order to satisfy —"

"Repressed infantile longings," she said.

"What?"

"Something Freud said."

"That's good," Ed said. "'Repressed infantile longings.' That about sums it up, except there's nothing infantile about the satisfaction. That's grown-up stuff."

"I know, Ed." She reached across the table and touched his hand to reassure him that she was not being cute, devaluing his account. He had not touched his coffee, and now he lit another cigarette with the brass lighter, running his thumb across the inscription. She said, "I was only thinking about connecting the dots and who gets satisfied and who doesn't. It's a child's game, after all."

"Not this game," he said. "They had to have a story for themselves, something plausible. Since no one would ever know the truth of the matter, they had to have something that sounded right, something that fit, something you can pass around to the critics on background. Doesn't the Mad Hatter seem perfectly believable in Alice's world? So they decided that there were a few Agency renegades led by me, the rotten crabapple in the barrel of Golden Delicious. Nothing wrong with the orchard, nothing *systemic*. The renegades went out of control, an appalling example of havoc when discipline breaks down, together with a regrettable lack of oversight on the part of Highest Levels, preoccupied as they were with the shooting war, the one in Southeast Asia, where brave American boys were being killed and wounded. The superb procedures malfunction, the random world taking its usual revenge. The second law of thermodynamics. Heisenberg's law. The law of unintended consequences. Murphy's Law. All heading in the general direction of the criminal law. Mistakes were made, owing to the human factor, and the in-house review will surely result in fresh procedures, even more superb than the procedures that failed, because the same men were putting them in place and everyone knew that experience was the best teacher, no? Can you hear the wagons circling, darling Sylvia? I could, so I fell on my sword."

"Oh, Ed," she said. "Those bastards."

"There was a script and we were all reading from it. And that's where we come to Wilson Slyde. The story broke in Slyde's column, the one he writes with that poolhall Marxist from Boston, the Irishman who went to Harvard and can't forget it and won't let you forget it, either."

"Cowards," she said. Sylvia was still back somewhere between Heisenberg and the law of unintended consequences.

He did not know how much to tell her about Wilson Slyde and Teddy O'Banion. The column was called "Our Side." They were nihilists, read daily in three hundred newspapers. O'Banion drove a Jaguar, so in the privacy of one's own home or office the column was known as the Jig and the Jag. Quite an ambitious piece of work was Wilson Slyde, scholarship boy at Milton, at Yale, at MIT, where he'd graduated with honors, thence to the Defense Department, then Langley, working for Harold Grendall. Hard not to root for Wilson, so bright, so unlikable, son of an army sergeant who served in Bradley's command during the big war and became fascinated with infantry tactics. When he came home he bought every book he could find on the Civil War, building a giant sandtable in his basement, where he refought Second Bull Run, Antietam, Chancellorsville, and Gettysburg. He advanced through the Franco-Prussian War and World War One, imparting all his knowledge and enthusiasm to his son. Wilson wrote his thesis at MIT on the tactical uses of nuclear weapons. When he went to work at Defense, and later at Langley, he wanted to parse the nuclear triad and the electronic battlefield as it applied to NATO and Eastern Europe. But his bosses dealt him the equal opportunity account and sent him around the country talking to the NAACP and the Urban League about what a superb job the administration was doing integrating the armed forces and the security services. He was holding the race card when the card he wanted was the strategy card. So he quit and started "Our Side" with Teddy O'Banion.

"And the first two deal with NATO's eastern flank and Soviet military preparedness and the syndicate people call him to say that while of course he could write anything he damn pleased and the syndicate would never, ever seek to censor him in any way, he could look carefully at his contract and understand that NATO and Soviet Threat were not what newspaper editors had in mind when they bought 'Our Side' by Wilson W. Slyde, Jr., and Edward O'Banion three times a week. Next time, perhaps — Crisis in the NAACP, or What Huey and Eldridge Really Want."

He expected Sylvia to laugh, but instead she shook her head. "That's a sad story."

"Lie down with dogs, get up with fleas."

"It's still a sad story."

"The Jig and the Jag have resentments enough to fill an abyss. So two weeks after my hearing ends and I'm hoping that the affair has blown over and I can return quietly to work, if not in my old job then in another job — you know that no tree crashes in Washington unless it's reported in the newspapers — Slyde commences a series on corruption in the security services, complete with quotes from the transcript. Odd thing is, I come out all right. But Langley is savaged and my cover, what's left of it, is blown. Question is, where did Wilson Slyde get his information?"

"Beats me," she said. "Where?"

He said, "Hard to say. End of story." Of course it could have come from any of the senators in attendance. It could have come from Red Lambardo. But Ed knew that it came from Alec Behl, because Alec was nowhere mentioned until the last piece, and then in sentences so respectful that Slyde might have been writing about Louis Brandeis. Those sentences, so admiring, so without Slyde's usual sarcasm, had the effect of making Alec an instant Visible. Slyde had the subtlety to omit any mention of Axel, and Red Lambardo was mentioned only in passing, "doing the best he could with a bad brief." The Slyde columns were picked up everywhere, even *Time*.

"What do you think?" she said. "Was it Alec?"

"What did he stand to gain?"

"You're right," she said. "He had nothing to gain."

Ed Peralta raised his hands, stretching, looking over her shoulder out the window.

"I wish he hadn't gotten involved."

Ed shrugged.

"Cowards," she said again. "It's Axel's fault."

He did not reply to that; she was off the point, and he had already said too much. The light was failing fast on Wisconsin Avenue; it was close on five o'clock. In his office he never noticed the weather, even the change of seasons. He had lived in an indoor paper world — estimates, proposals, memoranda, situation reports. Newspapers, magazines, an occasional book of current affairs or history, mostly European and New England history. He was born in Rhode Island but had not been back for many years. His family was gone. As a boy he had been a keen sailor and now he could not remember the last time he had been on a boat. His father had owned a Hinckley with teak decks and a set of red sails. A Wampanoag who lived at the boatyard in Jamestown taught him to sail, all the time spinning tales of the tribal lands up near Gay Head on Martha's Vineyard. Much later, Ed thought of his life in the government as similar to an Indian's on a reservation. You hunted on government land and bought your goods at the government store but you maintained your own rituals and worshiped your own gods. You stayed inconspicuous and encouraged your family to stay inconspicuous as well. When your children grew up, they went away. He knew the government's limitations but never wanted any other kind of life. He lived in a government within the government, and was accountable to that government. He liked knowing and not being able to tell what he knew. That, and the satisfaction that came from knowing a job and doing it well, and the many friendships here and abroad.

"Anyone stand up for you, Ed? Anyone at all?"

"Jesus Christ, Sylvia." He sighed, exasperated now. He had done everything but draw her a blueprint. She had been away from Washington for too long, had forgotten how things worked, how they had to work for the government to function. Sometimes you needed to sacrifice; that was the way it was set up. You could not believe the incoherence of the government until you had been inside it, attended the meetings and read the memoranda, the way things rocked and rolled on their own motion; you practiced damage control and then one day the fire was too big to contain and someone had to stand up. Someone had to say, "It's me, I'm responsible," particularly if he wasn't. Confession in hand, the arsonists agreed to take their gasoline and go home. They had to have a trophy, something to show for all the hard work they'd done.

"That was the point," he said patiently. "Keep everyone else away, far from the heat and the glare. Give them enough smoke and they'll forget about the fire. No character witnesses in my trade except sotto voce, over drinks at a party or in someone's office. Listen, Ed Peralta's a good man, got his cock caught in the wringer, maybe there's more here than meets the eye, maybe less, but Ed's okay, been with us a long time, don't crucify him. That's why your Alec was a godsend. Alec and his quiet manner. Alec and his friendships. Alec, his smoke and his mirrors. Best of all, Alec son of Axel."

She closed her eyes and did not speak. She remembered telling Alec years ago that she had never felt competent as a mother. Part of what she said was her usual exaggeration, but there was truth there, too, when she confided that she knew plenty but didn't think that what she knew had value for a child. She should have thought again, because her timidity had thrust her son into Axel's orbit as surely as if she had sent him aloft on a rocket. Now he was too far away to be seen by the naked eye.

"They're not cowards," Ed said.

"Would you call them friends?"

"My best, my closest friends," he said firmly.

"It's a terrible story you've told me, Ed. And so — meaningless."

He smiled broadly but did not want to begin a discussion on meaninglessness. It only led you into assassinations and war, to no profit. He was looking out the window again, watching the passersby on Wisconsin Avenue. He was trying to remember the Wampanoag's name and failing.

He said, "I hated doing it. I hated it personally, do you see? But there I was in the box. My friends were in other boxes . . ." He stopped suddenly, remembering the name, Alfred something. When the war came he joined the Merchant Marine for the wages; and if he was on the North Atlantic run, his chances were about one in five. He had forgotten what he was saying to Sylvia. That was what happened when you were out of the loop. You picked up bad habits, such as wanting to perform in front of attractive women. He did not think he had said too much and he thought that she of all people would understand life's ironies and paradoxes and where loyalties lay. Sylvia always had a grasp of the machine and was never bewitched by the purring of the gears, and that was why in the early days she was not trusted. She'd refused to shed her Gramercy Park skin. Even Axel had his doubts; and with that, his memory did another turn.

Sylvia saw the shadow cross his face, his eyes sliding away to the ceiling. She believed she had been too harsh with him and now asked gently what his plans were.

He said, "I do some consulting here and there, carefully. I have to keep my hand in somewhere to stay alive. I used to play a little tennis, but my doctor said that was a no-no. Now I sit around and read the newspapers, take a walk, and have lunch with the boys on Wednesday unless it's all business, and then I stay away. Did I tell you that Lambardo is sometimes there? He and Axel have gotten quite close. And La Bella Figura sometimes has a cocktail with us before we sit down."

She nodded. Paulina seemed to be all things to all men.

"I watch a ballgame on television. Once in a while someone calls me up and I agree to consult, read his tea leaves for him." He was looking at her strangely, remembering something specific and wondering if he should say anything. "Billie's got quite a thriving real estate business, did you know that? She and Alice Grendall."

"I heard," Sylvia said.

"You can't believe the prices," he said.

She laughed and said she could.

"I hate not working," he said.

Sylvia glanced at her watch. She and Willy had plans to see an early movie.

"I owe you an apology," Ed said abruptly.

"Don't worry," she said lightly. "Your secrets are safe with me. I don't understand them anyway."

"Not that," he said.

His tone of voice had changed and he was looking directly into her eyes.

"That woman," he said. "Years ago. You know the one I mean. I can't remember her name."

Sylvia knew at once that he meant Mrs. Pfister.

"The one who lived in Falls Church."

"What about her?" Sylvia said.

"She told fortunes."

"Yes," Sylvia said.

"We were involved."

She looked at him blankly, having no idea what he meant.

"We were listening," he said.

"You were listening to Mrs. Pfister?"

"There were so many people in and out. It seemed to us that half the State Department was visiting Mrs. Pfister, or at least their wives were. The news spread very quickly; you'd be surprised. And later on, years later, she attracted a real following, even some of the Kennedy people. What were we to think? At first she seemed harmless enough; swamis are a dime a dozen in northern Virginia. But then we received evidence —"

"What evidence?" Sylvia demanded. "Evidence of what?"

He did not reply immediately.

"What evidence?" she said again.

"I can't remember precisely what it was, or how we got it. It was information that we obtained. Someone talked or we sent someone over to check her out. We didn't know who she was or where she came from or who her friends were, and the séances were more than personal. It wasn't only health and love life, the way you'd expect, but other kinds of gossip, family business, finances. Then the husbands got interested and went to her to ask about government matters, personnel changes and their own futures. Foreign policy dilemmas. In the beginning we thought she was only a fad, like hula hoops or margaritas, and that she would fade, like any fad. But she didn't fade. You know Washington, everyone so quick to enlist, whether it's a hairdresser or a tailor or the new swinging freshman senator or a rising hostess. We were worried; who was she anyway? And what did she do with the information she learned? *We didn't know her provenance,* Sylvia."

"So you listened in."

"Yes."

"Eavesdropped."

"Yes."

"On me. With Mrs. Pfister."

"That's correct."

"And others," she said.

"Others, too."

"As we talked about our personal lives, ourselves and our husbands and what the future held. The things that were in our hearts."

"Some of it was personal, some of it wasn't."

"And how did you listen, Ed?"

"It's simple enough," he said. "Even then, with the basic technology we had. Nothing like today. Of course the tapes were very poor quality. They had to be enhanced."

"And who did the enhancing?"

"Our lads," he said.

"Your lads," she said pleasantly, the image evoking a troop of Boy Scouts bent over a tape machine. She was concentrating on keeping her voice level, as if this were any ordinary afternoon conversation.

"Even then there were some rough spots."

"I'll bet there were."

"Hard to hear."

"What did you hear, Ed?"

"It's too long ago; I can't remember. The usual things, bedroom problems, children problems. Indifference. Anxiety. Problems with parents. The men were more direct, I mean practical. I know that a few of the State Department boys were transferred overseas. They'd been indiscreet. You'd think they'd have had more sense, a swami in Falls Church."

"You'd think so," she said.

"The thing was." He looked at his hands and laughed his half-laugh, shaking his head in wonder. "She was amazing, some of her predictions and her excavations of the past. She was a phenomenon. We tried to figure out how she did it, but we never did. It was all so counterintuitive."

"Yes, she was a phenomenon."

"Well, she didn't have everything. She got things wrong. She'd confuse one event with another. But less often than you'd expect."

"And naturally everyone had a file."

"Of course," he said proudly. "We were scrupulous."

"There was a file on me, for example."

"That was nodis. Specifically you, nodis."

"What does that mean, Ed?"

"No distribution." When she said nothing, only looked at him pleasantly as if they had been discussing the weather or any neutral topic, he added, "It was kept personally by me for safekeeping. No one else saw it."

"Except your superiors," she said.

He shrugged at that.

"And the lads."

"For the enhancement," he said.

"And Axel."

His hands flew off the table and he shook his head vigorously. Not Axel. How could she think such a thing?

"Don't lie to me," she said.

He drew back, offended.

"So," she said, counting on her fingers, "there would be you, your higher-ups, the lads, and Axel. Who else?"

"I began by saying I wanted to apologize," he said stiffly.

"For what, Ed? Making the tapes? Keeping them? Showing them around? What, specifically, are you apologizing for?"

"Try to remember how difficult those days were." He had made a mistake of a kind he didn't often make, talking candidly to a woman. Women took everything personally. That was what you got when you tried to right a wrong, explaining that times had changed —

"Did you think Mrs. Pfister was a Red?" Sylvia laughed unpleasantly, leaning across the table, staring into his wounded face. "Reporting to Moscow, personal to Comrade Stalin?"

"We didn't know," he said.

"Ed," she said. "Save your apology."

"And you don't understand something else, how difficult it

was to keep the surveillance in our hands and out of Hoover's. In his hands the files would've been distributed all over town, congressmen, the Oval Office, this Pfister woman a security risk —" He went on to explain the competition between the agencies, Hoover's resentment, the never-ending struggle over turf and the heroic efforts to keep control of the product. He seemed to think she owed him thanks. But Sylvia was already rising, laying a five-dollar bill on the table, skidding the brass lighter across the table into his lap.

"Just a second now," he said angrily.

"Tell me one thing," Sylvia said. "Did Mrs. Pfister know she was being bugged?"

"I suppose she did," Ed said. "She knew everything else."

Sylvia and Willy lived only a few streets away from Alec and Leila but rarely saw them socially. Alec was very busy and Leila and Sylvia competed fiercely. Mother and son met for lunch once a month at Arthur's, a strained affair that usually ended in argument. Sylvia always managed at least one dig at Leila; and she was filled with rumors concerning Axel. Axel was buying a newspaper. Axel had given millions to the Democratic National Committee. Axel had seen Brezhnev at Tashkent. Axel had been photographed in a restaurant with Lauren Bacall. Axel and Paulina had quarreled and Paulina had returned to Rome, *ciao!,* more or less with Axel's blessing, Axel having grown weary of the Italian temperament. True or false? True, as it turned out, though Alec would neither confirm nor deny. Sylvia was particularly inquisitive about Ed Peralta's troubles, but Alec gave nothing, citing the sacred lawyer-client confidentiality. Superseding that of a mother and son? she demanded. Who exactly is Wilson Slyde? Alec compared the monthly lunch to returning service from Ken Rosewall.

Sylvia bought a house around the corner from the house Jack and Jackie Kennedy had occupied when he was a senator. Tourists were often present, talking in hushed tones and consulting guidebooks; and invariably they would stop in front of the wrong house, the Grendalls' or the Peraltas' across the street, standing on tiptoe and craning their necks to look through the heavy curtains to the darkened rooms within, as if the President and his family still occupied the premises, not Ed Peralta watching the Orioles on TV. Hard to imagine John F. Kennedy as a young senator, and Mrs. Onassis as a young mother still in her thirties. The street retained its unhurried between-the-wars flavor, as if the inhabitants were awaiting the visit of the horse-drawn ice wagon or FDR in his Cadillac, out for a Sunday drive with Daisy Suckley. In the summer the elms clouded the sky, casting the street in deep green shade. From the barnyard of Wisconsin Avenue or M Street anyone entering this neighborhood stepped back four decades or more. On quiet afternoons passersby could hear the music of Schubert or Brahms lingering in upstairs windows, easily imagine the woman of the house crocheting or writing a letter or reading a novel. Somewhere the ring of a telephone and the tap-tap of a typewriter competed with the whirr of hummingbirds; and then a sudden jarring chaos of jet engines as aircraft descended over Georgetown University and the Potomac River into DCA. In its evident somnolence and contentment the street recalled the quality districts of Richmond or Charleston, the chivalrous Old South of white magnolias and black maids in starched uniforms fetching the evening paper from the brick stoop, and then sweeping the stoop.

There were signs of wear and tear here and there, chipped paint and damaged clapboard and mottled brightwork, maintenance put off from one year to the next, owing to uncertainty; and it was hard finding someone who could do the work properly, who understood the original materials. Cars labored slowly on the cobblestones, careful to avoid the beer cans here and there in the gutter, debris from university revels the night before; no arrests, but a student was injured and a window was broken in the house next door to the Peraltas', Ed watching from his living room with a loaded Beretta in the pocket of his dressing gown, a circumstance that alarmed his wife when he told her later. Whatever happened to Georgetown University? It used to be the nicest school.

Sylvia began to enjoy herself in Washington, even reaching a truce with Ed Peralta, who sent her a dozen roses after their quarrel at Arthur's. She had become fascinated by the war after meeting Wilson Slyde, so hip and easy with his Chiclets smile and street slang, his panther's body and upper-class tastes. Wilson wore bespoke suits and a gold Rolex and drank only Courvoisier and soda. She was near hypnotized, listening to him talk about the war, wondering why so many of the body bags were filled by black boys. Listen up here, you folks ever thought of forming a Princeton Brigade, sort of like the Abraham Lincoln Brigade in Spain, take some of the heat off my peasants? I mean a fine brigade of congressmen's sons and senators' sons, Cabinet secretaries' sons, sons of the White House staff, Mr. Charlie to fight the Charlies, you hear what I'm saying to you? Of course the war had dropped from view, over the horizon of Watergate. But Wilson would not let it go, returning again and again; and very late in the evening muttering how proud he was of his work in the early days of the war convincing the NAACP and the Urban League what a superb job the Army had done integrating the infantry, bringing full citizenship to all those black boys.

Sylvia looked forward to evenings at the Grendalls' or Peraltas', mainly because Wilson was usually there, smiling his cat's smile while he flirted, so cool when he occasionally admitted them to the world they knew only from their television screens and James Baldwin's books. They thought he had a secret and if they got to know him well enough he would tell them what it was, like Salk with his vaccine or Freud with Dora's hysteria. They thought Wilson knew the terrain of the black heart, not only what Huey and Eldridge wanted but what all blacks everywhere wanted and would settle for. Was the black heart divided against itself? The table fell silent when Wilson spoke, unless it was a military subject, the capability of the North Vietnamese Army or the Israeli Defense Force or the utility of the swing-wing F-III. Wilson's was the only black face she ever saw at a dinner table. She always wanted to ask what it meant to him, being the only black key on the Steinway, but she never did, because she knew he would turn her aside with some black jive she wouldn't understand or understand all too well.

Of course there were others at the table, strange characters from FDR's third term or Truman's first, a lawyer who had helped out at Nuremberg, an editor, and always a mysterious foreigner, a British M.P. or a French banker or Swedish diplomat, or the Israeli scholar, a geographer, it turned out, whose specialty was archaeological sites in the Sinai Peninsula and the Golan Heights, the sites in such proximity to Cairo and Damascus that you could see the glow of the cities after dark. Sylvia eavesdropped as Leila Berggren moved in, flattering him, inviting him to lunch at the Institute to give a presentation to her colleagues — and laughed out loud when he agreed at once, of course, dear lady, my fee is one thousand dollars. And for that I throw in certain neglected political questions, many of them thousands of years old.

The evenings began aimlessly enough but ended focused and fractious around the dinner table, cordials for the women, port for the men, and Courvoisier for Wilson Slyde. At the end of the evening the talk turned to the scandal or the war, sometimes both at once. The foreigners were tactful about the scandal, mostly because its details eluded them; and they admired Nixon. Wilson Slyde attempted to clear things up with the remark that all financial scandals were alike but a political scandal was political in its own way.

Sylvia always waited for Wilson to intervene with a theory, which he was careful to enunciate in a kind of purr, so seductive that listeners were not certain whether he was joking or serious or merely showing off. At the end he could be counted on to provide a little mathematical simile, as if to remind everyone that MIT was still part of his résumé.

This night he proposed that history unfolded like the books of the Bible, yet obvious that some books were more important than others. You could not have the Bible without Exodus, Ecclesiastes, and Job, though you could do without James or Deuteronomy. Without James and Deuteronomy the Bible would be a poorer book, an uncoordinated book, but still a great book.

Job and Ecclesiastes were the Lincoln and Roosevelt administrations, years of great suffering and climactic decisions, momentous years without which the American Republic would be a very different republic. Yet it was only chance that had thrust Lincoln and Roosevelt forward at the propitious moment, unless you believed that the nation was under God's supervision, a proposition that he, for one, doubted. Wilson argued that Lincoln's great soul was present at all times, the *pi* in any discussion of circumference.

Naturally war was the greatest burden, and it always arose from oppression; there were no exceptions to this rule. The present war would have to be endured and its full consequences borne. The war was a burden on every back, though heavier on some backs than others. Indeed on many backs the burden was a feather, though the feather would grow with the years. In time it would become an intolerable weight.

Wilson's right, Ed Peralta said, much as I hate to admit it because he works for the damned newspapers, vultures . . . This was a long speech for Ed, who had grown quiet lately, preferring to listen to the after-dinner arguments instead of participating in them.

In one itty-bitty town in Georgia fifteen boys died, Wilson said. Five of them were given the choice of the Army or the penitentiary so naturally they chose the Army because they'd never heard of Vietnam. They didn't know there was a war on. Didn't teach Vietnam in that one-room schoolhouse they went to, the one with the cracked blackboard and no chalk, and no maps either, so these boys didn't know there was a war on out there in that Asia.

Loyal boys, Harold Grendall said, his voice so low it was almost inaudible. Patriotic boys; they served their country.

Wilson leaned forward and showed all his teeth, an expression somewhere in the vicinity of a smile. He picked up his Cognac and drained it, refilling at once. He opened his mouth to reply, then didn't. The subject was too serious. Just because the fish were in the barrel didn't mean you had to shoot them. Still, someone had to stand up for the troopers.

Wilson said quietly, That's horseshit, Harold. You shouldn't say it. You shouldn't even think it. You dishonor them.

The war is quiet now, Harold said. Our troops are out, mostly.

Unless he decides to reinforce them, Wilson said.

Impossible, Harold said. The plan was to cut and run, and that's what he's done.

Leaving the casualties on the battlefield, Wilson said.

It's late, Sylvia said. She looked at Willy.

Willy said blandly, Does anyone here know them?

No, no one at the table had ever met the Nixons, except for Wilson, who had interviewed him a dozen times, but that was different, a ritual dialogue, a dumb show.

Oh, Harold said, to shake hands with at some embassy function or the Alfalfa Club dinner or the Gridiron. The locker room at Burning Tree, Echo House for one of Axel's birthday parties, in and out in an hour, never drank anything. Thing about him is, he has this enormous head. Biggest head on a small man I've ever seen; you'd recognize him as one of the background figures in a Jan Steen tableau of Amsterdam burghers, his features unmistakably Dutch or German. You have to see him in person. He has specific gravity and draws your attention, and then you notice the head. And inside the head was a large brain, teeming with schemes and populated with his own repertory company of dead or forgotten souls, the Rosenbergs and Hiss and Harry Dexter White and Owen Lattimore, Whittaker Chambers, Jerry Voorhis, Helen Douglas, Checkers, and that bastard Cohn. Play the Nixon card, he'll lead you to trick after trick in every game that's been played in this town for the past twenty-five years. He's a phenomenon, all those suspicious characters crowded into this huge head.

Wilson was staring at Harold, waiting for him to continue. He had the beginnings of a column forming in his mind, something to do with slavery of the body and slavery of the mind, and the Nixon Court.

Go on, Harold, Willy said. This is fascinating.

Harold said, But I can't say that I've passed more than an hour in his company and I've lived in Washington for forty years. I suppose it's a political thing and a social thing, too, if I'm honest about it. He never cared for Yale men. Never cared for intelligence officers either. Maybe he was suspicious of people who knew more secrets than he did. He's been here forever but has never seemed permanent, as we are. He's always returning to someplace else, California or New York. He's always wanted to rule us but never wanted to live among us. He's an alien; he's a product of the West Coast. He brought his West Coast values to our city. He had a terrible mother, you know. He's an unhealthy organism in our midst. Really, he's an intruder. He's the one who breaks into your house and steals the family silver, and violates your wife on his way out. Willy, why are you smiling?

He's been here since nineteen forty-six, Willy said.

And never fit in, Harold said.

Congressman, senator, vice president, President.

It's amazing, isn't it?

I'd say — he fit like a hand in a glove.

Oh, you're wrong there, Willy. He's a low-life.

He's the glove, Willy said.

He wanted it so badly for so long and now he's got it, two terms of the presidency. But he's not satisfied. Of course the object cannot possibly satisfy the desire. It never does.

Sylvia said, Sometimes it does.

Harold said, Hardly ever.

Sylvia said, It would depend on the object, wouldn't it?

The head's too large for the body, Harold said.

Sylvia turned to stare into the cold fireplace. It would not be Steen, master of the decorous domestic life and the voluptuous after-hours, Steen's crowded surfaces: unbuttoned blouses and cracked oyster shells on the tavern floor, spilled beer and a lewd grin below glazed eyes. The wages of wealth, according to Jan Steen. The didactic Steen would be incapable of capturing the incongruity of Nixon's mighty head atop his light and awkward body. The head worked miracles of intrigue while the body lurched and stumbled, the effect that of a virtuoso striking all the right notes while mutilating the tempo. What a dreadful time the President must have had as a boy, to be so undersized and uncoordinated. Of course at schoolboy sports your head could carry you a far distance; the art of evasion was not for the timid or the slow-witted. But eventually the bigger and stronger boy would catch up and beat you senseless. Strength and speed were to an athlete what intuition was to an artist and foresight to a politician. Axel had told her once that a boy never forgot the lesson of the gridiron. Certainly Nixon never did. They used him for a tackling dummy. It would be wonderful to see what Rodin would have done with him, Nixon's head in bronze in the same gallery with Clemenceau and Balzac. Only the head, though. Rodin would leave the body to the viewer's imagination.

You'll be rid of him soon, Willy said.

Yes, Harold said. He's finished. He'll go back to California. That's the last we'll ever see of him.

Wilson Slyde said, The boys at the paper have him over a barrel, and he knows it. So you can argue that it doesn't matter what he does. He has no defense. He's incapable of telling the truth — what good has that ever done him? And it's unprofitable for him to lie. Nothing will change because no matter how fast he runs, the pack will run faster. I wonder if he can hear the baying of the hounds? I'll bet he sees the lynchman's noose in his dreams at night. With Nixon, everything's personal.

Well said, Harold said.

Very interesting, Willy said, his smile as broad as a Halloween jack-o'-lantern. He said, I have a theory; maybe you'd like to hear it. Nixon is Washington's Jew, despised and feared. He's never had full citizenship in the federal city. They don't like his background, altogether too cosmopolitan. They don't like his friends. If only they get rid of Nixon, Washington will be sound once again. They want him to put his pots and pans in his peddler's cart and move along to the next village, where they'll never have to see him or his like again; and his friends, too. Next thing you know, they'll want to pin a yellow star to his blue serge suit —

Oh, Willy, Wilson said. Superb!

7

Trust and the
Perception of Trust

〜

SYLVIA AND WILLY fled to Nantucket after Nixon's resignation. Willy was revolted by the frenzy of self-congratulations,
and Sylvia could not find the struggle so necessary to her work.
The capital went suddenly flat, exhausted by the interminable
crisis; and she was alarmed when she heard that Alec was somehow involved in the conversations between the White House
and the various committees overseeing the impeachment process. Ever conciliatory, Alec was said to have invoked the prece-
dent of General Grant at Appomattox Court House — uncondi-
tional surrender, but tell him he can keep his horses; he will need
them for the spring plowing. All parties sought the most convenient exit in order that the long national nightmare be ended at
last. Or, as Willy observed, things were getting a little too close
to home.

Alec's role was mysterious; and it had to be said that Sylvia
wanted to believe that he had no role at all and it was Axel
meddling behind the scenes. Everyone wanted to have a piece of
the scandal of the century. Not to have one would be like living
in San Francisco in 1906 and sleeping through the earthquake. So
the rumors persisted, one day Alec acting on behalf of the White
House, the next on behalf of one of the congressional commit-

tees. Willy thought that Alec's natural role was to represent both at once, Alec a kind of corporation counsel retained by Washington itself, the authority that was here today and here tomorrow and the day after, Alec the nimble mouthpiece seeking to preserve confidence at a time of terrible uncertainty; put another way, he was a bankruptcy referee protecting assets. Alec himself refused to comment, except to observe in a general way that a citizen had a duty to be helpful. Those who lived in Washington had a special responsibility, because the capital was home, the place where you earned your living, where your children slept; you had a loyalty to it, and it to you. Question, really, of civic pride. So it was natural that any helpful activities would be private, removed from the destabilizing public glare. Don't we all want to think well of ourselves? Nixon's crimes were terrible, but a pardon was necessary.

Filled up with Scotch one night, Willy listened sullenly to yet another assault on Hannah Nixon and the rootless ambiance of Southern California and at the first pause in the conversation introduced the criminal mothers of tyrants past. Tamerlane and his mountain of skulls, Stalin's systematic starvation of ten million Ukrainian peasants, among other horrors. Those mothers had plenty to answer for, perhaps the weather of the gloomy Caucasus was responsible, the air so thin no love could breathe, and their little boys became monsters. Willy tactfully avoided mention of Adolf Hitler. Then he turned suddenly and accused Alec of contriving a cover-up worse than anything Richard Nixon had contemplated. Another Washington shell game, now-you-see-it-now-you-don't, and one day there he was, waving from the Marine helicopter to his tearful staff. How fortunate the public was spared the anguish of a trial, which inevitably would have involved Washington itself, home to Richard Nixon for most of the past thirty years. Where do you think he learned his tricks? Whittier, California? Perhaps the trial would have involved other Presidents, and how they did their business. And how their staffs did business, and with whom. The intimidating public glare indeed! More like a Star Chamber, because while justice may have been done, it was not seen to be done. What remained were the tapes themselves, thousands of hours of loose talk and false hopes. What bad language! How coarse he was! And Big Head was an anti-Semite, along with three-quarters of the peoples of the nations of the earth. Genteel Washington was appalled at the stink of the locker room in the Oval Office itself. Do you think, Alec, that perhaps there's the smallest bit of snobbery here? Furious, Alec stormed from the room and refused to accept his stepfather's apology, which was insincere in any case.

That was unnecessary, Sylvia said.

He's more like Axel every day, Willy said.

He's just a boy, she said.

He was a boy, Willy said. He's a grown-up now.

So Washington lost its savor and they returned to Nantucket, for good, as it turned out. Sylvia knew that you could as easily live in one place as another; there was no public arena at all on Nantucket. For some years she maintained a correspondence with Billie and Ed Peralta and with the Grendalls, and then the correspondence languished. She no longer followed the news closely. Ford became Carter and Carter became Reagan. On Election Day 1980, she forgot to vote. She was tending her garden, preparing for the usual vicious winter, and that night watching the election coverage she wondered what politics had to do with life as it was lived. Now and again in the Sunday paper she would see Axel's name or Alec's, Axel meeting some foreign supremo at a resort you never heard of, Alec refusing comment on the pending hearings except to say that his client would be cleared of all charges. One night she saw Alec on the evening news and was surprised by how well he looked; but of course he was divorced now and sometimes divorce was a tonic.

Sylvia was experimenting with long-line verse, alone every afternoon in her upstairs study, watching Willy surf-cast on the deserted beach; he fished rain or shine, winter and summer. The struggle, she found now, was the tide climbing the low hill of sand, reaching and then falling back. She watched Willy's curvy line glittering in the sun, Willy in silhouette against the nervous ocean. Lobster boats moved offshore and she thought of dinner, lobster grilled, a green salad, chess with Willy beside the fire. She listened to cello sonatas, mostly Brahms, feeling her pencil on the paper like a bow across strings, an andante and then a diminuendo, almost a sigh. No rush; there was plenty of time. She was trying to draw music from the paper, trying to bring her crowded childhood to life, thinking all the while that any soloist needed accompaniment. Rostropovich needed Serkin. Even du Pré needed Barenboim. The cellist could supply the muscle, but the pianist set the pace, the gait of the piece. Sylvia was thrilled with her long lines, working now in a vernacular tongue. Slang she had not heard in years came back to her, and the look of her bedroom in the early morning light, her calico cat, a doll she loved, a nanny she didn't love. She was trying to arrange the characters as you would in a play. As she wrote she watched the tide; saw Willy stretch his arms and heave the line beyond the breaking surf.

Axel was in the room, and so were her father and her grandchildren, and poor Fred Greene and the Nazi officer in the Paris café so long ago, and the girl in the beret. She tried to remember the name of the brigadier's mistress and could not. She remembered the museum at Calcutta and the curator unlocking the vault to get at the drawings, and her own surprise. She conversed with her difficult mother, dead the year she left Axel. She remembered her dismay when she realized beyond doubt that one day she would occupy Echo House. She looked at Constance and saw an antique version of herself, an appalling prospect. She remembered her excitement when she realized she could leave Axel, that she was not a piece of property or a head bolted to an iron plinth. Watching Willy return, with his fishing rod on his shoulder and a fat bluefish in his fist, she decided she was the happiest she'd been. She thought, It's only 1982. I can have twenty more years of Willy and Nantucket. I will never run out of poems.

She heard the door close and the telephone ring and a moment after that Willy's knock on her door. She did not turn and presently felt his hand on her shoulder, and then his head close to hers. She knew at once that something was wrong and that it had to do with Washington.

"Ed Peralta's dead," he said. "Suicide."

Poor Billie, Sylvia said, and began to cry. She remembered Billie in the bar car of the Twentieth-Century Limited, appearing suddenly at their table, Axel looking up and smiling pleasantly as he would at any stranger. This is my place, Billie had said to the steward, but by then she and Axel were halfway down the car, his hand on the small of her back. She thought the heat of his hand would melt the cloth. She remembered the cloth against her skin and then they were embracing wildly in the vestibule, the train rocking and the night air unwelcome.

"Billie wants you to speak at the service," Willy said.

Of course the community was appalled and the newspapers understandably suspicious that the suicide came on the eve of hearings into the most recent Agency scandal. Ed's name still rang a bell. Everyone knew that he had been out of the intelligence business for years, but — did any of those people actually leave? Weren't they often called back into service, contract jobs in countries where they had special knowledge or friendships with figures in ruling circles? The answer was yes, but Ed was not one of these; no one wanted Ed Peralta back on the government payroll. He was worn out, ill, and bored beyond endurance. Axel said that his life was not worth the effort it took to live it, so he ended it; and Alec recalled that those were the exact words his father had used to describe his own condition at the end of the war.

A memorial service was arranged at the Friends Meeting House on Florida Avenue on a blustery spring day, the date and time never publicly announced but passed quietly from friend to friend, owing to the general commotion and the identity of many of the mourners, Ed's former colleagues, old now and deskbound or retired or semiretired but still more or less clandestine and determined to remain so. All the same, the more aggressive members of the Washington press corps were expected, because memorial services were political events and the intelligence community a subculture as mysterious as any in the capital. Wilson Slyde and a friend from one of the newsmagazines were among the first photographed. Axel and Alec entered together through a side door and were not noticed. Harold Grendall and Lloyd Fisher were both present and André Przyborksi unaccountably absent, out of the country it was said, Vienna or Rome. Someone suggested that the service be held in the chapel at Langley, but Billie tartly refused; and if the American press or the KGB or the Mossad or the Deuxième Bureau or MI-5 wanted to send their gumshoes to snap pictures, good luck to them. Everyone knew the identities of the old farts, and it was only vanity that kept their fedoras low over their near-sighted eyes.

Yet at the service Billie spoke touchingly of the love her husband had for intelligence work, its subtleties and crude hazards, its many demands and slender rewards in a world where secrecy defined success and publicity defined failure, as opposed to the political world, where things were the other way around. She concluded with an account of her husband's harrowing last days, when not even the prospect of a fine season from the Orioles was enough to give him hope. Of course this was the life he chose, and for the balance would have wanted no other. It was not for his family to disagree or make their own reckoning, or settle their own scores. She looked in the direction of her children, the son in tears and the daughter staring angrily out the window. They looked to be in their late forties, suburban people out of their element here. Billie waited for some sign that they would rise to say something about their father. When no sign came, she sighed and said she was glad her Ed did not live to see the present disarray and mismanagement of the agency he had loved and served for so long. The malfeasance. The misrule. The misprision. Billie was on her feet only briefly, blamed no one by name, and when she was finished, sat down.

Axel and Alec both spoke, Axel in his boardroom voice; someone later said that he sounded as if he were making a report to the stockholders, a bad year all around, profits flat because of the unsettled economic conditions and depressed consumer confidence, despite the notable achievements of the past. The truth was, Axel had neither patience nor sympathy with suicide. He spoke warmly of Billie, reminding the gathering that they had known each other for fifty years; she was a gallant woman and he admired gallantry. Alec spoke at some length, a droning summation of a life in public service. Truly in some sense Ed Peralta was a casualty of war.

Then from a bench in the rear of the room Sylvia rose and recited a poem, speaking in a lovely clear voice, conversational in tone. It took a moment for those present to realize they were listening to verse. The poem sought to capture Ed as he was as a young man, and Washington as it had been before and after the war, at the dawn of the modern world, and what the dawn forecast of the day to come. Sylvia made a number of obscure references, puns and wordplay that caused Lloyd and Harold to wince, look at each other, and listen hard. The witty parts made people smile, even Billie, though her children remained apart. Alec listened to his mother and thought that she would have made a great actress, her voice at perfect pitch and her manner commanding. But of course she had been giving readings for many years and knew how to lead an audience. Toward the end, her voice faltered, breaking, her hands trembling. She was reciting from memory and seemed to lose her way, but she gathered herself with difficulty and finished the poem, her voice barely a whisper in the vast gloom of the Meeting House. Gusts of wind rattled the windows.

Axel breathed heavily as he watched her, closely attending to each word. So far as Alec knew, this was the first time his father and mother had been in the same room since their divorce. It was possible that this was the first time they had seen each other in all that time. Axel's jaw muscles began to work when she mentioned the hydraulics of Washington and the brass cigarette lighter with its familiar initials, and the fist her hand made at something said, then unsaid, then enhanced, repeated, revised, and explained once again. You know how things go here in our capital city. You know who we are, the seer seen, the church fallen, bare ruined men. Axel snorted when he heard that. But he nodded in appreciation when she ended, bowing her head slowly and disappearing into her seat at the rear of the room. Alec turned to search out Billie Peralta, and when he turned back, Axel was already out of his chair and limping to the side door.

When Alec stepped outside his father was gone. Many of the older men had hurried away, though there were no photographers; the service had gone on for so long that they had wearied of the assignment, and there were other ceremonies that day. Alec remained on the sidewalk for a few moments, talking to Billie and her children. The son offered a limp hand and the daughter stared through him, eyes flashing in contempt. He did not know whether she was angry at something he had said, or only at who he was. Alec turned to find his mother at his elbow. When he congratulated her she looked at him strangely, shrugged, and walked sadly away, arm in arm with Willy. Then Wilson Slyde asked if he wanted to go across the street to the restaurant; he was lunching with Virginia Spears, the newsmagazine reporter much in the news. She was one of those who had become as famous as her subjects. Alec declined; he had appointments at his office. Billie and her children climbed into Ed's old Mercedes. Soon the sidewalk was empty except for Alec, Wilson, and Virginia Spears.

"We'll walk with you a ways," Wilson said. "We've decided to go to Melody's for the steak tartare."

The rain was blowing hard now. Bits of rain stung their faces.

"I liked your eulogy," Virginia said to Alec. He nodded, distracted, still back at the Meeting House, his mother reciting her poem and Billie sitting with her head bowed. Billie had shown no emotion when he spoke, but of course she held him responsible for Ed's forced resignation, illness, and death. There was plenty of responsibility to go around, but he hated it when Ed's daughter had looked so coldly at him, as if he had put the Beretta in her father's hand and commanded him to pull the trigger. It was all so long ago, the details forgotten by everyone except Ed and Ed's family. No one was proud of his role in the affair, but you had to put that behind you.

"The White House didn't send anybody," Wilson said.

"There was that one boy," Virginia said. "The deputy assistant something-or-other."

"No one official," Wilson said. "No one conspicuous. No one to show the flag."

Alec picked up the pace, eager to get back to his office. He had a conference call at four and a meeting with Billie and her children at five. He was executor of Ed's will and had to refresh his memory on its provisions. An awkward occasion all around, though the will was straightforward enough.

Wilson cleared his throat and said, "Virginia wants to have a word with you, Alec."

Alec looked at her, a slender woman, thirtyish, a blue silk scarf at her throat, alert brown eyes behind aviator glasses. She had the demeanor of an academic, her voice soft and well-bred, ironic around the edges. He did not know her well but he liked doing legal work for journalists, knowing about their wills and broken marriages. You built up a relationship, first of trust, then of friendship. You climbed the tree together. They told you things in the privacy of your office. And you told them things about cases you were working on and what you heard here and there. If your own name came up in connection with a political matter, they let you know about it; and if they had to write something they wrote it gently, with a wink. Alec made it a point to halve his usual fee, because journalists were such valuable friends. Wasn't it Wilson himself who had said that in Washington they were the *pi* in any discussion of circumference?

"I've proposed a story about you," Virginia said.

"I don't spend much time with the press," Alec said carefully. So it wasn't a will or a divorce after all.

She smiled. Yes, of course.

"A long story," she said.

"Listen to Virginia, Alec," Wilson said.

"I think it will be a cover story," she said.

Alec said nothing to that.

"Not the ordinary story at all; something different, something unique for the magazine. Of course the material has to be there.

The material has to be good. In fact, the material has to be superb. You can't imagine the competition; they find some cannibal in the heartland and they go apeshit. They can't get enough of body parts up in New York, and if it's not body parts it's some nasty little war south of the border. So the material has to be *really good.* It has to get their attention right away. And it has to be exclusive. *It has to bring the news,* Alec. In other words, I need access to your nearest and dearest."

"If you mean my father, forget it."

"He's part of the remarkable story."

"He's never given an interview in his life."

"Wrong," she said. "There was an interview in a British paper about the time of Desert One."

"Taken from a speech he gave, private speech, but the hack had somehow gotten himself invited. Printed the speech as if it were an interview. Axel spoke to someone and the little bastard was out of work before close of business next day. That's off the record."

Virginia sighed. They were stopped at a traffic light, wet leaves flying here and there. She was hoping for some help from Wilson, but Wilson was giving none, staring straight ahead and humming some dirge. She said, "It's so difficult when things are off the record. The chats we'd have, some of them can be on background only. I'm flexible on that point. But it's tragic when important material, anecdotes and quotes, are off the record. It makes my job impossible. I do take your point about Axel. Not that I won't make an attempt."

Alec was irritated by her voice, a schoolmarm's bray as irony had turned to sarcasm. She was almost as tall as he was and walked in a kind of lope, blinking behind her aviator glasses. When she gestured, Alec noticed that her fingernails were bitten to the quick.

"I'd like to start very soon, try to seize the march on the cannibals and the commissars. You see, we're bringing a new kind of coverage to Washington. We're interested in texture and nuance. We're interested in the faces behind the masks. We're interested in where the power really is as opposed to where it's supposed to be, and that's why we're interested in Alec Behl."

Wilson suddenly raised his hand to wave at someone across the street.

"Who's that?" Virginia Spears demanded.

"Biggs," Wilson said.

"Who's Biggs?"

"New man at the National Security Council."

"Never heard of him," Virginia said.

"You'd like him," Wilson said. "He's full of nuance."

"So," Alec said. "Give me an idea of the texture of the piece you want to write about me, your cover story."

She described two lines in the air as she spoke. "Attorney Alec Behl. The Man to See in Washington."

"The man to see about what?" Alec asked.

"Dey comes to you," Wilson said, jiving now on the sidewalk. "Dey comes to you wit de words, Nobody knows de trouble I's seen."

"Shut up, Wilson," Virginia said. "This is serious."

"An ole Alec, he lays on de hands, gives dem his blessing an washes dey feet, an sends dem away wiser an poorer."

Alec began to laugh. "I think you're ahead of things, Virginia."

"We are. That's the point, you see. We're ahead of the news."

"I'm not the man to see," Alec said. He named three lawyers, Visibles, looking all the while at the reporter and trying to discover where she was headed and what she wanted really, and how much she knew as opposed to what she would pretend to know.

"True enough," she said. "They're fine lawyers. They've been around this town for many years and they've had distinguished clients. They've rendered service to their country, when called. And they're old news, Alec. They're old frontier. They're on the downside of their careers while you're still marching toward the summit. And when they're gone, there'll only be you. You're asking about texture. That's the texture."

Alec looked sideways at Wilson, who now laid his forefinger on his right nostril.

"It's a new day," she went on, "and I'm not certain they understand the new day the way you do. Those many years ago, when Peralta landed in the deep shit, could they have handled Red Lambardo the way you did? No way. That was the key that unlocked the door for you, wasn't it?"

So she had done some homework.

"Of course I understand the sanctity of the attorney-client relationship. There are places I can't go. I appreciate that. A story of this kind, it's a partnership. I think you'll agree, it's got tremendous potential. By the way, you'd be dealing with me alone. This isn't a team effort. This is my idea and my story and if it's the kind of success I intend it to be, then there'll be others like it and those will be mine, too. You see, I'm part of this new day as well. The sun shines on us both, doesn't it?" Alec was listening hard now as she went through her multiplication tables. "I suppose in a certain sense you're my Ed Peralta. And my readers, why, they're Red Lambardo and the senators who snoozed through the hearing until they heard the texture of things. And then they sat up straight didn't they? Ramrods in their sorry spines because they were *interested*, isn't that so? They were interested in a well-prepared and subtle brief. And with interest comes conviction."

"Faith," Wilson amended.

They were hurrying now in the rain, traffic stalled on Connecticut Avenue, exhaust fumes caught in the heavy air. This part of the city always seemed to Alec like the main street of a state capital, Springfield or Indianapolis, with its small bookstores and boutiques, the buildings low and unconvincing. Then suddenly you came upon a general on horseback, but he was a municipal general, his horse rearing against the background of a travel agency and a jewelry store. This part of Washington was without aspiration or focus. For that you had to walk to Lafayette Park, the White House and the Treasury, the Washington Monument in the distance.

"Virginia thinks you're misunderstood, Alec." Wilson smiled winningly.

"Everyone needs a translator," Virginia said. "I want to be yours."

Wilson had paused to give money to a panhandler rattling his tin cup.

"Hard for me to know how I come out in all this," Alec said. "The wrong kind of story could be very damaging. We operate on trust and the perception of trust. If the facts are misinterpreted. If errors creep in. Well, then, your cover story could be a calamity."

Virginia Spears sighed heavily. Alec had misunderstood, as civilians had a way of doing, even worldly civilians who supposedly knew the score. So she tried again, speaking now in her reasonable corporate voice, the one she used with her editors in New York. She said, We inhabit a world of facts. At best the reporter has a supervisory role. You had supervision over the facts. They were in your care and you could release some and detain others. You could polish the shoes of this fact and comb the hair of that one and slash the throat of yet another. But you could not create them. They were conceived elsewhere and put in your charge, like children enrolled in a nursery. You had them on loan and when you released them they were gone; any mischief they created was their own responsibility. It was true that ancestry was often an issue, the source of understandable confusion and resentment. Not every fact came with a family tree. Some were aristocrats, others mongrels. Still others were orphans, parents and place of birth unknown. You were always careful with the orphans; some of them had unstable personalities leading to violent tendencies. They were unreliable, yet they too were often victims and deserving of sympathy. On certain specific occasions the reporter was encouraged to give approval or to withhold it, forcing the children to take responsibility for their own actions. So it was a question of the gene pool.

"Provenance," Virginia concluded.

Alec stared into the window of the travel agency while he listened to the reporter's fandango. He remembered that her father had been something in the Ford administration. Arms control or Angola, one of those two.

"A dirty business," Wilson said, clucking and shaking his head. "You have to change their diapers, too. Wipe the snot from their noses. Listen to their excuses such as the dog ate the homework. Give them baths and tuck them in at night and read them a nice nursery rhyme —"

"Be quiet, Wilson," she said.

"Call me next week," Alec said. "I'll think about it."

"I'll call tomorrow." Virginia hesitated, her hand resting lightly on Alec's arm. "I could give you the usual la-di-da, how I'll do the story whether you cooperate or not. But I'm not interested in that kind of outside-in story. I'm interested in the inside-out story, the one that can only come from you. Your story in your own words." She turned Alec's wrist to look at his watch, frowning, hastily shaking hands, explaining that she had to get back to the office, a conference call concerning the week's cover story, the destruction of the ozone layer and the catastrophic consequences of global warming. Our subscribers won't be disappointed, she said. We're going to scare the shit out of them, outside-in. She waved goodbye and loped away up M Street.

Alec watched her go, dodging raindrops.

"Get her while you can, Alec," Wilson said. "She's one of a kind."

"Is she going somewhere?"

"Television; she's made for it. Those legs! That voice!"

"A fingernail across a blackboard."

"She's Ms. Inside-out, doesn't even need to wear a wristwatch. She'll know someone who can tell her the time. And she loves her facts, particularly the orphans, the ones with the unstable personalities."

"Can she deliver?"

"I think she can. What's to lose?"

"Plenty," Alec said glumly, but that was for Wilson's benefit. There wasn't anything to lose. Virginia Spears only wanted in. She wanted a place at the table. She wanted to be part of it, faithful Boswell listening to Dr. Johnson put the fix in. Virginia Spears was avid for a peek behind the mask, thinking that she was staring into a man's soul when she was only looking at a second mask, the one that was even more untrustworthy than the first.

She would be interested in both dance and dancer, and it would be important to keep her focused on the first, where the feet go when you're preparing a pirouette, not the spin itself, not the actual doing of it, but the preparation for it, the process. Alec decided he would try to talk Axel into giving her thirty minutes, tea in the garden room at Echo House, let's see, on that occasion so long ago the President was seated *there,* and Tommy and Ben on the couch, and when Eleanor called I was instructed to say they'd already left, an urgent matter at the War Department, ha-ha, when all they were doing was drinking martinis. Some danger there, that Axel would take over the story. Virginia Spears would think she was sitting with Mr. Oracle himself, and if she phrased her questions properly, equal parts charm, tact, and bluff, she'd learn who really killed Kennedy. Of course Axel wasn't the real problem. Neither was Red Lambardo nor Harold Grendall nor Lloyd Fisher nor the others the reporter would seek out, to give her yarn the usual sweet-and-sour balance, the suggestive anecdote and the quote with the sneer behind it. The real problem was Sylvia.

That afternoon Alec called his travel agent and arranged for two seats on the Concorde to London and a third-floor suite at the Connaught, theater tickets, and a car and driver to take his mother and that bastard Willy Borowy to Sissinghurst or Blenheim or Henry James's cottage at Rye or any other place they wanted to visit in the glorious English countryside. Her birthday was in two weeks and she had been talking about a vacation in England, just she and Willy revisiting some of the old haunts. Alec told the travel agent to send the tickets and the other reservations to his mother by Federal Express. Add two dozen roses, he told the travel agent, and bill everything to the firm's account.

Alec and Virginia met the following Tuesday for an hour and

had dinner the following evening. They met for three hours on Saturday morning and spent the afternoon at Pimlico. Virginia won on a six-to-one longshot called Mr. Duck. Alec thought the interviews had gone well; any time the reporter got close to the heart of things, he pleaded lawyer-client privilege. Virginia was understanding but at one point lowered her pencil to inquire, almost plaintively, What is it exactly that you do, Alec? It isn't exactly law. It isn't exactly lobbying. Is it public relations? I think what you do is take people off the hook. There's a hook that they're on and you somehow move the hook or lift them off the hook or cause the hook to disappear or legislate it out of existence or, depending on the client, let it grow until it's the size of Alcatraz. I'm thinking that you're the neighborhood locksmith who hangs a brass key outside his shop, except with you it's a big black hook. Tell me this. Do you keep in touch with Old Man Nixon?

The clubhouse at Pimlico was not crowded. Alec and Virginia took a table near the window, watching the horses troop from the paddock to the starting gate. The jockeys looked tiny as toys atop the thoroughbreds, whose breath was steaming in the chilly spring air. After ordering drinks the reporter cleared her throat, took out her notebook, and said she would have to ask some questions about Alec's personal life, not all the gory details but the basic information. Most of the biopers would not be used, but they had to have it, in order to fill in the blank spaces and so forth and so on. The dossier was surprisingly slender, nothing of a personal nature published in the papers. It was obvious that he enjoyed a day at the races, betting modestly, losing the same way, and obvious also from the way he was staring at the travel agent's window the other day that he liked to get away from things. From the look of his office wall he didn't care much for contemporary art. Virginia admitted that she had made inquiries and, truth to tell, Alec wasn't often seen around town. Not at the usual embassy parties nor at the usual restaurants. Was occasionally observed at the symphony, as often as not with Axel. Was seen once or twice a season in the owner's box at the Redskins games, but people think that's a business afternoon, that you don't care much for the organized violence of the National Football League. They say you don't care figs for professional sports. Virginia smiled pleasantly and allowed the silence to lengthen. So what happened with Leila Berggren? And why are you living at Echo House with your father?

"I have two children," Alec said. "And they read the newspapers and magazines. So I'm not getting into any details about Leila and me and if you discover them yourself and publish them, I'll resent the hell out of it."

"I don't need chapter and verse."

"You're not getting chapter and verse."

"Now I'm very curious," she said, laying her notebook aside and steepling her fingers as she sat back in her chair, waiting. Her manner suggested an old friend ready to listen sympathetically to any confession, no matter how mortifying. Of course the facts would be carefully groomed before they were published.

Alec looked out the window at the track, the horses shying from the gate, high-stepping back and forth while their jockeys talked to them. There was a short form he could give the reporter. The long form was none of her business or the business of her readers. All marriages had a code. Probably even jockeys had a code, the words they spoke to their horses at the starting gate or in the homestretch, specific words spoken in a particular tone of voice. In Washington they lived by words, each métier with its own tongue, rules of syntax and grammar. They were all romance languages and collaborated at the margins, becoming a patois of their own — the language of the law, the legislature, the military, the university, and the newsroom. He and Leila lived for work, and their work was words. Their life together was animated not by who they were but what they did and how they explained themselves. Leila spoke an esperanto. She maintained that in another life she would have been a Silesian, meaning that she would manage in German, Polish, Czech, and Russian when she had to. Also Yiddish and Romany. She had so many tongues that Alec could not keep them straight. In bed one night watching the late news she announced a discovery: the most important work in the government was being done by outsiders, people like herself, consultants fee-for-hire. That was where the power was and the money, too; but you had to come on strong. Ventriloquism, she called it. You had to throw your voice, make them hear what they wanted to hear. But to be convinced they had to know that you were a part of things permanently, and for that reason she and Hugo Borne had taken a lease on a brownstone not six blocks from the White House. The old place in Foggy Bottom had become unsuitable. But the brownstone was expensive. She named a sum. Will you give me the money? I know you've got it. It'll make all the difference for us; for the first time we'll be going first class. We're just *this far* from a knockout and the doughski-dough that goes with it. He gave her the money and shortly after resigned as general counsel; only a fool had a wife for a client.

Once he ceased to be involved in her business he ceased to be involved with her and she with him. He wondered if they had both become so defined by what they did that they had no other dimension, like an agricultural economy with one cash crop. He was bored by her academic friends, weapons specialists, military strategists, economists, various geopoliticians. He himself had few friends, so they moved in her circle, and naturally her friends condescended to him, a lawyer uninterested in the great issues of national security, a lawyer who found it difficult to explain exactly what he did. Gradually he began to decline the small private dinners for the general or the deputy foreign minister. They might as well have been living in different cities, and in a way they were, with nothing in common except the one cash crop and their children. Their emotions were hidden inside the brick and marble of the federal city, their manner with each other a kind of amiable cynicism. Their lovemaking had all the passion of a tap on the shoulder. He did not know how this had come about and at a specific moment ceased to care. Alec would arrive home late, check the mail, read his children a story, kiss them good night, and go downstairs to see if the basement light was burning in the house next door. If it was, he called to the housekeeper to tell her he was going out for dinner. Tell Mrs. Leila not to wait up.

A minute later he was sitting with Sandrine Huet in her kitchen. Twenty feet away were the lights of his own house. On summer nights with the windows open he could hear the telephone when it rang and the voice of Ella the housekeeper explaining that Mr. Alec was not at home or Mrs. Leila either but she would be happy to take a message. Ella was hard of hearing and unpleasant generally, so her voice was loud and exasperated. If the caller pressed for details, her voice would grow cold and superior and she would ask again who was calling and explain that no one was home but the call would be returned when it was convenient to return it. Often the caller was Leila, working late.

He and Sandrine would close the curtains and eat in the kitchen and for many years whenever he smelled vindaloo sauce he would think of her in her jeans and pink sweatshirt pulling a bottle of wine from the fridge and asking how his day had gone, peering at the stove to check on the progress of the sauce. Tell me everything, she insisted, but rarely waited for his answer, preferring to describe for him the movie she had seen that afternoon at the embassy. Some fine things in it, she said, really very fine, the cinematography superb and the performances excellent. The sexy parts were charming. Perhaps the story was weak, lacking mettle. She had always loved the dialogue in French movies, a cyclone of words held together by centripetal force; but this conversation was aimless and without coherence. The pauses and silences were arbitrary. She rooted for the director, who was one of France's best. But at the end the thing went flat. The director didn't know how to end his story, so he left the boy and the girl on the suburban Métro, Direction Yvelines, sitting side by side holding hands, the boy looking out one window and the girl out another, waiting for Yvelines. At the end, the movie was without élan. I think we have lost our gift of narrative, Sandrine said. What has happened to us since Zola and Balzac?

The chargé d'affaires and her friend Avril Raye loved it, she said. But the ambassador's wife agreed with me.

The director's going to America, she said. Hollywood finally called. You drown us in Coca-Cola and then you take our movie directors.

America is a pestilence, he said. Especially Southern California.

Would you help me out? He's the chargé's cousin. He's only a boy. They'll eat him alive in Hollywood. He needs a lawyer.

With the greatest pleasure, Alec said. I know the best one in Los Angeles and he owes me a favor.

And it won't cost too much?

Not too much, Alec said.

Maybe he'll hate it and go back to France.

Maybe, Alec said.

Make him a contract with an escape hatch. Make them pay dearly.

Count on it, Alec said. Is he really good?

Yes, she said. He's one of our best and we don't have so very many. He has a vision. He knows what he wants to do with film, and he understands France very well. Maybe he'll understand Hollywood, too. He wants very badly to make an American film. I don't know why, unless it's the money. I suppose that's it.

It usually is, Alec said.

I hate it when we lose our good ones, she said.

If he's really good it won't matter.

She looked at him doubtfully and said, Now you can tell me about your day.

That always made him laugh, because one day did not differ from the next. Maybe he'd lost the gift of narrative or misplaced it in a hearing room somewhere. At least a movie director could choose among scripts and select one actor over another, and on a sudden inspiration rewrite the ending, or decide to make a film in Brentwood instead of Yvelines. Of course you would have to survive the critics. But the film would always be yours, no matter what the critics said. He refilled their glasses and said that his day was routine, not worth discussing. He would rather hear about events at the embassy. So she told him about the latest intrigue, a bedroom farce involving the chef, the chef's wife, the wife's lover, and the psychiatrist who lived down the street. When Alec asked her the chef's name, she said it was Henri, why? And he explained about the chef who had inhabited Echo House so long ago.

He loved listening to her and watching her move, as graceful as a dancer as she navigated the kitchen, all the while telling stories and holding her wine glass a few inches from her nose. Sandrine was near-sighted and excruciatingly shy. Crowds frightened her. At embassy receptions she tried to disappear behind the imposing suit of armor near the staircase; and that was where Alec found her one night at a dinner the ambassador gave for Axel. She stood with her face half-turned, concealed partly by chestnut curls that glowed in the light. She blushed when she touched her glasses with her forefinger, claiming she spoke English so imperfectly that conversation would be impossible. He moved slowly around her so that she could not avoid looking at him, but when she did, she recognized him as her neighbor, the one with the chic wife and two unruly children. He said something and she stammered a reply, looking at him sideways under her long commas of chestnut hair. When he introduced himself, she murmured a name he didn't catch. He spoke very softly, trying to forget the city he was in; he wanted to welcome her hesitant manner and evident embarrassment at being discovered. He went away and returned with two glasses of Champagne. When he asked her to tell him about the pictures in the room, she said she didn't know much about them.

Some of them belonged to the embassy; others were from the ambassador's private collection. She was sorry to be of so little help, but art was not her métier. She didn't believe in métiers generally. Sandrine spoke haltingly in incomplete sentences laced with incomprehensible French slang. When he complimented her on her dress, she blushed. When he asked her about the charm on the thin gold necklace at her throat, she smiled and said, no. She said no to a question about the ring on her third finger, right hand, and no to a question about the small scar on her chin. He told her his name and his age. He said he had never been to France. When he asked if she had ever been to the

Grand Canyon, she said maybe. He said he had always wanted to work in an embassy but that was out of the question now. She asked him what he did in Washington and he said, I live here. And I too, she said. He said something that made her smile and something else that made her laugh. She was so self-conscious. The women he knew were not shy. Perhaps they had been shy once but by the time he got to them they were as garrulous as senators, understanding that Washington did not reward hesitation or uncertainty. She still stood with her face half-turned from him but she was no longer blushing. Sandrine began to sip her Champagne, all the while inching around the suit of armor so that presently they were visible to the others in the room. She introduced him to her friend Avril Raye, who worked for the military attaché, and then the military attaché himself, a young colonel who regarded him with eyes filled with suspicion.

They remained standing beside the suit of armor until dinner, where, by good fortune, they were seated across from each other. He learned that she worked in the commercial section of the embassy, something to do with imports. Avril Raye was seated on his left, but the table never turned. The dinner was small and conversation general. Axel was witty and provocative that night and Sandrine laughed and laughed, and even told a story of her own. Avril Raye and the military attaché wanted to talk politics, but Alec's comments were perfunctory, his attention directed at Sandrine. Alec saw the ambassador's wife look curiously at Sandrine, and then begin to smile.

She's a great favorite of ours, the ambassador's wife said after dinner. We look on her as a daughter almost. She has not had an easy life. She is timid and perhaps does not have as much fun as she should. Washington is difficult for French people, so solemn and specific, so strenuous, so concerned with personalities. Sandrine needs someone reliable to care for her. Care about her, Alec said. That, too, the ambassador's wife agreed. Within the week Alec and Sandrine were lovers.

They talked often of France, Sandrine admitting that she was homesick for French life, the long Sunday lunches in Montparnasse or at her parents' farm in Normandy. She missed her parents and her brother. She was homesick for Parisian conversation, the mortal combat of the intellectuals, and afternoons shopping with a friend in the boutiques in the Place de la Victoire or in St.-Germain-des-Prés. She missed Mass at St. Sulpice. She still kept her little blue Renault at the farm near St. Aubin and one day would return to reclaim it. But meanwhile she had to earn a living and the embassy paid well. The routine suited her and she was very fond of the ambassador and his wife and Avril Raye, who was a true friend and had proved it time and again. She did not feel it was time to leave Washington, dull and stupid as it had become. She and her former boyfriend had had happy times in America, and then he went to Vietnam on temporary assignment. If you were a French journalist, that was where you went in 1970. He had been droll about the assignment, saying that he intended to meticulously inventory the American errors as the Americans had inventoried the French; and they were the same errors. She had not truly recovered from the shock of the telephone call informing her that he had found an American girl, also a journalist, and that they would be married in Saigon. It was natural that he would find an affinity with another of the same métier. That's usual, isn't it? There's so much to share.

They have two children now, she said. They live in Paris.

So I will wait a little longer.

And you, dear Alec, she said. I have no wish to leave you.

So I will live with my homesickness a little longer.

Months later, when Leila announced that she was leaving him, no mention was made of Sandrine Huet. Whether she didn't know, didn't care, or didn't want to open up her own life, Alec never knew. She called him a cold-hearted bastard with an adding machine for a heart, one of those men who should never marry, as other men should never drink or gamble. His passivity had become too much for her to bear, and in fact it was driving her mad. For herself, she intended to marry Hugo Borne. Alec agreed at once, a little too quickly to suit Leila. He insisted on keeping the house and agreed to have an evaluation made and pay her the sum in cash, whatever it was. She said the children would remain with her, along with Ella. Alec could see them on alternate weekends. Try to stay in touch for their sakes, she said.

A few weeks after the divorce became final, Leila and Hugo Borne were married at the registry office in Alexandria, so well known to the community that its address was given as the Street Without Joy. That night Alec and Sandrine planned a celebration, Champagne and chicken with the famous vindaloo sauce. When he arrived, she came to him from the telephone, clinging to him longer than usual, her fingernails digging into his back. When he asked her what was wrong, she avoided his eyes, excused herself, and left the room. A moment later he heard her on the telephone. My brother, she explained when she returned. He found her uncharacteristically distracted and careless in the kitchen. She drank one glass of Champagne and another and a third. He watched her intently as he told an especially gamy story about a senator and his secretary, the secretary threatening suit and the senator up for re-election. The secretary had letters and what she cheerlessly described as fashion photographs. How much did she want? And did she want it in small unmarked bills? No, she wanted her day in court.

He said, You can tell me now, whatever it is.

Sandrine looked away and said she was returning to France at the end of the week. Her doctor had given her bad news, news that she would rather face in the country of her birth, among friends. She was dreaming again of Montparnasse and the Seine at dusk and her little blue car at the family farm in Normandy. She stood with her shoulders hunched and her eyes averted, as she was when they first met.

She said, I'm terrified. I'm scared to death.

He said to her that she had to see American specialists, the best in the world. He would find out who they were and take her to them, at the National Institutes of Health or Mass General or Sloan-Kettering or wherever they were. We cannot allow this to defeat us without a struggle. She listened to him, smiling politely, amused in some region of her mind that he thought expensive doctors and mortal struggle the answer to a calamity. They had given her a death sentence with no appeal, which she had accepted quite calmly as she had been taught to do, really very calmly under the circumstances. The American doctor had been brusque. She never wanted to see another American doctor as long as she lived, though she knew that was a fantasy that would be unfulfilled. Still, there was not much time left and she would avoid them as long as she could. She drank another glass of Champagne, looking sideways over its rim out the window to the house next door, his house, all lights burning as if the family were still present. He was describing the very great advances American medicine had made, was making every day, brilliant researchers probing the very limits of biology. He held her hand while he spoke. His words tumbled over themselves in his rush to convince her of miracles. Finally he stopped talking and they embraced for many minutes while he listened to the beating of her heart.

Alec came to Paris at the end of the month. By then, Sandrine was in the quiet wing of the Hôtel-Dieu. He was with her every day for three weeks and then she was dead. The funeral was in a country church near St. Aubin, a Catholic service that seemed interminable, the priest speaking in a low incomprehensible mumble. The hymns were unfamiliar. He felt he had intruded. Her brother was cold to him, as if he were somehow responsible for her illness. Alec barely knew her parents, and they spoke no English and he no French. The ambassador's wife helped with translation, but she too was distraught and Sandrine's parents eager to return to their farm. They nicely asked him to join them for a meal and a glass of something but when he declined they said they understood. The ambassador's wife said they must get together in Washington. Sandrine cared very much for you, she said.

He drove away from the cemetery mad with grief, not knowing where he would go. He could not bear returning to his house in Washington with her empty place next door. Looking at it, he would always see the tricolor at half-staff. Where did he belong? Washington seemed now the leaden capital of a foreign country, as baffling as Sandrine's funeral service. Alec drove all night to Biarritz and then to Bilbao. Bilbao to Vigo, Vigo to Lisbon. He remembered that his father had visited Lisbon before the war, so he checked into the Ritz and stayed a week, driving to the racetrack at Estoril each afternoon and wagering absurd sums of money. The weather was dry and cool and he enjoyed standing at the rail watching the horses run, and returning to the hotel and having a drink at the bar, occupying the stool at the far end where his father had probably sat forty years before. He realized he was conducting a kind of vigil and in time he would have to return to the life he had made. His last night in Lisbon he called Axel from the bar, a rambling conversation that ended with the old man saying how sorry he was, that life was unkind and incoherent and lived always on the margins of chaos. Alec remembered the evening in Springfield so many years before, looking at Adlai Stevenson's bald head and tired eyes, and deciding he would never know anything of the spirit beneath the skin, the man himself forever unknowable, and finding satisfaction in that thought.

Cables from Lloyd Fisher followed him to Madrid and Seville and Ronda, urgent matters requiring his immediate attention, *return at once.* In Ronda he met a painter and his wife and slept with the wife. Then he drove to Granada to see the Alhambra and finally to Barcelona to look at Gaudi's architecture. He spent a week in Barcelona, prowling the Ramblas at night, gratified that he understood nothing that was said around him; then he got into a scuffle with a cab driver he thought was bent on assault, when all the man wanted was a light for his cigarette. He remembered Sandrine's tremendous affection for Paris, not for who she was in it but for the place itself, its essence; and then he admitted to himself that Washington was the reverse and that affection did not come into it except as a dividend. For himself, his work was all he had and Washington was home. In a sense the town was his, his own creation. He still could not believe she was dead.

Alec returned to the capital, sold his house, and moved to a place in Kalorama within walking distance of his office. There were bedrooms for his children on the weekends. Then the children went away to school and when they came home went to

Leila and Hugo's place in Cleveland Park, seeing him occasionally for meals. The house grew smaller as it emptied until it seemed to him the size of a squash court with the charm of a squash court. One night he looked around the place and knew it had no future; its only advantage was that it was near his office. So he called Axel and moved back into Echo House.

"The usual," he said to Virginia Spears.

"Irreconcilable differences?" the reporter asked.

"I suppose so," Alec agreed.

"Funny, that's what Leila said."

Alec looked at his watch and frowned.

"She said you both had different ideas of virtue." When Alec did not respond — indeed, his body was motionless — she smiled slyly and said, "Arguments about Nixon. Your role."

"I didn't have a role."

"Not what Leila said. And that your role helped bring down the marriage."

"Nixon was responsible for a lot. Not that."

"I'm trying to reconstruct the arguments about virtue, what you said and what she said and so forth and so on. I suppose it would boil down to who believed in what and why they believed it and how Nixon figured in. Wouldn't you say?"

"The marriage ended years after Nixon quit."

"Gotcha," Virginia said, with a sharp laugh. "Don't worry, I know Leila's off base. Still, we had a nice chat in that fancy office she has with the Twomblys on the walls and that desk the size of a tennis court. God, she's put on a lot of weight. Hugo, too. It's disgusting."

"They live well," Alec said mildly.

"After the irreconcilable differences there was a rumor you took a leave. Clients were left in the lurch. On the hook."

He said, "I took a vacation. People do that, even in Washington." And it had taken a year to repair the damage and longer than that to assure the faithful clients that he had not had a nervous breakdown.

"Have you had one since?"

"Of course," he lied.

"People say you're a lawyer who's always on call. Day or night, you can always reach Alec."

He turned to watch the horses break from the gate. He was trying to remember whether he had won or lost at Estoril, but the week was a blur. He had the idea that he had won again and again, betting hugely, returning to Lisbon with his wallet stuffed with escudos. The horses rounded one turn and another and came beautifully down the stretch. He looked at his ticket to see which one he'd bet on and saw it was number six. He and the reporter were sitting at the same table he and Sandrine had occupied one Saturday afternoon when she won a daily double, nine hundred dollars. She was yelling at the horse in French. Sandrine had brought him to the races, and her enthusiasm won him over and thereafter they went often when Pimlico was in session. The horses were reined up now and he looked at the tote board. The winner was number eight and both he and Virginia dropped their stubs in the ashtray.

"Who do you see now?"

Alec looked at her blankly.

"Women," Virginia said. "You're an eligible bachelor. You're as eligible as bachelors get in this town. Trust me, it's something I know about."

He wondered what sort of personal life Virginia Spears had, or if she had any personal life. He realized he knew almost nothing about her except what she did for a living. He said, "What about you? Do you have a boyfriend? A life after-hours? What do you do when you're not working?"

She looked at him, surprised. She said, The usual. She traveled in a crowd, mostly journalists and sources. There was no one special in her life at that moment. She supposed she lived a typical Washington life, an hour at the gym each morning, lunch, interviews, a party in the evening. She picked up her pencil and said that lately she was helping out at home. Her father was terribly sick and wanted her near him. She wanted to be there, too. You're lucky to have Axel, she said.

She was writing in her notebook. She explained that she was

old-fashioned and never used a tape recorder, too cumbersome and intrusive, and so much had to be edited out. Alec wondered what she was writing since nothing of value had been said.

"So there are no women. And now you live at Echo House."

"Axel and me, two old farts all dressed up with no place to go."

She shrugged and made another note.

"Don't make more of it than it is," Alec said.

"I wouldn't do that," she said.

The drinks arrived and Alec paid. The reporter continued to write. Alec imagined her notebook as an orphanage at recess, the illegitimate and unruly facts competing for attention. In the rough and tumble the weaker facts were mauled by the stronger ones, as the superintendent attempted to impose order.

Virginia looked up and said, "Have you had any success with Axel? I'd be grateful if I could have an hour with him sometime soon. I'm filing next week."

"I'll talk to him tonight."

"I'd appreciate it."

"Don't get your hopes up."

"Never, Alec."

"Maybe it'll work out; probably it won't."

"I've got these blank spots, you see."

Alec hesitated and then said the first thing that came to mind. "Don't forget we're a very long-lived family."

The reporter looked at him strangely and turned the page of her notebook. "I'd like to return, if I could, to the relationship you've had with Red Lambardo. When did you meet? I mean the date and the circumstances, and what exactly Red was doing way back then in the Kennedy administration."

"Lawyer-client privilege," Alec said, and when he thought to say he was sorry about her father, Virginia nodded and thanked him.

Ed Peralta's suicide left Axel worried and depressed. He refused to understand how a man could do such a thing, put a gun to his head in his own living room with his wife asleep upstairs, and leave that maudlin note. The event left Axel brooding about his own mortality, since Ed was younger and in better health, at least physically. Axel's aches and pains had multiplied and his world narrowed since the Republicans had come to power. They now had a thirst for government and the authority that went with it. So many of his old friends were gone, and the ones who remained were retired and living on memories. Feeding off memories was worse than feeding off the wretched food they served now at dinner parties, arugula, tofu, and raw fish; thin gruel, and it didn't look any better than it tasted. Ed was gone, Harold Grendall retired, André Przyborski returned triumphantly to Poland, and Lloyd Fisher obsessed with his golf game, though it had to be said that Lloyd still kept his hand in. Wednesday lunch was lively only when Alec or Red Lambardo stopped by to retail the latest gossip.

Moreover, the fortieth anniversary of D-Day was approaching and Axel wanted to attend the ceremonies, if to do nothing more than sneer at the broken-down movie actor who had inexplicably become heir to FDR and Harry Truman. That bastard Reagan was trying to repeal the modern world; only in America could such a catastrophe occur. And he would go to Omaha Beach and give his ghost-written speech and accept the applause of heroes, he who had never heard a shot fired in anger, he who had spent the war on a sound stage in Los Angeles. The man had no shame, yet there were those in Washington — serious people, men who had been around — who insisted that he was undervalued, both as a politician and as a man, and that was one other reason to journey to Omaha Beach, to see him eye-to-eye. Axel did not believe his health would permit a transatlantic flight, even on the Concorde. The seats were narrow and cramped, and when he arrived in Paris, what would he do? He wanted a place front row center with the other OSS characters and the veterans of the landing and the breakout. He wanted to put flowers on Fred Greene's grave. He did not see how he would be able to do this, so he sat in his Adirondack chair under the great elm next to the croquet court and brooded.

He often walked with two canes now, swinging his hips to

accelerate. Arthritis combined with the other pains to render him at times immobile; he thought of himself as a collapsed stick figure, a puppet abandoned by the puppeteer. At least he was still active; he was at the table, and now and again was even able to raise the ante, when the ante wasn't too high. In the last election his money was responsible for the election of at least one senator; one of his protégés was an assistant secretary of state, and another counsel to a Senate committee. He had placed Carl Buzet's boy in the Treasury. His black eyes were bright as ever, the skin of his face tight as paper. The long livid scar had the effect of narrowing his jaw. His nose had grown so that at a certain angle its tip seemed to touch his chin. But he radiated confidence and a kind of grandeur, a relic of a bygone golden age. Why was it then that he was never invited to the White House?

Alec found him in the Adirondack chair, tapping his canes on the toes of his shoes. Axel was muttering to himself, but that was normal. What wasn't normal was his request for a glass of red wine, the good Burgundy in the sideboard. The sun was almost down but it was still warm enough to sit outside.

Alec brought the glasses and they sat quietly a moment in the gathering darkness, Axel fussing with his cigar, finally managing to light it. He said, "How did it go with that idiot?"

"Lost every race but one."

"You or her?"

"Her. But she kept filling her notebook. I'm damned if I know with what."

"That's what they do. It keeps you off balance."

"And she had a chat with Leila."

"Naturally," Axel said. "I told you the interview was a bad idea. You wouldn't listen."

"She didn't care for Leila's Twomblys. Didn't care much for Leila's weight. And when Leila told her that an argument about Nixon broke up the marriage, she didn't care much for that either. But she'll use it because it's too droll not to use."

Axel blew a smoke ring and smiled. "Is it true?"

"We fought about everything, the defense budget, the

women's movement, the designated hitter, OPEC, Wounded Knee, Patty Hearst, *Chinatown,* and the legacy of Al Capone. Of course we fought about Nixon. She thought I was the one who got him off."

Axel began to laugh. "You never told me exactly what you did."

"Nothing," Alec said. "Spoke to a few people. Supplied some metaphors and scenarios that might have been useful, might not have been."

"People thought so," Axel said. "That's what counts."

"I'm going to ask you a favor."

"No," Axel said.

"You don't know what it is yet."

"You're going to ask me to talk to her."

"That's right, I am."

"I have given only three interviews in my lifetime. They were off-the-record interviews." He thought a moment and added, "I value my reputation."

"It would help me out," Alec said. "I'm asking you to see her for thirty minutes, here at Echo House. It would take some of the heat off."

"Off you. And put it on me."

"Don't be ridiculous. She'll be star-struck. She'll be the rookie reporter at the hometown newspaper who gets the interview with Elizabeth Taylor. Gosh, you have beautiful eyes. And such skin! You're as slender as a teenager. Do you mind if I call you Liz?"

"What if you're underestimating her?"

"I'm not."

"I'll think about it."

"I'd appreciate it."

"But I don't like it." Axel blew another smoke ring, sipping his wine carefully, glaring at his son. Alec always had a taste for the limelight, a mistake for anyone who wanted to exercise real influence. FDR never stood for it. These youngsters, perhaps it was different with them; but Alec had made his own bad bargain with the devil, so be it. Axel cleared his throat and told Alec about his ruined hopes for D-Day. He wanted to be there. Lloyd Fisher and Harold Grendall were already in Europe, bound for Warsaw to see André Przyborski, who seemed to be living very stylishly in a neighborhood near the Jewish cemetery, the one where if you looked hard enough you could find a Jew who died of natural causes. They were going to Normandy for the ceremonies. "I'd give my useless left leg to be there when they're there, but the journey's too difficult."

"I didn't know you wanted to go to D-Day," Alec said.

"I damn well do. But I can't."

"Why not? Car to Dulles, Concorde to Paris, car to Arromanches. That isn't difficult."

Axel shot a hard look at his son, who pretended to know so much but understood so little. "It is for me."

Alec thought a moment, swirling the wine in his glass, feeling his father's seething anger. Then he excused himself and walked back into the house. In the study he dialed one number and got an answering machine, dialed another and got Red Lambardo's soft voice, sounding as if he had just been awakened. They talked a moment of the current scandal, who was likely to suffer and why. Alec had some advice for Red on his own testimony the following week, and he had good news as well. The committee would treat him respectfully, mostly because they were trolling for sharks and they knew that in the present scheme of things Red was a minnow. He knew what the committee wanted to know but he did not know it firsthand. The counsel was a son of a bitch, though, and had to be watched carefully at all times. Alec lowered his voice and spoke in the usual code. He had one piece of information that might be helpful, both to Red and to Red's principals. Red was free to pass it on, under no circumstances revealing its source. As he spoke he could hear Red furiously making notes; and when he was finished, a low, satisfied chuckle.

When the pause came, Alec said he was calling to ask a favor, not a huge favor, perhaps not even a difficult favor, but one he wanted and needed to have. He told Red that his father was in a nostalgic frame of mind, as he almost always was these days, and wanted to go to the D-Day ceremonies —

"Don't worry about it," Red said. "That's an easy one. I'll get him a seat in the front row, but you've got to promise me he won't shoot Reagan."

"Well, thanks," Alec said. "More complicated than that."

"Tell me about it," Red said, his voice cooler now.

"He doesn't feel like traveling, even by Concorde. His back hurts all the time and he's using two canes and generally feels punk and complains all the time, you understand?"

Red Lambardo thought a moment. "If he can get to England, my guy can get him on the *Britannia* with all the other supremos. He probably knows half of them anyway. But I'd have to get on it right away."

"That isn't what I have in mind, Red."

There was a pause, and then Red Lambardo began to laugh. "You bastard. I know what you want. You want him taken care of tee to green."

"That's right, Red."

"You want him on Air Force One."

The call took longer than expected, and when Alec finished the old man was still sitting in his Adirondack chair, tapping his canes on the toes of his shoes, the wine glass empty now. He was staring into the middle distance, a sour expression on his face. He looked like a hawk at rest, alert but weary from the day's flight. Alec stood in the doorway watching him, trying as always to read his mind and failing, remembering when it seemed to him that his father could do anything, the ticket to Wimbledon and all the rest, and then his long absence. So much of his life was wrapped up in France, his Rubicon, a mighty Rubicon; and now he wanted to see it again. Alec wondered how often Axel thought of Nadège; he had not mentioned her name in years. But of course he thought about her all the time, Nadège and Sandrine were the ghosts of Echo House, present everywhere and visible nowhere, like Constance. Probably they had their own conversations late at night when he and Axel were asleep, dead to the world. No doubt Capitaine de Barquin put in an appearance also. It was almost dark now, but the old man seemed not to notice.

Alec brought the bottle of wine and refilled their glasses.

He said, "It's fixed. I fixed it."

Axel looked up, eyebrows raised.

"You're going with the President on Air Force One."

His father stared at him a long moment and then began to laugh, a deep sputtering rumble that caused him to spill his wine. He said, "What did you have to do to arrange this?"

"I spoke to a man who spoke to another man. They're thrilled at the White House. They're delighted."

"I'll bet they are. I'll be they're turning cartwheels. May I know the identities of these individuals?"

"You may not."

"If that son of a bitch expects me to contribute to his campaign —"

"That wasn't mentioned. That's not part of the deal."

"What is the deal, Alec?"

"A man owed me a favor. And as I said, they're thrilled."

"So they remember me over there."

"Of course," Alec said, surprised.

"What did you have to give them?"

"I didn't give them anything. A man was in my debt. He repaid the debt."

Axel sipped his wine and then he said sharply, "You're a lucky man, to know people who repay their debts."

"I didn't have to break anyone's arm. They were happy to do it. I think they're honored. As they should be."

"I'll have to buy a new suit," Axel said.

In the event, Virginia Spears's story was a triumph, the cover a photograph of Alec in his office on the telephone, the skin around his eyes crinkling with worldly amusement. Perhaps someone was telling him a joke, or the latest sexual peccadillo of Wilson Slyde, the price of beef in the Argentine, or the roughhouse that got out of hand in the Senate cloakroom the previous week. Alec was in his shirtsleeves, his feet resting on the bottom drawer of his desk, a yellow legal pad in his lap. He looked as handsome as a movie star, one of the old breed, with undeniable sex appeal along with obvious authority, Richard Widmark, say, or Jean-Louis Trintignant. One of Alfred Munnings's fox-hunting scenes was on the wall behind him surrounded by personal photographs — Alec with the chairman of the Joint Chiefs of Staff, Alec with the French ambassador, with Neil Armstrong, with Leonard Bernstein, with Dean Acheson, as a young man with John Steinbeck, as a very young boy with FDR in the Oval Office, as an infant in Senator Adolph Behl's lap in his Senate office, Behlbaver roses in the background. On the credenza behind his desk, peeping over his left shoulder, was a photograph of a much younger and very debonair Axel Behl, leaning on a cane under the porte-cochère of Echo House, his ruined face half in shadows but his bearing calling to mind a European grandee — and the photograph had pride of place, unless you counted the one in the silver frame face-down in the desk drawer, put there moments before the photographer arrived, Sandrine Huet in her Georgetown garden, Alec standing next to her, smiling openly in a way that turned him into a different man altogether from the one on the magazine's cover.

Alec Behl, the Man to See in Washington. Congratulations showered upon Virginia Spears, whose picture appeared alongside the by-line, the first time that had been done in the magazine's history. Everyone talked about the cover story, a masterpiece of the journalist's art, the inside-out account of a legal warrior who sought nothing more than simple justice from Washington's pig-stubborn bureaucracy and image-addicted political class. When the lambs were thrown to the wolves it was Alec Behl who defended the lambs, with no sanctimonious hocus-pocus, only a belief that leaders were accountable before their followers; and nothing was as it seemed in the federal city. When the Nixon scandals threatened to undermine the very legitimacy of the government itself, Alec Behl shuttled from one office to another, offering, as he said, metaphors and scenarios to bring the disgrace to an end and restore the people's faith. His efforts on behalf of the government — for it could be fairly said that he was representing Washington itself, pro bono — had a mighty effect on his own personal life, a painful and bitter divorce. Such were the realities of domestic life in the capital city. Moreover, at a time when American families were falling to pieces willy-nilly, Behl *père* and Behl *fils* lived together in the same family mansion that had been bought by Senator Behl in the last year of the first Wilson administration, a Washington landmark, for decades the venue of the capital's most sought-after dinner invitations. Axel Behl — agreeing to an on-the-record interview for the very first time in his long and conspicuous life — had been severely crippled for forty years as the result of harrowing wartime exploits so clandestine they could not be revealed even today — and when he expressed a wish to attend the D-Day celebration, it was his influential son who secured the invitation to ride aboard Air Force One with the President and his staff, who generously put aside partisan differences to recognize that American heroes belonged to no particular political faith. That, too, was in the finest Washington tradition of bipartisanship, and a reminder that in World War Two the nation had stood together, one diverse family —

Axel read the piece in disbelief.

"I guess I'm your father now," he said.

PART III

8

Echo House

❧

O_N THE FIFTH DAY of the heat wave there was no one about in Soldiers Cemetery. Even the mosquitoes had given up. The leafy crowns of the trees hung limp, exhausted, shading the gravel path, which undulated with the terrain. The path was uneven and overgrown, weeds tumbling here and there among the litter of gum wrappers and cigarette ends. The gravestones were warm to the touch and sticky as candy, yet the parched earth yielded a bright, fresh smell — unless that was the Cologne of the two old women in sun hats and light summer dresses who walked companionably arm in arm, following the path that was descending now but soon to rise. The women knew they would have difficulty rising with it. They were alert to the ragged roots of the great elms and the furnace of the afternoon sun, still high in the August sky. From time to time one of the women would rest a moment, her hand on a gravestone, idly noting the name and dates, and epitaph if there was one; and then she would move on.

They had not seen each other in many years and had met only by chance an hour before in the dress shop on Wisconsin Avenue, each recognizing the other at once with a sharp cry and an embrace. The salesgirls nudged each other and giggled because it was rare seeing two old parties so animated, delighted would be the word, thrilled to meet once again. They walked out of the shop and down the street until they came to the cemetery, not thinking of it as a cemetery but as a pleasant place to walk undisturbed in the shade. Now they were busy catching up, accounting for the many missing decades. They were both widows, husbands recently passed away, the events a blessing because the end was very painful and difficult though the men were brave. One was grimly elated because he had outlived Nixon, and the other — well, the other couldn't think about much of anything. They talked about their children and grandchildren, where they were living and how they had turned out; the grandchildren of one were estranged from their father and saw him only rarely, a common situation in the capital, where lives were so public and the hierarchy so rigid. Their grandfather frightened them and for good reason. Divorce always cast a long shadow, and it ran in families. And then their own medical bulletins, the arthritis and other complaints that came with great age, bad hips and failing eyesight and the rest. But, knock on wood, nothing major. Nothing threatening.

They had picked their way down the path, the woody ravine on their right. The descent was steeper than they thought, but they had made it all the way down and now were rising again, resting every few moments next to a gravestone. The sun burned through the crowns of the trees, hot as the tropics. Both women were sweating, unsightly half-moons on their dresses under their arms and on the bands of their sun hats. At last they reached the top of the hill, more or less where they had begun, and sank gratefully onto the wooden bench under the great elm. They were both breathing hard, disoriented in the heat. High overhead a helicopter chugged by.

Oh, Sylvia, Mrs. Pfister said. It's so good to see you. I knew we would meet again sometime.

I've thought of you often, Sylvia said, wondering where you were and what you were doing. Someone told me you had moved away.

Mrs. Pfister nodded slowly. She had moved back to Holland, where she was born, a small market town in the Ardennes with Roman ruins and two medieval churches, overrun at one time or another by all the tribes of Europe, even the French. The mercenary d'Artagnan was killed there. It was agreeable, speaking Dutch again, surrounded by familiar faces and of course the medieval churches. She was in Washington now visiting one of her sons. She had been in America for two weeks and that was long enough. She was eager to return to Maastricht.

Why did I think you were Romanian? Sylvia asked.

You didn't, Mrs. Pfister said with a grim smile. *They* did. On the days when they didn't think I was Romanian, they thought I was a Gypsy. Or Czech. Or Bulgarian or Russian or Polish. From anywhere but reliable bourgeois Holland, land of tulips, windmills, and Vermeer.

Sylvia smiled and looked away, past the gravestones to the street. Behind the trees she could see the soaring rooftop of Echo House. She wondered if she should tell Mrs. Pfister what Ed Peralta had said so long ago and decided against it. Everyone she knew lived in the past, and what was the point? She noticed the helicopter again, lower this time, circling as if it were patrolling.

Mrs. Pfister said, They spied on me, you know. And on you, too, and all my clients. They were worried about what happened inside my little bungalow, the cards falling the way they did and people talking as they do. They were afraid of private thoughts, what people think about when no one is looking. People are naturally interested in what precedes them and what lies ahead also. Your husband and his confederates thought I was a communist agent controlled by Moscow. They thought I was interested in their secrets, as if I didn't have enough secrets of my own. I set traps for them and they set traps for me. Some of their traps were clever and one day they had enough and came to me and said I would have to leave Falls Church. My status was "irregular." My papers were not in order. A complaint had been filed, though who filed it and why they never said. My gift was no help to me in this situation, so I packed up and went home to Holland. This was not what I wanted but I had no choice. They followed me to the airport and followed me after I arrived in Amsterdam. I would see them periodically in the market or at church, and then I spoke to someone and the Dutch authorities told them to leave me alone and they did and I haven't seen one for some time now. I could have saved them the trouble. But why bother? I have my gift from my mother and when she died my gift died, too. I think they have forgotten about me now. Perhaps they lost my file. I had no difficulty with the visa. It is the first time I have been to America since they expelled me.

They didn't forget about you, Sylvia said. They were embarrassed.

I embarrassed them?

They would never want it known that they were interested in a psychic. The publicity would have been dreadful. So they destroyed the file.

Mrs. Pfister allowed herself a small smile and then she said, They never knew about my husband. They seemed to think they knew everything but they knew nothing of him. It's easy to fall between the cracks in America if you know how. My Nick had more names than the devil. So they did not know of his existence.

Would it have made a difference if they had? Sylvia had heard a strange chill in Mrs. Pfister's voice. But when next she spoke, Sylvia realized the tone was one of triumph.

Perhaps it would have. My husband worked for them at one time.

Worked for American intelligence?

Not here, Mrs. Pfister said. Abroad. He was the Bulgarian. Not I.

Strange, Sylvia said, because she did not know what else to say. Mrs. Pfister was sitting straight as a schoolmarm, with her eyes fixed on the middle distance.

She said, Are you quite certain they destroyed my file?

As certain as I can be, Sylvia said.

Because I think that's one of them now, Mrs. Pfister said bitterly.

Sylvia looked up to see a young black man approach them. He had been in their vicinity for some time, watching. He was dressed in a black suit like a clergyman and moved most gracefully, like an athlete. Sylvia put her handbag behind her and told

Mrs. Pfister to do the same. The black man was tall and broad, with the looks of a street-corner tough, except for the black suit. He walked with his hands behind his back as if to emphasize his innocent intentions. He smiled politely and dipped his head in greeting.

Ladies, he said. Isn't it a warm day?

What do you want? Mrs. Pfister demanded, so coldly that the black man recoiled as if struck.

Your identification, he said curtly, uncoiling the chain around his neck and showing them a plastic card that stated he was William Block, an agent of the U.S. Secret Service.

We have every right to be here, Mrs. Pfister said.

And I have every right to ask for your identification. Give it to me now.

Mrs. Pfister handed him her passport. Sylvia fumbled in her purse for her driver's license and by the time she had extracted it William Block had returned the passport with a nod and a murmured thank you, ma'am. He looked at the driver's license and then at Sylvia and back again, twice.

He frowned and said, Sylvia Behl Borowy. Are you related to Mr. Axel Behl?

Sylvia said, I was married to him.

So you know the house? he said, gesturing across the street.

I lived there, Sylvia said. Many, many years ago, she added.

What a strange coincidence, the agent said.

Sylvia shrugged, finding her situation neither strange nor coincidental.

It's Mr. Behl's birthday, the agent said. His son is giving a party for him, and the President and the First Lady are expected later in the evening, along with many other notables. The agent explained that he was checking the neighborhood, routine when the President was out and about. He nodded and moved off, apologizing for disturbing them, wishing them a pleasant evening.

Then it was quiet once more. Mrs. Pfister looked at her wristwatch and rose slowly, looking around for other intruders. She said she was expected at her son's. She seemed to sway a little in the heat and admitted that she was tired. The two women embraced and agreed that it was a pity that neither of them had time for lunch, as Sylvia was leaving for Nantucket in the morning and Mrs. Pfister for Holland two days later. So it is unlikely we shall meet again, Mrs. Pfister said. Enjoy the rest of your stay, she said with a thin smile. I'm sure you will.

Mrs. Pfister walked off unsteadily. Sylvia watched her until she disappeared among the trees and gravestones, headed in the direction of Echo House; perhaps she would lay a curse on the old mansion, except it would be ineffective, because her gift had vanished; they were only two old women who had met in a dress shop and would never meet again. Sylvia was alone now in the cemetery. The failing light cast long shadows, and then a little breeze came up and she lifted her face to meet it. Dusk was always her favorite time, the day's work done and the long evening to look forward to. Something always turned up in the evening hours, an unexpected telephone call or a novel that beckoned from the bookshelf or an old movie on television. On the island she liked to drink a glass of wine and watch the lights of the ships at sea; and imagine Willy finishing up, one last cast before he trudged up the beach to join her on the terrace. She sat on the bench and thought about Willy's last days, aware suddenly of a commotion behind her. She turned to see a bright light and a tall young woman with a microphone; she was beautifully dressed in a cream-colored pants suit, Armani from the look of it. They were filming the old senator's grave, the rose and the inscription beneath; she could not remember the words now, only that Charles Rath had said them in German at graveside. The young woman struck a pose, pronounced a solemn sentence into the microphone, and then the lights went out. No doubt she was part of the media retinue surrounding the President at Axel's birthday, Axel kept alive by a formidable combination of state-of-the-art pharmaceuticals, round-the-clock nursing care, and Behl family genes, durable as walnuts. She wondered if she should crash the party, give them a taste of what life had been like in the old days, when Echo House was an inner sanctum, with as many secrets as a tomb. Sylvia rose slowly, losing her balance for a moment; and then she abruptly sat down again, savoring the gathering dusk.

Television crews were assembled in the street, each arriving sedan illuminated by lights that, if not brighter than a thousand suns, were not much dimmer, either. The pavement reporters, of course, were of the junior group; their senior colleagues, including the young woman in the Armani suit, were inside as guests. The usual blank-faced sentinels were in place here and there on the grounds, wires running from their ears, Goethe's gazebo their command post. The stun grenades and tear gas canisters were stacked beside the great poet's bust. A communications van was parked up the street. A small group of neighbors had assembled on the sidewalk to watch the show, the evening news live.

Inside, agents of the Secret Service were intentionally conspicuous, dressed in dark suits and basic black dresses, whereas everyone else was in full fig. The word was out that the President and his wife and the White House chief of staff would arrive together, so there was an excited buzz in the foyer. Nearly a hundred people had gathered in that room and in the living room, where a pianist from the National Symphony played selections of American music. White-coated waiters circulated with trays of drinks and hors d'oeuvres. The back lawn, in partial light, looked inviting, but the doors leading outside were locked on orders of the Secret Service, for what exact reason no one knew, but assassination threats were constant and the President's bodyguards hated large gatherings preceded by publicity, necessitating vettings of guests and staff, an inherently unstable environment, though just at that moment the only unpredictable element was a rabbit bouncing on the croquet court.

Alec was talking to a French diplomat while occasionally glancing at the staircase that swept away in the great curve to the second floor. At the summit the landing was empty and the double doors shut. The old man was in his dressing room, awaiting the proper moment to make his entrance. That would not be until the President arrived. Meantime, Alec acted as official greeter, shaking hands with the men and kissing the women and sending them in the direction of food and drink. The French embassy had sent Champagne and a giant truffle in a satin-lined box and the Russians a tub of caviar. There were cases of vodka and Bernkastler, Havana cigars, a jeroboam of slivovitz, nuoc mam, Swiss chocolate, and bundles of flowers. In a rare display of double-edged wit, the President and his wife had sent a door-mat with the presidential seal woven by prisoners at the federal penitentiary, Atlanta.

Alec always enjoyed his encounters with Avril Raye. She had been a friend of Sandrine's, and her apartment a refuge after he returned from his vigil in Southern Europe. They spent long evenings at her table drinking Bordeaux and talking about France; and when she was puzzled about this or that event in Washington, he did his best to unravel it for her. But mostly they drank wine and talked about France and only later did it occur to him how subtle she was, and how kind. She was a big woman and liked to say that she was successful in her work because she looked like a concièrge; and was unsuccessful in her romantic life for the same reason. He knew what interested her this evening, the administration's nominee for ambassador to Paris. She pointed out that her government was pleased; Bud Weinberg was a known Francophile and spoke the language beautifully. But there had been no hearings and he was not seen "around." So obviously a problem had developed and Avril wanted to know what it was.

"Bud Weinberg's a good man," Alec said. "Everyone likes Bud. But he has a son who associates with people he shouldn't associate with and he's supposedly seeing a woman who is not his wife. And there's a twist that you'll appreciate. The stories about the woman may be false. Probably are false."

Avril Raye rolled her eyes.

"But he can't kill the rumors. He knows the source but he can't kill them. The more he tries, the more he's accused of cover-up. The more he's accused of cover-up, the deeper the swamp gets. Bud's finished. They're casting around for someone else. Keep your ears open tonight; you'll hear chatter about Bud. Bud's been out of the loop too long. Bud doesn't understand the modern world. Bud stepped on his dick and then shot himself in the foot. Why won't Bud get out of the way so we can get on with it?"

Avril began to laugh. "Who's the source?"

"A gentleman who has his own nominee. A gentleman with important business in France who'd like his own man living on the Faubourg Ste. Honoré when it comes time to mount the take-over."

"I know who that is," Avril said slowly.

"Sure you do. That's why I told you."

"The Hollywood thug."

"None other."

"And there are no women?"

"That's what Bud says. I believe him. And there he is now. He's gone to the Venerables for advice. Bad idea."

Bud Weinberg was standing in the archway to the living room with Harold Grendall, Lloyd Fisher, and a much younger man whom Alec recognized as a lawyer from one of the small K Street firms. Alec couldn't remember his name but he had grown up in Wesley Heights and his grandfather had been a great friend of President Kennedy. Alec reckoned the combined ages of the four men at more than two hundred and fifty years. Harold and Lloyd at ninety-plus, Bud at sixty, and the boy lawyer at thirty. They spanned living memory but they all remembered different things and drew different lessons. Bud was talking and Harold and Lloyd were leaning close, avid to collect each detail. They were seldom in on things now and when given the opportunity devoted their full and undivided attention. The lawyer, too, was listening hard.

Wilson Slyde was eavesdropping from a safe distance, aware that Bud was making a mistake talking to the Venerables. Harold and Lloyd and their *salon des refusés* had been out of step with every administration since Eisenhower's. They were as long-lived as the French impressionist painters and in later years came to resemble them, with their out-of-date clothes, long hair, irregular habits, and singular insights. Harold Grendall was Monet's double, as wide as a barge with cheeks as smooth and pink as a lily pad. Lloyd Fisher was as bent and shrunken and saturnine as Toulouse-Lautrec and as mischievous. Washington honored the Venerables but didn't know what to do with them and their sarcastic sermons of reproach. And from the look of things, that was what Harold was getting into now, his heavy finger wagging at Bud Weinberg's chest, Lloyd at his side nodding vigorously. Easy to imagine Harold's complaint; it had not varied in twenty-five years: the cowardice and ignorance of the young, their disloyalty and carelessness, their twenty-second attention spans, their arrogance and self-absorption. When they quit the battlefield they didn't have the courtesy to shoot the wounded. You couldn't even call them cynics, since they knew neither price nor value.

They're going to hang you out to dry, Bud.

They're turds. They're creatures of television. They don't care about government, they care about elections. They live by image. Die by image, too. That's why they care so much about "perception." They don't believe in anything.

They're 'fraidy cats.

Bud Weinberg was attentive but stepped back, as if to distance himself from Harold's tirade. Harold's voice had risen so that those in the vicinity could hear him easily. There was some nervous laughter and one or two of the younger men had turned their backs. Wilson Slyde edged closer so as to miss nothing.

They had come to the capital's generational fault line. It was an argument over the inheritance. The old men seemed to exist as a rebuke, relics of the empire that had mastered the Depression and fought a two-front war, in which all able-bodied men participated, as opposed to departing for Sweden or declaring themselves homosexual or sheltering in law school or faking murmurs of the heart, and still had resources left over to rehabilitate the nations of Europe and Asia while defending them against the Stalinist scourge; and at that critical moment managed to assemble the most talented cohort of public servants since the Founding Fathers, men who were poor when they entered government and poor when they left it, often with dam-

aged reputations, owing to the recklessness of Senator Mc-
Carthy.

And the Venerables were not shy about reminding everyone
what Washington had been and what it had become, a self-in-
fatuated money-grubbing iron triangle of stupefying vulgarity,
vainglory, egoism, and greed, worse than Rome because at least
in Rome there was lively sexual license, orgies and the like.
These people wouldn't know an orgy if it patted them on the ass
and said, Please. The present-day crowd along with their un-
speakable arrogance were intolerant. They were sanctimonious.
They were puritans. They were budget-cutters, cheap Charlies.
In his mountainous contempt for contemporary Washington,
Harold was fond of repeating Mandelstam's epitaph for St. Pe-
tersburg: "Like sleeping in a velvet coffin."

This estimate of the nation's capital at the turn of the millen-
nium did not go unchallenged. To younger Washingtonians the
opinions of the old men seemed anecdotal, dated, nostalgic, and
partial, a loud fart from another time altogether, more unreliable Cold War propaganda. They not only had their own stories
about what Stalin had told Chip and what Chip had told George
and what George had said to Tommy and what Tommy had
told the President; they had their fathers' stories about what the
President had told Cohen and what Cohen had told Corcoran
and what Corcoran had said to Frankfurter and what Frankfurter
did. All very well and good, but weren't these more ghosts from
the past come to terrorize the present? There was another way
to look at it, and that was that these most talented public servants since the Founding Fathers, with their admirable modesty
and high intelligence, had bankrupted the nation fighting fool-
ish unwinnable wars and encouraging dubious insurgencies, all
because of what Stalin had told Chip and what Chip had said
to George, et cetera. And they had declined to levy the taxes
needed to pay for the installation of the New Enlightenment,
their American century. And when the Russian empire had
reached its megalomaniacal limit, it collapsed. Even so feckless
an operator as Mikhail Gorbachev had brought it to its knees;

and now it existed as a collection of impoverished semifeudal states, with grotesque arsenals of nuclear weapons, wholly dependent on the forbearance and generosity of the West, and all thanks to the paranoia of Chip, Tommy, and George, and to that list you could add Harry, Ike, Joe, Edgar, Foster, Jack, Bobby, Dean, Allen, Bob, Mac, Lyndon, Hubert, and Behl, Grendall, Fisher, Peralta, and that Polish agent provocateur Przyborksi, not to mention the unindicted co-conspirator Richard Milhous Nixon, who had poisoned the well for a generation, nearly destroying the nation's fragile faith in its political processes. Hell, yes, the country was in a sorry way and Washington sorrier still. The Treasury was empty. And as for 'Nam — could it not be humanely said that the true victims were those obliged to dodge and weave to save their skins, nobly refusing to be led like lambs to the killing fields? Victims, yes — and heroes, too, answering a higher call.

But these complaints went unsaid. In the amiable setting of Axel's birthday party there was no point refighting the generational quarrel over the size and value of the inheritance; certainly it would be churlish to do so.

The young lawyer turned away, leaving the old warriors to circulate as loud-mouthed curiosities, publicly congratulated and privately despised, the oldest creatures in the zoo and the most troublesome.

The room was brilliantly lit, flowers everywhere along the walls. A barrel-shaped glass vase of red, white, and blue roses, arranged in the French tricolor, rested in the fireplace, pride of place which the ambassador duly noted. Everyone knew that the old man was a great friend of France and that Charles de Gaulle himself had fixed the rosette of the Légion d'Honneur on his lapel, for his wartime exploits and other services to the nation. There had been so many stories about Axel Behl's moment in Aquitaine that Paris sent a team to investigate and establish the truth once and for all. They discovered a hospital record in Poitiers and the report of the gendarme who had found the mangled Jeep. And there the trail ended. No one could account for the twenty-four hours before the accident. The agents ventured deep into the countryside and learned nothing, the peasants so suspicious and closed-mouthed, unwilling to say anything beyond a muttered *comment?* The agents searched for a château, which according to the rumors had been occupied by the two Americans the night before, a château with a vineyard, it was said; but there were dozens of châteaux, and all of them had vineyards. The owners were polite but uninformative. Of a massacre in August 1944, all those questioned were adamant: there had been no massacre because the Germans had gone, routed by Patton. When the investigators inquired into a massacre of French civilians, they were turned away with a shrug and a sigh. So the mystery remained a mystery, though the chief of French intelligence was convinced that everyone was lying and that something most untoward had occurred. One always liked to tie loose ends, but in the meantime Monsieur Behl had performed a number of very valuable services; and his son was no less helpful. Of course the government had a dossier on Alec Behl, courtesy of Avril Raye.

The pianist was playing Jerome Kern but no one was listening. The crowd pulled and surged through the front door, swirling, spilling into the foyer, pausing to greet and be greeted, commencing animated conversations, only to abandon them at the sight of a new arrival. The current was interrupted here and there by eddies of countercurrent, guests stepping out of the way to talk privately or to inspect the artworks, the Hopper over the fireplace and the Caleb Bingham next to the grandfather clock, and the Homer and the Hassan looking oddly out of place, their frames suggesting a cottage on the Maine coast or Cape Cod. Conversation ascended in a crescendo to the ceiling, where it collapsed, crashing to earth. The glass chandeliers trembled in the din.

Weinberg's here; did you see him?

He's an embarrassment —

God, it's warm. Why can't they open the windows? Someone should say something to them.

It's the Secret Service. Damned Gestapo.

Waiters were perspiring as they moved with trays laden with

glasses of Perrier and flutes of Champagne, many more of the former than of the latter. On the sideboard the tub of caviar sat in a puddle of melted ice and the foie gras had started to run, not a pleasant sight at all, and at that moment Mrs. Hardenburg seized a waiter by the arm and told him to replenish the ice at . once and to place the foie gras on a cold platter before her reputation as caterer and social organizer was ruined. And fetch another bottle of Stolichnaya while you're at it, she told the waiter, because on this warm night people wanted something cold in their hands. The strange fact was that while the young and middle-aged sipped Perrier or Champagne, the old people were assembled three-deep at the bar, demanding a gin martini or vodka and tonic or Scotch over ice, in some cases their fingers so bent by arthritis and beset by nervous tremor that they had difficulty holding the glass, and indeed it often clicked against the rings on their fingers.

Everyone had arrived except the President and his wife and the White House chief of staff. A few of the guests were from Europe and the West Coast, a few more from Boston and New York, but mostly they were Washingtonians, each now with his or her little white envelope indicating the table for dinner. There were ten tables of ten, visible now through the double doors, crystal and silver glittering in candlelight; a full moon was rising over the lawn. Envelopes were already being compared, because it was no secret who would be at the head table with the guest of honor. Yet, if one looked around at the distinguished gathering, a bad seat would be hard to imagine. Well, Harold Grendall would be a bad seat. Lloyd Fisher would be worse. André Przyborski would have his hands all over you like a teenager in heat; of course André was gone but his spirit was present. They should be sent to the children's table, where they belonged.

"Lovely party."

"Thanks so much for having us."

"Hello, Alec."

"Virginia," Alec said. He kissed her on the cheek, avoiding the aviator glasses; he noticed she was wearing a tiny gold Cartier wristwatch, the watch peeping out under Armani's creamy silk sleeve. Her voice was newly modulated, the better to butter up a microphone. She had begun to look like Katharine Hepburn. Alec said, "Do you know Avril Raye?"

Virginia Spears nodded at Avril and turned back to Alec. "Is that Bud Weinberg, the one talking to old man Grendall and Lloyd Fisher?" She pointed at the three of them still standing in the wide archway leading to the living room. Harold was talking and the others were laughing. When Alec nodded, she said, "Will you introduce me?"

"Sure," Alec said. "Why?"

"I hear things."

"It's all right," Alec said. "You can talk in front of Avril."

"He has a son, doesn't he?"

"So I've heard."

"Well," Virginia said. "His nomination's kaput."

"Planning on doing some filming?" When she smiled enigmatically, Alec added, "Quite a campaign against Bud."

"The usual," she said with a shrug. "No surprises. Bud Weinberg's put the White House in a mighty bind, and while that doesn't bother me, it bothers them. And that makes a story for me." While she spoke she watched the three in the archway. "I heard he's a nice guy but's got shit for brains. Some after-hours irregularity, too, I hear. Never mind. I'll introduce myself." She swept a glass of Champagne from the tray of a passing waiter and hurried to the side of Harold Grendall, who stopped talking at once.

"Watch out for her, Avril," Alec said.

"I know who she is."

"She was fine when she needed you but she stopped needing people a long time ago. When you talk to her, have your own record."

"I never talked to reporters," Avril said. "Iron rule, no exceptions. I'd leave instructions that I was not in, ever. And then — I don't know when this happened but it seems like yesterday — the only way I could get a message to your government was through people like Virginia Spears. No one reads their mail in this city, and if you get to see someone he's so anxious to explain how difficult his position is and how numerous his burdens that he can't listen to you. I tried to cultivate them, including that one," she said, nodding at Virginia Spears, who had her arm on Harold Grendall's arm and was looking at him as if he were the thirty-year-old Spencer Tracy, "because I had a very important message to send to your national security adviser, the usual NATO trash but it was important to us. And I thought, quite frankly, that with her there might be some female solidarity. That's what I kept reading and hearing in your glorious free press, women helping women because you never get a break with the men. And then I discovered that my time was past. I discovered that they don't want to talk to me. They won't waste their valuable time talking to me because France is not high enough on their food chain and my name hasn't been in the papers so I couldn't possibly know anything and, for me, it was simply too infra dig to tell her plainly — listen, chérie, I'm the resident SDECE here and I have some information to trade so answer your telephone and let's make the bouillabaisse."

Alec began to laugh.

"Virginia Spears, she's disgusting. She probably thinks I'm the embassy sommelier or the ambassador's mistress, though come to think of it, if I were the ambassador's mistress I'd be a reliable source, a middle-aged French bimbo who reads the old man's mail. And I'll tell you something else, Alec. Remember what Monsieur Jefferson said, that if he had the choice of a government without newspapers or newspapers without a government, he wouldn't hesitate to choose the latter? He got his wish."

"You can do better than her. What about Wilson Slyde?"

"I know Wilson. I've met Wilson with you."

"Isn't Wilson good enough for you?"

"I've known him forever. Tell him something, he forgets it. Ask him anything, he waffles. Wilson knows what he knows but doesn't know anything else, you dig? In the old days Wilson was up to speed on everything, but he hasn't been abroad for five years and has no desire to go. He used to know more about the French Army than I did. I don't know why you can't let people be themselves, and earn a living doing what they want to do and are good at. *Merde.*" She paused, irritated, because an unwelcome face was bearing down on them. She said quickly, "God, I'm tired of America. I've O.D.'d on the capital of the Free World. I've been here so long, I've lost control of my own slang. I can't talk to my nephew because I miss half of what he says. I know your argot better than I know my own, and if you're French there's no worse fate. I miss the theater. I miss Paris. I miss Paris more than I can say, and do you know what I miss? I miss the crowds, being carried along by them, enclosed by them, cohabitating with them on those narrow sidewalks that Americans hate so. I'm going to retire at the end of the year and return to my leet-le flat in Mont-par-nasse and spend my time on sidewalks, going with the flow. What's wrong?"

"You remind me of Sandrine."

"Yes," Avril said and appeared to blush.

"Sandrine had a blue Renault. She was homesick for her *car.*"

"The language, too," Avril said.

"And oysters from Normandy."

"It was a long time ago, Alec."

"What difference does that make?"

She looked away and said that she had had too much Champagne.

"It's all right," he said.

"Not all right," she said. "I'm sorry."

Alec was silent as one of the women in basic black approached.

She said, "They've been delayed."

Alec nodded. The woman was attractive. Someone had told him that female Secret Service agents strapped pistols to the inside of their thighs, but he could not see how this would be efficient, and as he looked at the agent, lithe as a fashion model, he decided that he had been lied to.

"We had a message. They're still at the White House."

"A crisis of the national security?" Avril asked.

"I would not know that, ma'am," the agent said, smiling falsely.

"I'm sure it's routine," Avril said. "It usually is."

"He's always late, isn't he?" Alec said.

"They're all late," she said. "All of them. Always. It's one of the things that sets them apart from you and me. They're never on time and they're never, ever early." She put her finger on the button in her ear and listened, her eyes all the while patrolling the room.

"The many burdens of public life," Alec said.

She nodded crisply, still listening.

"But my father is very old."

"Your father," she began.

"You can tell the White House that they don't have to worry, he knows the drill. My father loves drama. And he's never on time, either." Alec leaned close to her and asked her to open the doors to the lawn. "It's stuffy in here. No air."

She shook her head firmly. "No way."

"Why not?"

"Orders," she said, and moved off in response to some mysterious summons.

"What was that about?" Avril asked.

"Control," Alec said. "What it's always about." But on the lawn something moved, and he briefly saw the silhouette of a rifleman near the high hedge. That was unusual. They had not had men on the lawn four years ago. They'd had them on the roof and in the Observatory and billiards room and across the street in the cemetery and among the elms, but not on the back lawn. But four years ago it had been raining heavily and the President had only put in an appearance. Even so, they were able to open the doors. He hoped his father had not seen the rifleman.

"Something strange here," Alec said. "Security's awfully tight."

Avril thought a moment. "We had a report last week. We didn't give it much weight, but we passed it along like a good ally."

Alec smiled. "Because the *Times* wouldn't take it?"

"*Au contraire,*" Avril said. "If there's something involving *your* interest, we get a hearing right away. We're invited straight to the

seventh floor. We get coffee and Danish and expressions of grati-
tude and respect and a nice pat on the back before we're sent on
our way."

Alec turned to greet new arrivals.

"Great party, Alec. Where's your father?"

"Upstairs, Admiral."

"Feeling shipshape, I hope."

"Never better," Alec said as the admiral turned to shake hands
with one of the service secretaries, Alec couldn't remember
which service. The admiral's wife ghosted along behind him like
a destroyer in the wake of an aircraft carrier. When she saw Bud
Weinberg put his hand on her husband's arm, she stepped deftly
between them, sweeping the admiral away with a short nod to
Bud.

"Word's out," Avril said. "Bud's persona non grata. We need
another ante in the kitty. How about you?"

Alec shook his head.

"Paris would suit you. It's ideal for a bachelor and much hap-
pens behind the scenes. My government would approve. Would
it ever."

Alec nodded at someone across the room. In his range of
vision were an anchorman, two Supreme Court justices, the
chairman of the Senate Foreign Relations Committee, an under
secretary of state, the Spanish ambassador, and the Speaker of
the House. Wilson Slyde was talking to the Speaker's new wife,
a svelte beauty who worked for one of the newspapers. Alec was
half-listening to Avril as his eyes patrolled the room. He knew he
would benefit from a change of scene, a different atmosphere on
a different continent, but he could not imagine living anywhere
but Echo House. Nights like this one made everyone stand a
little taller. All capitals suffered by comparison; and then he remembered Constance's prediction and realized that it had come
true at last. He thought that in its own way Washington was the
world's subconscious, momentous and unpredictable, the uneasy presence at every table. He could not bear working in a city
where he did not know the rules and the contents of the many
closets. He would never live in a city where he would have to

read the papers to learn the news, to voluntarily diminish himself, banished to a suburb of the world. The Speaker caught his
eye and winked.

"Admit it," Avril said. "You're bored."

"Not bored," Alec said. "Never bored."

"Stale, then."

"I like it here."

"Let me tell you a story," Avril said. "Stop me if you've heard
it. But it's your sort of story. It was going the rounds of Cairo
last week. True story. There was an army officer who kept pigeons. One night he heard the cat chewing under the bed and
knew at once that the cat had eaten the pigeons. He was beside
himself, because he loved his pigeons. He fetched his service
revolver and shot at the cat, missing the animal but striking the
wall of his apartment. The bullet went through the wall and into
the apartment of his neighbor. The neighbor, a very old imam
who happened to be blind, was taking a bath in a large porcelain
basin. The bullet struck the basin, shattering it, whereupon the
imam rushed into the street shouting that the world was coming
to an end. Chaos theory, according to the Egyptians."

Alec smiled. He had heard the story from Red Lambardo and
he guessed that was where Avril Raye had heard it, too.

"You heard the story," Avril said, adding a pout.

"Only once before," Alec said.

"Guess where I heard it?"

"I know where you heard it."

"Mrs. Pfister," Avril said.

"I didn't know you were a client," Alec said slowly. "And I
never would have guessed. I'm surprised that Mrs. Pfister is still
alive."

"Oh, yes," Avril said. "Very much alive. I saw her the other day.
She's given up her cards and lives in Holland. They expelled her,
you know. I think Axel had something to do with it."

"Axel never had much use for seers. Events foretold or events
recovered. He thought it was a form of hysteria. My mother
went to her after the war. Sylvia swore by Mrs. Pfister."

"Everybody did," Avril said. "First time I went to her, years and years ago, my first tour in the embassy, she looked at the cards for what seemed an eternity. She said, 'You are one of four children. You will never marry.' Again she was silent and I sensed she was struggling. She said she saw a body in a tiny casket, a young girl with chestnut curls. I thought nothing of that because I had no children and no one close to me had small children. And then later when Sandrine died I realized she had been talking about her. She was right about the other things, too. She had an amazing gift. Of course you had to keep an open mind. You had to be open to possibility. When I saw her yesterday she didn't look well. She's very old now." Avril was about to say something more, but Alec was turning because the woman in basic black was at his elbow with a message.

"The President will arrive in ten minutes."

"Crisis over?"

But she was hurrying away toward the door. Suddenly there was purposeful movement of the women in black dresses and the men in suits; and more were moving through the doors to take up their stations here and there in the foyer and the living room; and just as suddenly they seemed to vanish through various doors, into the library and the morning room and onto the lawn, leaving the party where they had found it, noisy and filled with anticipation. Even the waiters stood at attention.

"Mr. Behl? I'm Agent Block. If you have any questions —"

"No questions," Alec said.

"Sorry for all the confusion," he said apologetically.

Alec excused himself and hurried up the staircase to the second floor. He found Axel in his wheelchair reading a book, a glass of Champagne untouched on the table next to him. His face was ashen but he mustered a smile and murmured something. He said, "Gaaard," the word so garbled that Alec did not know what it was. When the old man repeated it, Alec knew he meant Fred Greene, dead now for more than half a century.

Alec said, "Rest in peace."

Axel nodded, remembering.

"Are the rest of them here?" His voice clear now.

"Everybody and then some."

"No," Axel said. "Them. I mean *them*. You know who I mean."

"In a few minutes. The SS is sweeping the house for terrorists right now."

"Will they find any?" He was smiling, the right side of his face drooping like a clown's. "I wish the children were here, too. They'd enjoy the commotion, the cameras and so on."

"They're with Leila and Hugo."

"It's Waltz Night, isn't it?"

"Leila and Hugo never miss one and they see to it that the children don't, either. They want the children properly introduced. So they go to Waltz Night and take golf lessons at the Chevy Chase Club."

"I guess they don't like us much. Truthfully, they chose Waltz Night?"

"Waltz Night," Alec said.

"Incredible," the old man said. Then, "I want you to make me a Scotch and water."

The nurse poked her head in, frowning when she saw Alec at the sideboard cracking ice. When he looked at her she shook her head sharply and withdrew. Alec handed the old man his Scotch, then made a martini for himself, leaning against the mantel, careful not to disturb the photographs. There were half a dozen ordinary photographs in glass frames, most of them grainy and out of focus, mainly of young men, some in uniform and others in baggy suits and Borsalino hats. The old man called them his rogues' firmament. The room was quiet except for subtle vibrations from the first floor.

"Avril Raye's here," Alec said. "And guess who she saw the other day? Mrs. Pfister."

"Impossible," the old man said. "She can't be alive. She's older than I am."

"Still alive," Alec said. "Still selling snake oil." Alec told him the story of the army officer and the imam, but it seemed to lose something in translation, because the old man did not smile or give any sign of having heard.

"Sylvia believed her," Axel said slowly. "Believed every word she said. She went once a week, first lunch, then her hair appointment, then Mrs. Pfister. She was a troublemaker. She was remorseless, worse than any Stalinist. He believed in Siberia, she believed in a deck of cards; and there was no appeal from any ruling she chose to give. So many people were going to her back in the 'forties and 'fifties that the boys got nervous; they thought she might be a blackmailer or working for the other side. So they bugged her house and in that way learned who was pregnant and who was having trouble at the office and who was having lunch with a handsome stranger. Mrs. Pfister had quite a clientele. There was a character in Policy Planning who went to her all the time for advice on the Cuban threat until he had a visit from the boys, who told him to stop. Mrs. Pfister knew more about the State Department than Foster Dulles . . ."

His voice had strengthened as he talked until now he sounded like a young man. His hand was steady as he sipped his Scotch, staring at the photographs on the mantel. Suddenly he laughed, but when next he spoke it was without humor, his voice silky dry and clipped at the edges.

"Sylvia was one of the first, when we returned after the war. She hated Washington so, its coldness and rationality. So she decided to go to Mrs. Pfister for the irrational and was eager to pass the poisoned cup to anyone who was interested, and many were, though it took a while to catch on. It took about a decade, as a matter of fact." Axel moved his shoulders left and right, settling in. "Mrs. Pfister. I haven't heard her name in years. She went out of fashion for a while and we lost interest. Then in the 'sixties people couldn't believe what was happening in front of their eyes. Nothing was working. The country was collapsing and Washington was responsible. So they turned to the spirit world. They turned to psychic mumbo-jumbo, worried about their draft-age sons and what the North Vietnamese would do next, and their own change of life. Everyone lost their nerve, chased by the past and terrified of the future, so they went to Mrs. Pfister. It was a hell of an embarrassment. We shut her down."

"She must have been right some of the time."

"She was," the old man replied. "That was the trouble."

"Avril went for years. Swears by her."

"Avril's been away from Montparnasse for too long."

Alec debated whether to tell the old man about the young girl with chestnut curls in the tiny casket and decided not to.

"She was remorseless," Axel said abruptly. "But Sylvia never saw it that way. Sylvia said Mrs. Pfister only wanted to see people in touch with themselves, whatever the hell that means. She wanted a sunny future for everyone. Basically, she was on the side of women." He paused, his eyes narrowing. "Basically, Stalin wanted people dead."

Alec said nothing to that, but he wondered what prediction Mrs. Pfister had made for his mother.

"Eddie Peralta took charge. We got rid of her, sent her back to wherever she came from and made certain she stayed there." He looked up. "How did we get on this subject?"

Alec said, "The imam."

"I heard that story forty years ago." He looked at his watch. "Are they doing a good job down there? Is the silver polished? Are they using the good crystal?"

"They're fine. Your man in the Kremlin sent caviar."

"I should hope to God he did."

"And I put the French roses in the fireplace."

"Good, good."

Alec was looking at the photographs. There was one of Eisenhower and another of Colonel Donovan, and one of Fred Greene with his arm around Marlene Dietrich, both of them grinning; it was a photograph taken somewhere in Scotland before the war. There was one of Axel sitting on an ammunition case, cleaning his rifle with great concentration, his helmet rakishly cocked to one side as if it were a fedora, a cigarette hanging conspicuously from his mouth; Alec thought of an author's dustjacket photo. And next to that was the shot of a dead German infantryman, his eyes wide open, his stiff fingers touching the Iron Cross that hung around his neck. By itself front and center was the photograph of the girl in the beret, the shot gray and out of focus. Alec noticed that the glass in the frame was smudged with fingerprints.

The old man was silent, watching his son.

He said, "God bless her."

Alec nodded and stepped back.

"All these years. I hate the Pfister woman for what she said about Nadège, and Sylvia for asking her. What did she know about it? Nothing."

"What was that about, actually?"

"We could have used her in the war."

Alec didn't know whether he was talking about Nadège, Mrs. Pfister, or Sylvia.

"She could have come with me on the interrogations. That's what I did, you know, because I spoke German. No one else did. We captured one of their intelligence people in 'forty-three, and after the formal interrogation, which was useless, we began to talk about Goethe and the manuscript known as the ur-Faust. He became emotional and I thought he would break down and tell us what he knew, but he didn't. Thinking about Goethe stiffened his spine. He was contemplating the German soul, never a simple thing. We didn't get the time of day out of him. Ten years after the war he sent me a book he'd written about Goethe and inscribed it: To my American Mephisto. It's in there somewhere." He waved a hand at the bookcase.

"I'll go downstairs now," Alec said. "I think they've arrived." He had felt a minute change of pitch in the room's vibration.

"He would have talked if she'd been there, and how."

"You should come down in five minutes."

"I wish she were here tonight."

"Who's that, Dad?"

"My Nadège, the girl on the bicycle." The old man's voice had thickened and he was squinting. "And Fred. We had quite a time together in France, living in one place and another, always on the run. We were coordinating people who didn't want to be coordinated. We were all so wild. Fred had a temper to go with his red hair. He'd spit in the eye of a President. He gave the count a hard time, too." The old man sipped thoughtfully at his Scotch, giving the impression of a man who counted on his audience to read between the lines.

"Five minutes," Alec said. "Don't be too long; they're waiting downstairs." He rose and stepped to the door, standing there with his hand on the knob.

"I've been thinking about Ed lately. In my father's day you could have spoken to a man and killed that investigation. I should have done more. I had the ways and means. I had enough on Lambardo to put him away for good. But I thought the thing would resolve itself. I never believed they'd sacrifice Ed. Ed was their loyalist. The Peraltas are Spanish, you know. Old Spanish family, bluebloods. In Spain they're serious about loyalty." He shook his head sadly and waved in the direction of the book-case, as if the answer were to be found on the shelves — *The Federalist Papers*, Forrestal's diaries, Freeman's Lee, Sandburg's Lincoln, General Grant's memoirs, Lippmann's *A Preface to Morals*, Adams's *Democracy*, *Huckleberry Finn*, Parrington's *Main Currents of American Thought*, Bailyn's *The Ideological Origins of the American Revolution*.

"The Spanish people. Beautiful people, and so badly used." He flinched then, shuddering, his head turning, the scar livid in the grayness of his face, the scar a fault line that reached to the center of his skull. He sighed heavily, losing breath, leaning forward in his wheelchair, fighting for balance, his starched shirt creaking.

Alec moved quickly to his side, supporting him; and then he heard the old man mutter something from a distant region of his mind, a woman falling in a storm of gunfire —

Axel looked up suspiciously, his eyes hooded and without focus. But the episode passed and he lifted his chin defiantly, growling, "Don't worry, I know where I am."

"I know you do."

"God, how they fought. The Spanish."

"Are you all right now?" The old man had a wild look in his eye.

"Last time I believed in anything, until I met Nadège."

Alec nodded; an encounter more than half a century past. Of course what the statesman forgets is as important as what he remembers. The same thing was true for nations.

"How passionate the Spanish were! Mystics in their souls, anarchists in their hearts. The Enlightenment never got that far south. The Enlightenment stopped at the Pyrenees." His voice was thick but color was returning to his face. He brought his hand up, extending his finger as if it were the barrel of a revolver. "You asked me what it was about, Nadège, Sylvia, and Mrs. Pfister. It was what it's always about, possession. They want to own your heart. They gaze at a portrait on the gallery wall and they want to be both viewer and artist, canvas and paint. Mrs. Pfister said that Nadège died and that I was responsible. But she was alive when I left. I never would have abandoned her, you see. Axel Behl would never do such a thing, never. It's only a feature of the accident that I can't remember a thing. But you put it behind you because you have to. Isn't the important thing to forgive yourself?" He made a fist, then moved his fingers in the direction of the mantel, smiling suddenly as he welcomed a new thought; the old one had vanished. "Bring me the picture of Fred and his friend."

Alec handed him the photograph of Fred Greene and Marlene Dietrich.

The nurse looked through the door; noise from downstairs came with her. "Is everything all right? I heard something." The old man looked at her as if she were Marlene Dietrich, tilting his head and half-closing his eyes, the debonair look he had when he was a young man.

Alec said, "We're fine."

"She gave Fred an original print of *The Blue Angel*. I kept it for safekeeping when we went to France. It's around here somewhere."

Alec looked at his watch.

"I live in a museum."

Alec opened the door.

"Everyone's dead now," the old man said with sudden enthusiasm. "I helped make the city of the dead and now I live in it, the last corpse. Many of them I don't even know. Millions."

"Mr. Behl," the nurse said.

"All that's missing is the crêpe and the coffins. The pallbearers are already here. Do you think our commander-in-chief can deliver a suitable eulogy?" Axel glared at the nurse. "What do you know about it, Marlene? Not a damned thing. You're out of it. You're not au courant." He looked at her, blinking. He knew he had made an error of speech but did not know what it was. He finished his Scotch and set the glass carefully on the table next to the untouched Champagne. He turned to Alec and said quietly, "I'll be down in ten minutes. I'll use the elevator."

"I'll come and get you," Alec said.

"Fine."

"It'll be a fine party," Alec said.

"I need a fresh shirt," Axel said to the nurse.

Alec closed the door softly and stepped to the banister. The old man had more angles than a mountain face and his memory was as relentless as a dentist's drill. Good luck to his dinner partners, arrived at last. The President and his wife and the chief of staff were standing in the foyer, smiling broadly, shaking hands with everyone in sight as if Echo House were a hotel ballroom and the birthday party a political rally. The White House photographer sauntered along beside them, casually checking the settings on her Nikon and then shooting one-handed, giving notice that this was an informal assignment, a professional's grace and favor. The pianist was in mid-riff and the waiters moved respectfully to one side. Mrs. Hardenburg served the late arrivals Champagne. The President appeared entirely relaxed, an official at ease and confident in friendly and familiar surroundings. Probably he thought that all private houses in Washington were, to some degree, his own. The other guests wore worldly faces as they stepped forward to shake hands and say a few respectful words, everyone standing straight as soldiers on parade. Even those who knew the President well were composed, and perhaps them most of all. Familiarity bred deep respect. The photographer maneuvered discreetly a few steps away, her legs now together, now apart, as if she were dancing.

There were men in the room who believed that if the cards had been dealt fairly, they would be the one striding through the door at Echo House discharging an aura of authority and inevitability, and burdens splendidly borne. Those who did not know the President well were wearing the faces of the people they wanted to be or thought they were — Voltaire, Dean Acheson, Aristotle, Walter Lippmann, Henry Luce, Jacqueline Onassis, Joan of Arc, Edith Wharton, Duke Ellington or the Duke of Marlborough, Ahab, Anna, old Sartoris, Gatsby, or Portia. Probably that was the trouble with being President; you never met a natural face; the face was always rearranged to suggest someone else. Of course that could be the fun of it, too, if you were a President with an appreciation of hypocrisy and a gift for abstraction. Alec watched the President shake hands with Harold Grendall, Harold beaming and moving in close, saying something private into his ear, the President smiling gamely and noncommittally, patting Harold on the arm and sauntering further into the crowd. There were many old faces who deserved a nod. Bud Weinberg was one of the first, the President rewarding him with a double handshake and a warm smile, the sort of spontaneous open-hearted greeting that had become a signature, Bud replying with a helpless grin that announced, of course he couldn't know about the wretched rumors surrounding the nomination to Embassy Paris; the President was a busy man with a full plate of life-and-death issues; when the chips were down and he was fully focused, the President would certainly do the right thing. He always had before. The photographer continued to move with the President, shooting with one hand. Alec hurried downstairs to greet the President's wife.

"How are you, Flo?"

"Don't call me that," she said, but she was smiling as she said it.

Mutual friends had told him she had aged terribly and they were not wrong. Her hair was gray and thinning and her voice tired. She was limping, a sprained ankle caused by a skiing accident, according to the explanation given by the White House. She asked after Axel and then in a voice so low it could not be heard more than a foot away thanked him for inviting them; it was rare that they had an evening out in a private house among friends. The White House was a prison worse even than Sing

Sing, with smirking Secret Service louts for jailers. The place
bristled with weapons and you couldn't move five feet without being photographed by that tart who thinks she's Cartier-
Bresson but's just another political payoff like everything else in
this rancid town, so why don't you come over sometime for a
drink, say around three in the afternoon. I'll raise Lester Lanin
from the dead and we can dance a waltz. I never see you anymore, Alec.

Alec said, "You need a vacation."

She took a glass of Champagne from the waiter at their elbow.
"A vacation's not allowed. We're allowed to go places, the West
Coast or Vermont. We can go scuba diving or skiing. But it's
never a vacation, because there are people wherever we go. How
can you have a vacation when you're surrounded by Secret Service louts and three hundred television cameras?"

"Sorry about your ankle," he said.

"So you've heard the rumors, too."

"I heard skiing."

"You heard wrong," she said.

"Don't worry, with the press on the case we'll soon get to the
bottom of things." This was a joke but she did not smile. Her
expression was distant and unreadable and then he realized she
was watching the photographer focus on the President and Avril Raye. On impulse Alec said, "Can you do anything for Bud
Weinberg?"

She looked at him coldly and said, "No."

"The stories aren't true, you know."

She laughed harshly. "When did that matter?"

"Bud's a good friend," he said.

"Talk to Red. Red's handling it."

"You could help."

"It's Red's worry. Red's good at worrying. Red's been worrying for other people for years and years. What I know for sure
is that Bud Weinberg isn't *our* worry. The President has other
things on his mind. And so do I. Talk to Red." She glared at him
and sneered, "But thanks so much for asking. That's why I was
so pleased to come to Echo House tonight, so I could talk to

you about that bastard Weinberg, and remember that the White House is with us wherever we go."

She took him to say hello to her husband. Alec remembered to thank him for the doormat, but the President only smiled suspiciously.

"My idea," the President's wife said, and they moved on.

Then Red Lambardo was at his side, asking where the guest of honor was and rolling his eyes when he was told that the old man was fortifying himself with Scotch and would be down shortly.

The chief of staff said, "It's good to be back at Echo House, the real world. It's been a while since I've seen you, Alec. Been so busy lately trying to reorganize things in the West Wing. It's been chaos. Can I put you on the list for dinner next week? It's for the German chancellor. Let me know." He was admiring the paintings, the Homer and the Hassam specifically, when he lowered his voice. "I'm glad to be here, truly. Wish the old man well. Your father's friendship has meant a lot to me over the years."

Alec thought, Everything that rises must converge. He watched the President's wife take another glass of Champagne, laughing now at something Avril Raye had said. There were half a dozen women surrounding her but the photographer had been banished to the dining room. He said, "Axel takes pride in the success of his younger friends. Always has."

The chief of staff lowered his voice still further and confided that Axel had sent him a memo on the Russian situation, superb memo that contained information he had not known. The State Department and CIA were similarly in the dark. So he was able to put the President in the picture and they were both grateful, as Alec would see when the evening commenced. Red Lambardo smiled broadly and inside the smile Alec could recollect the man in red suspenders he had met years before with Leila. Alec remembered his nonchalance describing an afternoon with "Jack" around the pool in Palm Beach, and later his mysterious Working Group. Red had implied they would overthrow Castro together. Castro then seemed a greater menace than Stalin had ten years earlier. No man had worked harder scrambling to the top of the tree, and now he was there, a loyalist whose devotion reached beyond party or institution to the President personally.

"Axel knows the country backwards and forwards," the chief of staff said. "One of the things I regret, I never traveled much. Never had the time, and I suppose Washington was always my town. The other places are just suburbs, as you've said so often. Amazing. He made his first trip to Moscow in the nineteen-thirties."

Alec said, "Care for some caviar?" Mrs. Hardenburg was hovering near them, two plates in her hand.

"No caviar, thanks. Caviar gives me gas. My doctor has me on a salt-free diet. You can't be too careful."

"Red," Alec said. He wanted to ask the chief of staff about Bud Weinberg, and if there was anything to be done and whether his own name fit into the scheme of things.

"The nineteen-thirties was an awkward time to go to the Soviet Union," Red said. "It was like Hanoi in the 'sixties, a controversial thing. Trip like that gets into your file and there's no way to get it out. He had some trouble with McCarthy, didn't he?"

"Some trouble," Alec said.

The chief of staff heard something in Alec's voice and frowned. "Strange period. Thank God it's behind us, nameless accusers, all the rest. Joe was strange. The people around him were strange. But he was a victim, too, you know. He was a victim of his circumstances."

"He was the circumstances, Red."

The photographer was maneuvering in their vicinity, setting up a shot, but the chief of staff waved her away. "True, but isn't there another point to be made here? Joe had a substance abuse problem. He had a chemical dependency. He was beaten as a child. Someone told me just the other day, he was abused by his father. And people didn't like Joe's manners. Senator Joe was a little coarse for Georgetown." The chief of staff shrugged; point made. He fluttered his hand at someone nearby, tilting his head to examine the Homer, a dory adrift on a featureless ocean. "The media didn't do its job. Of course the times were different. Different atmosphere. In some ways I prefer the media the way it was, don't you?"

Red Lambardo smiled thinly and moved closer. "Axel tried to put one over on me. Along with the memo he sent me a letter from some refugee organization that supports the Spanish exiles, 'Our Republican friends living in the vastness of the Pyrenees blah blah blah . . .' Christ, I didn't know any of them were still alive. Axel's comrades live longer'n crocodiles, all those Pepes and Pablos buying dynamite to blow up Franco's tomb or carbomb the king. Axel suggested a thousand dollars. But we have our own homeless, our poor Vietnam vets doing their damnedest to cope even after all these years. Who are they in the Pyrenees anyway? I don't know them. I don't give a crap about them, out of it for sixty years, singing the *Internationale* and waving the Red flag, fuck them."

"There are only a few of them left, old men and some women. Trying to get by."

"Forget it," Red said. "That kind of trouble I don't need. You've got to watch your back in this town. Particularly when you give money. God, Washington's a hard place."

"Try the Pyrenees some time."

"People just waiting to slice you up when you make the wrong move." He squinted at the Homer. "You can't be too careful. That's how people get marginalized once and for all. They go off the screen. They're untouchable, more trouble than they're worth."

"Like Bud Weinberg?"

"Exactly," Red said.

"He doesn't know where he stands."

"He better find out."

"He wonders if he has any support at your place."

The chief of staff sighed and shook his head. "Weinberg was helpful to us in the campaign. He raised money in places we didn't expect. So we owe him. But we don't owe him as much as he thinks we do. He doesn't understand that we operate in a different reality. *This is the White House.* He doesn't understand the fundamentals of the world we live in."

"The rumors are false."

"I'm glad to know that, Alec. But it depends on who you talk to, doesn't it? Buddy Weinberg's got some enemies and they're smarter than he is. They threw smoke and Bud didn't stop it. He miscalculated. He said, What the hell, I'm innocent. But you know as well as I do that smoke's fire. There's no difference between them, except that in some ways smoke's worse because it's so formless, you see, like a cloud in the sky that's Abe Lincoln's beard one moment and a white bunny rabbit the next. I'm talking perception here. Bud didn't get ahead of the curve. So he's an embarrassment and he's got to withdraw, the sooner the better. Someone has to tell him that and make it stick. It's not going to be me because I don't want the White House anywhere near him. You want to?"

"Why not you, Red? You got him there."

"I never thought I'd have to draw diagrams for Alec Behl. So I'll just say that I've better things to do with my time. This is pissant stuff compared to the rest of our agenda." Now Red watched the President's wife approach with Avril Raye. He tried to place Avril and failed, a fat lady who was always around. She wasn't political; he knew that. He thought she was someone's wife but, Jesus, she needed an aerobics class or fewer cashews. "No one gives a damn about France. We could send old man Grendall to France, no one'd care. We could send Wilson. We could send you. But we're not sending Bud Weinberg, so have a word with him, Alec. Help us out. It'd be a favor I wouldn't forget." The chief of staff stepped back because the women were almost within earshot. "And drop over to the White House some afternoon; our First Lady could use some reliable company. She never sees her old friends anymore and we're not so pleased with some of her new friends. Why is it that people think they can make new friends in the White House? It's always a mistake. You have to stick with the friends you have and hope they fit in and if they don't, tough shit. Isn't that true in life generally?"

"Sorry I was cross with you, Alec," the President's wife said. She smiled dully. "I've gotten so grumpy lately."

"We all have," Alec said.

"The President's waiting," Red said.

"And I like it when you call me Flo."

"We've been friends a long time," Alec said.

"I've taken up bridge, did I tell you? I used to play bridge in Oak Park eons ago and now I'm playing again, two tables in the private quarters. We have some lunch and then we play, my buddies and me. And I see my life dribbling away around the bridge table. It's a high-stakes game but that isn't the reason. I never see my old friends anymore, so many of them are irritated at the White House, one thing and another. I can't keep the problems straight. I was explaining it to Avril. She pointed out that if you were our ambassador there'd be good reason to go to France. Can you believe it, I've never been. I've never seen the Louvre. I've never seen a château. Jackie Kennedy used to travel abroad all the time, Europe, the Aegean. In India she met a maharajah. I guess in the early days the White House was everything she hoped it would be; and then she needed a vacation like any ordinary person, so she went abroad. If I had an escort then I could see Louvre and the châteaux of the Loire."

Alec nodded. Her voice had risen and he had an idea she was about to break down.

"A private visit," she said. "You could take me to the châteaux. And along the way we could lose the Secret Service. Avril could arrange security."

"Yes, of course," Avril said, her eyes worried, turning to Alec for help. A dozen people had gathered around them, listening in. They were smiling at what seemed to be repartee. Virginia Spears leaned forward, looking hard at the President's wife, knowing at once that something was not quite right. The First Lady, talking intently to Alec, was unaware that she was spilling her Champagne.

"We'll see," Red said quietly. He put his hand on her elbow.

"No press," she said again.

"You could go incognito," Alec said, trying to keep things light.

"A new haircut?"

The others around them began to laugh. How droll. The President's wife hadn't changed her hair in twenty years; it was a signature as distinctive as her husband's striped shirts, evidence of stability, a stubborn refusal to follow fashion.

"I thought I'd love it," the President's wife said, her voice rising again. "Who wouldn't love it? So many worthwhile things to do and all the time in the world to do them and everyone watching, inspecting you while they listen to every word. At first you love it and then you think you can't do without it and they can't either, the cameras and the attention and admiration because you're the President's wife and live in the White House and — the good you're doing, being there. You should read the letters sometime, they'd break your heart. Except when you leave, the sick are just as sick and the elderly as old and the children as famished and the dispossessed as insulted, and the flood waters are still rising. I'd thought about it so long, even in my dreams at night. I'd read everything and talked to the people I admired. Jackie was so reticent, no help at all, when I talked to her in late 'sixty-two, I guess it was. I thought she had a secret and didn't want to let me in on it. Do you think she had some private knowledge that she dared not share? Of course I was so young then, just a freshman congressman's wife, even younger than she was."

"The President's asking for you," Red said loudly. The others had begun to stir, a nervous silence becoming a kind of expectant hush that spread in the foyer, people turning their heads at Red's harsh voice.

"— and then later, after the assassination and all the stories, I couldn't bring myself to ask her again. Wouldn't it have been indecent? Jackie, how did you manage to save yourself?"

"Flo," Alec said gently, and at the name the President's wife smiled warmly, her eyes brimming.

"Well, well!" Red Lambardo cried. "And here he is at last! Here's the birthday boy, Axel himself!"

Alec looked up. The old man was gliding through the upstairs doors, the nurse behind him. He was guiding the wheelchair himself, pausing at the top of the curving staircase to observe his party. He was bathed in yellow light from the chandeliers, the scar a dark line on his cheek; but his white shirt was dazzling and he wore a red rose in his lapel. He looked down, his eyes half-lidded, smiling crookedly. Something almost boyish about him, Alec thought, except he was not in motion as a boy would be but still as a piece of sculpture. His hands were clasped in his lap. Red began to clap. Presently the room was loud with cheers and applause, the President cheering loudest of all, then raising his glass in a toast.

"Mr. Behl?" Agent Block was at Alec's elbow.

"Later," Alec said. He bent to listen to something the President's wife said, but Red intervened, removing the Champagne glass from her hand. She began to clap politely as he led her away, Virginia Spears trailing close by.

"There's a lady at the door," the agent said.

"You take care of it," Alec snapped. The applause diminished. His father had a distracted look on his face, as if he were trying to remember something.

The President waited for silence. At such moments those in his vicinity believed he was nearly godlike in his ability to command a room, the great authority of the presidency merging with his own personality and becoming indistinguishable from it. They felt the spirits of Jefferson and Lincoln and FDR hovering close by, offering a benediction. Were they not in a certain sense his brothers? And Lincoln and FDR had visited this very house, drinking and dining while they settled matters of state. When the President looked left and a shadow crossed his face, only Red Lambardo knew that the Man's sense of well-being was evaporating, dying as the applause died; he had seen his wife's troubled expression, and knew what it portended. It was so unfair, she had become such a burden, a liability all around, a threat to his equilibrium. The President had expected things to be perfect, and now they weren't.

It was time to speak but still the President waited. The chief of staff knew that he intended to reprise the career of Axel Behl, no easy task, since so many of the old bastard's contributions to the life of the nation were sub rosa, made many years before and dubious even then, not precisely illegitimate but surely on the margins of the law. No one now living, not even the Venerables, could say with absolute confidence exactly what these contributions entailed, except that everyone had been talking about them in the abstract for years, praise for a long-retired conductor whose most brilliant performances had never been recorded. So the President faltered, his celebrated fluency collapsing under the weight of uncertainty; and those in the room would call him to account for any error of fact or judgment. He was fond of enumeration, four-point programs, three-stage negotiations, two-step solutions, always upbeat; Lambardo watched the Man's face grow dour and knew now that his own ass was on the line, for failing to prepare a proper speech. Of course Red assumed he'd know, a figure as celebrated as Axel Behl. But summarizing the career was like describing an iceberg, seven-eighths below the surface. Red had no idea of the shape of things in the darkness and the cold. So much of what Axel represented seemed to be personified by the grandeur and formality of Echo House and its many ghosts, along with the eminent living now gathered in the foyer in a spirit of comradeship and celebration. If only the American people were as good and competent and compassionate as their government, Red thought but did not say.

And then the Man smiled, the one-hundred-watt smile that took your breath away with its whole-souled ardor; and Red knew he'd reached down deep and found the elusive key. The President's voice caught, as it had a way of doing at moments of high improvisation. At that exact moment Red knew why this Man was President — in the absence of a great war or a mighty depression he could give the people a sense of who they were and the splendid destiny that beckoned. The President picked up his cadence, his voice throbbing with the vibrato of a cello. He wanted to give them a brief sermon.

Let us praise the character of Americans who choose a life in the arena. Let us praise the passion for politics and government despite its many disadvantages, the slanders, the misrepresentations, the pettifoggery and the condescension, the unwholesome cynicism of the critics. You need the hide of a rhinoceros and the mind of Copernicus! So Axel Behl was a man very much like himself and the many other fine men and women who served the government — and here it seemed to occur to the President that Axel had always shied from the arena, preferring work in the shadows, the master craftsman who sharpened the swords and prepared the bulls but did not remain for the cutting. The President heard the anticipation in the foyer and lowered his voice another half-octave.

"A patriot, an exemplary Washingtonian, a Washingtonian of principle, honor, and vision, one of us through and through, a true man of state. On behalf of our grateful nation —"

The President put out his hand like a relay runner awaiting the baton, and Red Lambardo slapped a long blue box into it. The President eased off its cover and raised the golden medal high above his head.

"The Presidential Medal of Freedom to you, Axel Behl!"

The President's voice echoed in the foyer while the old man waited, expressionless, his hands still folded in his lap. There were cries of approval, then a crash of applause. The photographer was maneuvering behind the President, shooting upward to pose him and the old man in the same frame. Red Lambardo had retreated, saying something now to the President's wife, knowing that his Man had lost his way in the beginning but had recovered in fine style; and standing behind the chief of staff was Sylvia Behl, a horrified look on her face. Axel looked like death itself. She leaned heavily on Agent Block's arm, and then Harold Grendall was at her side.

Alec moved to the foot of the staircase, motioning to the nurse to turn the wheelchair in the direction of the elevator. But she was watching the old man and did not notice his son and could have done nothing if she had, for Axel was deep in thought and would move only when he was ready. Alec started toward the stairs. His father was staring at the President, who was nodding and accepting congratulations. Everyone agreed that his remarks had struck just the right note, modest yet assertive; they boosted everyone's morale. He stood now with the medal in his hand, wondering if he should follow Alec. Then he decided against it. Conversation rose again amid the merry crush around the bar.

Alec had paused at the bottom step, allowing the drama to build a little. The waiters commenced to pass Champagne and the pianist to play *Happy Birthday,* everyone singing with full throat. Sentiment was never wholly absent from the capital, so there were a few moist eyes watching the old man at the summit of the staircase, bathed in the yellow light of the chandeliers.

Alec gave his father a little wry salute, but the old man's half-lidded eyes never moved. He seemed not to hear the music and the applause and perhaps he was in another place altogether, his eyes fixed on a point just over Red Lambardo's shoulder and widening as if he had seen an apparition or some half-remembered figure from the distant and irrecoverable past, unwelcome from the expression on his face, which seemed to be one of unambiguous astonishment, as if the events of his life had returned in one appalling spasm and he was now reliving each one. He made an abrupt motion with his hand, the push-pull of putting a car in gear; and then he slowly pressed both palms over his eyes and waited. The applause and singing died, replaced by a nervous rustle — and then he shuddered, his head snapping forward, eyes still covered, his body swaying.

The wheelchair glided forward on its own motion, the front wheels slipping over the top step of the staircase. The chair leaned slowly sideways and fell with a crash. The old man was thrown into the banister. Someone cried out and the nurse made a frantic lunge, too late. The empty chair hit the second step with a bang as loud as a pistol shot, and then another and a third as it tumbled violently end over end, Axel rolling behind it. There was a series of brittle snaps, the noise a dry stick makes when it is broken, and Alec knew these were the sounds of his father's bones. Still, Axel Behl fell cautiously, as if he knew there was no urgency in his descent.

A woman screamed, the scream echoing and joined by others in the stampede to avoid the chair, entirely out of control as it careened from one step to the next and finally to the floor, where it broke apart, the pieces sliding wildly across the marble, people scrambling to avoid their path. The old man followed at a distance, his body dropping tactfully from one step to the next, his limbs flapping like a rag doll's, his head bloody and tormented as if beaten; and still he had uttered no sound or given any sign that he was aware of the disaster, except his obvious discipline in remaining sightless, his palms over his eyes until the very end. At last he came to rest near the foot of the stairs.

A waiter dropped his tray with a terrible crash. There was uncontrolled movement everywhere inside the noise. Alec had waited on the bottom step, at first shocked and immobile but finally beginning to move to intercept his father, when suddenly he was on his back, knocked down by a Secret Service agent who was rushing to the President's side. Now three agents surrounded the frightened President and hustled him from the foyer to the safety of the garden room. The agents were shouting to one another and waving their ugly weapons, telling people to stand clear or to lie down, the President's life was in danger.

Alec did not understand why this should be so. The President had nothing to do with this catastrophe. When he looked closely at his father at last, Alec knew he was dead. He could not be otherwise; there was something terribly out of place with the body and its position on the stairs, one leg bent at an impossible angle, the other curled under him. Blood was on his face and shirt, and that too was unnatural. Alec felt violent movement all around him. The President's wife was surrounded and carried away struggling, roughly handled by the young women in basic black. She was followed by the photographer and Red Lambardo, both crouching as if under fire, covered by Secret Service agents, their guns poked like pikestaffs at the terrified company. The presidential party was hustled out the front door and then to the driveway, where presently were heard sirens and the squeal of tires. Two agents remained at the door, kneeling, with weapons in their hands. One of them was the attractive agent who had spoken to Alec. Her skirt was hiked up around her thighs and she was looking wildly left and right, talking nonstop into the tiny microphone on her lapel.

Alec struggled to rise and to bring himself to the present

moment. He had no idea how many minutes had passed. He saw his father lying on the third step, his foot caught grotesquely in the balustrade. Both legs were broken and blood was still leaking from the wounds on his skull, the blood thin and pink as a child's watercolor, leaking down his face and staining his wing-collared shirt. Blood oozed from his eyes and collected on his cheeks. His eyes were half-lidded so that you could not see the irises.

Alec raised himself on one arm. The nurse was creeping down the stairs, sidestepping pieces of the wheelchair. Two older men were at Axel's side, gesturing helplessly, their faces horrified. They were holding glasses of Champagne. The nurse roughly pushed them aside and bent to press the old man's neck. With a brusque motion she closed his eyelids, then wiped her fingers on her skirt.

Alec heaved himself to his feet with difficulty and went to his father. The moment when the wheels paused at the top step was still in his mind, a still photograph that would not vanish. Axel had the look of a man who had seen his accuser, Nemesis herself. Defiance gave way to something like contrition, and he bowed his head. Alec saw the rubber wheels moving forward and back and forward again, and the chair falling and his father falling with it, his hands over his eyes and his bones breaking.

He took Axel's hand, the skin stretched and wrinkled as fine paper, warm to the touch, dry and manicured as it had been moments earlier, when he was talking about Marlene Dietrich. "A doctor," Alec said.

But the nurse looked at him blankly.

"A doctor!" Alec roared, furious at the semicircle of faces above him, yet knowing at once that there was no doctor. Doctors were not part of the Behl circle, except for an amiable psychiatrist with a special practice. There were writers and editors and diplomats and politicians and bankers and lawyers and industrialists enough to administer a small nation. But there were no doctors.

Avril Raye had come up behind him now and put a hand on his shoulder. She said, "Alec, dear."

"It was a stroke," the nurse said authoritatively.

Alec said to Avril, "Did you see the way he dipped his head and raised his hand as if he was surrendering?" Avril nodded. She had been standing next to Sylvia.

The nurse said, "He was talking strangely after you left."

"He was talking about the war," Alec said.

"He was talking to his photographs," she said.

"Same thing," Alec said, pointing at the broken body, looking for all the world like a battlefield casualty, even the tuxedo with its red rose and ribbon of the Légion d'Honneur. He removed his own jacket and covered his father's torso and face, knowing this would be the last time he would see it.

People had begun to gather around him, murmuring expressions of sympathy. Someone asked if he wanted a drink. The old man's death had been so violent and so unexpected that people were confused in their reactions, uncertain what to do or say. A few of them were still holding drinks and others were already slipping out the front door, wanting no more to do with this evil. Alec could see the television lights illuminating the street and the elm trees. He could hear raised voices, reporters demanding admission to Echo House to see the disaster for themselves. The two Secret Service agents were still at the door, but they had holstered their guns and were conferring earnestly with a District policeman. Suddenly the three turned to look at him, their expressions apologetic.

Then Harold Grendall and Lloyd Fisher were at his side. They were perspiring heavily. Bud Weinberg was behind them. Harold laid his heavy arm on Alec's back and murmured how sorry he was, what a dreadful affair. He began an involved anecdote about a premonition he had had years ago but did not finish. Well, Axel had had a good life. They all had. We've had the best of it, Harold said bitterly, and now maybe it was time for all of them to go.

"They thought there was an attack on the President's life," Harold added sourly. "They thought they heard shots."

"Gunshots?"

"Axel's wheelchair banging into the wall and on the stairs. I don't know what they thought, Alec. It was just an accident. I don't think they understand accidents. The look on Lambardo's face was something to see, all right. He probably saw himself an also-ran in the obits."

"Morons," Bud Weinberg said.

"Let's get some air in here." Alec turned to a waiter standing nearby and asked him to open the doors, but he refused. The Secret Service had given orders. The doors stayed closed until the President was safely inside the White House. Alec looked outside. The rifleman was standing on the croquet court, smoking a cigarette.

"Alec," Harold said. "Sylvia's here." He pointed at her sitting quietly on a chair in the dining room, glaring at Constance's portrait. Alec had to look twice, she seemed so very composed, even the glare. He rose painfully and limped to the bar to pour two glasses of Champagne. They sat together sipping Champagne. When Alec said that Axel apparently had had a stroke and was unconscious when he fell and therefore had no pain, Sylvia glanced at him sideways and said that he had been in terrible pain for half his lifetime and would not know what life was like without it and that therefore what Axel felt or thought or believed in his last moments could only be imagined. He was not interested in pain, his own or others'. He was forever alone. What he felt or thought or believed generally could only be imagined, because he lived in a world that did not value confession, and he trusted no one. Axel was the last aristocrat. He was always brave, Sylvia added, when it suited him.

"I don't think he had much of a life," she said.

"You'd get some disagreement there," Alec said. He saw that she had been crying, but her voice was steady now.

"Probably," she said. "I don't care."

"He had a magnificent life," Alec said.

"At least I had Willy," she murmured. "Poor Axel. He never wrestled with angels."

"A wonderful life," Alec said stubbornly. Then, "How did you get in?"

"Agent Block let me in," she replied. "He said you approved it, as if I needed your approval to enter Echo House."

They sat a few more moments in strained silence, staring across the dining room through the foyer to the staircase, where the dead man was. Alec looked at his watch, realizing suddenly that Echo House was now his alone; and he was head of the family. He swallowed some Champagne, but it tasted like salt. He helped his mother to her feet and they walked slowly from the dining room into the foyer.

Sylvia said, "Do you mind if I keep this?" She held the Presidential Medal of Freedom by its ribbon, swinging it back and forth. "The President dropped it. And I picked it up."

Alec caught the medal in midair. "It belongs to Echo House."

She let it go, smiling her wry smile. "I suppose it would, wouldn't it?"

"Definitely," Alec said and put the medal in his pocket.

"The President seemed to lose his way, didn't he? As if he wasn't quite certain who Axel Behl was. I guess he didn't know that Axel won the Cold War singlehanded." She smiled maliciously. "How quickly they forget."

Alec smiled at that. She had a point.

"I wish Willy were here," she said sadly and walked off to join Harold and Lloyd.

"Mr. Behl?" It was the Secret Service agent. "I'm very sorry."

Alec looked at her.

"Things happened so quickly and we were on double alert tonight. We didn't have time to evaluate the situation. I've called an ambulance for your father." She drew him aside and said there was another problem and she was sorry to bother him with it, but. She nodded at the doorway, where the District policeman stood, hat in hand. The other Secret Service agent had vanished. "The news media wants to come in."

Alec said, "No."

"Because the President was involved, they say they have a right. They're being insistent. Frankly, they're making a fuss and holding us responsible. It's because the President was here, you see. They're concerned that facts are being withheld and it's the fault of the Secret Service. I promised I'd speak to you before we left. And as a matter of fact, they're already filming." She pointed out the front door, where the lights were close up now and much brighter than they had been. Cameras were panning the foyer, then focusing on the body and moving up the stairs. The District policeman was standing on the threshold, looking grim.

"What do they think is being withheld?"

"They don't know. That's why they want to come in and ask questions, to satisfy themselves as to the facts of the matter. You know how they are. They don't want to be intrusive. They feel your pain."

"No, they don't," Alec said. He got the attention of the District policeman and motioned with his hand, Shut the door. With a nod and a smile, the policeman obliged, and suddenly the foyer was much darker. Alec heard shouts outside and the ringing of the doorbell. He was light-headed in the stale indoor air, thick as mucus. "Will you tell that waiter that it's all right to open the back doors."

She nodded at the waiter. "Do you think you could speak to the media yourself?"

The doorbell continued to ring. Alec glanced into the dining room, where Virginia Spears was leaning against the sideboard making notes. Her gold pen glittered in the light and he guessed that in a moment she'd be over for an interview, asking him what the President did and where Lambardo was when the accident occurred. And where exactly was the First Lady, who seemed so strange earlier in the evening . . . One of the other journalists was on the telephone, speaking rapidly, apparently narrating from memory, for he had no notepad; he stared at the corpse while he talked. Almost everyone was gone now, leaving the foyer a disheveled and forlorn place. It had the depleted look of a stage set after the performance, all the energy absorbed by the audience. The doorbell rang now at one-second intervals.

"Alec?" Virginia Spears touched his arm.

"No comment," he said.

"I was in another part of the room. Is it true that the President ducked behind his wife when he heard the shots?"

"I have no idea," Alec said. "Go away."

"Won't take a sec."

"Go away," he said again.

"The story won't go away, and how," she said. She put her pen between her teeth and headed for Harold Grendall.

"That god damned doorbell," Alec said to the Secret Service agent.

She was listening to the microphone in her ear. "The ambulance is outside."

"Tell them to come in through the side door. No press."

"This is no longer our affair, Mr. Behl. Our responsibility is to the President."

Then the medical team was suddenly in the room, standing uncertainly a moment before moving swiftly to the dead man. They verified his condition, then removed Alec's tuxedo jacket and replaced it with a blanket. No one said anything while they went about their business. Alec described the accident, giving his father's name and age, his place of birth and his occupation, fumbling with the last, finally saying "statesman." He had to speak loudly over the ringing of the doorbell, which had begun to sound to him like a piece of reductionist music. The coroner's man made notes and handed him a form to sign. When he asked if there had been witnesses, Alec said there had been many witnesses, including the President and his wife and the White House chief of staff. The official nodded sympathetically. Then they put the dead man on a stretcher and departed, leaving Alec alone with Harold Grendall, Lloyd Fisher, Avril Raye, Bud Weinberg, Wilson Slyde, Sylvia, two dozen waiters, and the pianist. Virginia Spears had departed with the medical team. Mrs. Hardenburg manned the telephone, which had begun to ring again and again.

Alec stood alone staring at the front door. He heard voices outside. The doorbell dueled with the telephone; but at last the back doors were open and a warm breeze moved gently through the rooms. He realized he was sweating and straining to see beyond the closed door, where the reporters were clamoring for attention, a noise like the growl of animals. Of course they were furious at being left outside while their more esteemed colleagues had been invited in, an obvious competitive advan-

tage; and to a degree the witnesses were also accomplices to the
events, whatever the events were. An outline was already being
composed, Alec was certain of that. No one quite knew how
they went about things, selecting quotations and slices of what
they called color, and texture to go with the color, and context
to go with the texture, all of it supported by the unruly facts that
gave their work its authority. No wonder they called the finished
product "pieces." He remembered Axel watching the election
returns in Springfield, 1952, and remarking that it was like watching the invention of gunpowder.

Alec was blinded when he opened the door. One microphone
brushed his chin and another his ear. A camera's lens was a foot
away, and then a second and a third. One of the reporters cursed
loudly when he was elbowed aside in the crush. The lights were
so bright, Alec could not see beyond the immediate vicinity,
but he imagined he was looking into the nucleus of an atom,
all swirling particles, some magnetic, others electric; they only
wanted to coalesce. He waited until the reporters stopped shouting and then told them what had happened inside, ending with
the observation that the President and his wife and the chief of
staff had returned downtown. The news was no longer at Echo
House; try the White House. When he paused for breath, the
questions began again, the angry voices rising in the warm night
air, circling and colliding, swarming. Alec listened another moment, then turned and walked back into Echo House, slamming
the door behind him. The bell rang for a moment but the thumb
on the button was without resolve, and in seconds was withdrawn.

"Good job," Wilson Slyde said. He had been listening with
Bud Weinberg.

Alec was about to make a sarcastic reply when he saw the
tears in Wilson's eyes.

"My people have respect for age," Wilson said. "And I liked
the old bastard."

"Stay a minute," Alec said.

"I'll say good night," Bud put in. "Sorry, Alec. This is a terrible
thing." Bud smiled wanly, a worried middle-aged man in a rum-

pled tuxedo. He looked adrift and aware that help would not arrive any time soon. "Strange thing was, I needed to talk to him. I needed Axel's advice."

"I know what he'd say," Alec said. "Don't let them off the hook."

"They're not on the hook," Bud said unhappily. "I am."

"They are," Alec said. "They just don't know it."

Bud Weinberg smiled wistfully. If he had had a white flag he would have raised it. He said, "For a while I thought it was anti-Semitism. It was the only explanation I could think of, and then I heard the rumors. Absurd rumors that I tried to laugh off, forgetting that in Washington you don't laugh anything off ever. In a way, anti-Semitism's a lot simpler, don't you think?" He patted Alec on the arm. "Thanks for the advice. All condolences, Alec. We'll all miss your father; one of a kind." He turned away, then paused for one last inquiry. "What do you know about Red Lambardo? He's behind it, I'm told. What's his problem? I know he was bagman for the campaign, and we've spoken once or twice on the phone. Why is he involved?"

"Maybe he has his own candidate for Paris." Certainly Red was involved. Look far enough along the Amazon of Washington gossip and Red would be lurking somewhere in the shallows, helping things along, rumor's assistant, innuendo's counselor. Alec said, "Do you want to fight?"

"My wife advises against it. She's the one who's hurt, really."

"She's a smart woman," Wilson said.

"I raised about seventeen million for them in the campaign."

"That should get you something," Alec said.

"If you were me, what would you do?"

"I'd talk to Wilson here," Alec said. "You need someone to tell your story. In a time of trouble, everyone needs a personal journalist."

"I don't know if it's worth it," Bud said.

"It won't begin and end in a day," Alec said. "A campaign of this kind, it takes time. You've got to want it badly."

"I've wanted Embassy Paris for as long as I can remember."

"Everything comes with a price," Wilson said.

"Seventeen million," Bud said.

"That's the down payment," Wilson said.

"I don't understand this town," Bud said, turning again and walking away, this time for good.

Alec watched him go, then called to the others, Outside, for a nightcap on the croquet court. He asked Mrs. Hardenburg to prepare a table, caviar, foie gras, Champagne, and Scotch. Glasses, plates, the wine in a bucket. Take the rest of the food away. Take the phone off the hook. Do the clean-up tomorrow. Everyone can go home except for the pianist. He asked the pianist to play French cabaret music, Piaf and Trenet. He filled a glass with ice and poured Scotch over the ice. The old house seemed suddenly lighter, weightless, as if it had been relieved of a great burden. He thanked Mrs. Hardenburg and said she could go home, too.

But Mrs. Hardenburg only whispered, Oh, my goodness.

The President's wife was striding through the dining room, Agent Block at her side. She smiled archly and said she had had an argument with her husband, the thoroughly frightened President of the United States, and decided to take the evening off and return to Echo House to pay her respects. She wanted to be among friends. She hoped she wouldn't be in the way.

She said, "Make Flo a drink, Alec."

The croquet court was glossy in the moonlight, so bright that the stakes and wickets cast sharp surreal shadows. The air was very warm, with thick Southern heat boiling up from the tidewater. Alec could smell the bluegrass, freshly mown that morning, and the vaguely medicinal scent of eucalyptus. Inside, the lights of Echo House went out one by one until there was only a single lamp burning in the garden room and another upstairs in Axel's sitting room. Alec's throat caught when he remembered the rogues' firmament, Fred Greene and Marlene Dietrich, the girl on the bicycle, the dead German infantryman with the Iron Cross at his throat, and the old man himself, his helmet tilted like a fedora. This was his father's history, and now it was as extinct as he was. A shadow passed between the upstairs lamp and the window, an alarming sight; but it was only the nurse, tidying up. One door closed followed by another until at last the house was silent, except for the pianist softly playing *Les Amants d'un Jour*. Alec tried to remember the last time he had been alone in Echo House and could not. The old man was always in the vicinity, within earshot. Without him the mansion seemed depleted.

They sat on the long bench beside the magnolia. Alec occupied the Adirondack chair.

"To Axel." Lloyd Fisher rasped, raising his glass.

"Rest in peace," Avril Raye said.

Sylvia asked. "What do you remember right now, Harold?"

"Lenin's squint," Harold said, his voice soft in the darkness. He reached to touch Lloyd on the arm, but when he spoke again it was to no one in particular. "I remember when Lloyd and I and Axel went to visit that Russian, filthy little flat somewhere near the Montparnasse cemetery. The Russian kept talking about Lenin's squint. Millions dead, a revolution made, and the thing he remembered most was Lenin's squint."

"We tried to recruit him," Lloyd said.

"We paid him some money and all we got for it was Lenin's squint."

They were silent a moment.

"I just saw a shooting star," Lloyd said.

Harold rose stiffly and moved awkwardly to the table, where he spooned caviar onto toast, careful to add a sliver of onion. "It's Axel, telling me to shut up about the exiles. I can't remember why."

"The source," Lloyd said.

"He fell away from the party," Harold said. "A lot of them did, the old Reds. Hard for them to ignore the terror in front of their eyes, friends murdered or sent to the Gulag. They lost the center of things, their reason for being. The ones who escaped the trials went into exile to write their memoirs and their poems, trying to recapture the way things were supposed to be. They had plenty of life left but nothing to do with it except remember."

"Americans don't go into exile," Lloyd said. "Except tax cheats."

"I went to Nantucket," Sylvia said.

"You're different," Harold said.

Sylvia laughed and began to stroll around the croquet court.

"I don't know where we'd go, Lloyd," Harold said. He filled his glass and the other glasses, staring into the sky as if the shooting stars held the answer. "We're so high here, the heavens are in sight. No city glare. It's like being in Montana."

"It's why I always hated the Observatory," Sylvia said from the lawn. "I could never see the stars, only the glare of the buildings and monuments. On a clear night it hurt my eyes."

"I liked it," Alec said.

"I knew Kerensky and didn't like him," Lloyd said. "Terrible windbag. He shouted at people. He thought the only reason you didn't agree with him was that you couldn't hear him. So he shouted all the time. To the end of his life he thought he was the sole legitimate head of the Russian empire. He emigrated to Australia and bored the bejesus out of them. Died in nineteen-seventy, but the truth was his life ended when he left Russia. God, they loved their country. Loved her to death."

"I'm not going anywhere," Harold said.

"Happiest days of my life," Lloyd said.

"This town," Flo said. "Either you're born to it or you're not."

"Everyone here is from someplace else," Alec said.

"Except you," Flo said.

"I always preferred London," Lloyd said.

"Axel loved France," Harold said, his voice breaking. He fumbled a moment, then reached to take Lloyd's hand and the two old men sat in the darkness, holding hands like lovers.

"Paris," Wilson said softly. "There was a time when I knew the order of battle of the French Army better than I knew our own. I lectured once at St. Cyr on Falkenhayn's artillery strategy at Verdun. The cadets gave me a standing O. I was so proud. I wanted to go to the embassy as military attaché. I knew some of our musicians who were living in Paris and there was a singer I was sleeping with." He paused to listen to the piano, ragtime Piaf. "She was from Martinique, wonderful voice. Sang at a little place near Sacré Coeur. But they had other ideas for me and of course at that time they didn't want Sambo anywhere near the Faubourg-St.-Honoré. Embassy Paris was my ambition in those days, and I didn't see any reason why I couldn't go back as ambassador, once I'd done the things they wanted me to do. And now I couldn't afford it. And I couldn't get confirmed if I could afford it. A lot of water under my bridge, Alec."

Alec poured Scotch into his glass and drank, the liquor spicy as it went down. He looked for Sylvia, but she had vanished.

Wilson helped himself to the foie gras. "You should go, Alec."

"Yes," Avril said. "Get out of Washington for a while, Washington's dead."

Alec hesitated. Unlike everyone else he knew, he had no sentimental thoughts of Paris. He had no friends in Paris and his only memory was of the Hôtel-Dieu in the afternoon. If he went to Paris, what would he do there?

Wilson said, "What do you think, Flo?"

"Alec couldn't get confirmed either."

"Of course he could, if we made an effort —"

But the President's wife did not reply, only sighed and smiled a neutral smile. None of them would ever leave, not her, not Harold or Lloyd, not Alec, not Wilson, not Avril Raye. They were bankrupts in debt to the same hard-hearted creditor, the one who never took no for an answer. "That isn't the way we do things," she said mildly. "You know that, Wilson. You of all people."

Alec said, "What would happen to Echo House?"

But the others were occupied with their own thoughts, and the question went unanswered.

"Another shooting star," Flo said.

Harold pointed skyward as a star vanished. They were silent again. In the neighborhood somewhere a dog barked, and when Alec looked up he saw a vague fluorescent glow and fireflies and beyond the fireflies two slender shadows cheek to cheek. He imagined they were the golden couple come to eavesdrop, their first rendezvous since the anonymous year 1947. The shadows moved fluidly here and there, touching and then breaking apart and becoming one and finally flickering, flames with insufficient oxygen, then evaporating altogether, back to wherever they had come from. Washington had always been populated by ghosts, and now Alec knew that his father was present over his shoulder, delivering another interminable lecture about the nation's promise. He raised his eyes and saw a curtain move in the upstairs study, the silhouette behind it unmistakable. She was looking at the pictures and turning the pages of the scrapbook, trying to reclaim what had once been hers, or understand what it was about Aquitaine, 1944. Alec raised his hand, motioning for her to join them. But the curtain closed decisively into place as Avril murmured something incomprehensible in French. The silhouette vanished. The fluorescence in the sky expired, for there was nothing more for the cameras to photograph. Harold and Jack began to reminisce again; Wilson and the President's wife were tête-à-tête, out of earshot. Alec sat back in his chair, his eyes on the windows of the upstairs study, waiting for the curtain to move once more. This was the house he had inherited and the life he had made and he could not rid himself of either one; he guessed he had another thirty years to live.